KATE & ANNALISE
Their Books of Days

A Novel by

Patricia G. Raab

Kate & Annalise
Their Books of Days
Written by Patricia G. Raab

Edited by RaeAnne Marie Scargall

Associate Editors: Kristin Schlingman, Griffin Mill

Proofreader: Lyda Rose Haerle

Layout by Michael Nicloy

Cover Illustration by Joseph Lerche (grandson of author, age 17)

ISBN 978-1945907609

PUBLISHED BY NICO 11 PUBLISHING & DESIGN
MUKWONAGO, WISCONSIN

www.nico11publishing.com

Be well read.

Quantity orders may be made by contacting the publisher via email:
mike@nico11publishing.com

Printed in the United States of America

For William Raab, my husband, for his unending support of my love for writing.

For my children, Marcus, Gretchen, Paul, Sarah, Kristin, and Heidi, who have made me so proud with all of their amazing accomplishments and for their encouragement along the way in the writing of this book.

For Helen and Linda, your willingness to read the first of many trial versions of this book and your persistence that I complete this novel.

BOOK ONE
Kate's Story

CHAPTER ONE

Kate could barely hold her eyes open, curled up alongside Gerrit as his Hudson Essex motorcar cruised toward Chicago and their new life together. The wedding she dreamed about for so long had now come and gone. Everything was perfect, from the beautiful September day to the outdoor reception in the backyard of the parish house where she grew up. Kate Conner was now Mrs. Gerrit Jansz.

Officiating the service were Kate's father, Pastor Conner, and her brother, Pastor Daniel.

Kate, youngest of the Conner clan, knew her father was disappointed that neither of the two Conner daughters had gone to college.

Ida, the oldest, grew up wanting to be a pastor like her dad. She practiced giving fire-and-brimstone sermons from the pulpit when he wasn't around. Being a pastor had also been Daniel's dream. When the coast was clear, the three would sneak into church. Daniel led the choir of three, but his passion never ramped up to Ida's level, which usually included punctuation on the rim of the pulpit. Little Kate was always the designated parishioner in the front pew.

Ida grew up to marry Jake, an Iowa farmer. Daniel, who never married, finished his Bible studies and was assigned to a parish in Joliet, a city in Illinois.

Kate should have gone to college except for her dream of marrying her best friend, Gerrit Jansz. Now, instead of a dorm room, she was on her way to a basement apartment near downtown Chicago.

When Kate yawned, Gerrit suggested she sleep awhile. She didn't need any encouragement to snuggle alongside Gerrit. "Don't you two go to sleep," she teased. Since Daniel still didn't have a car, whenever Gerrit went back to Iowa for a weekend visit with Kate, he'd swing by to pick him up in Joliet and deliver him back to his parish on his return to Chicago, "I've got early service tomorrow," Daniel said, "so I really appreciate your giving me a ride back, especially since you've had a pretty exhaustive day—no, weekend."

"Now that the wedding is over, maybe we could find some weekend to go car shopping?" Gerrit suggested.

"I think I'll also need a few driving lessons," Daniel said, laughing. "I'm ready for a car, but I'm not ready for a fancy one, like your Essex." Both laughed.

"Shhh," Gerrit said. "Better not wake Kate."

Kate was mesmerized by the city lights of Chicago.

They never dim. How can people sleep with all those lights shining in their windows?

In the weeks before their wedding, Kate thought often about taking the train into the city to see what it was like. She'd never been to Chicago, nor had she ever been on a train. Anywhere. One thing she knew for certain: she could never get on a train and go into Chicago alone.

Kate found a map of the city at the library back home and tried to find some of the streets Gerrit talked about. But even when she found them on the map, she knew she'd never find her way from the train to the street where Gerrit lived.

She knew better than to ask if Gerrit and she could drive in over a weekend so she could get used to a big city. Poppa would never approve an out-of-town trip with Gerrit until they were married.

"I hope the windows have shades," she mumbled to herself.

The arrival at the apartment was disheartening. She helped Gerrit unload the suitcases and boxes, stacking them down the steps to their front door. Kate was left to stand guard while he drove around the building to the parking area. *No need to worry about anyone trying to help themselves to our clothes and wedding presents—there isn't a soul in sight.*

Judging from the sound, rain isn't far off. She handed gift boxes down to Gerrit who stacked them in what must have been the parlor. Before lightning started in earnest, they'd gotten the last gifts inside. Kate found her small suitcase with the things she needed the first night. Gerrit closed the curtains on the eye-level window overlooking the sidewalk.

"It really is a basement apartment," Kate whispered to herself.

"Don't worry," Gerrit piped up. "You'll get used to it." He whistled as he moved into the next room where she could see a bed and dresser.

Kate and Gerrit had been best friends throughout their school days. When Gerrit left to study at a business college in Chicago, he and Kate were already planning to get married as soon as he finished his studies and had his degree. That, Gerrit promised, would be in September 1926. And it was.

Their wedding was held at the Methodist church in central Iowa where her Poppa was the long-time pastor. Kate was thankful Gerrit's part-time job at a downtown bank turned into a full-time job when he finished his exams.

The more Kate worried about the challenge of living in Chicago, when Gerrit was at work, the more anxious she became.

Now that she was moving in, she realized she'd better not even think of walking up those steps to the sidewalk. Instead of worrying, she concentrated on making their living space look homey.

She didn't have money to buy things, but she could look in magazines to see the kinds of things she'd like to have—someday. Wooden furniture would be nice, with white or soft yellow curtains. The only windows in their apartment overlooked the busy sidewalk outside their parlor. Curtains would give them some privacy.

Would they live in this apartment a long time? Would they ever have a house? In Chicago? Her space probably would look a lot like her momma's did when they started out. She smiled at that. In many ways, she was like momma. Ida was like poppa. Gerrit, an only child, resembled himself.

Ida never worried how things looked. She filled their farmhouse where she and Jake lived with whatever furniture or fabrics caught her fancy. Kate wanted her home to be restful and welcoming. Ida didn't care if her house was restful. But then again, neither was Ida.

Kate never knew anyone who lived in an apartment. Maureen, a schoolmate, and her mom and dad, lived in an upstairs flat that belonged to her grandmother, who lived downstairs. Kate always tried to see inside, but all she saw was a hallway, never rooms.

She tried to imagine furniture Gerrit would like. For starters, she hoped he had his own mattress on their bed. Mattresses at home were hauled out to the backyard every spring for a good beating. You certainly couldn't do that in a Chicago apartment where the yard was a sidewalk and busy street.

She decided to quit worrying about the parlor and concentrate on making the kitchen more usable.

"I know Ida and Jake gave us a set of everyday dishes, but they have to be washed before we can use them, and we first need to empty the cupboards so the new things can go in," she said. Gerrit was too busy emptying boxes in the parlor to hear what she was saying.

"Actually, I'll just do that on Monday while you're at work. It's still our wedding day, and I don't feel like emptying and rearranging cupboards or washing dishes."

They'd already decided to open their wedding gifts on Sunday. "We can work on that together tomorrow afternoon," Gerrit said as he came back for another box to empty. He returned, paused, then suggested, "If we're not worrying about dishes, we could put clean sheets on the bed."

By the time Kate re-made the bed, Gerrit had sandwiches and coffee set out on a parlor table.

So far, she'd gotten a good look at the cupboards in the kitchen and bathroom. The small linen closet had a second set of sheets. But the bathroom cupboard had only one bath towel, two face towels and wash cloths.

"Tomorrow will be interesting when we unwrap wedding gifts," Kate said. "I know Daniel got us towels, but I don't know if they are kitchen or bath. If we don't get bath towels, we'll share the only one you have," Kate said.

Even Gerrit laughed at that possibility.

Kate needn't have worried about dresser space for the few clothes she brought. The only dresser had four large drawers. He emptied two of his for her things. The bedroom closet wasn't very large, but there were empty hangers for her two dresses and Gerrit's two suits and several white shirts. Although she'd never moved before, it didn't take long to get her things put away. But being a wife was more work than she imagined.

With everything organized—although not decorated to her daydream standards—Kate found the days while Gerrit worked long and lonely. She stood at the window overlooking the street, watching shoes pass by on the sidewalk.

After a few days, she decided she had to at least go outside and see what Chicago had to offer. Well, almost. She started up the stairs to the street, then pretended she'd forgotten something and hurried back down. A while later, she tried again. No one on the sidewalk took notice. Everyone was in a hurry. When the door was closed, she had no sense of traffic, people and noise. Just opening the door a crack let the racket in.

The next day she tried again. When she and Gerrit went out in the evening or on Saturday to shop at a nearby store, the traffic and people didn't bother her. It was only when she faced it alone that her heart raced.

Was she afraid of people, or was she frantic about getting lost? She was married and living in Chicago. She had to come to terms with that.

If she went for a walk and kept notes, she could retrace the route and get back to the apartment. Why hadn't she thought of making a list of streets in her neighborhood? She found a notebook and pencil in her jacket pocket and made notes of which way she turned to get to another street and even wrote the names of department stores and shops to find her way home.

The first days she walked only a few blocks, but everyday her surroundings became more familiar, and she increased her pace. Before long, her morning routine was a brisk walk around the neighborhood, paying attention to the clothes people wore. She began to feel at home.

One day, she walked the opposite direction toward the bank where Gerrit worked. It wasn't far. She saw other buildings like theirs, but only one with basement windows. She knew Gerrit picked their place so he could walk to work. And the rent was probably cheaper than those on upper floors, where tenants could see Lake Michigan. It was a perfectly logical choice for him in order to save money to buy a farm where someday their children could run, play, and do chores.

It took a long time for Kate to get up courage to go into a big store. The smaller shops were less intimidating. Department stores had huge display windows with room settings. She was anxious to go inside and look for things she'd been thinking about for their place. Curtains. Furniture. Dishes. Gerrit finally admitted that all their current furniture came with the apartment.

"Settling into marriage isn't as easy as I thought. For goodness sake," she added, "why am I whispering? There's no one around to even hear."

Gerrit never seemed concerned about how she found her way around and home again. He was far more interested in how his weekly paychecks were adding up for their farm-in-Wisconsin account. On one of her outings, she found a Methodist church not far away. She jotted down the times of Sunday services and even peeked inside when she saw someone going in on what must have been her lunch break. She ventured in for a quick look and nearly fell over when the organist started playing chords and a few hymns like momma played. It was so dark in the choir loft it was impossible to see if it was a man or woman at the keys. She'd have to remember how to get back there on Sunday. Would Gerrit go with her? At least the first time?

"Wishful thinking," she whispered to herself.

She thought about writing to Ida to tell her about the fancy pots and pans on display. That's when she realized she was talking to herself, but no one noticed.

Momma, she thought, *I'm going to send you some magazines I bought at a store. There are articles that tell how to arrange furniture, what kind of rugs to put in front of your davenport and what curtains are in style. I never realized there was a right and wrong way to arrange things.*

What kind of furniture would look good in a farmhouse? Would there be furniture stores in the town where they'd live someday? And how would she buy even used furniture and haul it home to their farm? Were there secondhand stores that sold used furniture? Eventually, I'd like a rocker. It wouldn't make sense to buy furniture in Chicago then truck it to a farm in Wisconsin.

She'd need a sewing machine and lessons on how to sew. Why didn't she ever ask Ida or momma to teach her to sew? At least curtains. Eventually, she'd sew good enough to make clothes for herself and their children.

Thinking of everything she'd need to keep house, she decided it was time to take a nap.

Gerrit found her sleeping when he got home. She hadn't even started supper.

"Tell you what," he suggested. "I think we could walk to the restaurant where I sometimes ate. They had good soup and sandwiches. Are you up to it? If not, I could buy a couple sandwiches and bring them home. You all right? You look a little peaked."

"I went on a long walk. I don't even remember eating lunch. I found a Methodist Church. I'd like to go there some Sunday. Someone was in the choir loft playing the organ. Very loud! It was beautiful. I'll write Momma and tell her about the church. I think I'd like a sandwich, if it's not too far."

Gerrit's Sunday routine was checking Wisconsin farmland listings in *The Chicago Tribune*. He said people keep telling him that farmland is cheaper in Wisconsin than in Iowa or Illinois. Not sure about Minnesota.

After several months of wandering around near their apartment, Kate was bored. She was tired of the same displays, especially without money to spend. And because Gerrit was determined to keep adding to his farm savings, he took every Saturday shift posted at the bank, usually leaving her alone six days a week.

One Sunday she decided to join Gerrit on his Sunday afternoon shopping in the farmland listings. Except she was shopping for a job. Until she realized she was in a family way.

Her job search ended with a flourish one Monday morning when she wadded up all the newspapers she'd saved and deposited them in a sidewalk garbage can.

Home again, she put a little mark in the corner of a calendar date that she suspected had been the day of conception. She added a tiny pencil speck in the bottom left-hand corner each day, hoping those dots would add up to nine months. She stopped that routine the first morning she had to make a run for the bathroom. Day after day, she faced morning sickness until Gerrit finally heard her in the bathroom and came looking. She splashed her face with cold water and tried to smile, but she knew she wasn't a pretty sight.

Gerrit folded her into his arms and tried to do a celebratory skip and hop, but that only set off another round of miseries.

Before heading to work, he put a bucket next to the bed. Bending down to kiss her goodbye, he whispered: "At last, we're getting a start not only on our farm, but also our first baby."

She heard Gerrit's feet going up the steps. If she could have gotten up to look, she wouldn't have been surprised to see his shoes skipping along the sidewalk.

She was soon asleep.

Kate never asked if he told anyone at the bank about his wife, but when he didn't come home with suggestions for a baby doctor, she knew she'd better find one herself.

She also had to find a sewing machine.

After writing to Momma about the baby, Kate had a surprise visit one Monday afternoon from her brother, Daniel. Now that he had his own car, he could fit their mom's treadle sewing machine in the back seat and deliver it to Kate's apartment in Chicago.

The next morning, Gerrit left without waking her. When she got up, she found ten dollars and a note on the table: "Buy some yard goods to make a new dress for yourself. Love, Gerrit."

It took several tries, but eventually she got the hang of cutting out patterns and sewing the pieces together. She made four everyday dresses and a fancier one for church.

Kate never passed the sewing machine without laying her hand on the wooden box that covered it. A touch of home.

Then she found a resale store where she discovered clothes donated by people who worked downtown. She didn't even need Momma's machine. She found maternity clothes that fit her growing size and a woolen shawl she could wrap around her shoulders to ward off the chill of early fall.

She knew from Gerrit's gleeful trips to the bank on Saturdays that money was growing in their farm fund. Then, one day, he laid the ad section in front of her while she drank her tea and pointed to one. It was, he said, in the far reaches of north-central Wisconsin.

"Sounds perfect," Gerrit said. He had already called about it and learned it was near Lillehammer, obviously a little town with a lot of Norwegian settlers. From there, it was a half-day trip to Milwaukee and Lake Michigan. "The same lake we have in Chicago," he added.

Kate had an appointment with the doctor that Tuesday. When she asked him if she could ride along with Gerrit to look at property, the doctor had a one-word answer: "*No.*"

So, Gerrit took holiday time off, rolled out the Essex, and on a sunny, warm fall afternoon, waved goodbye and drove north. When he returned two days later, she was waiting anxiously to hear if it was their farm.

"Well, yes and no," he began. "We have enough for the down payment, but they aren't sure we are the buyers they want. They expect us to move up there when the sale is final. I said you could live on the farm. I told them the doctor would not let you move up there until after the baby was born and you have recuperated several weeks."

I could tell they weren't sure that would work. But I explained that I wanted to keep working at the bank to get enough money, not just for the down payment, but to make payments on the property and still have money to buy chickens, cows, horses and machinery to run the farm. I reminded them that's why the property was foreclosed on in the first place—the couple who started the farm didn't have the money to keep it going. The bankers agreed. So, it looks like you and the baby will be tenant farmers until I've worked enough to give us a good start.

"Do you think you could live there by yourself with the baby for maybe a year? I'd come up when I could."

"Do you mean I'll be up there all by myself? You're not coming up there with me for a whole year?" Kate started to cry. It's only two weeks until the baby arrives. And after a couple weeks for recuperation, you're going to put me on the train and ship the baby and me off to Wisconsin with a bunch of strangers? I don't have a car. I don't drive. How will I even get to a grocery store?"

"But," Gerrit said, "you didn't hear the best part. There are neighbors just down the hill from our farm and they promised they'd look after you and the baby.

"Helen and Harald Iversen are the best neighbors we could ever have found. They have a large farm and all their boys are now married and have farms and children of their own. Our farm is also part of an Amish community—you remember them in Iowa, going from farm to farm on Sundays for church meetings. Amish farmers helped my pop when his rheumatism got too bad for him to climb up to the haymow to throw down feed for the cows.

"How can I possibly do this all by myself? What about washing baby clothes and diapers, day after day? I'm sure there's no washing machine. Probably not even a wash bucket that I could fill with hot water and then another to rinse the soap out. You have no idea how I'm supposed to manage all of this, even if we have nice neighbors."

"Does the farm even have electricity? You said those original farmers didn't live there very long. Is there even a house that's livable? How could you ever have promised to send me away for a whole year? What am I supposed to do for a whole year alone, except for a couple of neighbors down the hill?"

"The only time I've ever been on a real farm was when I visited Jake and my sister Ida's farm and the few times I was at your mom and dad's farm. What if something happens to the baby? How would I get into town? I'd have to walk down the road to the Iversen's to ask them to drive me and the baby into town to see a doctor. How will that work in the middle of temperatures below zero with a baby in a buggy and snow all around? You can't expect busy neighbors like the Iversen's to drive me into town whenever I need anything. Even a doctor!"

"You mean, the only way we can buy this farm is if I move up there and leave you in Chicago? We wouldn't have any way to keep in touch with each other except by mail. We won't even have a telephone. And how are you going to get me and the baby up there? In your Essex in the middle of winter?"

"If it's too bad for me to drive you up there, *we* will just get on the train. That might be better anyway, because we could ship some of the things you'd need, like your mom's sewing machine and the baby bed your sister Ida wants you to have. I looked around when I was up there, and they had a small thrift store right in Lillehammer. They even have a hospital. When I met the Iversen's, and they heard what we might have to do to get the farm, they said: "Don't worry, we'll look out for your wife and the baby until you move up here.""

That night Kate couldn't sleep. She tried to imagine what it would be like to be alone in a farmhouse overnight. *I never liked sleeping alone in the dark and often went into Ida's room where I snuggled close before drifting off.*

From then on, plans moved ahead. Ten days later, Fletcher arrived – all six pounds, three ounces. *The next four weeks raced by, and then there I was, packing up our lives for the train trip from Chicago to Lillehammer and our farm.*

Besides Gerrit, Kate knew she'd miss her walks around downtown Chicago.

Gerrit had a surprise for Kate. She couldn't believe her eyes when she saw the large cupboard on the platform when they got off the train.

"This sideboard is the first piece of furniture for our farmhouse," Gerrit said.

"Side-what?" Kate asked. "Remember, we had a big cupboard in the dining room at the pastor's house only it was called a buffet," she said. "It was where we kept the good dishes for when the bishop came for lunch. Whatever it's called, it's big. Maybe it won't even go through the door into the house," Kate lamented.

Leaning against the buffet/sideboard was the baby bed Ida sent along for Fletcher.

Once they collected their suitcases and other parcels and packages, their neighbor Harald Iversen and two of his sons pulled up, hauling a hay wagon behind the Model T. Harald and his boys lifted the buffet off the train platform and laid it flat on the hay wagon. The baby bed was easy to tie down. The Iversen boys tied the suitcases on the wagon rack, with some of the smaller packages piled in the backseat of Helen's car.

After a quick round of introductions, the Iversen and Jansz parade got underway. Kate tried to remember all the details of the trip so she could write about them in the journal she planned to keep of her life alone on the farm.

The next morning was scary. When you are accustomed to the day-and-night clatter of streetcars and traffic, it's strange to be awakened by silence. Gerrit was already up and pacing. He said Harald had gone back to their farm to get milk for our breakfast. Gerrit started stacking dishes in a large cupboard in the kitchen.

The sideboard he bought in Chicago and hauled on the train to Lillehammer, was a perfect fit in the main room alcove around the corner from the kitchen. They'd brought only a few dishes—enough for Kate and the baby. Kate already had a shopping list of things she needed. At the top was a reminder to buy dishes, glassware, kettles, and flatware.

How in the world did I expect to get to stores? Kate wondered.

What she didn't know was that Gerrit bought a pony and courting buggy for her. The pony was in the grazing area behind the barn, and the buggy was in the carriage house near the house. Gerrit showed her how to hook up and un-hitch the little buggy and return the horse to pasture. He reminded her that she was not to hitch up the buggy until spring. If she needed to go to a store for supplies, all she had to do was ask and Harald or Helen would take her.

And did she know that Grammy Iversen lived there with them and was always ready to rock a baby to sleep?

There were groceries in the cupboard and bread, butter, jam and jelly, eggs, bacon, corn flakes and oatmeal. She also didn't have to fret about trips to the grocery for starter supplies, like fresh eggs or milk. They were already in the new icebox Gerrit bought when he signed the papers for the farm. There also were several loaves of homemade bread and a batch of breakfast rolls—and even a batch of baby formula already bottled and cooling in the ice box. Helen said Grammy Iversen took care of that, just like she'd done with all the Iversen children and grandchildren.

Harald said Helen and Grammy hauled over a bedstead from their big empty house. It was a present from the Iversen's so Grammy and Helen would have space to set up a quilting frame in a now-empty upstairs bedroom. Grammy had three quilts waiting to be stitched.

Kate was overwhelmed. She'd grown up in a community where neighbors always seemed to know what a family needed, and they'd always find someone who had extras to share. But things like that didn't happen in downtown Chicago, where they only learned other tenants' names by looking at mailboxes.

The original owners of their farmhouse didn't leave any furniture, except for a very large cookstove in the kitchen. Next to it stood a large wooden box that held split logs and kindling. There was plenty more neatly stacked in the woodshed.

Gerrit said: "There should be enough wood to last until spring for both the wood-burning heater and cookstove." And when the wood box starts to run out of wood, Harald would bring in a few armloads to fill it up again. "You only need to ask," Helen told Kate. "Harald keeps an eye on that shed and decides for himself when you need more logs and kindling."

But water was another thing entirely. The pump was close to the north side of the house, across from the doorway into the woodshed. There had been an outside pump at the parish house in Iowa. Often, Ida would prime the pump, then go back out a few minutes later to start pumping water up and into the kitchen bucket. On wash days, Ida and younger brother, Daniel would take turns pumping and carrying until the washtubs were filled nearly to the brim. Besides Ida and Daniel, their mother, Annalise Conner, had a hired girl on Mondays to help with the wash

The Conner's washtubs stood on benches in the basement. Momma would do most of the scrubbing, pouring washing powder over the towels, shirts, underwear, and socks, rubbing them on the washboard. Then she'd swish each half-clean piece through wash water before dipping it into the first-rinse bucket and cranking it through the hand wringer into the final-rinse water. After another run through the wringer, it all dropped into a basket to be carried either outside, to hang on the clothesline, or in the basement, where it was pinned on a line or draped over a clothes bar. In damp weather it sometimes took days to get clothes dry.

By the time momma and the hired girl got everything scrubbed, rinsed and pinned, Annalise Conner was so exhausted she could hardly get upstairs to the comfort of her own bed. Now, Kate would have to manage all those steps alone. A wash day in warm weather was less strenuous, but it still took time, especially since clothes came off the line as soon as they dried. They still had to be folded and put away in cupboards and closets.

Washing grownup clothes was one thing, but the every-other-day schedule for baby clothes and diapers was grueling. Somehow, she'd manage.

Gerrit didn't get back up to the farm until spring. The loneliest time was Christmas. The Iversen's invited Kate and Fletcher to spend the day with them, but she didn't have money to buy presents. No matter. She made quilted potholders for all the Iversen families, sewing them on her mom's treadle machine.

At the last minute, she thought about the box of dried apple slices Nana Conner sent. On Christmas Eve, when the Iversen clan was gathering after finishing farm chores, Kate slipped outside and up the hill to get the apples her mom and dad sent for Christmas. They were a treasured holiday treat at the Conner's, since Annalise, Kate, and Ida used to work all fall picking apples, slicing them, and laying them on tables in the sunny backyard to dry. They had to keep them covered so bugs couldn't feast on them. Sometimes it was frustrating because it took so long, even on warm days, to get them dry enough that they wouldn't mold.

Since she knew what was in the box, she hadn't bothered to even open it. She brought along a large shallow basket she bought at the Chicago resale store. The size and shape of the slices were perfect for tempting hungry children and keep them from dipping into the bowls of candy and cracked walnuts.

When the men came back from doing chores at their farms, the rest were ready to bundle up and go to Christmas Eve services at the nearby Lutheran church. Grammy Iversen said she was too tired and volunteered to stay with Baby Fletcher so he wouldn't get cold and over-tired. When they got back from church two hours later, there wasn't a peep from any corner in the house. Grammy was in her big feather bed in the back bedroom, and Fletcher was snuggled under an Amish quilt in the iron baby bed most of the Iversen children had used.

Kate's basket of apple slices was emptied, refilled, and refilled again. It was the perfect gift they could all share, even sleepy children curled up on the floor, wrapped in quilts, dozing until morning light.

In the daylight, Kate was surprised to see a large balsam holiday tree decorated with colorful ornaments and a few candles. Where did that come from?

A large kettle of oatmeal was bubbling on the stove, and plate after plate of pretty holiday bakery had been set out. There weren't enough chairs for everyone to sit, but the kids shared space on chairs or found more pillows to bring down from upstairs so they could sit on the floor. The menfolk hitched their sleighs to the teams of horses that spent the night in the big barn. Early that morning, they'd driven back to their barns to do the morning milking, then hurried back for the day's celebration. It was the biggest, most amazing holiday Kate had ever seen. She was still learning all the Iversen names, but everyone there knew hers.

They'd all brought small gifts, most of which were handmade, to give to one another. For Kate, there were endless supplies of jams and preserves, jars of dill pickles, and loaves and loaves of breads filled with nuts and fruits. The breads, they assured her, would last a long time. She could leave most of them in the ice box in her basement. From the looks of it, she thought the bakery and jams might last until next Christmas.

She'd taken the presents Gerrit sent her and was surprised to see where they'd come from. There were plenty of clothes and baby toys for Fletcher—even little shoes and socks to keep his feet warm. For her, there were hand-knit sweaters and a long winter coat, plus the snow boots she'd forgotten to bring along when she moved to the farm. And the surprise? Seeing the labels sewn into the clothes and the price tags he'd left on, there was no doubt Gerrit had done his shopping at the resale store.

When Helen's daughters-in-law saw what was in the box, they thought it might be fun to take a midwinter holiday trip to Chicago on the train. And when they found out that Kate often shopped there when she lived in Chicago and even knew the owner, they were ready to leave the following week. Their husbands told them they didn't need fancy wardrobes to do farm chores.

They tried talking Kate into putting on an impromptu fashion show, but first she had to settle Fletcher with his morning bottle. When his tummy was full, he didn't mind Helen's granddaughters dressing him in his new clothes and parading him around.

The day disappeared before anyone was ready for daylight to be gone.

Kate hadn't really thought about Gerrit all day, except when she was trying on her 'new' sweaters and watching the little granddaughters dance about with Fletcher. Had he spent the entire day alone in the apartment? Or had he and other people from work without family in Chicago or the means to travel, join in other co-workers' home celebrations?

Kate had made several woolen scarves to keep Gerrit's neck warm on those cold, dark walks to and from the bank. She'd also found a pair of brown leather gloves with fur lining that she knew he'd appreciate. All that day, thoughts of him only occasionally crossed her mind.

It had seemed like a daunting ultimatum for Kate to stay alone at the farm, but it really wasn't all that difficult. While she knew the bankers wondered what a young mother with a baby in a buggy could do to start a working farm, she found she could pick stones in a swampy field that ran the distance from the graveled farmyard down to the mailbox corner. So while Gerrit was salting away his paycheck after paying the monthly farm mortgage, his rent, and food, Kate was carting stones in a wheelbarrow from that stretch of field to a growing pile on the side of the carriage house. She had plans to line the borders of her flower and vegetable gardens with some of the stones. She'd already hauled some to the growing orchard. The stones weren't very big, but they did define the space.

Kate still had no idea how long Gerrit was going to stay in Chicago before he had enough money saved to move to the farm.

The blessing in all this was having good friends like the Iversen's, who looked out for her and even invited her to go to church with them. Kate always appreciated Grammy Iversen's eagerness to take care of Fletcher when she went to church guild meetings to work on quilts for the missions. Even though it was sometimes months between Gerrit's trips, Kate found it didn't really matter. She had developed her own life with plenty of friends who had gotten to know her. It wasn't that she stopped loving Gerrit, it was that she learned she could fend for herself, even being alone on a farm miles from town.

Kate realized she'd grown up.

With her growing self-assurance, she was already planning ways to redecorate the farmhouse. Not that she had much time to work on it (or money to make it happen), but she could page through magazines, clipping out ideas.

Fletcher, meanwhile, was also growing up. He didn't always ride in a buggy. Over time, he learned to crawl, then walk along holding onto a wall, and finally, walking by himself—but only when the road wasn't all torn up after heavy rain. On the days she needed milk, she had to take the baby buggy. Fletcher always objected to the cold jars bumping his legs.

During the months before Fletcher was born, Kate rarely had anyone to talk to all day. Most people in the apartment building went to work in the morning, and at the end of the day, all they wanted was to eat supper and go to bed. Before moving to the farm, she worried that she'd be too far from neighbors to have friends. She was pleasantly surprised when women invited her to join their church guild. They often had potlucks in the parish hall or, in warmer weather, out on the lawn.

The other women had farms that had been up and running for a long time. Kate was still dreaming about having cows to milk and more chickens in the coop and clucking around the farmyard. She still couldn't imagine how Gerrit planned to run the farm without having a job to pay the mortgage. But the bigger question was how he could possibly work a farm after a childhood that left him weak, often gasping for air from his allergies to hay and silage.

He must have had a plan, but he never told her what it was. She knew someone else would have to milk cows morning and night. Perhaps he expected she would do that. Sometimes when she was sitting in her rocker on the enclosed porch, she'd stare off at the small barn. There wasn't room for a good-sized herd of cows to wait in stanchions to be milked and turned out to pasture.

Months zipped by. Kate gave scant attention to Gerrit's past. Perhaps he had just been exaggerating his barnyard allergies. He could, of course, help clear the land for planting crops and grazing cattle. He'd need a houseful of kids to help with the hard work of clearing the land for farming. But Kate long ago figured out what was behind Gerrit's determination to have a large family. It wasn't the need to have children do what he couldn't, but, rather, it was to surround himself with children—to hear them playing games in the front yard or riding bicycles with friends who lived nearby.

She remembered how it used to irritate him when he'd come over to visit that there were always kids around. Ida had a lot of friends who'd sit on our front porch, sometimes just to sing. Daniel also had friends, but he'd sometimes settle for just hanging out with Ida's or Kate's visitors.

Kate's family was never pleased with her choice of Gerrit for a husband, even if his business school studies earned him a good career in banking. Gerrit just didn't want his only son to grow up an only child. But what if he was?

She'd brought a half-dozen books from her father's library, tucked into the packing boxes she took to Chicago after their wedding and then to the farm. Sometimes after Fletcher was settled for the night, she'd get one of poppa's books and sit in the rocker next to the big kitchen range where the day's fire had settled into warm embers. The familiar edges of the nameplates inside the covers were comforting. Sometimes, tears of bitter loneliness—and fear—spilled onto the fading ink that reminded borrowers to return the book when they finished reading it. She often carried a book to bed with her, careful to tuck it under her pillow so she wouldn't damage the treasured pages when she slept.

She missed poppa's study with his shelves of books. When she couldn't find something on one of his shelves, she could walk just a few blocks to the public library. The Iversen's promised to take Kate to the new library in Lillehammer sometime when they went to town for shopping. It would be nice to have something new to read when Fletcher was sleeping. That's when she felt most alone. During the day, she could always walk to the Iversen's, but when darkness set in, she had no choice but to lock the door and go to bed.

Kate's days were always busy, but it was the hours after Fletcher was asleep when she was most homesick for Gerrit. He usually wrote a page or two to her every month or so. She tried to write him every couple of weeks, mostly about Fletcher and how much he'd grown. Did Gerrit miss her? Did he even think of her?

He hadn't written for some time. His last letter was about how he'd been moved up the banking ladder and now had his own office where he reviewed loan applications. Probably meant more money in his pay envelope. She knew he was a hard worker and had a friendly personality, but with what she was hearing about banks closing, he might lose his job. Then what would they do for money to make the mortgage payments?

While the big issues of how to run a farm kept dogging her days, that wasn't her biggest problem. She didn't have any idea what day of the week it was, much less the date or even the month. Although she asked Gerrit to mail her a calendar, he never did. If she had a notebook she could write little paragraphs every day, giving her a record of her early days at the farm. That way she'd have a starting date so she could keep track of the weeks—but more important, she'd have a record of her early days at the farm. The next time she and Fletcher walked to the Iversen's, she asked Helen what the day and date were. She wrote it on an old envelope she had in her pocketbook. From then on, she tried to write daily entries on a grocery sack she kept in the kitchen cupboard. The next time Helen and Harald stopped at Kate's, they not only had a notebook, they also had a wall calendar. It would be the first of dozens of little notebooks she kept in a drawer in the sideboard.

When she put Fletcher to bed and the house was quiet, she wrote the date and first entry. She thought about copying the messages she'd written on the grocery sack, but instead, she folded the bag and put it in the bottom of the drawer as a reminder of how determined she was to keep a history of her early adventures.

May 15, 1928

Dear Days,

Helen and Harald brought me a little notebook so I can keep track of our lives here. They said it was a belated "welcome to Wisconsin" present. Figuring back from the date we arrived here, I realized we've been here more than six months.

Helen said Mother's Day was last Sunday. May 13. If I'd had a calendar, I would have known in time to send something to momma. I can still make a card. Fletcher and I will walk to the corner tomorrow and put it in the mailbox. I hope I can find clean paper, an envelope, and a stamp. Otherwise I'll have to wait until we go to town. Sometimes it's such a bother to be so far from stores. In Iowa, if we needed something, we just walked to the store.

I hope my notebook will be as special as the ones momma kept. I remember her sitting at the kitchen table after supper dishes. She never let us look at what she'd written. She said we'd have time enough to see it after she was gone. We couldn't imagine a day when she wouldn't be there. I can still hear her voice as she sang hymns as she stirred a kettle of something on the stove, or kneaded the dough to make bread and breakfast rolls.

Fletcher is getting so big. He's trying to walk and I have to laugh at how he holds up the wall. He jabbers a lot, but I hope he starts saying

17

words real soon. But I don't often talk to him. I read stories. Sometimes we even sing. Sort of. It's such a long time between Gerrit's visits. I hope Fletcher remembers he has a poppa.

Fletcher likes to work in the garden with me. I'm planning to spade up a little garden behind the house. I'd also like to have apple trees so I can make apple butter and apple pies. Maybe even learn to can applesauce. I also want to make dried apple slices like mom sent last Christmas.

I have a lot of dreams for our farm and I'll need to keep good records.

And so, another day has come to an end!

Kate

The few chickens had been a blessing in their ice box. Gathering eggs every morning meant food for eating and supplies for baking and cooking. She'd learned to bake bread in her mom's kitchen. Helen made sure Kate always had enough flour to bake bread and sometimes cookies or a loaf cake. She knew if Kate ran out of anything, she could take a quick hike down the road to get a fruit jar full of flour or starter. Usually there was a surprise or two in the buggy. It always paid to be careful so nothing unexpected fell out when she lifted Fletcher out. Grammy Iversen always found little things to send home with her. Sometimes it was a jar or two of raspberry jam to go with the fresh bread. When the surprise was applesauce, Kate got so lonesome for her mom she had to wipe away the tears so Fletcher wouldn't see her cry. Kate's mom, Annalise, always used every apple in the orchard.

Gerrit's trips from Chicago were nearly impossible in winter when snow drifts blocked anything on wheels. Sometimes the train would get him to town, but the snowed-in roads out to the farm made getting home impossible. Those weekends he'd just sit in the depot until the train headed south again.

May 18th, 1928

Dear Days,

Guess what? Harald drove his 'Johnny Popper' tractor up the hill this morning so he could plow the ground for my garden. I told them how I tried spading the rock-hard dirt behind the house. So now, thanks to Harald, I have a big enough patch so I can plant lots of things. He also brought a present: apple tree seedlings that grew up uninvited in his orchard. After he plowed my garden and I raked it nice and neat, Fletcher and I dug holes for planting the seedlings. Then we got a pail of water and gave each one a drink. We'll look for tomato plants and maybe lettuce seed when I ride to town with the Iversen's next week. Funny thing...I found I even talk to my seedlings, telling them they need to grow because I have big plans. Momma used to talk to her plants. I think she even sang hymns when she pulled weeds or gave them drinks. I'm going to say prayers over mine. There are so many distractions during the day I often find I haven't even said "Good Morning" to God. So, if I pray while I'm weeding and watering, I will do two good things every day.

I'm so happy I have you to talk to about our new life here on our farm.

And so, another day has come and gone.

Kate

It would be many years before the seedlings would grow big enough to produce a few apples to munch, much less cook up into apple butter and pie slices. All summer, Kate's daily walkabout included a visit to check that the seedlings weren't wilting.

She saved small bits of kitchen scraps in a covered bucket under the sink. From time to time, she emptied it into the garden where she mixed it with dirt and shoveled it around the plants. Eventually, Harald told her, it would help break up the clods and nourish the soil.

He showed her how to hill potatoes, corn and beans. She hoed around her tomatoes and pumpkins. Best of all were the green sprouts of lettuce she picked to put on a roast beef or chicken sandwich or in salads. The pumpkins would be good for pies and a jack-o-lantern for Fletcher.

Life settled into a neat book of her days. She set up a rain gauge so she'd remember by looking in her daybook how much it rained during a certain season. But she didn't need her book to remind her of the day the sky turned pitch black in the afternoon before it poured rain and a tornado roared across the land as she hid Fletcher under the sideboard.

May 28th, 1928

Dear Days,

Yesterday was so scary I'm still shaking. After the storm, Harald and Helen came up to make sure we were okay. Harald was driving his tractor and pulling a wagon on behind. I could see Helen hanging on for dear life as the tractor went back and forth across the road to get by trees that were uprooted and tossed around.

They came to take Fletcher and me down the hill to spend the night.

Fletcher was taking a nap when the lightning, thunder and roaring wind started. I grabbed him out of his crib and pushed him under the sideboard where he would be safer. I pulled the rocker close, holding the little white leather Bible Grandfather Fletcher gave me when I was Confirmed. But I was too terrified to say or even think any words. I just clutched the Bible as the howling wind crashed overhead, dropping stuff it gathered up elsewhere on its way to our farm. Fletcher and I were safe with the grove of pine trees protecting our house. Even after the storm passed, it was a long while before I could scoop Fletcher into my arms. He just cowered in the corner. We walked over to look through the hole where a windowpane had once held out the rain, sleet and snow. Later, when the rain stopped and the wind calmed, I got Fletcher dressed for a hike down the road. I knew Harald would have some scrap wood I could nail over the broken window.

Then I heard it—the sound of a John Deere popping up the hill. Harald had loaded supplies unto the wagon. He and Helen waved as they pulled into the yard. They'd come to see how we fared and what might need fixing. But first, they insisted I gather up some things so Fletcher and I could stay overnight. Harald brought wood and found a piece that fit over the broken window. He propped it up with a broom handle anchored it in place by the back of the Morris chair. He said he'd come back tomorrow to fix it properly.

Then Fletcher and I climbed on the wagon for the ride to their house.

Helen said Grammy had a pot of soup simmering on the woodstove. It would, she said, be the best medicine for soothing our shattered nerves. Harald dropped us off at the back porch where there were lanterns set out to light our path. He drove the tractor to the machine shed near the barn, then followed us into the house. We marveled that the strong winds hadn't even tipped over the three wooden porch rockers that still creaked back and forth in the gentle breezes.

And so, a quiet night!

Kate

Kate remembered tornadoes in Iowa, but this was different. Now she was responsible for a little boy and herself. As they ate, the Iversen's talked about serious storms and decided that when it looked bad, Harald would come to get us.

Harald and Jim, the hired man, just started milking when the wind tore through. After they finished eating, Harald went out to see how the milking was coming. Jim was finished and anxious to have some of Grammy's soup.

Grammy slept in the downstairs bedroom, just off the kitchen. There was a little iron bed in the room, but Fletcher almost always curled up in Grammy's bed to nap. Grammy Iversen had a lot of grandchildren but most of them were already in school. She was happy to have Fletcher to take care of.

CHAPTER TWO

February 7ᵗʰ, 1930

Dear Days,

Do I dare hope this time I could be expecting? After so many sad days when the baby I dreamed of didn't grow, maybe this one will be different. I'm so excited. I'd like to let Gerrit know that maybe we'll finally have another baby. This one seems to be doing all the right things. I don't have much energy, and I nap every afternoon when Fletcher sleeps. But the best part is my summer dresses are getting a bit snug. Maybe next week I'll ride into town with Helen and Harald so I can buy yard goods to make bigger dresses. I probably should make an appointment with Dr. Chandler. Every time I lost another baby, he'd pat my shoulder and tell me not to get my hopes up about having any more. Please God, let this baby be healthy and come out to live with us.

And so, another day. Goodnight!

Kate

Helen and Harald were always anxious to have Kate and sometimes Fletcher ride to town for shopping day. If they went in the morning, Fletcher usually went along, but if they didn't go until afternoon, Fletcher stayed with Grammy so they could nap.

June 30, 1930

Dear Days

Harald stopped at the bank this morning so I could cash the check Gerrit sent last week. Gerrit never asks what I do with the money. I'm afraid

23

*to tell him my news for fear it will end the same
way as the others. Helen, no doubt, figured out
what I had to shop for today. She said she had to
pick up thread and buttons at the general store.
But instead of finding buttons and thread, she
walked right over to the yard goods aisle and
started picking summery dress material. I'm
worried. Dr. Chandler told me I had to rest a
lot and that meant hiring someone to help with
the farm work until baby arrives. He said it's the
only way I'll make it to term. I believe him. Let
this baby come to live with us.*

Kate

When Gerrit came again in late May, Kate had more than an expected baby to tell him about: there were young apple trees in the grove behind the house and a rosebush Harald planted in the grassy circle across from the front porch, which was covered in roses last summer.

Gerrit was thrilled at learning a second son was on the way. He talked about going back to Chicago to close out his life there and move to the farm for good. But Kate knew that wouldn't be the answer. He was many wonderful things, but a farmer still wasn't one of them. Besides, she knew they'd need money coming in until the farm could bring in enough to pay the bills.

In the end, he took the train back to Chicago.

July 5th, 1930

Dear Days,

*Guess what? A letter from Gerrit arrived
yesterday. He said we had to get a telephone at
the farm. We need one, even if it is expensive.
He said he made inquiries to find out how soon
telephone would be available. He said he was so
used to having a telephone, and he wants one
up here so he can stay in touch until our new
baby arrives.*

A happy Kate

Dr. Chandler's due date for the baby was right on target. Helen and Harald drove her into town in plenty of time and took Fletcher back with them until his poppa came. By the time Gerrit's rental car pulled into the hospital lot, baby Annalise had arrived. She had a healthy set of lungs that could be heard up and down the small hospital hallway. Baby was fine, but Kate was less so. When Gerrit found her, still sleeping off the effects of her ordeal, he was shocked at how exhausted she looked. And how beautiful.

Kate never made a fuss about his not coming for long periods of time. Sometimes it was the bitter cold, or sleet and ice, or just too much snow. And on softer days, Gerrit could get so wrapped up in the cadence of his life there that he often forgot about the farm he'd bought and the woman and child he'd delivered up there to 'man' the operation until he was ready to be a farmer. The last time he'd been up was early spring when Kate told him she was going to have a baby in fall.

He kept putting off quitting his bank job, and there it was—early September—and he most likely still wouldn't have left Chicago if he hadn't gotten that phone call from Helen, letting him know Kate was about to have the baby.

"Aren't you coming?" Helen asked. "Dr. Chandler said he expects Kate to deliver any day, which was why he asked you to come to the hospital."

It was probably guilt that made Gerrit finally go to the bank president and tell him he was needed Up North to help his wife who was due to have their second baby in a few days. Who could argue with that? Gerrit had been a valuable employee, and the bank was reluctant to see him go. But they wished him well. His last paycheck would be ready by the end of the day.

The timing was so tight there wouldn't be time to say goodbye to the many friends he'd worked with at the lineup of teller stations. But he would make it around to thank the bank officers. And since he'd been expecting this phone call, he'd already gathered his things so he could be on the eight-forty train to Wisconsin the next morning.

Most of the long train trip north he spent fretting over how he could have left Kate and Fletcher alone for so many months. Years? He knew Harald and Helen looked out for her, but she was alone day after day, making her own way with the help of a little boy who was now three years old.

It didn't feel like a good beginning for his new life with his own family. He was so consumed with the need to have a farm he hadn't seen the skewed irony of it. All those years, running away. Now he was face-to-face with his own farm and the struggle to make it work. Even without anything to trigger an asthma attack, he could hardly breathe.

To avoid dwelling on his past, he focused on his to-do list for this first week. Most important: hire someone to run the farm. A tractor. Farm implements. A barn full of milk cows. A couple horses. A used car to replace the Essex he sold months ago.

Gerrit's life was bundled into two suitcases and a tall box his mother left for him. When he gathered his bags and box to get off the train, he had a moment of dread. He certainly didn't deserve the life he was stepping into. A wife who handled a pregnancy and delivery. Alone. Who worked the little farm and raised their son. Alone.

While he had the advantage of a good job to grow his farm equipment account, all he had from the sad, lonely years of his childhood was in a box his mother left for him at the Conner's. This was the first time he faced up to what he'd done to his family. He was determined that his life with Kate and their children would be different.

The three blocks Gerrit walked from the train depot to the hospital was barely enough to get his demons under control. Quitting his banking job was enough trauma, but memories of his childhood during that long train ride unnerved him.

Inside the hospital, he set the box and suitcases in a corner of the lobby and went to the reception desk to inquire if Kate was there. He found her asleep in her second floor room.

Gerrit didn't know how long he'd been standing there watching her. Nurses came and went. Still she slept. The sky dimmed from bright afternoon sunlight to twilight. Lights in nearby houses came on. He thought of Fletcher having supper in the Iversen's kitchen.

Kate stirred. Her eyes opened, not quite taking in where she was or who was with her. She smiled. "Did you just get here? Have you seen her?"

"She's so beautiful. Like her mother."

"I want to name her after my mother," she said as the nurse took the baby out of the bassinet and handed her to Gerrit. Kate marveled at how easily he held the little bundle. She wasn't what he'd expected, but she knew his heart didn't mind. They'd figure out how to run a farm with one little boy and his baby sister.

Gerrit handed the baby to Kate. "We have to call Pastor Conner and your mom. Later, when they let you up, we can put you in a wheelchair for a ride down the lift to the first floor. I saw a phone booth near the desk. I talked to your dad before I left Chicago."

When a rattling cart stopped outside the door, Gerrit realized it was time for Kate to eat. The young girl who carried in the tray explained that Kate could have only a light snack. "The lunchroom for visitors and staff is on the lowest level," she said. "They have sandwiches, soup and good coffee until eight o'clock."

Gerrit pulled a chair over to Kate's bedside and sat down, leaning his elbows on the bed so he could touch the wrinkled pink skin of his newborn daughter. The nurse came in to tend the baby so Kate could eat her red gelatin.

There was so much to talk about—plans to discuss, missing time to retrieve. But not now. Now was the time to bask in the joy of a second baby. Kate didn't know Gerrit's luggage and box of treasures stood in the corner. He hadn't told her she wouldn't go back to the farm alone. That he'd come to stay, find a job, and stock their farm with more than the few dozen chickens she'd been tending. She didn't know that the week she'd be in the hospital would be a busy one for him...settling in, getting acquainted with Fletcher, shopping for a used car, and finding someone to run the farm.

A nurse's aide pulled the shade, closing out the darkened sky. When it was time for Kate's bedtime back rub, Gerrit walked downstairs to the phone booth and dialed the Iversen's. It was a number he knew well, since he called most weekends to find out how Kate and Fletcher were. He knew Kate would never tell him what her lonesome life up here was really like.

Helen and Harald were anxious to meet the latest addition to the neighborhood. Perhaps tomorrow after church. "Sunday's always a good visiting day," Helen said.

Gerrit wouldn't tell her what the baby's name was. "You'll have to ask Kate," he teased. But the two women had long ago discussed name choices. Helen knew Annalise was Kate's choice.

When Gerrit got back to the room, Kate had already dozed off. He didn't trust driving out to the farm so late at night. He figured the pillow and blanket in the recliner were for him. Annalise had been moved back to the nursery where she and the night nurse took turns dozing. Despite interruptions for pills and vitals, Kate slept soundly. Gerrit was restless, anxious for the day to start.

As the morning sky brightened, he ran down the long list of projects lined up for the day—before remembering it was Sunday. Car and farm implement dealerships certainly weren't open. If the Iversen's came to see Kate and the baby, perhaps he could get some tractor advice from Harald. He figured he'd need something strong enough to pull stumps from the swamp that stretched east from their barnyard to the mailboxes. He remembered the day he'd come up from Chicago to look at the farmland he'd already made an offer to buy. Sight unseen. It certainly didn't look like Iowa farmland, but the price was agreeable. He figured, after it was cleared and plowed, it would start looking like Iowa. Then he remembered home was Wisconsin. Iowa was where he'd grown up, but it had been several years since he lived there.

Although he knew the Conner's missed their daughter, he was sure they probably would never make the trip to see Kate. Her Methodist upbringing was misplaced here, where the closest Sunday service was at a small, sparsely attended Lutheran church. Kate generally walked to the Iversen farm early Sunday morning for the one-mile ride to attend church with them. Kate's letters to Gerrit often told about the fun she had and the people she met at church activities. It was a life Kate made for herself and Fletcher.

Gerrit was never much for church-going of any denomination.

Helen and Harald brought Fletcher when they came in the afternoon. While Kate showed off baby Annalise, Fletcher took a quick look, then went off to stand beside Mr. Iversen.

All too quickly, the sunny afternoon slipped toward twilight, and the Iversen's gathered their little houseguest and headed home for milking and the supper they knew Grammy would have in the warming oven.

Kate finally had the promised ride to the phone and a call to her family. When she heard her Momma's voice, she struggled to keep from crying. She hadn't seen them since she moved to the farm. Before that, her brother Daniel had often driven into Chicago to pick her up so they could go to Iowa after he finished his Sunday services. They'd head back early Monday morning, and he'd take her into Chicago before heading back to his church in Joliet. She envied his weekends with their parents.

She could tell by her voice that Momma was overwhelmed that Kate had named the baby Annalise after her. It had become a Conner tradition to pass along family names to the next generation. Just as Annalise and Pastor Conner named their younger daughter Katherine in honor of her grandmother, Annalise was thrilled to tears knowing her name had now been passed on to this new grandchild.

Back upstairs in the room, Gerrit noticed that Kate's face had lost its pallor as they talked about their future life in this still-rustic area of Wisconsin's Northwoods. While she was relieved to learn he would not be going back to Chicago, she was worried how they'd manage without his salary to pay the mortgage and buy cattle and equipment for the farm. And when he told her about their need for a car, tractor, *and* cows, she was almost frantic. She didn't have any idea how much money he'd accumulated, nor how much it would take to keep the farm running without a weekly paycheck. As the day faded and Gerrit left to go out to the farm, Kate realized she hadn't brought her daybook to the hospital. Writing a page about the days that stretched ahead would have to wait, but she couldn't let that day end without saying her goodnight prayer.

Sept. 9, 1930

Dear Days,

And so, another wonderful day. Our baby girl is finally here, and I'm so happy! But the best news is that Gerrit isn't going back to Chicago. He said he has a good chance to get a good job, so he can hire someone to run the farm and he can go into town to work. The best of both worlds.

Kate

CHAPTER THREE

Gerrit wasted no time getting settled in Lillehammer: a new baby, a full-time job at the courthouse and a neighbor's son who was interested in hiring out as Gerrit's farm manager. He had a shopping list of equipment he needed for the farm and a car for getting him back and forth to work.

Kate would soon be going home from the hospital with Annalise, her mother's namesake. And Amish neighbors would help get the family settled in now that the baby would be coming home from the hospital.

The biggest worry for Gerrit was making sure he spent his savings wisely so they could buy what they needed without running out of money. Gerrit figured he'd better not get too far ahead on his equipment list.

Harald said he had an old tractor we could use until we can buy our own. And reminded Gerrit that the Amish use MANpower, never POWER equipment!

Gerrit needed a car. He rented one, but wasn't sure it's what he wanted.

"It's scary to spend so much money without a job," Kate told him.

"Don't worry," he said. "Harald's sure I got the County Treasurer's job. After that, we'll talk to Aaron Mellen, our Amish neighbor, about hiring one of his sons to run your farm."

On the drive into town, Gerrit asked Harald why he didn't take the Treasurer job himself.

He didn't answer right away. The Iversens had a long history in the County. Harald was third generation of the Norwegian family in Wisconsin. Most of those who came when the Iversens did, settled in Minnesota. But the Iversens preferred Wisconsin.

"Their original home was a small log cabin just a few miles from the Harald Iversen farm. The log cabin has been vacant a long time. His son, my dad, built this house we live in, although it didn't start out nearly so large. We bought good land, raised good crops, and had a large herd of milking cows and other livestock, including plow horses."

"I had an older brother. Farming wasn't his thing, but when the structure for the County was set up, he got involved. Ultimately, he was County Chairman."

"My brother was always anxious to do a little farm work in summer when things got busy. He used vacation time to help with haying and harvesting grain."

Harald was lost in his own world for a few minutes before explaining what had happened to his brother:

"My brother, Nels, was using our best team of draft horses to gather the bundled oats stacked in the field for drying. He had a wagon load and was crossing the ditch at the edge of the field when a couple deer spooked the horses, causing the wagon to tip. Nels had no time to grab the hayrack to stop his fall. He landed on the ground before the wagon tipped over—on top of him."

"When I heard the horses and Nels' screams, I raced like a wild man across the field. He was unconscious and his body limp when I got to him, and we couldn't revive him."

"Nels and I were very close, but we weren't a bit alike. I'm no politician. So that's why there hasn't been another Iversen in the courthouse. I still miss him dearly."

Gerrit seemed puzzled by Harald's history. "From all the stories I've heard, you may not conduct board meetings, but you sure 'run' this County. Anytime anything needs doing, you're the one they go looking for. Your family has had an incredible role in getting this area settled."

"One thing I've never figured out is why this town was called Lillehammer. Now I know," Gerrit said. "Or think I do. It's probably the place in Norway where your family emigrated from."

Harald was quiet for a bit. Finally, he said, half to himself, "I know that's the name of a town in Norway, but I'm not sure if that's where the Iversen clan is from. I always thought they just liked the name. Up here, in what started as a very hardscrabble place, the name probably added a little beauty to their surroundings."

Gerrit was quiet for a few minutes. "I can't imagine how sad it would be to lose your brother, your best friend."

After hearing Harald's story, Gerrit felt himself sinking back into the melancholy that haunted his train ride. Faced with stories of how other families grew up, he couldn't imagine how he could have been so uncaring. When Gerrit went away to college and a job, his parents were left without anyone to care for them as they got older.

His parents never mistreated him. He didn't remember his dad ever raising his voice, even when Gerrit told him it wasn't his job to help with farm chores.

Gerrit remembered nights when he couldn't breathe. His mom would come running to help as he gasped for air. She rubbed his back until his breathing settled. He remembered poppa in the doorway, looking worried.

In the morning, momma let Gerrit sleep rather than send him to school. She always made him oatmeal, even in summer.

As a kid, he was desperate to get away from the farm and all the things that stifled his breathing. He missed so many days of school, but his mom always brought his schoolwork home so she could help him keep up with his class.

When his mom got lung cancer, he often heard her struggle in the middle of the night, frantic to get air in her lungs. Pops rubbed her back until it calmed down. She used to help with the milking until she was too weak to go out to the barn. Gerrit remembered wanting to help her like she helped him, but he never did.

What Gerrit didn't know until much later was that his dad sold off most of his dairy cattle because he couldn't keep up with the milking. The neighbor, who bought most of the small herd, told Gerrit his dad had so few cows left it seriously depleted his income, and his warning that things would become more desperate came true. Regardless, Gerrit was removed from the farm. He wanted to be anywhere but there.

The worst was when they died. First his dad, whose heart just gave out. He remembered the sad little funeral. Although they didn't officially belong to his congregation, Pastor Conner arranged a service for him. The church was filled. Annalise Conner played the organ, and choir members sang hymns that Mrs. Jansz said her husband liked. In his eulogy, Pastor Conner called him a hardworking man who had a very hard life.

After he was gone, Gerrit's mom put the farm up for sale and moved in with her sister. It was Pastor Conner who called to let Gerrit know his mom had died, and it was Kate and Ida who stood with him during the service. With all the missed opportunities to make a difference in their family, standing there without them was the saddest day of Gerrit's life.

Before heading back to Chicago, Pastor Conner told Gerrit his mom left a large wooden box for him. Something rattled inside when he lifted it. His toys and treasures? Carefully folded on top was the quilt his mom made for his little bed. It was weeks before Gerrit had the courage to look under the quilt. It was all he had left of his childhood. His family.

Gerrit was so caught up in his own memories he didn't realize Harald was waiting to climb the steps to the courthouse. Thanks to Harald's advance work, Gerrit had a job offer as County Treasurer, and Robert Stanton could now retire. With that arranged, except for the County Board's vote to make it official, Gerrit stopped for a quick visit with Kate while Harald picked up supplies at the mill.

Then they went to their next appointment: shopping for a car. Gerrit would have liked Kate's help, but when he saw the robin's egg blue Plymouth, he knew he found the right one. He parked the car so Kate could see it. With a little help from a nurse's aide, she walked to the window. Kate wasn't sure if it was a good running car and worth the money, but she sure liked the color and shape.

CHAPTER FOUR

Gerrit's next stop was to see their next-door neighbor, Aaron, an Amish farmer. As they sat around the kitchen table having coffee and slices of homemade bread, Noah, the eldest, joined them. He didn't drink coffee but ate at least two slices of bread spread with apple butter. Eventually, Aaron called in his second son. "Samuel, this is Mr. Jansz, our neighbor. He needs farmhand help. I thought that might be a job for you."

Although Gerrit liked both young men, he thought the older boy, who had more experience, could easily work alone. That would be a huge benefit since Gerrit knew almost nothing about farming. The younger son probably knew more about farming than Gerrit could learn in a year—but he didn't say that out loud.

While the boys deferred to their dad, Noah said he was interested in working at the Jansz farm because he was anxious to someday have enough money saved to buy his own farm.

That made sense to Gerrit, but Aaron was still mulling the situation. Finally, Aaron asked Samuel what he would like to do.

"I think I'd like a little more time working with you on our place. Noah has been doing this for a couple of years and knows more than I do. I think I'd be too scared to do everything by myself," Samuel admitted.

"So, that settles it for now," Aaron said, looking across at Noah, who wore a broad grin.

Gerrit seemed pleased with the negotiations. "We only have one heifer now, but I'm hoping to buy a few more head in the next week or so. We have chickens and a horse that will need tending, and my wife's garden needs looking after. She's just had a baby and is still in the hospital. So, we'll start slow and easy with the things she's been taking care of."

They agreed on wages and routine for getting the work done.

Aaron's wife Nellie, who had gone somewhere in the house to take care of an unhappy baby, came back to the kitchen. "You'll also need help with housework and looking after your little boy, as well as the baby," she said. "I know you don't have family around to help, so when your Kate is home, let me know. My Aunt Cora lives not far away, and she's often here helping me. She's a widow and likes to stay busy. She knew Kate was about to have her baby, and she talked the other day about helping her once the little girl arrived. It is a girl, isn't it?"

When Gerrit asked what he should pay her, Nellie looked upset. "Oh, no," she said. "Neighbors help one another. We don't expect pay for being neighborly. So, that's settled, and you'll let Noah know when Kate and the baby are home. I will come with Cora the first few days. I don't think she's ever helped in an English house. I'll also help with the washing."

Gerrit couldn't believe his good fortune. He didn't have to figure out how to make a farm work and could earn his livelihood in a more enjoyable way. And someday he'd be able to take his wife and children to Iowa, where Kate could show Pastor and her momma that Gerrit was a good provider for her and their children.

There was only one problem that Gerrit didn't know how to handle: the tractor he hoped to buy. Amish use horses, not tractors. Aaron Mellen, an Elder, grimaced when Gerrit suggested that perhaps the young man could learn to drive the tractor. It was a question that was not raised again nor ever answered. The English had their practices, old-order Amish theirs—even though Noah would eventually learn to handle some chores with a tractor.

CHAPTER FIVE

After visiting their Conner grandparents in Iowa for the first time, Fletcher and Annalise had a large bag of children's books to take back to the farm with them. On the long ride home, Kate sometimes sat in the backseat between them so both children could look at the pictures as she read. Most of the books were stories Kate remembered her Momma reading to her when she was little. But many of those books had already been shared with cousins and the children of family friends. Fletcher and Annalise each had a new book with the same nameplate inside the cover that Pastor Conner used on his own books. Their names were printed on the label and signed by their grandparents.

The trip home was very sad for Kate. She could see her dad was failing. He could still preach a good sermon, but she knew it tired him out so much that he was happy for a nap in the afternoon. There were still not enough hours in a day for Nana Annalise. But there were shortcuts—bread from the bakery and Sunday dinner from the grocery store deli. And a parishioner who was happy for a little extra income when she helped with the wash, cleaning, and parish office every other week. Kate was happy when she saw her mother was willing to hire help so she could enjoy family visits and have time to visit sick parishioners.

Yet nothing could prepare Kate for the phone call she received barely four weeks after they'd returned to the farm. Pastor Conner's voice was barely a whisper as he tried to tell Kate that her mom had died in her sleep.

"Oh, Poppa. No! No! She can't be gone."

The Pastor couldn't say the sad news again. Kate knew she'd have to make the trip back to Iowa alone, and what was worse—she knew that would be followed by another. She and Poppa Conner cried without saying another word until finally she said Gerrit would put her on a train to Iowa, probably the very next day.

Grammy Iversen insisted she could take care of the children while Kate was gone for her Momma's funeral. She had it all figured out. There was a little cot in a bedroom upstairs. They could bring that down so Fletcher and Annalise could both sleep in Grammy's room. Kate knew Fletcher would just climb into bed with Grammy like he always did, curling up with her for their afternoon nap.

Kate packed her things in an old carpetbag but kept her little confirmation Bible in her pocketbook. As she had done that long-ago day when a tornado spiraled over the farmhouse, she clutched the book but didn't remember saying the words to even a single prayer.

The miles inched along as she replayed her childhood of wonderful memories. Cookies in the kitchen. Special holiday programs at church. Concerts and plays at school where brother Daniel was always the star, especially the talent-show every February. There were always ball games where some cousin or another was the one making the winning run or hitting the tiebreaker. In a town where they seemed to be related to everyone up and down the block, there was never a time when kids sat around complaining there was nothing to do. The big problem was getting into the house before Momma's curfew.

Pastor Conner, along with Pastor Daniel, presided at Momma's funeral. The church filled with relatives, friends, and parishioners who were such a part of their lives for so many years. Kate prayed that she could provide as happy a life for her two children, even if their home was much more isolated. Momma Annalise had made it all seem so simple, but Kate learned long ago that was an illusion—there were hard days, anxious nights, tears. Kate just remembered the reassuring hugs, a kiss every night at bedtime, and promises that they would grow up and have wonderful families of their own.

Later that long, sorrowful day, Ida and Kate sat at the kitchen table. Ida moved the cups of tea she poured for them and reached for Kate's hand.

"You were always most like our Momma," Ida told her sister. "That's what I remember most about her, sitting here at the table, writing, reading, or just having a cup of nighttime tea. She always relished the quiet when she could sit alone, thinking about that day and what her plans were for the next days."

"I know she told us we couldn't look at her notebooks until after she was gone, but I don't think I could open even one of those little books and read what she'd written about our life here. Remember, she used to tell us that someday one of us would write a book about our family growing up here, across from Papa's church and sharing our lives with all those good people who came here every Sunday. You know," she told Kate, "you're the only one who can write that book. Daniel never would, and I never could."

Kate didn't answer, but she knew Ida had it right. Ida couldn't be bothered with writing in the little journals Momma gave each of us every year on our birthday. Kate's were always filled and packed away in that cardboard box in the attic. Daniel certainly would have had a lot to write about on his pages, but Ida never asked him if he had. Were his in the attic, or did he have them with him at his parish?

Four months later, Pastor Conner collapsed at his pulpit. He'd have loved that, Kate thought as she rode alone to another funeral. Daniel, the second of the Conner kids, had called to tell her they were now the oldest generation. Losing their dad was tough—he'd been chiseled from a tower of granite. There was no doubt where they were now. Together.

After the church service and committal ceremony at the cemetery, family, friends, and parishioners gathered in the parish center for the ceremony that began the healing from a terrible loss. With the room nearly overflowing, Kate noticed that extra tables, marked with the names of other congregations in town, were needed to accommodate all those who'd come for the funeral. Pastors from area churches, town officials, and business owners were there. Many asked for time to voice their sorrow at losing such an amazing man of God. Then it was Daniel's turn to thank them for their kind words and for sharing in the family's grief. But he thought they needed to hear a little more about this man who'd led the Methodists for so many years. It would be, he said with a smile, a bit more down to earth than the accolades that accompanied the service.

"I think you all know my sister, Ida. She's the one who thought she would succeed our Poppa in his pulpit," Daniel announced. "Ida and Kate, perhaps you could tell them what I'm talking about."

The two sisters looked at each other, then started to giggle. They walked up to the microphone.

Kate started: "Ida was forever practicing her sermons, sneaking into the church when poppa was busy somewhere else. She'd climb the stairs into the pulpit, after making sure that I was seated at attention in the front pew, waiting with baited breath for her fire-and-brimstone diatribe. Delivered full throttle and accentuated with fingers pointing at the chief sinner sitting in the front pew—me—and threaten me with where I'd end up as her fists pounded on the shelf that rimmed the pulpit."

She added: "Daniel always knew better than to tag along with us because he knew where we'd end up, and he lived in fear of our poppa walking in on one of Ida's rants."

The whole room erupted into laughter.

When things quieted down a bit, Kate continued. "Our poppa sometimes took a nap on Sunday afternoons. We kids were always shooed outside by our momma so he could get a good rest. One Sunday, I'd gone to play with a friend. Daniel was somewhere else, and Ida was left to her own devices. Poppa was only half finished with his nap when the doorbell rang. Momma hurried to answer it, thinking it might be someone collecting for a local charity. Instead, it was Mrs. Flanagan from the Catholic Church. She was so upset she didn't even waste time on pleasantries. Instead, she delivered a hasty message that something terrible was happening across the street in Pastor Conner's church.

"There's a lady screaming at the top of her lungs. I can't make out what she's saying, but it's very, very loud," Mrs. Flanagan said in an excited voice.

"By that time, Pastor Conner, in his bare feet, had come down the stairs and flew out the front door and across the street. The main door of the church was locked, so he hurried around to the side where he knew the sacristy was unlocked. Inside, he found Ida. Even without an audience, she'd worked her lungs up to full volume, but that wasn't the half of it. She'd been trying out the volume control on the new pulpit speaker system, which the church council had bought so pastor wouldn't have to talk so loud on Sundays. A slight twist of the knob would have been enough to carry the sound down past the Lutheran, Catholic, Baptist, and Presbyterian churches. While Pastor shook his finger at his eldest daughter, he rushed the pulpit and flipped off the amplifiers. Ida considered climbing over the rim of the pulpit and making a run for it. By that time, Mrs. Flanagan had gotten inside the church and stood there, not knowing whether she dared laugh. I can't say that was Ida's last sermon, but it was the only one she ever screamed into the loudspeaker system."

"Ida didn't grow up to be a preacher, but she was most like Pastor Conner in his real work in this congregation—the gentle words he said to people when he wasn't preaching. He never raised his voice to us, despite all our hijinks, and he always had as much time as anyone needed to talk things over, solve a problem, or share a good laugh. "That little office in our house was the heart of this parish," Kate said. "Find joy in the stories you remember about him."

Ida added only a few words: "He was a man who loved his wife dearly, put up with his kids and their shenanigans, and, in time, packed up and went home to the Man he served up to the end.

The full room sat in almost-stunned silence. Kate couldn't believe she'd had the courage to tell stories about some of the human things that happened in the parish house and in the church. But it was a house that had held a growing family and now was vacant and ready for a new pastor.

Ida, grinning from ear to ear, hugged her sister and brother. Life had been such a joy for all of them growing up there. "You were right," she whispered to Kate. "I admired our Poppa all my life and wanted to grow up to be just like him, but shouting sermons wasn't the answer. It was his quiet voice and the gentle, caring way he handled people and the work of the parish."

As the crowd thinned out, parishioners and other visitors took time to thank the Conner children for sharing their poppa with them, not only every Sunday, but any hour of the day or night when someone needed him in that little office near the front door.

"It's now our sad duty to pack up the lives we lived here and let another pastor take his place."

Sept. 15th, 1933

Dear Days,

Saying goodbye to Aunt Ida and my brother Daniel was almost as hard as saying goodbye to Momma and then Poppa. I know Fletcher and Annalise are well cared for, but I had to get back home to them. I've been rewinding my own childhood, and I am hopeful I will have learned all of momma and poppa's lessons so well I can give my little ones the same kind of childhood. I know we won't be having any more babies. Perhaps if I hadn't worked so hard in the garden and picking rocks in the fields, I could have had another one. Or two. But Dr. Chandler said those first years on the farm and the babies I lost took a toll. He said I should be thankful we have two.

And so, another day. I'll be home soon. Home on our farm. Thank you, for our wonderful parents and for the two little ones waiting for me at home.

Kate

Sept. 17, 1933

Dear Days,

I'm sorry I didn't have time to write for two days. I just felt so lost knowing momma and poppa are both gone. That first day, all I could do was sit in the kitchen rocker.

I think our little Annalise grew while I was gone. Her hair has changed from golden straggles to reddish-gold curls. She looks more like Nana Annalise every day.

Fletcher had a hundred adventures to tell me about when we brought him home from the Iversen's—rides on the tractor with Grampy Harald, gathering eggs in the henhouse with Grammy. He helped her candle eggs, so they didn't put one in the carton that had been fertilized. The Iversens made weekly trips delivering their fresh eggs to stores and customers.

When the Iversens eventually give up farming, perhaps the children and I could take over their egg route, gather and candle eggs, and put the best into cartons that Gerrit can deliver when he goes to work in town.

Maybe in time I'll learn to drive and could go on my own to deliver eggs. Gerrit doesn't think much of that idea. It isn't that he'd worry about my traveling by myself or that I wouldn't find my way home. Rather, it's that we'd need a second car. He argued that there wasn't any need for me to drive into town during the week since he could stop for things I needed on his way home for supper. And we could all drive into town on Saturdays when he didn't have courthouse hours. But that can all wait for the day the Iversens retire.

Big news: my apple trees have little apples growing on them. The blossoms from early spring are turning into real apples. The joy of that dream quickly dipped into a trough of sadness, remembering the dried apples momma made from the trees behind the parish house. Packages of the sun-dried fruit were always good sellers at the church fall festival.

I'll have to stop at Carl's Hardware Saturday to see if he has one of those new electric machines that dry fresh fruit quick and easy.

Next Tuesday when Helen drives her eggs around to customers, Annalise and I will go along. Now that Fletcher is in first grade, he's at school until the bus drops him off at the farm late in the afternoon. By that time, we should be back from town and have apples drying in the new food-drying machine on the porch. Gerrit never pays much attention to what's happening out there when he hurries through to get out of his suit and into his farmer gear. Fletcher is old enough to wear barn gators like his poppa when the two hurry out to check on the milking. Fletcher's job is holding the cow's tail so it doesn't dislodge the milking machine. Sometimes Gerrit lets him strip the final drops of the day into his own small bucket. The barn cat usually gets a few good slurps for her supper before they head back to the house for their own.

Another busy day.

Kate

Sept. 24, 1933

Dear Days,

I think I'm going to look for plastic bags instead of wax paper to package the apple rings for the Lutheran church festival next Sunday. If only momma could see the huge pile of dried

*apples on the breadboard, ready for packaging.
I hope the shoppers will like them as much
as they did at the Methodist fall festival in
Iowa. The dryer hasn't shut off in a week. The
instruction booklet had a lot of suggestions for
preserving foods for soups and other recipes for
winter meals and treats. I think I'm going to
have to buy another food dryer.*

Thank you for such a beautiful fall day.

Kate

The apple rings were a hit, and when neighbors learned she hadn't exhausted her apple harvest for drying, they put in orders to buy more when those were ready. Customers wanted dried fruit they could eat long after the fresh apples shriveled up or went bad. Now with an even bigger food dryer ready to be plugged in, she'd give up on canning applesauce and only make dried apple rings. Gerrit had no idea how much her business added to the money she banked during the apple season.

Kate had long-since learned to drive a car, which made deliveries easier.

Oct. 1st, 1933

Dear Days,

*Every time I think about how Ida and I
passed up our chances to go to college and
maybe even qualify for jobs like being teachers
and how sad that made our parents, I could cry.
Will Fletcher and Annalise grow up and break
my heart? I'll do the best I can to nudge them
into making good choices as they grow up.*

*But I'd best get to bed. Another day has flown
by.*

Please help me make right choices for my life.

Kate

BOOK TWO

Annalise's Story

CHAPTER ONE

Annalise watched from the window of her upstairs bedroom at Aunt Ida's house, three blocks from the high school she would be attending for the next four years. It was the first time she'd been away from home without her family.

Ida, Pastor Conner's oldest daughter, moved to Wisconsin years earlier to be close to Emily and Tom, her daughter and son-in-law, after Jake could no longer manage their Iowa farm. Ida tried to take care of Jake and the farm but in the end she had to sell it. When Emily and Tom graduated from Iowa State, they both got teaching jobs at the same high school in Wisconsin. Emily worked only a little over a year before she learned they were expecting a baby. But, when Tom was killed in an icy car crash, Emily lost the baby.

Now, both Ida and her daughter, Emily, were widows in Wisconsin.

Annalise first met Aunt Ida and Cousin Emily during one of her mom's infrequent trips to Milwaukee for a checkup with a heart doctor. She couldn't remember her mother ever talking about heart trouble. She knew Nana's family had some heart problem history, but so far it hadn't stretched down to the Conner clan. Still, Kate wasn't taking chances.

As a sacrifice to ensure that his wife's heart would not be troubled by his pipe- and cigar-smoking habits, Gerrit stopped smoking. His cigars and humidor disappeared, as did the thick blue smoke that floated over his desk. He still had his tray of pipes, but didn't keep even one cigar to smoke during his walk across the farmyard to check on the milking. With the smoke gone, he thought he didn't have to worry about Kate's heart.

Poppa didn't go along when Kate took Annalise to visit Ida. He had money enough set aside to pay college expenses for Fletcher and Anna, but with the hefty savings from Anna's dried apple slices, he knew she had enough to pay her college-prep-school tuition, plus room and board at Ida's.

Although Pastor Conner and Nana Annalise were both gone, Gerrit was still intimidated by the chasm he created when he married their daughter Kate and moved her out of reach, first to Chicago, then northern Wisconsin. He was always dismayed that Kate's parents never took a train to Chicago to visit Kate when Fletcher was born. Instead, Kate and Gerrit took Fletcher and Annalise to Iowa so they could meet their grandparents. Fletcher remembered them, but Anna was still too young to figure out who those people were. Nana Annalise was thrilled to meet her namesake, who also was a look-alike of her own baby picture.

Like Kate, young Annalise took some of her storybooks along with her when she moved to Aunt Ida's her freshman year at St. Michael's High School. Originally a boy's-only school, the diocese opened enrollment to girls a year earlier.

Fletcher, who would be starting college next year, could have gone to the same Milwaukee school. But he was content to ride into town with Poppa during Anna's time at Aunt Ida's. It apparently had never occurred to Fletcher that he could have gone to the all-boy high school in Milwaukee. He was old enough to do a farmhand's work with the milking but was excused from morning chores while school was in session. Weekends when there were no meets were for training for sports, especially running.

Annalise had wanted her brother along when they drove down to Aunt Ida's at the start of the school year. But Fletcher had other plans: "I've been training all summer to get in shape," he said.

Kate remembered watching when Gerrit tried out for track and field. There was never any doubt he'd make the team, and eventually was voted captain. But Fletcher inherited the same breathing problems his dad had. Also like his dad, he tried to hide them by conserving energy, running all-out only when it really mattered.

Poppa was determined his son would succeed. Poppa never complained when he had to drive Fletcher into town on Saturdays for training and meets. One day, Kate was home before Gerrit and Fletcher got back from an out-of-town meet. They'd stayed for all the events, anxious to find out where Fletcher placed in overall scoring. When they saw Kate's car in the second bay of the new garage, Fletch jumped out before poppa's car pulled in alongside. He had ribbons to show his mom.

The house seemed surprisingly empty, despite there being only one less person at the table. Fletcher could be overflowing with excitement, but he never worked up the same energy as Annalise—even when the topic was as mundane as an update on her latest bank tally or reading a thank-you letter from a new apple-slice customer. It would take a little getting used to life without Anna.

Aunt Ida, on the other hand, was getting used to a new level of energy in her home.

Kate had cautioned Anna not to babble. Ida lived alone for many years, and the chaos that surrounded her when Emily was growing up ended long ago. Annalise tried her best to talk slower and more quiet, but it was a losing battle. Then she noticed that Aunt Ida was always waiting for her after school. She was interested in how the day had gone, who Anna met, everything that was so exciting about coming all this way just to go to high school. Although she was a Methodist like the rest of the Conner clan, Ida said she'd like to meet this Father Cleary Nolan, who was the principal of the school and pastor of the parish. Perhaps he could come to supper some Sunday night. She knew pastors of any denomination always had meetings or appointments every night of the week, except Sundays.

Ida and Father Nolan worked out a Sunday night when he would be available. He even brought a container of ice cream and a jar of raspberry jam for topping, carefully wrapped in layers of newspaper to keep it from melting.

Over supper, Ida monopolized the conversation with a never-ending list of questions about Roman Catholics. When she ran out of those, she switched to an explanation of the Methodist faith she'd grown up with. Surprising, Cleary Nolan seemed to know more about her faith than even she did. It was an interesting conversation that went on long after the last dribbles melted in the ice cream dishes. One weekend, when Kate was coming to visit Anna, Ida convinced her to stay longer, promising an interesting Sunday supper guest. Kate was surprised to see a man with a Roman collar when Ida sent her to answer the door.

Anna left the dining room as soon as she finished eating. She excused herself to finish a book report for English class. She closed her bedroom door, but when it got stuffy, she opened it a crack. Eventually, she closed it again to keep out the conversation that kept intruding on her struggle to compose her report. A long while later, Kate called Anna down to say goodbye to Ida's guest. Rather than come downstairs, she leaned over the banister and told Father Nolan she'd fallen asleep and would see him the next morning at Mass.

Kate was taken aback by how easily Anna mentioned her plans to attend Mass. Perhaps it was just the way Catholics started every school day.

The next morning, Kate drove Anna to school then headed back north. Her head was awash with a replay of the previous evening's conversation. Was this really the best type of school for her daughter? Suddenly, she realized how askew her own thinking had become. Raised Methodist, she attended the little Lutheran church a mile or so from the farm. Even though it now was possible for her to drive into town to the Methodist church, she continued to attend services at the Evangelical Lutheran church where she helped raise money for new hymnals by selling spiced apple rings at the fall festival. Over several years, apple money bought paint for the shabby, white clapboard siding, then evergreen trees that would grow into a windbreak along the driveway to the church grounds.

Gerrit always teased Kate and Anna about their dried apple rings, but he was happy to plant the spruce tree seedlings that had grown into a substantial snow and wind buffer at the church.

The traveling pastor who served the Wisconsin Lutheran Church down the road announced that he'd have a special meeting after services the following week for members who wanted information about family burial plots. Over the years, Kate had walked through the cemetery many times. Years earlier, she dreamed of her remains being taken back to Iowa so she could be buried alongside momma and Pastor Conner. Over time, she realized she and Gerrit would instead be laid to rest in that country cemetery where they'd be among friends. She hadn't thought about it since her parents died. She could finally face the reality of how settled she'd become in this place she called home.

In the time Kate lived at the farm, she'd gotten to know many of the original settlers. Now, many more were laid to rest west of the church. It was hard to miss the Iversen monument where Grammy was buried. Kate always stopped to talk, keeping her posted on what was going on in the neighborhood and how the children were growing up. They'd had happy times when Kate and Fletcher were alone at the farm. He was just a baby when they moved there. Now he was a senior and thinking ahead to college. She knew Grammy would be pleased to know Fletcher was courting her great-granddaughter, Cynthia, who was planning to study nursing at the state university in Madison.

"But you already know that," Kate whispered. Then she patted the headstone and left the white rock she carried with her that morning. Someone told her it was a Jewish custom to leave a stone on a grave marker. Someone else said it was an old European custom. It was now a tradition she took as her own.

When she got back to the house, Fletcher said Aunt Ida called to tell them she and Emily had business there the following weekend and would stop in to say hello. Annalise, who had a forensics competition that Saturday, would not be along. She had arranged to stay with a teammate so she wouldn't be alone on Saturday night.

But Anna didn't go to the forensics meet. She woke up with laryngitis and could barely whisper. Had she practiced her speech so much that she brought on a bad sore throat? Her teammates wished her well and went off in search of top-place awards and the promise of eventually making it to state finals. Anna fixed a warm honey tea to soothe her throat and went back to bed.

After sleeping off and on all day, she woke to the knocker banging on the front door downstairs. She thought about ignoring it but then decided Aunt Ida's neighbors, not knowing she was out of town, might be at the door and worried when she didn't answer. Anna put on her bathrobe and went downstairs. The knocking didn't stop until she twisted the key to unlatch the door.

"Father Nolan, what are you doing here?" Annalise asked.

"The coach said you missed today's meet due to a sore throat. I thought you might like some warm soup along with the team's results," Father Nolan said.

She reached for the jar of soup, but instead of handing it to her, he stepped inside and closed the door.

"Are you feeling better?"

"I just woke up."

"Is Ida here?"

That's when Anna knew she needed to keep a record of what happened in Ida's house when Father Nolan invited himself in on a Saturday night when she was alone.

"Why are you here?" Anna asked again.

"I thought you might need some warm soup to help your sore throat. Will Ida be back soon?"

"I'm not sure when she'll be back."

He asked again about Ida, but again Anna hesitated.

He knows she's gone, maybe even that she's out of town. Otherwise, she'd have made her own soup for my supper.

"I heated this soup before I walked over here tonight, so I'll get a bowl out for you and you can eat it while it's still nice and warm."

He opened the cupboard door and took out a bowl. He had more than enough soup in the fruit jar to fill the bowl twice. "I even brought crackers."

Anna prayed he'd leave as soon as she ate the soup. But he didn't.

He read the forensics results as she stirred the crackers around in the bowl. She scooped out a small spoonful and tasted it. It burned the inside of her mouth.

"This doesn't taste like chicken noodle soup," she said. But Father Nolan just ignored her. "Have another spoonful," he insisted. "I can't," she said. And didn't!

"When will Ida be home?" he asked again.

"When she gets here," she said. "You don't have to wait for her. Just leave!"

While she sipped the still-warm noodles and broth, he urged her to finish it all. Then he read the competition results.

Still, Father Nolan remained at the table. Annalise got up to rinse the bowl, leaving it to soak in the sink, then announced rather impolitely that she was still not feeling well and needed to go back to bed. He didn't take the hint. Instead of going to the front door, he started toward the stairs.

"I'll tuck you in," he said.

When she didn't follow, he crossed to where she stood leaning against the front door jamb, too frightened to move. He put his arm around her and encouraged her to walk with him up the stairs.

Maybe all he really wanted was to make sure I'd get back in bed safely—then he'd leave.

But he didn't. He pulled out a small cruet from an inside pocket and poured some liquid into an empty glass on the bedside table. "This will help the sore throat," he whispered. "Try a little. It's like the toddy my mother made when I had a sore throat. It will help you sleep."

I swallowed a couple sips, but it tasted worse than ever. He said he added orange juice to make it sweeter.

"You need to drink it, then crawl under the covers and go back to sleep."

He held the glass up to my mouth. "Try just a little more."

"My mother always fixed a toddy for me when I got sick. I used to get bronchitis, and she'd give me a few sips of this, so I'd sleep without coughing."

When I took the last swallow, he pulled a chair over to the bed. I laid back on the pillow and Father pulled the blanket over me.

"I promise, you'll sleep like a baby and by tomorrow morning you'll feel better. When you've dozed off, I'll let myself out so you can sleep."

Annalise did sleep all night, but she woke early the next morning with a wretched headache. *Besides the toddy was there something else, maybe in the soup?*

The coverlet and bed sheets were all rumpled. When she realized she didn't have her pajama bottoms on, she found them half under the bed, in a wadded-up heap. When she picked them up off the floor, she saw there were blood spots all over the pajama legs.

And there was a very painful ache between her legs. *What happened while I was asleep? What did he pour into that glass, insisting I drink all of it?*

I tried to remember last night, but all I could recall was him helping me up the stairs and into bed.

Instead of putting the wet pajama bottoms back on, I took a bath. Afterward, I put on clean pajamas. I put the soiled pajamas in an empty box from the closet shelf. I tried sponging the stains, but most were already dry. What will Aunt Ida think? I'm afraid to tell her who was here last night.

I crawled back in bed, avoiding damp spots on the sheet, and tried to sleep. But I couldn't stop crying. Was it the unexpected house call from Father Nolan and his stupid soup and stupid toddy?

October 24, 1943

Dear Days,

I thought I should write down everything that happened to me last night when Father Nolan was here. I called the forensics coach to let her know I couldn't go to the meet because I could hardly whisper.

It was already dark when I heard someone pounding on the front door. I thought Aunt Ida had come back and couldn't get in. Or was it a neighbor wondering why there were no lights on?

I still felt woozy, but I was careful walking down the stairs. When I unlocked the front door, I was surprised to see Cleary Nolan. He comes here sometimes to have Sunday night suppers with Aunt Ida. They mostly talk about religion and education. Father said he knew I hadn't gone to the forensics meet because I had a sore throat, so he brought some chicken noodle soup his housekeeper left for his supper. I didn't want him to come in, but he did anyway. He went out to the kitchen, took a bowl out of the cupboard and filled it with soup. He insisted I eat it all, but it had a very funny taste. And made me sleepy.

I did eat it. When I finished, I told him I had to go back to bed, and he'd have to leave. I went to the front door and opened it, but he didn't go out. Instead, he said he'd help me up the stairs so I wouldn't fall. He even went into my room and told me to get into bed. He said he'd sit there until I fell asleep. But first he pulled out what looked like the little pitcher with a stopper they use at Mass at the school chapel. He said he made some toddy like his mother made for him when he was sick. He poured it into a glass and told me it would help me get a good rest. It smelled awful. The next thing I knew, it was morning. There was a terrible ache between my legs. And my bed was a mess. Did I have a nightmare? Then I realized I didn't have my pajama bottom on. I found it on the floor half under the bed. When I picked them up I saw bloody spots. And more spots on the sheets. I put them in an empty gift box in the closet and took a quick bath, and put on clean pajamas. I tried sponging the blood off the sheets, but it was dried on. Then I remembered the soup bowl and knew Aunt Ida would wonder about that, so I went downstairs, washed the bowl and put it back in the cupboard.

On my way back upstairs, I decided I'd make sure the house door was locked. That's when I noticed the house key, that hung on the first hook was missing. But the door was locked. The only way Father could have gotten out, locking the door behind him, was if he took the key and locked it from outside. If Aunt Ida asks about the key, I don't know what I'll tell her. I know she'd be upset if she knew Father had been here.

I've used up so many pages of my notebook, but I wanted to write everything I could remember from last night. Momma always said our little notebooks are a good place to write things we don't want to forget. And while I don't want to remember how scary it was to have him in the house, I wanted to write it all down in case I ever needed to remember what happened.

Annalise

CHAPTER TWO

Annalise hadn't told Aunt Ida anything about the priest's visit, especially regarding the blood specks on the white sheet. Ida probably just figured Annalise had started her monthly period and unintentionally stained the sheet. But Annalise wouldn't have another period for months.

By the time Annalise—and Aunt Ida—noticed something was wrong, her friends at school undoubtedly also wondered why this petite new girl was starting to look a little pudgy.

Aunt Ida first talked with Emily about what she suspected. Then she called Annalise's mother and asked her to drive down for a visit on Saturday. In the meantime, Ida and Emily made an appointment for Annalise with Emily's doctor. It was uncomfortable for Ida, but the family's conversation with the doctor sent young Annalise into a panic. How could they think she was pregnant? She didn't even date boys. She never even talked to boys at school.

Kate was frantic, wondering what happened to Annalise that called for this hurried trip. When her mother arrived Saturday morning, Annalise started crying and couldn't stop. Ida hadn't questioned her niece on how this happened. That was her mother's place.

When Ida went out to the kitchen to make sandwiches and tea, Kate sat on the sofa with Annalise. Kate kept asking questions without answers: "How and when could this have happened?"

Sobbing, Anna tried to explain she didn't have any idea. Except...

She thought back to the day she was home alone with a sore throat and how Father Nolan brought a jar of soup. At first, she couldn't remember the name of the tonic, but then the word popped into her head. "Father brought a jar of soup, then insisted I drink the toddy he brought for my sore throat."

When Kate heard the word 'toddy,' she knew exactly what that priest had done. Here was her beautiful Annalise, who barely started monthly periods, was raped by a Catholic priest from the school and was now pregnant. Ida said the doctor they saw at the clinic confirmed Annalise was three months pregnant.

Kate's first thought was to call Gerrit and ask his advice, but she knew that was a conversation they needed to have later with a cup of tea on the front porch when no one else was around. She promised Annalise she'd handle that when they got back to the farm. She did call home, but simply told Fletcher she wouldn't be back until late tomorrow afternoon and Annalise was coming home. She started to say..." but she couldn't lie about the events unfolding for all of them. Instead, she hung up and took a minute to calm herself. Nothing in her life could ever have prepared her for this.

After lunch, Kate settled Annalise down to rest, then left for the first of several appointments she arranged. Then she went looking for the priest. She started at the neighborhood parish where the rector lived. When the housekeeper showed her to his office, he seemed surprised to see her.

Kate didn't make polite conversation. Father Nolan extended his hand across the expansive desk to greet her. When she didn't accept it, he motioned toward the chair opposite his own. But Kate leaned across the desk, glowering in his face. The door was slightly ajar, the protocol when a woman meets with a clergyman. She shouted at him about what he'd done to her daughter.

He went around the desk to close the door. He knew the housekeeper was close by, listening.

"The doctor who saw her said she is three months pregnant. That seems to match the time when you brought soup for her, knowing she was alone in her aunt's house. Then you gave her a toddy, a supposed 'home remedy' for her sore throat. When she passed out from the alcohol you made her drink, you raped her." Kate's heart was pounding.

His face showed no reaction. If anything, a slight smirk settled around his mouth. She had, after all, no proof. Besides, Kate's daughter would not be the first—nor last—to become pregnant after playing around with a boy from school.

He interrupted her tirade, insisting her accusations were false. He walked around to the side of the desk, so they were face to face. Although considerably shorter than Kate, he seemed to stretch himself taller before accusing her of repeating lies her daughter told her.

"How dare you come here and accuse me of being responsible for what your daughter did with one of her friends. I will thank you to leave. I presume you'll take your daughter home with you. I will advise the school office to refund your second semester tuition and send her current records to your home address. If you like, I'll have the secretary clean out her locker and send any personal items to you. Tell her we enjoyed having her and wish her well."

"I'm on my way to see your bishop," Kate said. "I'm sure you'll hear from him."

As she turned to leave, he hurried around to open the door. He held out his hand but again she didn't acknowledge his gesture.

Kate couldn't stop shaking. When she left his office, she saw the housekeeper across the way, obviously listening to voices from the principal's office. While she didn't care who heard her accuse him of doing this to a student, she hoped the housekeeper didn't hear a name to prattle to her friends.

Annalise was pregnant, and his visit with a jar of soup was a poor disguise for his real intentions that Saturday night. Kate had no way of knowing about the soiled pajamas her daughter had folded into a box on a shelf in her closet. What could possibly be the value in those?

When she mentioned she was on her way to his bishop's office, the priest's face blanched to a pale shade of gray. Kate had only a general idea where the bishop's office was, but when she found it, she realized she never made any effort to get an appointment. But right then, she didn't care. If he was in, she expected he'd see her. Unless, of course, Cleary Nolan alerted him she was coming.

She rang the bell at the lower-level door identified as the bishop's office. Since she parked close to that door, she figured someone would have seen her approaching. When no one answered, she rang more insistently. This time, she heard shoes on the stairs.

When the door opened, she saw it was the bishop's housekeeper, not his secretary. Kate was flustered at seeing a woman in a housedress and apron, carrying a dust rag. She didn't have an appointment. "I'm only in town for the day and it's very important," she said.

The housekeeper laid her dust rag on the radiator and asked Kate to follow.

Answering her tap on the door, a male voice told her to come in. When it was Kate who stepped inside, he seemed surprised to see a visitor rather than the cleaning woman. Kate tried to calm herself by imagining this was no different than the people who called on her father.

The bishop, who apparently had been reading letters, set them aside and stood up to greet her. That's as far as the pleasantries went.

"I regret barging in," she started, "but a situation has occurred involving my daughter and a priest of your diocese."

He sat down again. "How may I help you?"

She took a deep breath.

"My fourteen-year-old daughter has been raped and is now three months pregnant. She's only in her first year at St. Michael's High School. She didn't even realize she was raped because she had been plied with a lot of alcohol, and who knows what else, on the pretext it would ease her sore throat. Then she fell into an unconscious deep sleep."

The only person who visited Anna when she was home alone, was one of your priests, Cleary Nolan. And don't even suggest she was fooling around with a boy. What she remembers was answering the front door and finding the high school principal holding a jar of soup.

She tried to get him to leave, but he insisted on staying. He put his arm around her and helped her up to her room. That's when he poured his 'toddy' in a water glass and made sure she drank it all. Then Father Nolan re-filled it as he sat in the rocker beside the bed."

Kate noticed the bishop shuffling impatiently, realizing she raced through the details.

"Please hear me out, bishop. Her private areas were sore."

Kate's sister, Ida, with whom Annalise was living, and her niece were at Kate's farm that weekend. Somehow the priest found out she was alone. He even had the audacity to ask if her aunt was home.

"I'm sorry," the Bishop interrupted brusquely. "I need to keep on schedule."

"Just a few minutes longer," she said. "My daughter said when she went downstairs the next morning, she saw that the house key, which normally was on a rack near the front door, was missing. But the front door was locked. The only way it could have been locked from the outside was with a key. That key reappeared a week or so later when Father Nolan came over for another meal. At that time, my daughter knew she'd been raped but had no idea she was pregnant."

"The irony of all this, was he continued to show up for occasional Sunday suppers as if nothing happened. That's when he returned the key. And Annalise always found an excuse to stay in her room upstairs when he came for supper. At school, she religiously avoided him.

The bishop looked annoyed. Was he even listening? Did Father Nolan call to warn him Kate was coming to his office?

"I had a meeting with Cleary Nolan this morning, and he, of course, blames it all on 'boyfriends.' He's the one who was there that night when my daughter was sick and alone. I wanted to put you on notice about what we know happened. That ultimately will lead to a young girl having a baby. We could take away the problem if we believed in abortion, but we do not. Someone will have to cover the medical bills. Her doctor is concerned about her very young age and this pregnancy. Besides medical bills, the baby's father will have to provide support."

While the bishop promised to have a conversation with Cleary Nolan, he said he was confident there was nothing to the girl's accusations. He said he believed it really was just a story by a frightened young girl to get herself out of the trouble she and a schoolboy got themselves into.

"Making such a scurrilous accusation against a well-respected clergyman is uncalled for," the bishop scoffed.

His preachy tone and words didn't sit well with Kate. After all, she grew up in a parish house. The bishop seemed surprised when she explained that her father and his father before him were Methodist pastors. She'd heard plenty of Sunday sermons about making amends for wrongs they commit against one another.

Kate responded angrily, "How dare you claim this story isn't true? You have no right to defend him without even calling him in."

The bishop held up his hand, a signal to stop.

"And may I remind you that, just because your daughter made up this story to get herself out of a predicament, coming here and accusing this diocese of being responsible for her problems will not work. And if she decides to keep the baby, that's her choice, and yours."

The bishop's discomfort at this conversation was beginning to show, but Kate didn't back down. "We know Father Nolan gave her alcohol from a cruet that Annalise recognized as those used in the school chapel."

The bishop's secretary came in to announce his next appointment. That was supposed to be Kate's cue to leave, but it didn't work. She'd grown up with those situations in a parish office.

She again demanded to know how medical bills his priest caused would be paid and how this young girl was supposed to raise a priest's child, since they weren't Roman Catholic.

"It's a good thing my father is deceased and not a witness to this mess," Kate said.

The bishop opened a desk drawer and took out a notebook and a sheaf of papers. But Kate knew that trick and stayed seated.

"This isn't something you can just dismiss by accusing my daughter of lying about what happened to her. And while I'm certain your priest will lie to you, you have to consider the harm you do to your church if you let a clergyman get away with doing something so terrible to a child."

Kate continued: "I wonder how many other innocent young people he's done this to. He seems to have a well-practiced routine. There's no doubt he'll keep on.

"I know Roman Catholic clergy take a vow of celibacy—and this priest is no celibate. Nor does he follow what my father used to regard as his most important role: to protect the children.

"I don't care how often he confesses his transgressions. My daughter was brutalized, and had her innocence stolen from her."

Kate laid a piece of paper in front of the bishop with her name, address, and phone number.

"Annalise and I will expect to hear from you in the next few days, not with excuses, but with what you plan to do about it. My daughter's life was ruined while she slept. His sins will be fodder for gossip if we don't get this settled. This baby is not going away, neither is my daughter. Her father very reluctantly allowed her to leave home to attend this high school. We were assured it had a good reputation and safe environment."

The bishop remained seated until Kate was out the door.

She wondered if he'd even bother to call the rector. Father Nolan probably assumed Annalise was too young to get pregnant.

But her next worry was Gerrit's reaction when she tried to explain why Annalise was home with a car full of clothes and books.

Ida and Kate started packing Anna's things. They left her school jumpers in the closet. Ida would deliver them to the school office Monday.

The physical activity cooled some of Kate's anger. She packed Annalise's textbooks in a box and put them in Ida's car so they could be returned. Ida said she'd empty Anna's locker and send everything to the farm.

They'd have to see what the priest and bishop would do. Probably nothing.

Ida had beef stew simmering in a Dutch oven, which would be ready to serve when they finished piling the boxes and bags in the car.

There wasn't much left to say as they ate.

Emily arrived just as they were ready to leave. She had a little package tied with pink and blue ribbons. "Your first gift for baby." Emily looked across at Kate, then to Ida, wondering if the gift was a mistake.

"Thank you," Annalise whispered as she hugged Emily.

"We pray every day for you and the baby. We don't know how it all fits together, but we have to rely on God to help you and this little one."

Annalise just smiled as she climbed into the front seat for the long drive home. She was worried what Poppa would say. The backseat would announce that something had gone very wrong.

Annalise dreaded all the 'whats' she'd be asked when they got to the farm—questions without answers.

What would Poppa do?

What if he was ashamed of her?

What would Fletcher say?

What would they tell friends and neighbors?

What about school?

What would she tell the kids in her class about why she came home?

What would they think of her?

What if she didn't go back to school? What if she couldn't go back? What would she do until the baby was born? After the baby arrived? She couldn't just show up on a Monday morning as if she were just a new kid in town.

And what would it be like to be a baby's mom?

There weren't any answers.

After she settled down, Anna pulled out a new notebook for keeping track of her days now that she was home.

January 20th, 1945

Dear Days,

Momma and Aunt Ida whispered to each other while they were packing my things in the bedroom. They thought I was asleep. The bishop insisted the principal could not possibly have done anything so awful.

Momma said she might have shouted about what the priest did to her daughter. She told him: "Don't make excuses before you know the truth from the priest."

Momma told Aunt Ida I have to finish school, then go to college. She said she and Poppa would help with the baby until I was ready and able to do it myself. They didn't hate me or blame me for something someone else did to me. She said the new baby would be part of our family, and I'd never have to give it away. The baby would be loved by all of us together. Isn't that a wonderful idea?

Annalise

P.S. I need to remember to get my last daybook out to show mom and pops. I forgot I'd written all the things I remembered from when Cleary Nolan came with the soup and toddy. Maybe momma could show that to the priest and bishop, so they'd know I was telling the truth.

It's been scary to read this over and over. The answer is always the same—he raped me.

I don't have much confidence that anything will come of all this. They just keep denying it.

I doubt we'll ever get the truth out of the bishop's office, much less from Father Nolan. Give me courage to get through this. I'm so sorry I can't finish high school at St. Michael's. What if I need to be home-schooled? This isn't right.

Annalise

CHAPTER THREE

Poppa was on the front porch, working the rocker back and forth. When Kate made the sharp turn into the driveway, the rocker was still rolling back and forth but he was out the storm door and down the steps.

It apparently never occurred to Gerrit to just call Momma at Aunt Ida's and find out why she had to rush down to Milwaukee. Was Annalise sick? In trouble? Expelled?

When Kate pulled up in front of the steps, Gerrit saw the back seat was full of boxes and suitcases. He knew. She was expelled. She had no business going to a school so far away from home.

Annalise was afraid to get out of the car. Fletcher tried to open the door, but she wouldn't pull up the door-lock button.

On the other side, Gerrit opened the door for Kate, but she hesitated before she got out. "I'm so tired," she said.

"Fletch, your mother and I have things to discuss and you aren't included. I thought I told you to take your sister inside."

He tried again, but except for his mother's door, all the others were locked. He knocked on the window and motioned for her to unlock her door. Seeing it was Fletcher, Annalise pulled up the lock button and got out.

Kate saw that Annalise was finally out of the car. "Fletcher, maybe you could take your sister up to her room so she can rest.

Annalise saw the look on Gerrit's face. *Was he angry at what happened to her? But he didn't even know what happened to her.*

"Your mother and I have things to discuss."

Fletcher and Annalise went inside.

Kate and Gerrit walked around the yard. Talking. She told him of the priest's Saturday night visit when Annalise was home alone, sick. He'd brought her a jar of soup and later fed her some sort of alcoholic drink. She passed out from whatever she ate or drank.

When she woke up on Sunday morning the bed was all rumpled up and she didn't have her pajama bottoms on. She found those wadded up on the floor next to the bed.

Three months later Ida and Emily mistrusted what had happened and took her to Emily's doctor. After examining her, the doctor's diagnosis was simple. "She's three months pregnant."

"Three months?" Gerrit's face blanched. "She's going to have a baby in six months. She's only a kid! I knew it was a mistake to let her go so far from home to go to high school. "Now what are we going to do?" Gerrit muttered. "An abortion?"

Meanwhile, upstairs in her bedroom, Annalise is telling her brother what happened to her when she was sick and alone at Aunt Ida's.

They were interrupted by Kate. "We think it's time to sit down together and plan how we're going to handle this. Think you both can come downstairs for a pow-wow on the porch?"

Their serious conversation on the porch went in many directions and covered many questions. At one point Annalise began talking about motherhood. "That's foolish talk," Gerrit said. "You are a long way from being able to deliver and raise a baby at your age. And you are not going to drop out of school."

"What about reporting the rape to the police, I suppose it would have to be those down in Milwaukee," Fletcher added.

"I'm not going to tell the police anything," Anna sobbed. "If we did report it, then it would get in the newspapers and we'd all be faced with that for the rest of our lives."

"Your mother said she'd already reported all of this to the Milwaukee bishop. More stories to circulate," Gerrit said. "You and that baby will have that millstone hanging around your neck forever."

"I don't think so," Fletcher said. "I don't think churches are too eager to have all of their information plastered in newspapers. They like good publicity, but stories about a possible priest rape isn't something they want in headlines."

Anna stopped crying. "I think we can raise that baby like it was just one of us. It would be part of our family. I could go to school and take care of the baby when I got home. Momma could take care of the baby while I was at school. No one would know the difference."

"We'd have to have a good doctor who didn't spread this story all around," Anna said. "And they don't always put new baby arrivals in the newspaper. I looked for new babies that should have been listed and some never showed up."

"I think it might work," Kate said, but Gerrit wasn't ready to accept that.

"It has to work," Anna said. "Momma lost babies she wanted to have. This would give her one more to raise. We can share!"

"I suppose we could at least think about it," Gerrit suggested. "I'm not saying anything for sure, but we could think about it."

65

Next, Kate explained to Gerrit what happened at the Chancery. For one, she didn't have an appointment with the bishop and made accusations about what the priest rector had done to their young daughter. And she not only demanded money for doctor bills and ongoing costs of raising the child, she insisted the priest first apologize for what he'd done.

"And that probably will never happen," Annalise said, quietly to herself."

"Kate," Gerrit said, "you really are something."

"Not me," Kate said. "Annalise! She's the one who has worked out a plan to raise this baby as our own. It's not going to be easy. It's going to take all of us, even you Fletcher. Probably even some of our neighbors," Kate continued.

Annalise would have gone upstairs to her little room off the landing, but she wasn't ready to leave.

She watched as Fletcher paced back and forth across the lawn. When Kate finally told Annalise to go up to her room and rest, she went inside. Fletcher followed her upstairs.

"You can come in for a few minutes," she said. "I'm so tired and nothing seems quite real."

She knew it was her choice to tell her brother what happened. She was confident he wouldn't tell his friends or kids at school that she had been raped by a priest and was now three months pregnant.

After she explained the details of that night and the days since, they sat a while without talking. Finally, Fletcher slid off the bed and went to his room. It was a story he couldn't comprehend. How could a clergyman do such a thing? To my little sister? She's only fourteen.

A high school freshman. Now what?

"That priest should go to jail for doing that to Annalise. Didn't anyone think to call the police down there? We talk about getting justice for Annalise, for our family, but it seems we just want the priest or diocese to pay the baby's expenses. This is a real crime!"

Looking out the window across to the woods on the other side of the road, Fletcher pondered what he should do. Not say anything to anyone about that law? Talk to Pops?

He tiptoed down the steps and went looking for him. He knew his mom was already in bed, probably asleep. It had been a very long, very sad day.

Fletcher found Pops on the porch, staring out the window.

"Can I talk to you?" he asked. Gerrit was startled by his son's question.

"Anna told me what happened. Did anyone report this to the police? Rape is a crime," Fletcher whispered. "There was a kid who was a runner for a school we competed against last year. We ran against him early in the season, but when it came time for the championship meet, he wasn't there. He was a top-notch runner. When I asked why he wasn't on the roster, one of his teammates whispered that he'd been arrested for raping a girl in his class and since he was already eighteen, he was now in jail. Everyone figured he was a shoo-in for a big athletic scholarship to a fancy Ivy League school, but that's never going to happen. His teammate said if he even did go to college, he'd probably be paying his own way."

Gerrit stood there, speechless. "You're right. This was a serious crime. I know everyone is tired and upset, but we need to figure out how to handle this. We don't live where this occurred. This would have to be reported to authorities there, and if they decide to check it out, that's where the court jurisdiction would be. That's a huge complication but one Annalise is entitled to pursue. Go ask your mom and Annalise to come here."

Gerrit pulled the porch table away from the wall so the four of them could face each other—Fletcher and Anna on the bench, Gerrit and Kate on chairs opposite. Gerrit started: "Fletcher, tell them what you just told me."

"We have to remember rape is a crime," Fletcher said. "It has to be reported to police."

Gerrit looked as if he'd let his family down, but his voice was firm. "We have to report it to the police where the crime occurred. If their investigation showed a rape was committed, they would arrest the person, and he'd be charged in court and have to stand trial and, depending on the verdict, could go to jail."

Annalise shook her head. "I can't do that!" she whispered. "There'd be stories about me in all the newspapers around here and Saint Michael's. They'd take my picture or get one from the school to put in the paper. If I keep this baby, think of the life the baby would have. Everyone would know the baby's father was a priest. The baby would never live it down and neither would I. Nor would any of you! We'd always be the family that sued a Catholic priest for rape. I'd always be a girl who did something to cause a rape. *No!* I won't do that. I don't want to carry that weight for the rest of my life. That would be the worst thing I could do. To me! To the baby! To us!"

"He doesn't deserve your goodness," Gerrit said. "If he committed a crime, he should be held accountable."

"This is what I think," Annalise continued. "If I reported him to the police, he'd be investigated and there'd be stories about us in the paper. And if he had to go to court, more stories. So, *no*, I won't go to the police, here or anywhere. I'd have no control over anything. Everyone would know and talk about us. Kids and their parents would point fingers. I'd have to move where no one knew us."

"Oh, Annalise," Kate said. "I never thought about that. A lawsuit? That wouldn't be justice for any of us, least of all you. It makes sense to keep this information to ourselves and with those we trust, regardless of what the diocese decides to do. That's all the justice we can expect. It's not fair, but I have a feeling we'll weather this, and in time might even be surprised how it works out."

"I was so mad when I heard what happened to my sister Anna," Fletcher said. "The courts would take a very dim view of putting a popular priest on trial for an accusation from a high school freshman who moved there to attend his school. There'd be gossips who'd spread stories that the girl was just lying to cover up her own loose morals."

"It's true," Gerrit said. "Once a situation gets into the legal system there's no way to stop the stories and gossip. When a case is set in motion, it would be completely out of our hands and our control. Fletcher, you and Annalise had the right idea. Take it to the bishop and I can guarantee he won't be rushing to the courthouse and headlines. I have a feeling he might have his own tough justice to dish out."

Kate suggested they draft a covenant that would spell out how they would deal with the information in order to protect Annalise's privacy, the baby, our family. Think about it and we'll talk again," Kate said. "Now, let's go to bed."

CHAPTER FOUR

After an early breakfast, Kate and Gerrit left for church. Anna was still asleep.

When they got home, Gerrit went upstairs to check on Anna. She quickly slid her daybook under her pillow and leaned back against the headboard.

"I see you've been writing," he said. "Your momma and I have been praying. For you." Gerrit pulled the rocker closer to the bed. "She's much better at this praying than I am, but I'm learning."

"I'm still trying to sort it all out, trying to decide what's best for you. For us. I know you're determined to have the baby, but given your age and how this all happened, I can't see why. . . ." He looked toward the floor with a sad expression.

"Poppa, because it's a baby. You can't just give babies away. I think about all the babies Momma couldn't have when you were in Chicago, and I know that was a sad time. You wanted a big family. Well, two isn't a big family. So, if God wants me to have this baby, I won't say no."

Annalise reached for his hand with pleading in her voice. "But I'll need your help. Momma and I will work together to raise the baby as part of our family until I'm ready to be the baby's mom. Won't that work?"

Her dad stopped rocking and stared at Annalise while pondering. *Here she is, just fourteen, barely starting high school, and she's come up with some pretty grownup decisions about how to deal with this family crisis. I still see her as a little girl, but she hasn't been that for a long time.*

There's no doubt in my mind she can raise this baby. She might still question a decision that seemed right in that moment, but for sure she'll follow through on whatever she committed to. She's amazing for such a young person. That baby is going to have one heck of a mom!

Annalise said when she first realized she might be pregnant, she talked it over with God and He agreed. She didn't think He liked how she became pregnant, but He'd certainly be happy she was giving the baby a chance for life.

"Well, that's all decided. I think it must be time for lunch. Something smells good," Gerrit said, helping Anna up.

Downstairs, Fletcher was helping Kate set the table on the porch.

"I invited Cynthia for lunch, but her family was going to the gift opening for the cousin who got married yesterday. She asked me to go, but I wanted to be here with our family."

Fletcher put his arm around his sister and gave her a hug and a big smile.

"It'll be Momma's secret," Annalise whispered. "I guess I'm just the delivery person," Annalise said, and laughed. "But I suppose we'll have to tell Dr. Chandler."

CHAPTER FIVE

It was an errand Ida dreaded but one she couldn't escape. She'd promised to see Father Nolan early Monday morning. She'd lain awake since five-thirty. By six-thirty, she knew she might as well start the day. It would have been easier to confront him if it hadn't been for all those pleasant Sunday-night suppers in my kitchen. When she thought of Annalise and the reason for this morning's errand, the muscles around her heart started to constrict. She headed to the bathroom to get ready. Although anxious to do what she'd promised, she just needed time to think, to talk to her Poppa and God. And have a cup of coffee.

She'd just turned on the shower when she heard the phone. Knowing it undoubtedly was Emily, she left the water warming up and went to answer it.

"Hello," she said, plopping down on the edge of the unmade bed.

"Aunt Ida?"

"Annalise?"

"I know you're going to get the things in my locker," Anna started. "I just wanted to tell you how sorry I am that you have to do such a thing for me."

"Anna...."

"I remembered I didn't tell you what my locker number was. It's seventy-three. It's down the south hallway where all the freshmen classrooms are," Annalise began. "I think I have a sweater folded on the shelf and my book satchel. Most of the books belong to the school—we just rent them. But there are a few of mine." Annalise described them for her.

"You should stop in the office when you get there to remind them who you are and that I won't be coming back. Eventually I'll be able to get my things from you."

Aunt Ida didn't have the courage to tell Annalise what her plans were for visiting the school. "Okay, Anna. I was just about to step into the bath when you called—don't want the tub to overflow. I'll call back early this afternoon."

At the school, Ida stopped at the office, just inside the front door. She hadn't bothered to call for an appointment, nor did she forewarn them she was coming. She put on what Pastor Conner used to call "a sunshine face," but was still sketchy about her early morning visit.

"My niece, who has been boarding at my home for this school year, has had to go home unexpectedly. She will not be returning. I've come for her personal items from her locker. I know the number and where it is. But first I need to talk to Father Nolan. I don't have an appointment, but I know he'll see me."

That approach, Ida thought, put this receptionist at a disadvantage. Obviously, Father was in—the receptionist went to his door and tapped lightly. Ida walked quickly to the end of the counter, rounded it, and came up behind the young lady.

"Come," his cheerful voice answered.

But the smile in his voice didn't remain when he saw who was standing there. She didn't give him a chance to suggest she needed an appointment. She stepped inside the door and shut it firmly.

"I presume you know why I've come," she announced. "And unless you want everyone in this school to know why, we'll keep this door shut. But if you prefer having it ajar, my voice is loud enough to carry up and down the hallway."

He motioned to the chair in front of his desk, but she didn't sit. Leaning forward, she told him she'd come to collect Anna's things from her locker, "and unless you want the questions to start, you needn't walk me down there. Before I go, I want to make sure you understand that what you did—forcing your way into my home when Anna was there alone that Saturday night— was unforgivable."

With her voice rising in anger, Ida continued: "What you did was sinful enough, but your audacity – coming back for suppers at my house even after you raped Annalise – that is doubly unforgivable.

"May God help you if you ever commit this vile act on another student. And, by the way, Annalise kept the pajamas she was wearing the night you were there, including the bottoms that you stained, then pulled off and left in a heap on the floor."

Ida didn't wait for a reply.

She hurried down the south hallway to locker seventy-three. She put Annalise's things in a shopping bag and stacked the textbooks on the office counter just inside the door. The secretary handed her a signed receipt for the textbooks.

"I'm so sorry to hear that," the secretary whispered as she glanced uncomfortably toward the still-closed door. "She's such a lovely girl, and I know the students really liked her."

"Anna will have no use for her uniforms, so she asked that they be given to students who could use them."

When she got outside, Ida was surprised to see her daughter's car parked behind her own.

"When you didn't answer your phone, I knew where I'd find you," Emily said from her open car window. "I thought a fresh cup of coffee and toast with orange marmalade would add some sweetness to the day. I'm guessing you did all the talking and chatter box didn't have a word to say."

Ida nodded.

It was early afternoon before she returned home. The phone was ringing.

"Hi, Kate," Ida said into the receiver. "I've been at Emily's. You'd have loved my soliloquy. The secretary said everyone really liked Anna. Now, have you heard anything from the bishop?"

CHAPTER SIX

It took Anna a few seconds to remember where she was—and why. She reached under her pillow for her morning Daybook. Morning sounds drifted up the stairs. *Poppa's booming voice, but what is he saying? He's talking to Momma. I can't make out her words either. Was I dreaming?*

Today Poppa's going to register me for school. I remembered that. Tomorrow I'll be in school with classmates I've known for eight years. They won't hesitate to ask why I've come back. What should I tell them? That I was raped and now I'm pregnant? They'll figure that out soon enough.

Some of them will smirk. Raise their eyebrows. Giggle behind my back.

Later. I can't deal with that now.

She reached over the side of the bed, pulling the wastebasket within easy reach—just in case. She swallowed hard, then rolled over, burying her face in the pillow. She started sobbing when she heard Poppa's footsteps.

He tapped quietly. "Anna? You awake?" He sat on the edge of the bed. "I know you're worried, but we've figured out a way for you to stay in school."

Gerrit's voice was gentle. "I'm going to get you registered when I drop Fletcher off. They don't need to know why you're home. Let them think you were homesick. Fletcher will be with you, and no one will dare tease you about giving up on your fancy school and settling with the home crowd."

"Pops," Fletcher called. "I'm going to be late!"

"Hold your horses, Fletch. Your sister and I have business. I'll just drive faster on the back roads. In between the ruts.

"You'll start tomorrow. We don't have your transcripts, but you have eight years of records on file."

"Anna, just stay in bed. Your Momma made oatmeal. She'll bring some up. No tears.

Anna smiled and slid back under the blanket.

Momma came in with the oatmeal and a handful of apple rings. "It's good to have you home. We can spend time planning. There's a lot to do while you're waiting for a baby."

Tuesday morning, Fletcher and Annalise waved to their dad as they walked up the front sidewalk into the high school. Fletcher said he'd go with her to the office to pick up her schedule, but Annalise said she'd rather go by herself. Fletch reminded her he'd see her at lunch.

When Anna left that morning, she was determined to face her classmates as if it were any other Tuesday, but now she wasn't so sure. *If they start teasing me about coming back, I'll probably break out in tears. Worse would be if they'd try to find out why. It isn't any of their business, but I don't want to confront them with attitude. I need their friendship and support, even if they couldn't possibly know why.*

She didn't have to worry. Although the room was alive with conversation, that stopped when someone noticed her in the doorway.

"Annalise! When did you get back?" Another: "Coming back to school?"

"Looks like it," she said. "I missed you all."

The homeroom teacher checked her seating chart and pointed Anna to an available desk. "Welcome," she said, and asked the class to quiet down while she took attendance.

The worst was over. They didn't have time to ask hard or embarrassing questions.

At lunch, she took her paper bag and followed the others down the hall. Looking around, she thought the building was shabbier than she remembered. She didn't have much of an appetite for the roast beef sandwich Momma packed. After a bite or two, she re-wrapped it and put it back in her bag. She managed a few apple slices but left the cookies.

Fletcher and several friends stopped at her table. He reminded her that Pops would be at the school by four-thirty "The school library is usually open until at least four, sometimes four-fifteen. I'll try to leave a few minutes early from practice, but most days I'm out a little before four-thirty. If not, Pops just waits."

After Fletch and his friends left, Anna looked around the nearly empty room and spotted Ellen, sitting alone at a table near the door. She waved. Seeing Ellen took her back to a time when her world wasn't so complicated.

"Annalise! I heard you were here. You back home for good?"

"Yes, and yes," Anna said, trying to mask the quiver in her voice. "I looked for you this morning, but I guess you're in the other homeroom. I got lonesome and a little homesick, so here I am."

Anna sat with Ellen while she finished her lunch, then walked with her outside. It was like old times at junior high.

Anna had a hard time staying awake after lunch. The bell finally rang, signaling time to move to the next class. The dismissing teacher shouted out the overnight assignments as students hurried out. Anna made sure she had the homework written in her notebook, even if she had no idea which textbook it was.

At the end of the day, she circled back to all her teachers, to make sure she knew the assignments.

Anna was a little surprised that no one hung around to ask about her decision to come home. After she left last August, no one except Ellen kept in touch. *It's as if the others don't want to get re-acquainted.* But I can finish the school year here, then decide where I'll go next fall. There's probably another parochial high school nearby. *Then she remembered she couldn't go away to another school. She'd have a baby waiting for her.*

She hurried down the hall to the library. It was a small room with only a few shelves for books. It was a pleasant space, except for the dark-green shades that blocked the sun from peeking through the three floor-to-ceiling windows. In front of each was a small wooden table and two chairs.

At four, she packed up her things and went outside to wait. She tried sitting on the concrete, then leaned against the window casings that flanked the wide entryway door, but it didn't take long for that option to get downright cold. Finally, she stood with her back against the brick wall, hoping Fletcher would finish soon.

He didn't show up for another half hour. By then she dozed off while leaning against the sunshine-warmed bricks.

"Time to go home," Fletcher announced. "Pops is here."

CHAPTER SEVEN

Fletcher decided it was just too nice to spend a glorious spring day in a classroom. It was a perfect day to ditch school. His senior year was winding down. Final exams started Monday, by Friday, his high school days would be history. An opportune time to play hooky.

The bell on the wall above the front door started clanging. That bell will be one thing none of us will miss." Fletcher said.

"I don't think colleges have bells," Ken chimed in.

"Your dad's here," Charlie said, pointing to the car at the curb.

"Something happened," Fletch said, looking around for his sister in the freshman lineup. He hurried toward his dad's car.

"I got a call from your mom when I got to the office," he said. "We need to find Anna and head right home. I've signed you out for the day."

Usually Fletcher sat in the front seat, but that day he held the door open for his sister and climbed into the back seat with her.

"There's been a terrible accident at the Iversen's," Gerrit said. "They think Mr. Iversen had a heart attack. He fell off the tractor, and without anyone steering it, it hit something near the machine shed and tipped over. The milk hauler found him, but it was too late."

Without more conversation, he started the car and headed to the highway.

Anna couldn't stop crying. Fletcher reached for her hand. Since mom and baby Fletcher first arrived at the farm, the Iversen's were like family. When the car reached their graveled intersection, poppa turned left toward the Iversen place. The farmyard was already filling up with cars and Amish buggies. He pulled his car alongside one of the buggies, which was parked next to their mom's car. Fletcher jumped out, hurrying alongside Gerrit. Anna stayed in the car. She looked for her mom and Mrs. Iversen. They stood together. Anna could see their mom was crying. Mrs. Iversen said something to her, and they headed toward the car where Anna waited.

Momma opened the door and reached inside, catching hold of Anna's hand as she slid across the seat. Mrs. Iversen waited.

As Anna moved to hug Helen, the tears streaming down her cheeks turned to sobs.

"My dear girl," Helen whispered. "He was a wonderful man and we'll miss him. You were his pride and joy – the daughter we didn't get to keep. Now, no more crying. We'll do what we did for Grammy. We were the luckiest people to have such wonderful neighbors. Helen looked up as another buggy pulled into the yard. "The Mellens. I don't know how word traveled so fast in an old-order Amish Community without telephones. She squeezed Anna's hand and walked over to greet them.

Kate took Anna aside. "I think you had best go home and rest. I'll get you settled; then walk back. No sense having two of our cars in the yard. Do you see Poppa?"

He thought taking Anna home was a good idea and offered to give Kate a ride back.

"Helen is busy with people, so I won't be missed. I'll walk back."

Gerrit walked over to the ring of men near the tractor. There were whispered questions about what would happen to the farm. For now, neighbors would pitch in and set up schedules for milking, but that wouldn't last, because their own work would fall behind.

The women always set out a nice lunch after a funeral. Because Mr. Iversen was a friend to so many, they'd need a lot of food. Kate and Annalise always made and baked baskets of homemade dinner rolls for the funeral lunch. They packed them in large baskets to carry down the road to the church.

"Having something to do helps," Kate told Anna. "My poppa told the ladies in his church that fixing food to serve the family and mourners was a holy way to show their respect to the deceased."

Kate looked at her daughter across the porch table. "And now, little girl, you'd better get under the covers. I'll lock the door when I leave."

Anna was asleep before Kate reached the end of their driveway.

When Kate entered the little church that night,she was in awe of the vases of forsythia, which adorned the main altar.

The next morning, the pall bearers carried the casket out to the horse drawn hearse for the short walk to the church. At noon, the bell tolled the funeral cadence as Pastor Wickert led the older Iversen grandchildren with Gerrit and Fletcher, carrying the casket to the church for the funeral procession. Family followed. Kate and Annalise sat midway down the aisle. Anna looked around, surprised to see many Amish neighbors standing in back. The horses waited patiently for the service to end, then carried the casket to the burial site next to Grammy's grave, where bunches of lilac covered the grave site.

The service included one of Harald's favorite hymns, "The Old Rugged Cross," which Grammy often played on the pump organ in their parlor.

The noonday sun captured gentle colors from the stained-glass windows, sending flickering shadows throughout the space. The moving color was mesmerizing, and Anna felt her eyelids drooping. Gerrit and Fletcher sat in the front pew across from Helen and her sons. When the organ music stopped, the pastor asked if any mourners wanted to share memories of Mr. Iversen.

Annalise was surprised when Poppa walked to the pulpit. It was a proud moment to hear him reminisce about the years their families were neighbors. Gerrit told how his wife prayed through a terrible storm, begging God to save her and baby Fletcher.

"I expect you all have stories to tell," Gerrit said with a nod to the congregation. "Harald was the kindest person you could ever want for a neighbor. We could never repay his goodness, but we could, in turn, practice the neighborly lessons he lived by. Rest in peace, dear friend."

Kate smiled as she wiped away tears. Anna tried not to cry.

Several others had stories to tell: Harald's booming laugh that made worries melt away, and his "forever smile" that never sagged.

Then it was time to carry his casket out to the cemetery where the ground had been opened for the burial. "I will miss you forever, Mr. Iversen," Annalise whispered as she collapsed on the ground.

Mr. Mellen, the burly Amish farmer, quickly scooped her up and carried her back into the church. Following him were Kate and several Amish women. He laid her on a back pew and Kate thanked them, urging them to return to the services. Anna was coming to and trying to sit up. They sat in the quiet church for a while before they went back outside.

While most of the others went inside for lunch and more stories of the good neighbor they just buried, Mr. Mellen walked his horse and buggy over to where Kate and Anna stood, offering to take them home.

"We'll ride back with Mr. Mellen," Momma said as Anna snuggled under the blanket.

The angle of the sun had changed when Anna woke to voices downstairs. Footsteps on the stairs said they were on their way to check on her. She tried to sit up but still felt too tired. She settled back into the pillows and felt her eyes closing again. Momma pulled the sheet up around Anna's shoulders and straightened the blankets, then hurried out. A few minutes later she was back with Poppa.

He shook Anna awake and told her he was going to drive her to the hospital. He carried her downstairs. Fletcher held the car door open. Momma climbed in the back seat with Anna. Minutes later they were heading toward the highway.

Anna could hear voices but couldn't make out who it was and what they were saying. She woke up when she was lifted onto a bed.

The door opened and closed again. She heard voices from the hallway. Who was this doctor who was checking her over? It wasn't Dr. Chandler.

Then they all came in. She'd have to stay in the hospital for several days so they could keep an eye on her and the baby.

In the confusion of the past days, Anna had forgotten about the baby. *Could she lose it?*

CHAPTER EIGHT

After a week in an uncomfortable hospital bed, Anna thought she was going home. She didn't. Then when she thought she was going back to school, she spent several more weeks in bed at home.

"Maybe even through the summer until baby arrives," Dr. Chandler said, his hand resting on her shoulder. "I'd rather not do anything to encourage this baby to come early. You'll have to do your schoolwork in bed. We'll try letting you up to go to the bathroom and take sponge baths. No tub baths. And you won't be coming into town for appointments at my office. I'll come out here on Saturday mornings to check on you. At least until we know what's going on. A car ride on these country roads isn't a good idea for you. I'll see you in a few days."

After he left, Kate pulled a chair up to Anna's bedside. "We were afraid you'd lose the baby after you collapsed. You lost some blood, and that's not good. But it seems God expects you to have this baby. "And you can't argue with God. He always has the last word."

They sat quietly as Anna tried to cope with the idea of spending spring and summer in bed. Poppa promised her a weekly supply of library books and Fletcher brought her lessons home every night and took her finished work back for grading. And no one needed to know why she had to stay in bed.

Picking up Anna's assignments was an easy routine. At first, some old friends asked about her, but they eventually realized they wouldn't get any answers. Only one girl asked if she could visit some Saturday or Sunday. That answer was easy. "Doctor's orders—no visitors!"

Sitting on the front steps of the school, Fletcher tried to sort out what had happened to their lives. His sister was shut up in their parent's bedroom. She only rarely could eat at the table. Mostly she ate in bed from a tray.

Mr. Mellen fixed a chair with wheels so she could use the commode in the bathroom and take sponge baths at the sink.

Fletcher was pre-occupied on the drive home—his sister's confinement, his graduation coming up, and she couldn't go. Did he dare hope that both Mom and Pops would be there? He knew there couldn't be a party—but that didn't matter. Relatives from Iowa wouldn't drive all that way just to have potato salad, fried chicken and lemonade. But if Aunt Ida and Emily came, that would make the day more special.

Some of his friends invited him to their parties, but he knew that wasn't something he'd enjoy, especially those shindigs at the lake. Somebody always drank too much.

Momma usually waited for Pops at the screen door. That way she could give him an update, but that afternoon she wasn't waiting there. Fletcher panicked. Something happened. Then he remembered. This was the day for Ladies Guild. He poured himself a glass of milk, taking it with him as he took Anna her homework.

"Here's your assignments," Fletcher said, offering her the milk he originally poured for himself.

"Thank you," she said, reaching for the glass. "I just woke up. Is Momma home?"

"No," he said as he went back for a second glass.

Fletcher wondered where Pops disappeared to. He almost always stuck his head in the doorway to say "hi" to Anna.

Fletcher parked himself at the foot of the bed. "As long as Pops is outside somewhere, do you think we could have a talk?"

Anna settled back.

"I was sitting on the front steps at school and missed having you there. I'll be gone next year, and you'll probably be going to school in town again. You think?"

"Probably. Momma will take care of the baby while I'm at school, and I'll spend as much time after school with the baby as I can." she said. "I still can't believe I'll be a mother. Changing diapers, bottles. Watching him or her grow up."

Fletcher stared. "Do you ever think about what happened? How he gave you something to drink so you'd pass out like kids who drink too much?

"I sometimes wonder if he never expected anything to happen…that he didn't know I was grown up enough to have a baby."

"You always sound grown-up," Fletcher said as he reached for her empty glass. "It was my job to watch out for you."

"You know, Fletch, we had everything arranged. But when he showed up that day, I had no way of stopping him."

"I'm home," Momma announced as she came around the corner."

Kate was surprised to see Mr. Mellen standing at the screen door, because it wasn't Friday. He usually didn't pull into the yard when he dropped Sarah off on Fridays for the weekly cleaning.

"Good morning, Aaron," Kate said. "Good to see you. Anything wrong?"

"Nope," he said. "Your husband stopped over yesterday to arrange for me to make a cradle. I picked out some patterns I thought would be perfect for Anna's baby. This is my favorite," he said, handing her one. "The design is very simple but has very classic lines. I used this pattern for one of our girls. Come to think of it, I think it was Sarah's." He handed her the sheaf of patterns. "Take your time deciding," he said, as he got back into his buggy.

Kate and Gerrit had talked about having a cradle made, but he never told Kate he already ordered it.

May 13, 1945

Dear Days,

It's been such a long time since I've written on your pages. Today is Friday, and Sarah is coming to help Momma with the cleaning. Sarah and I got to be friends when she went to the township grade school last year. Most of the Amish kids go to Amish school farther up the road. She told me she wants to go to college so she can become a nurse and help people in the Amish community. She's so excited because she'll be going into town next fall for high school. Most Amish kids only go up to eighth grade, some not even past sixth grade, especially if they are needed at home.

Sarah's the oldest of the four Mellen girls. She missed a lot of school this spring so she could help her Momma with Jacob, their new baby. He had some problems, and Mrs. Mellen was so worn out that she had to spend time in bed. Staying in bed all day is hard.

I'm glad Momma asked Sarah to help her. She never has a lot for her to do, so Sarah and I sometimes just sit and talk. Sarah's a year younger than I am. Their school year is different

*from ours. They have as many days as we do for
a grade, but they have school six days a week in
winter because they help in the fields in spring
and fall. It works out. Time to go. I hear Sarah
on the porch.*

Anna

Sarah stuck her head in Anna's room to see if she was awake. Anna hadn't felt like getting out of bed that morning, but since Sarah was there, she was happy to have her help getting to the bathroom. After washing up, Anna sat in the rocker while Sarah pulled off the dirty sheet and spread clean ones over the mattress.

"My dad brought his cradle patterns for your parents to look at," Sarah said, then paused. "Oh, dear—I think it's supposed to be a surprise," she said.

Anna and Sarah never talked about the baby, but Sarah knew it sometimes was necessary to stay in bed so the baby wouldn't arrive too early. She never asked about the baby's father.

The sound of voices from the front porch faded. Sarah said her dad had errands in town. From the sound of his buggy wheels, he was in a hurry.

Kate came in to see how the bed-changing was coming. Now that the washing machine was filled with hot water, she was ready for the first load of sheets—from Anna's bed. Anna hated wash day. Even with a hot water heater in the basement, there always seemed too little to keep the washer and one rinse tub full and warm. It was a good day to hang wash on the line around back. Anna could see the leaves moving ever so slightly on trees around the yard, trees Momma planted eighteen or so years ago. The apple trees would be in blossom soon. If only she could be up and about to tend to her apple business. The extra money would help with the baby's expenses.

Anna watched the sheets and towels flap in the breeze while they ate lunch. After they finished, Kate worked the Maytag, running bath towels through the wringer, then carrying them outside to pin on the line. Sarah cleared the lunch plates and put cookies on a saucer for Anna. After she helped Anna back to bed, Sarah washed the dishes and put them in the rack on the table to dry.

Sarah finished her list of chores. The warm wind made quick work of drying the wash. Sarah loved folding clothes and putting them away in drawers and closets. While she straightened Anna's stacks of clothes before adding the freshly laundered ones, the two girls continued talking.

"Have you decided on a name for your baby?" Sarah asked, unexpectedly.

If Anna was surprised, she didn't show it. "No, but now that school is almost over, I'll have time to think about names."

"My mom always makes a list of baby names when she's in a family way. We all add names to the list, but she has the last word. My dad has more say about a boy's name. Will the father help name your baby?"

"No!" Annalise said sharply, immediately embarrassed at her heated answer. She liked talking to Sarah about the baby but not any details about what happened. "I don't plan to ever see the father or let him see the baby."

The porch door slammed. Fletcher was home. "All done except graduation."

"Cheers," Annalise said in a sing-song voice. Learning always seemed easy for Fletch, but regardless, she knew he still worked hard.

Sarah gathered the rest of the laundry to carry upstairs and put away. Anna was grateful for the interruption.

"We passed your Pops on the way home," he told Sarah as she left the bedroom.

When Sarah was finished upstairs, Fletcher was still talking to Anna, so she waved goodbye and hurried out to the driveway. She knew her dad would be anxious to get home and start chores. Perhaps it was having a friend her own age to talk to, but Sarah never got as tired doing chores for Kate as she did at home. But then, things didn't get as messy at Kate's because they didn't have small children leaving toys and crumbs all over. But they'll find that out when Anna has her baby, Sarah thought.

Sarah was puzzled by Anna's answer about the baby's name. Funny she wouldn't want the baby's father to have a choice. Even more puzzling was how emphatic she was when she said he'd never even see the baby. Maybe he didn't know she was pregnant.

Aunt Ida and Emily were coming for Fletcher's graduation. So was Helen Iversen. Maybe. It was so soon after Harald's funeral that Kate thought she might not feel up to it. Kate had hoped Helen might stay with Anna so she wouldn't be alone so many hours while they were at graduation, but all that changed when Harald died.

Instead, Kate asked Sarah if she'd stay with Anna for the two or three hours they'd be in town that afternoon. She knew the girls got on well together and it might be fun. Of course, Sundays were meeting days for Amish families. If Sarah couldn't skip the full day of church, Kate would have to find another neighbor who could be trusted with Annalise.

She needn't have worried. The Mellens were happy to be asked.

On the Friday before graduation, Sarah talked with Anna about things they could work on when she was there on Sunday.

"Do you knit?" she whispered to Anna as she fluffed the pillows before helping her back to bed.

"No," Anna whispered back, although she didn't know why they were whispering. No one was in the house to overhear anything they were talking about.

"Do you have knitting needles?" Sarah asked out loud. "My sisters and I sometimes whisper just for the fun of it. I'll bring needles and yarn for both of us. We knit a lot in our family. I think you will like knitting. Maybe when you learn how, we can use better yarn and you could even knit a blanket for the baby."

Annalise had been feeling sorry for herself since it wasn't possible for her to go to the graduation. But when Sarah suggested teaching her how to knit a blanket for the baby, she forgot about having to stay in bed.

When the Mellen family climbed into their buggy for the trip to church meeting that Sunday, Sarah rode along as far as the Jansz farm. They drove into the farmyard and Mrs. Mellen and Sarah got out. Sarah had a knitting bag she'd sewn yesterday so Anna would have somewhere to keep her yarn and needles. Kate was surprised at Sarah's early arrival and especially pleased to see Nellie, her mother, with her.

"We'll collect Sarah on the way back from meeting, probably about four thirty," Nellie said. "If they aren't back by then, we'll just wait. So, don't hurry. This is a big event. Maybe in four years there will be a horse and buggy in the schoolyard when Sarah graduates."

Kate had made a plate of sandwiches for the girls. Most everything for the party was already in the refrigerator—bowls of fruit, potato salad, sandwiches, Jello, ice cream and other treats. Especially pink lemonade.

The house seemed so quiet after everyone left. Although Anna wasn't feeling her best, she was anxious to learn how to make something with two needles and a ball of yarn. They practiced casting on stitches then took a break for one of the sandwiches and a glass of lemonade. Annalise was surprised at how easily she mastered the first part of knitting, but after lunch, she preferred a nap rather than make sense of knit and purl. Sarah could see her friend was having trouble staying awake. She suggested a short nap and said they'd start again later.

While Anna dozed, Sarah read her Bible. She had markers in the pages for the day's scripture readings. It was such a part of her Sunday she forgot to watch the time. It was almost two o'clock and Anna was still asleep.

A pounding on the porch screen door frightened Sarah. She didn't know whether to answer the door or pretend she hadn't heard. The banging woke Annalise. Sarah walked to the kitchen where she could see who was pounding on the locked door. It was a man in a black suit and white shirt with a round white collar. A priest!

"Is this where Annalise lives? I have to talk to her."

"No! Now leave!" Sarah scolded.

"I've driven a long way. I could say what I have to say, then leave."

He started rattling the door and Sarah was afraid he'd pull it off its hinges.

"Please!" he said again.

"No!" Annalise pleaded as she ducked under the blanket. She recognized his voice—Father Cleary Nolan. *How did he find her?*

Sarah set her Bible on the bedcovers.

When the priest saw her, he stopped shouting. "Is this where Annalise Jansz lives?"

Sarah stared. What did he want? Then Sarah realized who he might be, and she stood there, not knowing what to do.

"Does Annalise live here?" he asked again.

Sarah nodded.

"I'd like to talk with her," he said, his voice growing more professional.

Sarah was more certain this man had something to do with Anna's baby. When she looked at Anna before answering the door, she saw what? Fear? Anger?

"I'm sorry, she's resting and can't come to the door," Sarah said politely. "Maybe you could come back another time when her mother is here."

He shook his head. "I'm sorry I came unannounced, but I have to talk with her. I don't live nearby. I'm here now."

She can't have visitors," Sarah said. "Why don't you write her a letter?"

"No!" he said, his anger returning. "I have to see her today while I'm here."

Sarah knew that opening the door was the worst thing she could do. But she couldn't stand there arguing through the screen door. If she let him inside, that would be a real worry for Anna. But if she relented and let him in for only a few minutes, she could control how long he could stay inside and enforce where he stood to talk to Anna.

Father Nolan followed her in.

Anna couldn't stop shaking when she saw him come toward the bed. She slid farther under the blanket, barely seeing the smirk on his face.

"How are you?" Father Nolan asked, his tone ingenuine. "I was surprised how easy it was to find you. I just asked at the filling station in town, and they gave me excellent directions."

Father Nolan barely paused before continuing, clearly disinterested in any response. "I hate to interrupt your nap, but I had to talk with you. I had to see the bishop last week, and that conversation did not go well. He was so angry because your mother and he had a very contentious meeting. I just wanted to tell you—in person—what I told him."

"I told you only five minutes and you've used up one of those minutes already," Sarah said.

Anna saw what Sarah had in her hand. The knitting needles. She held one up and pointed it at him. He ignored her, inching closer to where Anna was still hidden. Sarah tapped it in her hand like a pendulum as Father Nolan continued his rant.

TRUTH OR FANTASY?

"I don't know where this fantasy story came from," the priest said, trying to moderate his angry voice. "There's no truth to the lies your mother told the bishop about me. And I demand those lies cease. I don't know how you got yourself into such a mess, but believe me, I had nothing whatsoever to do with it."

"Ha!" Anna said, pushing some of the blanket away from her face.

"If your family continues to spread false stories, I will see my attorney, and you will have to answer to a judge. I'm a Catholic priest, and I take my vows of celibacy very seriously. I did my best to look out for you when you attended our school, and this is how you repay me? I don't know what happened, but my bringing a jar of soup over when you were sick did not cause you to be pregnant. I'm warning you. Stop the lies!"

"You're the one telling the lies," Anna said, her teeth clenched. "And I will thank you to leave. Now!" She shouted. "Get out and don't ever come back. You know what you did to me and you can't lie your way out of it." By now she was sitting up in the bed, glaring at the man who had turned her life upside down. "I don't ever want to see you again! Ever! Now get out!"

As the priest turned to leave, Annalise saw the doorway was blocked by a gray-haired lady with a knit shopping bag over her arm. Helen!

"And who are you?" Helen asked the man in the black suit. He was surprised to see someone standing right behind him. He tried to get past her, but she deftly cut him off.

"Sir," Helen continued, "I asked who you were and why you are in my neighbor's house. What is your business here?"

"That, ma'am, is none of your business." He tried again to shove past her, but she stood her ground.

The priest grew more flustered. "I brought a message for Annalise that is none of your business. Now, if you would please step out of my way, I'll be going."

Anna finally found the courage to call out, rising from the covers. "He's Father Nolan, the priest who was the principal of the high school I went to for a few months. He's the one who raped me and made me pregnant. He claims he had nothing whatsoever to do with it, but he drove all the way up here today, just to threaten me to never blame him for what HE did to me. He said he'd take me to court if anyone from my family ever pointed a finger of blame at him again. But some day the truth of it—evidence he left behind— will show up. And it WILL!"

Anna's courage surprised her when she heard her own voice deliver that message to Father Nolan.

Sarah lost any of the bravery she tried to project when the priest first arrived, but she was grateful Helen was blocking his escape.

"Yes, I think you need to leave now," Helen said. "I know Kate knows how to reach you and your bishop. I gather you didn't come to offer an apology nor inquire about your former student. But never mind," she said. "I'll let Anna's mom and dad know you were here, what you said, what you didn't say."

"And do have a nice drive home," Helen said as the unwelcome visitor hurried out to the porch, where he was surprised to see someone else coming in. Aaron Mellen. He'd parked his buggy right in front of the porch steps.

"Everything alright in here?" Aaron asked as he held the door open.

"It is now," Helen said, feeling her legs give way a bit as the angry priest shoved past Mr. Mellen.

"Oh POPPA," Sarah said. "We were so-o-o scared until Mrs. Iversen came. He didn't hear her come in, so she heard some of what he was YELLING at Annalise about. He was VERY angry at her."

Mrs. Mellen, clearly sensing something was wrong, brushed the priest aside as she made her way to the two girls sitting on the bed. Sarah smiled at her mom, then went back to check on Anna.

Annalise held out her arms to the friend who ran interference, trying to keep the priest away from Anna. Sarah exhaled a breath of satisfaction, wrapping her arms around Anna. Relieved!

Sarah whispered: "You sure you're okay?"

"I'm fine, now that he's gone. He really frightened me," Anna said. "When I heard his voice shouting through the screen door, I almost forgot that I can't just get out of bed and hide in the closet," she said.

"You were really brave," Annalise said to Sarah. "So was Helen!"

Helen and the Mellens were still talking in the kitchen when they heard another car drive up. Was he coming back?

Anna heard her dad's voice as he hurried into the house. "Was that Father Nolan I saw storming out of our driveway? How did he get in here?"

"It's all okay," Helen said. "Sarah stood up to Father Nolan, but it was still very scary for the girls. He even scared me the way he was shouting."

Gerrit said when he figured out who barreled out of their driveway when he was about to turn in, he was tempted to make a U-turn and go after him. But that wouldn't have solved anything. Besides," he said, "chasing a car that is trying to get away is always dangerous."

Sarah and Anna recounted the details, starting with the pounding and shouting.

Helen had been visiting Harald at the cemetery and was nearly at her driveway when she caught sight of a man wearing dark clothes going into the Jansz house. "Too dark for such a nice, sunny day," she said.

"So, instead of turning in, I drove up the road but didn't recognize the car, or the man in the black suit," she explained. "So, I pulled into the driveway and parked my car in front of his so he'd have to back up to get around me. I left my car door ajar so he wouldn't hear it close. I tiptoed into the bedroom and watched him shout at Annalise. I could see she was very frightened. And I didn't budge when he tried to hurry out."

Kate hurried over to the bed, where Anna sat wrapped in a blanket.

"What was he doing in our house? Who let him in? And why?" Gerrit asked again. The question didn't have an answer.

Annalise hesitated at first, but then relayed the priest's message to Kate. "Father Nolan started shouting about the 'lies' you relayed to the bishop when you made a recent, unannounced visit to the chancery. And Father Nolan will file a grievance with the district attorney against you if she told any more lies about him."

"Those weren't lies," Kate said.

"How did he get in our house?" Gerrit asked again.

Anna said, "He banged on the door and kept shouting to let him in. Sarah said she was afraid he was going to pull hard enough on the screen door that he'd break the door or yank it off its hinges. Finally, Sarah gave him five minutes inside and then he had to leave."

"I was really scared when she did that because then he'd be inside the house. But Sarah reminded him he had only five minutes to talk and then he had to leave.

"Except he couldn't because Helen blocked his way. Father Nolan hadn't heard Helen come in the house so she heard a lot of his yelling at Annalise. And then Sarah's parents came in and he was anxious to get out of their way.

"And Momma, he kept shouting that you told the bishop lies about him being the father of this baby. That's when Helen came in, she just stood where he couldn't see her. When Sarah wouldn't open the door, he stopped shouting a little to get her to unhook the door. He threatened me. Said he'd have a lawyer after me if I accused him of being the baby's father. I was so afraid."

"Oh, Momma," she cried out.

Kate was shocked at the audacity of his coming to their house and demanding to be let inside and threatening their daughter.

Gerrit disappeared into the kitchen, coming back a few minutes later to say he tried calling the city police but didn't get an answer. Probably tied up with graduation traffic," he said. "We'll talk more about this tonight," he told Kate.

When Ida and Emily arrived, the whole story was retold again. To help defuse the stress of the priest's unwelcome visit, Kate and Gerrit insisted the Mellens stay for Fletcher's party. The children clambered out of the buggy and ran around playing tag while waiting for the food.

In all the stress and confusion, Fletcher almost forgot the good news he got at his graduation. He was surprised, and pleased, that the Green Bay Teacher's College he planned to attend had given him a renewable four-year scholarship—if he did well. It would cover tuition and books. He had already saved enough to pay his dormitory room and board from his job scouring milk pails and milking machines at their farm milk house. He also was banking paychecks from his Ben Franklin dime store job.

The sunny afternoon was quickly slipping away.

The Mellen family hurried through their meal so they could get home to do farm chores. Sarah reluctantly went with them.

Ida and Helen replenished the platters and bowls on the table for the next group to eat. Helen took a plate of food home with her. She had questions to ask her son who was buying the farm.

Fletcher helped with the evening milking, but he had more than enough activity for one day and was anxious to stretch out on the daybed on the porch.

Ida and Emily decided to stay overnight, and also were ready for an early bedtime—after they cleared the food and dishes away. They planned an early start for home in the morning before the highway got too busy. Gerrit would sleep in Anna's little bedroom since Ida and Emily were already dozing off in Fletcher's double bed, both upstairs. Kate would sleep in the downstairs bedroom with Annalise.

Anna kept drifting off as she tried to reflect on the day's events. The bedroom was wrapped in whisper-soft quiet, with gentle voices drifting in from the porch, but not loud enough to keep her awake.

"I'm so sorry I missed your graduation," Anna mumbled to Fletcher, when he stopped to check on her on his way back from a bathroom stop. "Was it fun to be handed your diploma? And a scholarship! Maybe I'll get one when I graduate. But first I have three more years of high school. And a few other things." She smiled at her own understatement. "I hope my day won't be as eventful as yours was today." Her voice trailed off.

It didn't take long for the sounds of sleeping to fill the farmhouse. Only Kate and Gerrit were still awake. They wanted to soak in the joy of their son's graduation, but the day's unexpected visitor weighed heavier on their minds. Kate couldn't stop thanking God for sending Helen to their house.

Gerrit was too restless to sit for more than a few minutes in the back hallway, illuminated only by the moon. Kate poured each of them a glass of iced tea left from the party.

"Maybe we should visit the bishop again," Kate wondered. "He never responded to my visit in April. The least he could have done was let me know that he met with the priest and the outcome of that."

"I never thought we'd hear from him," Gerrit said. "We are, after all, not Catholic."

"But it would be common courtesy to follow up with someone who has brought a serious matter to your attention," she said. "If you can't get away during the week, I would pick up Ida and take her. This baby will be here in a few weeks, and that priest is still denying he had anything to do with Anna's situation. And how dare he show up on a Sunday afternoon, frightening Anna and Sarah with his liar accusations? Catholic or not, he was the principal of that high school she attended."

Then it was Kate's turn to start pacing.

"We'd have to make an appointment to meet with the bishop. I know the first time you went unannounced, but this call has to be more formal," Gerrit said. "I've been thinking I should talk with an attorney about Annalise's rights. Before we go blustering in, we need to be sure of what we are going to say and how we are going to voice any legal claims against this priest. The County Board has an attorney to handle its issues. I think I could ask him for a little advice. It's not his field, but perhaps he could recommend someone who has experience in something like this. It's not as if we can't pay the doctor and hospital bills and everyday baby expenses, but this man did, after all, cause her pregnancy. But, in the end, it's going to be her word against his."

"He's never going to admit anything at all," Kate said, her voice tight with frustration.

"Shhh," Gerrit cautioned. "You'll wake her."

They sat quietly for a long time. Gradually, their eyes grew heavy from the strain of the day.

"Let's get to bed," Gerrit said. "I'd like to get to the courthouse a little early, before most of the staff arrives. That way the county's attorney and I can talk undisturbed. If I can find out how we should proceed, I will either call from my office and reimburse the county for the call or go in late tomorrow so I can call from here. I'd rather you didn't make any calls," he added. "Anna would overhear and that might be upsetting for her. I'll let you know if I can arrange an appointment. You'd have to see if Helen could spend the day with Anna. I certainly don't expect this priest to make another trip here, but I wouldn't be surprised if he'd have someone else deliver another message."

Later that night, a car pulled into the driveway at the rectory of St. Michael's Church. Father Nolan got out, unlocked the side door to the rectory, and went upstairs. He set his alarm for six, having remembered on his drive home that he had the seven o'clock Mass.

The next morning, Ida and Emily had an early breakfast with Kate, long before Gerrit came down to join them. The sisters talked about scheduling another appointment with the bishop at his chancery office. Tops on their list that morning was how they should handle the priest's unexpected arrival at the farm yesterday. How should they raise the subject of the priest threatening to sue them if they raised questions about the priest's rape and sexual paternity?

They were still visiting in the driveway when Gerrit came outside. Kate was still expecting Gerrit to consult a county attorney about how to proceed with that line of questioning. But Gerrit had other issues to ask about. Fletcher!

Ida and Emily were anxious to raise questions about the priest's issues with Annalise, but Gerrit thought back to the conversations with Fletcher about the athlete who was in jail because he had raped a student.

Ida volunteered to make the trip to see the bishop with Kate if Gerrit couldn't get away.

"That's an option," Kate said, giving her a hug. "We feel we have to report what happened here yesterday, and we need to find out where the bishop's investigation is heading. If he's even investigating at all. I suspect Father Nolan probably was called in or else he wouldn't have driven up here to deliver his ultimatum."

"I saw him at my grocery the other day," Ida said. "He was already in line to check out, but then he just left his cart and walked out. I pushed his cart aside and went through in his place."

Ida and Emily left mid-morning. Kate hoped the stormy sky didn't follow them home. The swirling dark gray clouds looked ominous.

Kate woke Anna for her morning bath. The young girl seemed more fragile, but the baby hadn't shown any problems. Although none of them could bear thinking about the baby's father, they were anxious for Anna to have a successful pregnancy and a beautiful baby.

"How about a chicken sandwich or chicken salad for lunch?" Kate asked. "I saw the mail truck stop at the corner. I thought I'd better get it before it starts raining. It'll only take me a couple minutes on Fletcher's bike."

"A chicken sandwich would be good. And some potato salad," Anna said. "And lemonade, please. When you get back with the mail."

It had just started drizzling as Kate pedaled up the hill toward the farmhouse. She had the road to herself. The clouds were getting dark off to the west. The sudden deluge turned the gravel road into a swamp.

She caught a faraway flash of lightning and heard a distant rumble. *Thunder. I need to pedal faster.* Still, she got the bike back in the garage before the wind started. Rushing into the house, she closed the porch windows, then quickly circled the house to secure the rest. By then, the storm was howling, and rain beat against the house.

Kate went into Annalise's room. "I'll just sit here until the storm passes," she said. "Want the shades closed?"

Anna snuggled under the covers, hiding from the lightning. When the sky lit up, she could see the angry shape of the storm clouds.

Storms always scared Kate. This one passed quickly, but far-off lightning and faint rumblings meant it was being chased by another one. The soil had been unusually dry lately, so the rain would at least help their summer garden.

"I'll get our sandwiches made and bring them in here to eat. Anything else you'd like?" Kate asked.

"Maybe a small piece of Fletcher's cake."

They didn't talk as they ate. By the time she carried the plates back to the kitchen, the second batch of rain slammed against the windows. Lightning flashed again.

Just as the wind whipped itself into a frenzy, the phone jangled. She figured it was Gerrit, but she had no intention of answering it. She'd call him back after the second storm passed. Kate looked out to see if the wind had razed her tulips. She could see a little color, but most of the blooms were gone.

When the rain died down again, they were ready for cake and lemonade. Anna's slice was barely a sliver. "Better not crowd your stomach," Kate said. "You can have another piece after your nap. I've been thinking this bed looks awfully comfortable. I may join you for a nap after I do the dishes."

"Where's Fletcher?" Anna called after her mother.

"He went into town with Poppa. It's a Ben Franklin work day."

She turned from the window and saw that she talked Annalise to sleep. The daily nap was an enjoyable doctor's order. It was never a punishment on a rainy or cool day. It was harder to fall asleep when the sun was shining and a breeze kept the curtains in motion.

Kate dialed the courthouse number and asked for Gerrit. When he came on the line he was all business. "I got the diocese office and talked to the bishop's appointments secretary. He seemed to know what I was talking about but said the bishop is in Rome this week and will be backed up on appointments when he returns. I told him we had an unannounced and totally unacceptable visit from one of his priests yesterday."

"Did he give you an appointment?" Kate asked.

'No," Gerrit muttered angrily.

"Then I'll call," Kate said. "I told the bishop I expected to hear back in two weeks, even if all he had to tell me was that he'd scheduled a meeting with the priest. I'm inclined to think he never did that. But Father Nolan did show up here."

"It's starting to storm here," Gerrit said. "I'm going to hang up."

Anna seemed restless. Kate held Anna's hand, hoping that would calm her. They both slept until nearly four o'clock. They might have slept longer, except Noah woke them with his knocking. "He just stopped to make sure we were okay."

CHAPTER TEN

Annalise was groggy after such a long nap. A warm summer sun had dried up all the rain clouds. *If I weren't confined to this stupid bed*, she thought, *I'd just get up and open every window in the house.* She looked at the bedside clock and saw it was nearly time for Poppa and Fletcher to get home.

The Ben Franklin store where Fletcher was working this summer was at the opposite end of Washington Street from the courthouse. Fletch was waiting at the curb for his dad.

They rolled down the windows to dry off the humidity inside the car.

As Anna stretched and yawned from her nap, she looked over at her mom. Kate didn't look right; her face was flushed.

"Momma?" she asked. No answer.

Anna felt her forehead. It was very warm. Was it a fever, or just overheated from the blazing sun? How did you tell the difference? She reached over and shook her mom's arm, but still Kate didn't stir. She watched her chest move up and down. She was relieved to see that. Why wouldn't she wake up?

A loud knock at the door. Was Noah back for something? She heard the door open and footsteps crossing the living room. Anna was relieved to see Helen.

"I was worried," Helen said. "I didn't see any activity around your house all afternoon. Everything all right?"

Then she noticed Kate's closed eyes. She was usually such a light sleeper—no one could ever sneak up on her.

"Kate? Kate? Wake up. It's almost suppertime. It's Helen. I just drove over to see how things were going. Wake up," Helen urged, shaking her shoulder.

Finally, Kate's eyes opened, albeit reluctantly. "Helen, what are you doing here? Is everything okay?"

"It was, until I got here and found you sound asleep. Anna's been trying to wake you so she can get up and go to the bathroom. Just stay there," Helen said. "I'll take her."

When they returned, Kate was up and brushing her hair, squinting at herself in the mirror.

"I was so tired I don't even remember falling asleep," Kate said. "I guess we were more tired than we realized."

"Good thing I brought supper," Helen said. "I made a casserole this morning. It's way too much for me to eat, and I thought it would be fun to have supper with you. I just took it out of the oven a few minutes ago, so it should still be warm when Gerrit gets home. I hope you don't mind. I tried to call, but the storm must have knocked out your telephone."

Helen and Kate set the table. Helen, as usual, brought a loaf of her raisin bread—Anna's favorite. By the time Gerrit and Fletcher pulled into the driveway, everything was on the table, even the flowers from Sunday's party. For a treat, they wheeled Anna to the table.

"You must be getting anxious to get on your feet again," Helen said. She remembered having to spend long weeks in bed before her youngest son was born. With three older brothers already running around the house, Nana had been a busy grandma for several months.

"Is there still cake from the party?" Fletcher asked but answered his own question by bringing the last slices of chocolate cake from the pantry.

Poppa returned Anna to bed and went back to the table for a cup of coffee. When Kate went out to the kitchen with a pile of plates, Gerrit leaned over to ask Helen if something was wrong.

"Not with me," Helen replied, "but Anna and I couldn't wake Kate earlier. She napped all afternoon and was very flushed when I came over. I didn't like the way she looked." Her voice was a whisper. "She might need to see Chandler."

"Always happy to have you over for a meal, especially when you bring it," Gerrit laughed, avoiding Helen's concerns.

A car came up the driveway, its horn honking as it pulled beside the porch door.

"Fletcher? Were you expecting someone to come calling tonight?" his mom asked.

"I nearly forgot. Jerry and I made plans to go to the drive-in," Fletcher said. "Not with any girls. Just us," he added shyly.

"You'd better be back no later than ten-thirty, Gerrit reminded him. You have to be up early for work."

After Helen left, Gerrit offered to finish up in the kitchen so Kate could get Anna ready for bed. Kate didn't argue.

A soft breeze found its way into the front porch. Lightning bugs sparked as they flew around the yard. It was unbelievably peaceful. Gerrit slid his chair closer to Kate, reaching for her hand. Uncharacteristically, he didn't talk. They sat in silence until Kate pulled her hand away to stifle a yawn.

"I think we'd better get you in bed," he said as he stood up, stretched, then helped her to her feet. "I wish we could get someone in to help you with Anna. I think you're working too hard. You don't have to do all your usual household chores every day. Maybe we could get Sarah another day a week."

Kate did a wash-up in the bathroom before checking on Anna. She made sure the bell was within easy reach in case she needed something during the night. With a breeze drifting through the window, it would be pleasant overnight. She sometimes worried about Anna being downstairs alone overnight, but they were all light sleepers and would hear the bell. Kate kissed Anna goodnight.

By the time she got upstairs, Gerrit was snoring. Getting to sleep would be a problem, she thought, heading back downstairs to spend a night in her old bedroom.

Car tires crunching on gravel in the driveway didn't disturb her. Nor did the sound of Fletcher closing up the house, checking on his sister and surprised at finding his mother there. He tiptoed upstairs for what was left of the night. Morning would come all too soon.

Kate put on a smiley face in the morning, but she felt worse than the day before. Maybe Gerrit was right. Maybe she'd worn herself out with worry since the doctor assigned Annalise to bed rest. Later, she'd try to remember to write in her journal. It had been such a long time since she'd taken it out of the sideboard. She wanted to write about Dr. Chandler overseeing Annalise's care during the pregnancy. Kate worried about his weekly bill for farmhouse visits, but she appreciated his attentiveness to Anna's care.

Kate also realized she hadn't written a word about the crisis that required Dr. Chandler's care in the first place. She never answered the pressing question: What would she have done in her daughter's place? She'd been so consumed with caring for Anna and the unborn baby that she hadn't taken time to consider the reality of what happened to her daughter. She prayed every day that Anna and the baby would survive—and that Anna would have a fighting chance to go to college and get a job after graduation, But how could she help Anna come to terms with the terrible violation she endured? How could Kate help her daughter when she couldn't accept what happened!

But to lie there, month after month, knowing a baby was growing inside you and that the person who raped you was your high school principal? Kate always ended up thinking that she could never have done the same. And to that end, she tried to honor her daughter's decision. When school started in fall, she knew the baby would be her responsibility while Anna studied. Then college. But would she ever marry? What suitor would take on a spouse who had a child after being raped by a priest? It seemed inevitable she'd have to raise the child herself, always wearing the stigma of having a child out of wedlock, banished to a life of shame. And that shame would be passed along to the child.

Kate thought back to the almost-daily entries in her old journals. Funny how distressed she'd get when her days didn't work out little stuff, like rain when things to do required sunshine. Is that how Anna would continue her life, knowing that someone else hung a perpetual cloud over her that would forever dictate her every movement? Hearing Gerrit's usual morning pacing with his coffee mug and toast, she knew Anna would find the gumption to do what she set out to do, even if her plans had unexpected detours.

Fletcher, Kate knew, worried about his sister, but with his graduation came at least the respite from anxiety about unannounced quizzes, quarterly tests, and semester exams.

Poppa was getting anxious to get going to work that morning. "Better hurry, Fletch," he said as he stepped from the front porch back into the kitchen. He reminded his son, who was now downstairs and hunting for a quick bite to eat, that he had an early meeting with the Executive Committee. It was usually informal, but since the subject was finances, it was imperative he be ready to talk numbers.

Fletch took his bowl to the kitchen and put it in the warm water his mom had poured in the dish pan. He stuffed the sandwich she made for him into his bag and followed Pops out to the car. Kate stood at the screen door and waved before going back inside to find out why Annalise was ringing her bell.

"It feels like I've peed in my pants," Anna said, looking upset. "Maybe I need to go to the bathroom."

Kate tried to swallow the fear she knew had instantly flushed her face. Why had she waited until Gerrit drove off before answering Anna's frantic alarm? Maybe she hadn't wanted her dad and brother to know she'd had an accident and avoided calling out.

Kate prayed: "Please God, let it just be an accident."

But it wasn't. Kate got Anna changed and her bed re-made, putting a piece of oilcloth under her. She took the pillow away. "Don't move around," Kate cautioned. "I'm calling Dr. Chandler."

She left a message with Chandler's wife, who promised to get the message to him while he was still making rounds.

Kate wasn't sure if Gerrit was at the courthouse. Maybe she needed to find out what Chandler recommended before calling Gerrit.

She barely got back to the bedroom when the phone rang. Grabbing for the receiver, Kate nearly pulled the phone off the wall.

"Hello," she said breathily, expecting to hear the doctor's voice. Instead, it was Helen, wondering if she might like company for coffee. "I could use a friend right now," Kate said, swallowing hard. "All of these long days in bed haven't helped Anna." Her voice broke into sobs.

Helen instructed her to sit with Annalise. "I'm on my way. If we have to take her into town, I'm going with you."

Helen intended to come for coffee so she could observe what might be wrong with Kate. She knew things weren't going right in Kate's life, and she had an awful dread Kate needed to see a doctor herself—and soon.

When Helen arrived and came into the bedroom, she found the mother and daughter hugging one another, both trying not to cry.

"Dr. Chandler just called," Kate said. "He wants me to bring Anna to the hospital right away. He can get away from his office for a while, but he wouldn't have time to make a trip out here. He said not to bother getting her dressed in clothes, just bring her in bathrobe and slippers."

Helen and Kate wrapped Annalise in her robe and propped her with pillows so her feet were up. Kate had driven a lot since she'd gotten her own car, but she'd never had to deliver a family member to the hospital.

"Did we close and lock the door?" Kate wondered aloud. Helen told her not to worry; she knew where the key was, and she not only locked the door, but brought the key along so they could get back in without having to crawl through a window.

Despite the tension in the car, the thought of her mom and Helen climbing through a front-porch window brought a giggle from Anna in the backseat.

As promised, Dr. Chandler was at the emergency room entrance with a gurney, two orderlies, and a nurse, all ready to lift Anna out of the backseat. They made a hurried run inside, with Kate and Helen close behind. After they pulled the privacy curtains, Kate spotted a phone down the hall and rushed off to call the courthouse. The meeting, she was told, had just started, but they promised to get Gerrit to the phone. Calling her back later wasn't an option, she told them.

The Finance Committee meeting was postponed until Gerrit was back from the hospital. Family, they reminded him, always came first.

The hospital was only a few blocks away, but Gerrit wasn't one to walk when he could drive. He pulled into the emergency parking lot and ran inside. Chandler was still examining Anna when he got there. A few minutes later, he came out to talk to them.

"I don't think Anna's situation is too serious. She's lost only a little blood, and she's not having contractions. The baby seems to be dancing around in there, so that's a good sign that it's not in distress. But we're going to keep her in the maternity section for a couple days—just a precaution. I expect it will settle down and we'll be able to get this baby a little bigger before delivery."

"Say, Doc," Gerrit said, "I know we've imposed on you enough today, could you squeeze Kate in for a look-see sometime, maybe even today? She's been awfully tired and very pale, not her usual bubbly self. You know how busy it's been with graduation and company, but usually she can handle all of that with energy left over. She doesn't know I keep close tabs on her, especially now with all the extra worry and strain with Annalise."

"Let me first make a call to my office, then I'll take a quick listen to Kate's heart. The nurse will get Kate into a gown so we can hear what's going on in there. I'll give Kate a good going-over later this morning after my morning crowd clears out a little. No doubt about the stress Kate's been dealing with these past months. If things are sounding OK, she could take a trip upstairs to settle Annalise, but only for a few minutes, then back down here and we'll tuck her in a bed so she can nap a few minutes. You could hike over to your office and my nurse will call when I'm ready to check Kate over. Is Fletcher upstairs with Anna, or has he gone to work?"

He sends Gerrit back to the courthouse and finds out Fletcher is upstairs with his sister,

Later that afternoon, the nurse has Kate in a hospital gown and they get her under cover on the hospital bed. Chandler comes back, goes into the patient room with the nurse, and Gerrit leans up against the wall outside that room. Chandler doesn't come out right away. When the curtain slides open, Chandler comes out to talk with Gerrit. Tells him he needs to give her a good going over—he'll also track down the cardiologist and get his input if necessary. Her heart is running fast, but it's not out of control. "I'll have the nurse take frequent readings. It should settle down," he says and hurries off to check out another last-minute patient.

"The nurse," he said, "will stay close by so she can keep tabs on Kate. And Kate must stay in bed and above all cannot go upstairs to see Anna."

Gerrit finds Fletcher and reminds him to go to work. He spends a few minutes with Anna, then says he needs to check in at the courthouse and take care of a couple phone calls before going back to the hospital. Minutes after

Gerrit leaves, they send Fletcher running after him to come back. Things have gotten serious with Kate. The cardiologist started checking her over.

Gerrit was sent out of Kate's room while Chandler and the cardiologist continued to check her over.

Everything happened so fast that morning it had taken her breath away. Literally.

"Oh, Helen," she started crying again. "Now I've got to stay. My heart isn't pumping right, and they don't like the sound of my breathing. Those are two of the biggies," she said, trying to muster a smile. "Looks like you'll have to drive yourself home in my jitney. But be sure you get the key out of my purse so you can start the car and get into the house to pack up some things for me."

"No need to worry about your own robe and slippers just yet," Chandler said. "We can outfit you in the height of fashion, and if you have to stay a few more days that will be time enough to have someone bring a little bag with the things you need. In the meantime, we'll keep you in nightgowns and a robe. Maybe Gerrit could pick up a toothbrush for you.

"I'll come by after office hours to see how you're doing," he said. "I've ordered some meds for you. But under no condition are you to go wandering around looking for Anna. She knows you're here, and you know she's here, but both of you are to stay in bed. Period!"

Dr. Chandler called his office and told his nurse that he'd be delayed a few minutes longer. He gave her details about admitting Anna, and asked her to add Kate's name to his appointments for the day. "I'll check her here as long as she's handy, and I'll dictate details when I get back to the office."

"Maybe she's just coming down with something," the doctor suggested to Gerrit, "but I know how she operates, and if Annalise doesn't go home, Kate's going to be running back and forth to make sure Anna's okay. You and Fletcher will just have to do your own cooking and cleaning while your girls are lounging in this high-class hotel."

Chandler turned to Kate and said, "And I mean *rest!*" With that, he turned to leave, then turned back and held Kate's hand for a few seconds. "I forgot my bedside manners," he laughed, and again turned to leave. "Stay in bed!"

Fletcher was worried—no, scared—by seeing his little sister in that hospital bed, wires and tubes hooked up to her. It didn't worry him when he saw her day after day in the big bed in the downstairs bedroom at the farm. But in the hospital, she looked so little, so young, so vulnerable. The reality of what had happened to her and how it all might end was frightening. Or maybe it was just that the anger he tried to hide was taking over.

Gerrit was lost in his own batch of worries. He knew the possible outcomes of his young daughter's pregnancy. She might lose the baby, and if that happened, they would deal with it. He couldn't deny that he wouldn't shed too many tears if that was how all things worked out. Anna would recuperate from that trauma and move on with her life.

But it was his Kate who worried him most. She was the rock at the center of all their lives. She looked so small, so wilted in that hospital bed. After weeks of worrying about Anna, she was on the verge of collapse. Or was it something more serious? He knew Doc was worried, or he'd never have insisted she be admitted and told to stay in bed. To reinforce that, he had the nurse put up the side rails so she couldn't get up. It was scary seeing her there.

Before heading home at the end of the workday, he and Fletcher stopped in to say goodnight. When Gerrit leaned over the rail to kiss her goodbye, he was shocked to see how frightened she looked. He promised to stop in before going to the courthouse in the morning.

He waved goodnight, then went looking for Fletcher. He found him coming around the corner toward the stairs. He retraced Fletcher's route and went up to say goodnight to Anna, but she was sound asleep. He put a kiss on his finger and touched her forehead. Then he hurried out to catch up with his son.

What an unexpected day. That morning, his only concern was figuring out how they could both get away for a possible appointment with the bishop. Gerrit was never comfortable around clergymen. And church seemed like a waste of time for a young man who had plans to make a fortune in banking.

He cringed, remembering what he'd expected Kate to do all those years ago, living alone on a farm with a little boy…and being pregnant with Anna all alone…and going by herself to both her parents' funerals. The stress it caused her. He hated that he'd always found reasons to not leave Chicago and join his wife on their farm, just as he'd always found reasons to not visit his parents.

As their car slowed at the row of mailboxes on the corner, he pulled over so Fletcher could check theirs.

"Doesn't look like anything too important," Fletcher said, holding a small stack of letters and the weekly newspaper. They turned into the driveway and Fletch jumped out to swing open the garage doors. Kate's car was in the second bay in the garage.

Neither of them were hungry, even though they hadn't eaten since noon. In the icebox was the last of the chicken from the graduation party. Fletcher cut a few slices of bread for sandwiches while Gerrit checked the stack of letters. Fletch noticed that his Pop stared at one envelope a long time before reaching into a drawer for a knife to slit it open. He could see the stationery had fancy lettering at the top and a brief message typed below. He didn't have to ask where it came from.

Gerrit read the message and continued to stare at the sheet of paper. Eventually, he laid it on the table next to his plate and sat down.

"It's from the bishop's office," Gerrit said, exhaling. "We have an appointment next Monday at ten-thirty. Depending on how your mother and Annalise are doing, I may go alone. There's a phone number I can call to verify the appointment. I'd like to call and tell them that the chaos dumped on our lives because of what his priest did has continued to grow. It's not only made your sister's life hell, it also has affected your mother's health. These are serious situations. The medical bills are going to be substantial."

Fletcher had trouble focusing on what his dad said. The list of worries just kept growing.

"We have to go into town long before the Ben Franklin store opens tomorrow," Gerrit continued. "I'll be going to the hospital to check on your mom and sister. Figured you'd come, too."

Fletcher nodded, reaching for the pitcher of milk. He still wasn't hungry, but the cold milk tasted good.

Gerrit stared off toward the Iversen's house. It looked like there was still a light on in their kitchen. "I think I'd better give Helen a call to let her know we'll be leaving early and to thank her for bringing Kate's car back. She'll be worrying about the girls."

When Helen answered so promptly, he knew she'd been sitting near the phone expecting it to ring. She would've noticed their headlights.

"I was hoping you'd call," she told Gerrit. "I know you have work to do at the courthouse. I was thinking I would drive into town after lunch tomorrow and visit Kate and Anna.

"I can't thank you enough for helping us through all of this," Gerrit said in a quiet voice, breaking his usual thunderous tone. "I'll poke my head in tomorrow morning to find out how Kate's doing and perhaps get a chance to talk with Chandler. Fletcher also wants to see how his sister is getting on. You can call me at the courthouse if anything happens while you are there. If I can get away at lunch, I'll stop over to visit Kate while she eats. My plan is to get out of the office by at least four-thirty. I'll give you a call in the morning after I see Kate and let you know what they have planned for her for the day. No sense in your driving into town if she can't have visitors in the afternoon. Again, we really appreciate how you are always so willing to help us when things get topsy-turvy."

Next morning when he reached over for his glasses on the bedside table, Gerrit saw the bishop's appointment letter staring back at him. Suddenly it hit him. He hadn't called Ida last night to let her know Kate was in the hospital. It was too early to call her now. He knew she liked to sleep late. He'd call before they left for town.

He was about to knock on Fletcher's door but knew from the sounds that he was already getting dressed.

Gerrit went downstairs to wash and shave. He decided to skip fresh coffee, knowing he could buy a cup at the hospital cafeteria, but he thought a couple slices of toast and jam would taste good. They hadn't eaten much supper when they got home last night. Before he went back upstairs to dress, he dialed Ida's number.

"Ida?" Gerrit said when he heard the receiver pick up on the other end. "It's Gerrit. I should have called last night, but by the time Fletch and I got home it was the last thing on my mind. There's no easy way to tell you all of this, but both Annalise and Kate are in the hospital."

"Oh, dear Lord," Ida said. He could hear the fear in her voice. "What happened? An accident?"

"No. Anna had some bleeding, and when Kate called the doctor, he told her to bring her in so he could check her out at the hospital. He didn't think Anna was in danger of losing the baby, but he decided to be on the safe side and keep her in the hospital for two or three days."

"I've been worried about Kate, so I asked Chandler to take a look at her sometime yesterday as long as she was at the hospital" Gerrit continued. "He was happy to do that, but I wasn't expecting his report about her heart and lungs. I was hoping she wouldn't have inherited your family's medical troubles. Now she's also been admitted. I don't have any idea if this is something Chandler and the docs there can handle or if we need to take Kate to a larger hospital. Fletch and I will be heading to town in a few minutes. I don't know if I can even get to the courthouse today. No important meetings today, so I'm going to stay with Kate and Anna as long as necessary. Fletcher can go to work."

Despite her upbeat, cheerful voice, Gerrit could tell Ida was crying. "Did you want me to come?" she managed.

"I'll have to let you know about that. Helen said she'd be with them today so I could go to the office. So, no need for you to come rushing up here. I think Chandler just wants Kate to get relaxed before she goes home. I'll call you later. Perhaps when both are home, you could stay at the farm with us for a few days."

"I'd be happy to do that, Gerrit," she said. "Please call again so I can start planning when I should come."

As they had the night before, Gerrit and Fletcher drove almost the entire way into town without saying a word.

"Would you check on your sister?" Gerrit asked before heading off to Kate's room. He had his mind set on finding Chandler.

Fletcher found Anna wide awake and waiting for breakfast. She still seemed a little pale but looked better than she had the afternoon before. They talked a few minutes until Gerrit came to find them. Then the boys traded places. Gerrit thought Kate might go home that day, but he wasn't sure how that would all be ironed out. Kate would have to take it easy. She always tried to spend as much time with Anna as possible, and that's why, he thought, she'd gotten run down and her heart grew weaker. Maybe Ida did need to come for a few days until they were both on the mend.

Gerrit did not tell Anna or Kate about the letter from the bishop's office with a suggested date for a meeting. Any news from that bishop would probably put both over the edge. Still, they'd have to be told sometime.

Fletcher promised his sister he'd be back after work that afternoon. "Anything I could pick up for you?"

"Maybe something to read," Anna suggested. "Or maybe just pick up one or two magazines from the sunroom down the hall. That way you wouldn't have to spend money, and I'd still have something to do."

Gerrit walked Fletcher to the main entry. "I'll see you this afternoon, unless you have a few minutes over your lunch time."

Gerrit met Chandler in the hallway near Kate's room.

"Looks like you got some good rest," the doctor told Kate, pulling the curtain around the bed.

Gerrit left the room, trying to steer clear of the morning traffic in the narrow hallway. There was a clattering cart with breakfast trays wheeling from doorway to doorway.

"I'll be back after doctor finishes in there," the kitchen helper said to Gerrit as he pushed the cart past.

When he heard the rings sliding the curtain along the metal tubing circling her bed, Gerrit tried not to hurry in. Both Kate and Chandler were waiting.

"Heart seems to be settling down some," the doctor reported. "It certainly was racing yesterday. We've talked a bit about Kate's family's heart problems, so it's nothing we can ignore when it gets going that fast. I haven't seen Anna yet, but I'm thinking she might as well stay here, too—even if she's doing okay—since there's no one at home to look after her. Is there someone you can hire to stay with them for a few days when they do go home? Mostly just to fix light meals and help Annalise with the bathroom?"

Gerrit nodded. "I already talked to Kate's sister about it but wasn't sure when she should come. Maybe tomorrow?"

"Let's say tomorrow. Then if things aren't looking good, we'll try for the day after. I've cautioned Kate that she must take it easy for a while."

A half hour later, Chandler returned with a report on Annalise. "She seems in good spirits," he said, "and the bleeding seems to have stopped. The baby has a very good heartbeat and Anna's appetite is back. She licked her plate clean! Can't blame her. Those pancakes and sausage smelled so good I was almost ready to beg for a plate myself."

They all laughed. The doctor continued. "Kate, I'll be stopping in again before I go home for supper. You can get up for the bathroom and to wash up a bit, but you may not go upstairs to visit Anna. She knows not to expect you today. You both are under orders to stay in bed and rest."

Gerrit knew he had two days of work to finish in one, and Helen would be at the hospital soon enough. "If things aren't too frantic over there, I'll try to come back for lunch. If I can, I will."

He bent down to kiss his sleepy wife when a voice startled him. Helen.

He briefed her on Chandler's assessments. "I've called Ida to come for a few days after they're both home" Gerrit added. "At this rate, we're going to have a busy few months after that baby arrives. Bottles and diapers and baths. Hard to believe we're starting all over again. But Kate will love it, don't you think?"

He walked back to the courthouse offices, climbing the fifty-seven steps from the street up to the double doors leading to the foyer and reception area. That entryway never ceased to amaze him. It was such a grand building. The area's earliest settlers obviously planned an impressive future, since it was way too extravagant for such a little country town, even if it had a very powerful name like Lillehammer. Helen had once dreamed of working there.

The building held elegant full-length windows in the courtrooms and County Board chambers.

Gerrit was heading up to his office when the county clerk's secretary came running to meet him. She spoke quickly through her panting. "You've got to get back to the hospital as fast as you can. It's your wife. Something's happened."

Gerrit nearly fell down the steps to the street below. "How could something have happened? I just saw her sitting up in bed waiting for breakfast." He saw Fletcher at the window in the sunroom at the end of the main floor hallway. How did he find out so fast that something happened to Kate?

"Pops," was all Fletcher could say before tears rolled down his face. "Pops, she…"

Gerrit quickly arrived at the hospital, rushed down the hallway to his wife's room. Opening the door a crack, he saw there was room for him to go inside and closed the door behind him. What happened? The curtain circled the bed, and he could hear that they were doing something for Kate. He found an opening where the curtains overlapped and looked inside. Kate had a terrible bluish gray color and her eyes were closed. He couldn't tell if she was breathing, but it didn't look like it. Then the sobs started, and he couldn't stop. His Kate. How could she have died in the few minutes it took to run down the street and up the stairs?

Chandler bumped into Gerrit as he tried to move to the other side of the bed. "You'd better wait in the hall with Fletcher. We're still trying to stabilize her and there's no room for you in here. Please!"

Gerrit quickly exited the curtain but hesitated to leave the room. He wasn't used to being told he couldn't be where he thought he had a right to be. But Chandler was the boss in this room, so he went to find Fletcher. Then he remembered Anna upstairs and figured that's where Fletcher must have gone in the few minutes he'd been in Kate's room. What if he'd told his sister what he thought had happened to their mother? Anna didn't need that kind of news right now. He knew he should go up there and see for himself, but he felt his legs starting to cave and he reached for the wall to steady himself.

He didn't remember how close Kate's room was to the main reception area until he saw a woman rush from behind the counter to grab him before he slid down the wall. She steadied him until an orderly pushing a gurney came around the corner, saw what was happening, and caught him under his arms and onto a rolling bed.

The receptionist went back to her station and the orderly stayed with the gurney until a nurse was called to take over.

Finally, Chandler came out of Kate's room and looked around. Surprised at seeing Gerrit flat on his back on a gurney, it didn't take him long to figure out what happened.

"We've got Kate stabilized, but we're going to have to put her in our intensive care unit so we can monitor her constantly," the doctor spoke to him. "It apparently was a stroke, something I was worried about last night with that racing heartbeat. But it was settling down when she went to sleep, and the nurse's records from overnight showed it continued to settle down. I'm not sure what the damage is, if any. We have a heart specialist on staff here, but he's in surgery right now, so he won't be able to assess Kate's condition until he's finished. In the meantime, I'll hang around until he's back. I've had my nurse cancel my morning appointments, so I'll be close by in case something else happens. That's a possibility." He added the last part grimly.

Gerrit was usually a fast thinker, but his brain seemed to be operating in slow motion. He still couldn't make sense of what had happened to Kate in the few minutes it took him to walk to the courthouse. He thought of his children upstairs. He tried sitting up, but the nurse standing beside the cart put her hand on his shoulder, insisting he stay still.

"We don't need another patient," she said quietly.

Chandler knew what was distressing his friend. "Nurse," he said, "could you find a wheelchair so we can get him up to the second floor where his daughter is a patient?"

Gerrit did not relish a ride in that elevator. It squeaked and complained as it traveled between the two floors. But he knew there was no other way for him to get upstairs where Annalise and Fletch must be frantic. It didn't do any good to question how so much could go wrong in a few minutes on a beautiful summer morning.

"If I need you quickly, I'll send someone to get you," Chandler told Gerrit, who was now in the wheeled chair. "Otherwise, just stay with the kids. People survive strokes. There can be physical damage, maybe speech problems and other inconveniences, but those are things that can be overcome with time and treatment. Kate is young, unbelievably healthy, and a hardworking, optimistic person. And she's stubborn. Those are good qualities for battling a stroke."

A nurse clomped along the hallway, pushing Gerrit in the wheeled chair. She had a nice smile but wasn't much for chatting. She asked his name, recognized it as belonging to the woman in Room 108, and didn't say anything more until they had held their collective breath in the 'lift' and gone down the hall to Annalise's room.

Gerrit was pleased to see his children were not dissolved in tears. Fletcher had pulled a chair alongside Anna's bed and was watching her eat breakfast. The nurse asked if he'd like a cup of coffee and promised to bring one back for him. "With cream and sugar?"

"Only a little cream," Gerrit answered. And she was gone, the clomping of her heavy white nurse's oxfords getting more faint.

Gerrit had a hug for his daughter, who looked surprisingly adult during her brother-sister conference with Fletcher.

"Should you be going to work pretty soon?" Gerrit asked his son.

"It's only eight thirty," Fletcher said after checking the clock on the wall above the door. "No sense going in before nine, because the doors are locked and I don't have a key. I'll leave in a few minutes."

"How's Mom?" Annalise asked. "Is she going to be alright? What happened? Fletcher said she was sitting up in bed waiting for her tray. He said he started telling her how well she looked when he thought he heard her say something about a very bad headache. Then she stopped talking. Her lips turned blue and her head seemed to have sagged to one side. Her eyes were closed. He heard Doc Chandler running down the hallway. "I just wish I could see her."

No one said anything for a while. The nurse came in with the coffee as well as buttered toast, and a milk for Fletcher. Anna finished the last of her breakfast and lay back on the pillow. Her dad and brother sat on either side of the bed, each holding one of her hands. Fletcher looked like he was going to cry again but didn't when he saw his father's head hang lower. He knew it would distress Anna, even though she was unbelievably stoic about this whole crisis.

"Where's Helen?" Fletcher asked. Gerrit looked befuddled, remembering that she arrived just as he was about to leave. Fletcher said she seemed to have disappeared when they realized something happened to Kate.

Anna knew exactly where they'd find her. "There's a little chapel here in the hospital somewhere," she said. "I know she would have gone there to pray for Mom." That's when the tears welled up in her brown eyes. Fletcher left to find out where the chapel was and promised to bring Helen back to Anna's room.

Gerrit tried to eat a few bites of toast but just couldn't make his mouth chew. His body felt rigid. Fletcher returned with Helen. Gerrit had to stay in his wheelchair, but since Fletch had to leave for work, she took his chair on the opposite side.

For a while, the three were lost in their own worries. To break the unbearable quiet, Gerrit said, "Annalise, I think you are the only patient they have on this whole floor. I haven't heard a single sound except those we're making."

Helen's eyes were puffy and red from crying. When Harald had his accident and died, she had been so accepting, so stoic about losing her life partner. If she ever cried, Gerrit never noticed. But today, she was desperately upset.

In his effort to calm her worrying, Gerrit relayed the doctor's assessment of Kate's condition and what had happened. Then he sighed. "Wish we could go down and peek in at Kate. I just want to see her. I know we'd be in the way and we can't do that…but I'd like to whisper to her that we're here and we love her.

Gerrit hadn't taken the time to go back to his office to call Ida to tell her things had gotten worse. He had no idea when she should come, but it seemed like Anna was getting better while Kate would spend more time at the hospital.

"How do they treat stroke patients?" Gerrit asked Helen.

"Most of the Iversens who suffered strokes usually died almost immediately. Some lived longer and spent time at a home to get therapy to overcome the damage. They all were older than Kate and not in as good health."

Suddenly, the door into Anna's room opened and there stood Ida. Gerrit should have known better than to think Ida would wait to hear from him before driving nearly two hundred miles to see for herself. Hugs and questions tumbled over each other. But Ida already knew the information she needed. The family was in bad shape and needed her help. She could stay indefinitely. "Besides," she said with a wide grin, "that baby is going to make an appearance soon, and I want to be here."

At the same time, Fletcher had gotten to work and was already straightening shelves and store displays, thinking about his Mom and trying to pray. But he couldn't remember the words, so instead he just kept begging God: "Please don't let anything happen to Mom or Annalise and make the baby strong and healthy, but not so bossy like my sister."

CHAPTER ELEVEN

Dr. Martin Wetzel wondered where the worried family was. There was no one in the reception area or leaning against the hallway walls. He knew no one could be admitted to Kate's room except hospital staff. Then he remembered what Chandler had told him earlier, that there were two of them —a daughter in obstetrics and the mom in the cardiac unit.

Chandler, Martin knew, had gotten the woman stabilized. He probably was waiting in the room. Martin pushed the door open and saw Chandler standing by the bed, intently focused on the woman lying there. He looked worried.

Martin nodded and slipped the latch to unhook the side rail, easing it down. He needn't have worried about disturbing the woman. He instinctively started the familiar examination procedure. He had barely begun when the woman opened her eyes. She seemed to be looking for someone. Her husband perhaps. She turned her head to the left with some difficulty. When she saw Chandler, she tried to smile. He reached over the other side rail and took her hand.

"This is Dr. Martin Wetzel," Chandler said gently. "He's the heart doctor on staff. He'll be checking you over to make sure I've been taking good care of you. I've sent a nurse upstairs to tell Gerrit that Dr. Wetzel is here and will be examining you. Your family can't come in yet, but those who are able can wait in the hall until Dr. Wetzel is finished."

Whatever happened to Kate while she was at the hospital with Annalise didn't make sense to her. She tried to talk but the words didn't sound right and even Gerrit didn't understand her. Frustrated, she'd just cry. That made those around her uncomfortable. What was wrong? Had she fallen and hurt her head? Had something terrible happened that no one could fix? And why was she in bed with the side rails up? Were they afraid she'd fall out like a child? Why couldn't they hear her when she said her head hurt? She shut her eyes. The voices kept talking. They must have thought she couldn't hear. But she could. She just couldn't understand what they said.

Every time she opened her eyes, she was sure someone would hear what her lips were trying to say. She wasn't sure who that man was who wore a white coat and listened to her heart. He called her Kate. She knew that was her name. Everything was all mixed up. No one listened when she tried to talk. Maybe she wasn't really there. Maybe she wasn't talking at all.

Then she remembered. They were going to get a baby. That's why they were at this place. The baby might come soon. No, it wasn't time. They didn't even have diapers ready. Was it her baby?

Sometimes the light was on over her bed. Sometimes it was dark, and she couldn't see anything. The light and dark were unsettling because she couldn't figure it out. Sometimes there was no one around to ask what had happened to her. Sometimes people around her were talking. No one heard her. She tried shouting but someone only came in and turned on the light and covered her with a light cover. They'd talk softly and rub her arm. She'd doze off.

Her week of days was mixed up. One day she saw Gerrit. He bent down and kissed her cheek. That made her smile. She tried to say his name but couldn't remember how. Her mind knew the word but her mouth couldn't make the sounds.

Upstairs, Ida was doing a little checking of her own. "Annalise," she chided lovingly. "I was barely home and unpacked when the phone rang, and I had to put all my things back into the suitcase and turn around and drive back up here." After a careful hug, she turned to Gerrit, anxious for news of what was happening downstairs with her sister. "They wouldn't tell me anything when I stopped at the front desk except that you were all up here. What's going on with Kate?"

Before Gerrit could answer, a nurse stopped in to let them know the cardiologist was examining Kate and suggested those able should head downstairs to be available when he finished. That, Anna knew, did not include her.

Gerrit felt safe enough to walk down the steps on his own, leaving the wheelchair outside Anna's room. He and Ida followed the nurse down the stairs, promising Anna they'd come back after they talked with the doctors.

There were several chairs at the far end of the hallway. Although they had spent the entire morning sitting, neither felt up to leaning against a wall. They moved the chairs a distance from the main desk so they could talk without being overheard. Gerrit tried to brief Ida on what had happened after they got to the hospital that morning. Oddly, he noticed, Ida didn't cry. It was almost as if she knew exactly what had happened. After all, their family had an unsettling history of heart trouble.

Ida sat quietly for some minutes, her mind trailing back to that dreadful day when their mom died. But even worse than losing their mother had been watching their father blessing his deceased wife in the casket before the altar where they had led services for so many years. The terrible pain in his eyes still haunted her. Their parishioners always remarked what a matched set

Pastor Conner and his Annalise were. They had been playmates growing up, and no one was surprised when they decided to marry.

Although she'd lost her own husband six years ago after a long and painful battle with ALS, colloquially known as Lou Gehrig's Disease, Ida's sadness was tempered by the joy of knowing that his days of suffering were over. Jake had been a good man, but Ida had no more tears. She'd done enough crying in the back bedroom after the many days when she was overwhelmed with watching the pain he had to endure.

During the drive that morning, Ida had faced her dread of the day when their generation would pass on. Ida and her siblings had now moved to the front of the line. And, although she was the oldest, there was no guarantee she would be the first to go. Kate had always been the fragile one, or sickly, as Aunt Ella used to say. If a bug was going around, Kate was always the first to get it. Ida had prayed all those long miles that morning that whatever was wrong with Kate wouldn't be as bad as she imagined. She knew better than to upset Gerrit and Anna with her fears. Besides Kate, Ida was still frantic about Annalise. She would never understand how Anna could carry the baby, but she kept those thoughts to herself and prayed every day that she'd deliver a healthy (and not too premature) baby.

Gerrit, like Ida, was lost in his own thoughts. Finally, he pulled back to the present.

"Ida, I know this is a terrible proposition, but I don't know where else to turn," Gerrit began. "I have no family left, as you know, who would be capable of caring for not one invalid, but two. I can hire someone to help, but I need someone at the house to be in charge. We have no notion of what's happened to Kate, and I pray to God that whatever it is will be of short duration and she'll be back to her old self soon. But she certainly can't take care of herself and still do all Anna requires. Could you stay with us for a couple weeks? I don't know how long Kate will have to be in the hospital, or if they'd send her to a home where attendants would care for her. I know that would not be her ideal choice, because she'd get no rest if she weren't where she could at least oversee Anna during these weeks before the baby comes."

"Gerrit, of course I can stay for however long I'm needed. I have nothing to do that won't wait until things are back to normal here. That's why I had to get here today. Perhaps one of your Amish neighbors might know of someone who could help with the housework. I can make meals and do laundry, but my back and knees complain bitterly when I try to scrub floors." Ida attempted a smile.

"We'll find someone with young legs and lots of energy to help as long as you're there to direct traffic. Chandler thought Anna could maybe go home tomorrow, but he said he'd have to wait until the morning to see how things were going. We'll get the word from Dr. Wetzel about Kate and the care she'll need. I know our neighbor Helen is a jewel, much like you, who can just step in and take charge. Maybe when Kate is home again, you and Helen can trade off. Now that Harald is gone and she's selling her farm, she's anxious to find something to keep busy and out of her son's hair. She's got a lot of energy, and she's not quite ready to sit in a corner and knit slippers."

They laughed. Ida was grateful for the distraction. She never would have guessed Gerrit would be so good at laying out a plan in an emergency. But she wondered if he'd really thought all of this through—if he knew what he would be setting himself up for once she and Helen took over the household.

"You sure you're ready to turn your life and wife over to two widows?" she asked.

They were still laughing when the door to Kate's room opened. "Don't you know you're supposed to be quiet in a hospital? Laughing is not allowed." Dr. Chandler's teasing gave them hope that Kate wasn't as ill as they'd worried.

They hurried down the hall to where Dr. Wetzel was waiting. His smile was even more encouraging than Chandler's jokes. But the biggest thrill was seeing Kate awake. When Gerrit tried leaning over the side rail, his plan to kiss her on the forehead fell a little short. Kate tried to say something but couldn't find the words. A puzzled look crossed her face and she reached for Ida's hand—with her left, not her right. Again, she tried to say something, but her mouth couldn't form the words.

Dr. Wetzel suggested they find chairs and sit down. Ida figured he didn't want them standing over Kate, staring at her. When she started crying, neither Gerrit nor Ida knew what to do or say. Ignore the tears? Ignore her struggles trying to talk? Ignore the fear spreading across her face?

Gerrit held his wife's hand while the doctor explained what apparently happened to Kate.

"It was a slight stroke," Dr. Wetzel said. "Still serious, but not as bad as it might have been. The blood clot or whatever blocked the blood flow left her with some damage that should, in time, be reversed. It could be a long process, but people who have had similar experiences have learned to talk again. We haven't checked yet, since Kate just woke up before we called you in, but often the speech difficulty also includes difficulty with recognizing words and reading."

"I had a patient not long ago who is very bright, very active, and an excellent speaker. He thought all of that was behind him after his stroke and he was extremely angry. But he turned that anger into determination, and he worked on learning to say words again, recognize people he knew and call them by name. And, today, he's back in his college classroom, teaching. But that didn't happen in a few days. He was so determined we had to slow him down for fear he'd get so upset he'd bring on another stroke."

The doctor continued, "That hasn't happened. He learned to pace himself, stopping to rest rather than pushing himself. You'll meet him eventually. He has made it his mission to spread the word about what he did as encouragement to others who have suffered strokes."

"Kate, you will need to stay in the hospital for a week or two so we can get you started on the therapy to get your brain working again. When you are comfortable with the exercises and daily schedule for your recovery, we'll send you home with instructions and our little how-to manual for getting better. We will need to see you at least once a week for the first month, and after that, a little less often, depending on how you're coming along. It's important to take it slow. You'll make greater progress that way. I see you have a good crew to help you. I know Helen is planning to work with you on your exercises."

Gerrit looked at Kate and winked. He hadn't done that since she had walked down the aisle toward him. He saw her try to wink but it didn't work quite right. "I think that's the first thing I'm going to teach you. After all these years, you're going to learn how to wink."

Chandler was amazed at how swiftly Gerrit and his sister-in-law had stepped up to manage this monumental task. He had given Dr. Wetzel a heads-up about Kate and Gerrit's daughter's situation. The doctors knew it would only complicate their assignment to help Kate repair the stroke-damaged muscles and re-program her memory to retrieve what she had lost.

Gerrit suddenly remembered the letter from the bishop asking them to meet with him this week. Suddenly, he knew he'd have to make good on their request for an appointment to discuss the rape issue and subsequent pregnancy, regardless of everything else that had occurred. Although he hadn't talked with Ida, he knew if they could do it while Kate was still in the hospital, perhaps Helen could stay with Anna while he and Ida drove to Milwaukee and back the next day.

Ida didn't even have to think about it. "Of course, I'm going. I hope he's there, too. I'll gladly be Kate's stand-in."

The two doctors exchanged glances. Kate seemed to understand what the discussion was about because she tried to smile. The gratitude in her eyes, however, spoke louder. Ida realized that she was looking forward to confronting that bishop about what had happened to her niece, now more than seven months ago.

CHAPTER TWELVE

Anna didn't get her wish to go home because there was no one there to care for her. Dr. Chandler asked Dr. Wetzel to check her over to make sure her heart wasn't pulling the same stop-and-go rhythm as her mother's. He wanted to make sure there would be no surprises when it came time for Annalise to deliver.

Anna wasn't pleased. She thought she'd have a couple of days at home before Aunt Ida had to go with her dad to meet with the bishop. She knew there was no use even asking if she could go along.

The hospital routine had grown very boring. There didn't seem to be any other patients in the maternity ward. Or maybe they were just quiet. But babies weren't quiet.

Annalise amused herself by thinking up names. She reached over the edge of her bed to pull out the little notebook Fletcher bought at the dime store. *If it's a girl, her name will be Mary Ellen.* When she wrote it on the top line of the notepad, she thought it looked very proper. *Janet? Rosemarie? Grace? Joyce? Christina? Cristina? Kristina?* She studied the three variations of Christina and said it repeatedly to herself, wondering if it would look good on school papers and report cards. She then added a few new ones. But she always went back to Christina. It was a pretty name, she decided. For now, the baby would have to use the Jansz last name, as Kate and Anna had discussed. To avoid confusion of whose baby it was, if it had Anna's name, it would be as if it were her younger sibling, not her child. Then, if Anna ever married, the baby could still go by that last name, or instead take Anna's husband's last name.

"Such complications," she muttered. She certainly would never give the baby its real father's name, no matter what her dad and Aunt Ida worked out with the bishop.

She heard footsteps she didn't recognize. She also heard the squeaky sound of Aunt Ida's comfortable shoes. At first, she slid the little notebook under her pillow, then just laid it on the rolling tray that slid across the bed so she could write letters or stories or more baby names. There was no need for secrecy.

The unfamiliar sounds were from Dr. Wetzel's shoes. His morning rounds didn't take him long. Maybe his patient from surgery was already dismissed. Probably not, she figured. Doctors kept heart patients in bed longer than two or three days, and Kate was no exception. Anna didn't like having to go home without her, even if Aunt Ida or Helen would be there. If only she could go downstairs for a few minutes to see Momma for herself. To see if she had learned how to talk. And read. And move her legs.

Anna realized Dr. Wetzel had been talking to her while she was daydreaming.

"I was busy thinking of names for my baby and I didn't hear what you said," Annalise admitted. "I'm sorry."

"No worry," Dr. Wetzel said. "I was just asking how you were feeling and if you'll be going home later today, or maybe tomorrow?"

"Dr. Chandler said if you didn't find anything wrong, I could go home this afternoon. Otherwise I'll have to stay a few more days until my dad and Aunt Ida get back and can take me home. Helen is going to stay with me while Aunt Ida goes with my dad for a meeting," Anna explained.

"Breathe deeply," he said. "In and out. Now hold your breath until I tell you to let it out."

He put the stethoscope first on her chest, then against her back. She thought once she heard him mumble under his breath. Then he listened to the heartbeat in the artery in her neck. He wrote some notes on a paper snapped to a clipboard that had a pencil tied to it with grocery string. She thought she might have to try that trick, so she'd always know where her pencils were.

"Lie back," Wetzel said, all business as he placed the stethoscope in several spots around her stomach. I sighed a, "Hmm," before he twisted the stethoscope around his neck and helped her sit up so she could straighten her hospital gown. She looked around for any family members while the doctor wrote more things on the clipboard.

"Some good news and some not-so-good news for you today," Dr. Wetzel began. "Your heart is in there but not working in a regular beat. It wants to start and stop. Do you ever feel short of breath? Do you notice that sometimes your heart seems to be working awfully hard and might even stop for a beat or two?"

Anna had never paid much attention to her heart. It seemed to work just fine. It kept pumping. She thought for a few seconds, then realized that her heart did slow down sometimes when she'd put her fingers on her wrist like the nurses did when they checked her pulse. Other times, it seemed to race. Sometimes her heart hurt, and when it did, she often had to sit down to catch her breath. But since she'd been in bed or riding in her wheelchair, she didn't pay much attention to it.

Dr. Wetzel finished Anna's exam and said he was going downstairs to see Kate. "Dr. Chandler will meet me there. Then we'll talk to your mom about you. But for now, I see no reason why you can't go home later today, or you can just stay here until your dad and aunt get back from their business trip. Maybe that would be the best thing; I know Dr. Chandler wants you to get up more to keep everything moving, so we have to talk about a schedule for you to do without causing another situation like the one that brought you here the other day. There's no guarantee it won't start up again, but we need to figure out the best way to keep you from getting too sedentary without making more problems the other way. I'll be back up in about a half hour. If you're good and mind your Aunt Ida, I might have a little surprise for you later."

He cranked the bed up to a slight rise so she wouldn't have to lie flat. Then he pulled the wheeled tray back over the bed and handed her the notebook and pencil with her list of names. He smiled at her and said, "That will keep you busy for a few minutes. I'm anxious to see the names you are considering. My wife and I are having a baby in fall, and I'd like to look over your list so I can suggest some names for our baby. It will be our first. Are you choosing names for both a boy and girl, or do you think you know which you are having?"

"I thought I would start with girl names, because I have a feeling that's what it will be. But I will have some boy names ready, too."

"I'll bring Dr. Chandler with me when I come back," Dr. Wetzel said and left. His footsteps faded as he made his way to the stairs.

Anna and Aunt Ida worked on the lists of names, putting marks next to those that were favorites. Auntie had agreed on the Christina name, so they put a big circle around it, as well. Boy's names weren't so easy, she discovered. Maybe that was because she only had one brother and not many boys lived close to their farm. "Maybe we'd better ask Fletcher for suggestions," Anna said.

Before they got around to even starting a list of boy's names, the two doctors were back. "First, the surprise," Dr. Wetzel said. "We've decided if that old rickety elevator can find its way down to the first floor, we'll take you to see your mom. She seems to be having a good day today, and her heart is behaving better. We can only stay a few minutes—for her sake, not yours. She hasn't started speech therapy yet, so she probably won't be able to talk. But don't fret. We are confident she'll speak again. It could be a long process, depending on how she gets along in therapy. We have a nurse trained to help stroke patients learn to talk again. I can tell from her eyes that she is anxious to see you."

Then Dr. Chandler took over. He told Ida she'd have to practice some exercises with Anna that day. A nurse would be coming in to instruct them. "You've been lounging around far too long. You have to keep your muscles in good condition if you are going to deliver that baby in a few weeks," he told Anna.

Anna was excited about seeing her mom but scared to death about the trip back up to second floor on the elevator, although they made it safely.

Anna thought riding around in a wheelchair would be fun, but she quickly realized there was an art to steering it around without bumping chairs and beds.

"This is one of the first exercises you'll have to learn," Dr. Wetzel said. He helped her get close enough so she could reach between the bars of the bedrail and rub her mom's hand. Anna could tell she was trying to smile back at her. It was a little lopsided, but it was beautiful. She tried not to squeeze her mom's fingers too tightly, but she wanted her to know how happy she was to finally see her. It seemed like they had been cooped up there for weeks.

"I've started making lists of names for the baby," Anna said. That brought an even stronger smile to her mom's face.

Aunt Ida, thrilled at seeing her sister so alert, was anxious to get Annalise home where they could build up her strength. Once Kate and Anna were both back home, they could probably work together on exercises.

But first things first. Anna told the doctors she would be content to stay at the hospital until her dad and Aunt Ida got back from their meeting. It probably cost a lot of money to stay here, she knew, but she was leery of being too far away and unable to get back to the hospital—not for herself, but for her fragile mom. She had a lot of questions she wanted to ask but knew this wasn't the time; her mother might have struggled to make sense of the words. For now, maybe they should both stay in the hospital.

There was one question Anna couldn't wait to ask the doctors once she was back in her own room. "Why can't I just move downstairs into the second bed in mom's room?" Besides, then the doctors wouldn't have to run up and down the stairs or haul her in that creaky elevator when she wanted to go see her mom.

The two doctors looked at each other, then shook their heads in agreement that there was no reason for her not to spend a couple of days beside her mother.

CHAPTER THIRTEEN

June 23, 1945

Dear Days,

It seems like I'm the mom taking care of my mom. I still am not allowed to be out of bed for more than a few minutes, but at least I'm there to call the nurse in case Momma needs help. She still can't talk, but I know from the expression on her face when she's in pain or needs something.

Most of the time, I talk to her, hoping she'll forget she can't speak and just answer. But that hasn't happened.

Poppa stops to see us in the morning on his way to work, at lunch, and before he and Fletcher drive home. His appointment with the bishop was postponed because of a conflict with his schedule. So instead of driving down on Monday afternoon as he planned, he and Aunt Ida don't leave until Thursday afternoon.

The days drag by. There's not much to do. I've read some of the magazines a couple times, and the only books in the waiting room are for little children. Once, I thought about getting a child's book for Momma to try sounding out words, but the nurse didn't like that idea. They took her for exercise to get the parts of her body that didn't work right back into practice. I wish they would tell me where she goes, but they said they can't. If Poppa asks, they tell him.

Aunt Ida stopped in today to tell Momma and me that they were starting out. Ida left her car here at the hospital so Fletcher can get home tonight and back for work in the morning. She gave me her car keys and told me not to lose *them in my bed. I know she was just trying to be funny. I'm so worried what the bishop will say about me this time. He wasn't very nice to Momma when she went there right after she found out what happened to me. I sometimes think I'll never smile again. But when this baby is born, I just know it'll make me so happy I'll forget all this sad stuff.*

Maybe the bishop doesn't like us because we aren't Roman. Regardless, I did enjoy going to their school before Father Nolan did what he did.

Anna

Poppa and Aunt Ida planned to spend Thursday night at Ida's house in Milwaukee. Besides Ida's bedroom upstairs, she sometimes slept in the little bedroom off the kitchen downstairs. Anna didn't want her Poppa to sleep in the second bedroom upstairs because of what happened in there.

Anna needn't have worried. Ida slept in Anna's old room and Gerrit slept in Ida's. Since Emily offered to drive her mom and uncle to their ten o'clock appointment the next day, she decided to bunk overnight in the little room off the kitchen.

Emily knew her way to the bishop's office, but she allowed extra time for morning traffic. The meeting would probably take less than an hour, so they'd have no trouble getting back to Lillehammer by late afternoon.

Emily had coffee made and toast buttered when Ida came downstairs. Gerrit had been awake a long time before he finally got up. Despite all the chaos that had occurred in that little house, Ida's bedroom was a very pleasant space. Before getting into bed the night before, he'd sat in the old kitchen rocker Ida kept in her room, obviously a comfortable place for reading. There was a nice lamp next to the rocker, but he preferred the soft glow from a streetlight just down the road. He sat in the near-darkness and tried to organize his thoughts for their appointment. He kept remembering the look in Kate's eyes when he'd bent down to kiss her goodbye. She had things to remind him to say, but the stroke made it impossible for her to voice those words. *Never mind*, he thought to himself. *I can hear her words as loud and plain as if she were talking to me.*

Now with the sun coming up, he realized he was wasting precious minutes going back over the same list of details he wanted to tell the bishop. He took a quick shower, shaved, dressed, and went downstairs. Emily and her mom were already drinking coffee. Emily pushed back her chair so she could fill his cup, but before she did, she slipped two slices of bread into the toaster.

Gerrit usually faced each day ready to take on whatever came at him. This morning, though, he wasn't sure he could handle any part of the day.

When Emily set the buttered toast in front of him, Gerrit absentmindedly picked it up and started to nibble at a corner. He remembered that they'd never stopped at a restaurant in any of the little towns they passed through the night before.

"Ida," he said, "I just remembered we never got anything to eat last night. You must have been starving this morning. I'm so sorry. I was so pre-occupied with what lay ahead for us today that I never gave food any thought once we got in the car."

She laughed. "Heavens," she said, "I never eat when I'm upset, and I have been very worked up looking forward to today. But now that it's here, I've had some toast, coffee, and now good company. I know things are going to go well. I promise I won't get unruly or weepy-eyed."

Ida chided Gerrit to stop worrying. "I've talked to that bishop a couple of times on the phone. "I was always upset whenever I heard his voice, but he was always very kind. I would have preferred he sided with me about what had happened to Annalise, but he never did. I keep thinking back to my father and, in my memory, he talked that same gentle way to people who'd come to complain about something. When I first talked to Cleary Nolan about what happened, I was ashamed, later, at how I'd raged and ranted. For what? Poppa used to tell us kids, 'You never accomplish anything when you're shouting.' That was a lesson I forgot that day."

Ida sighed before continuing. "I've promised myself that today you will do all the talking. Kate was always so much better at speaking in a moderate voice. But I remember Kate telling me, while we packed up Anna's things, that she was very angry when she was in the priest's office. But who could blame a mom for raising her voice when she finds out her daughter has been drugged and assaulted by a priest?"

Emily gathered up the breakfast dishes and put them in the sink. "Have to get started," she said. "We need a calm trip so we aren't all frazzled when we get there."

Again, who could argue?

They were on their way less than a half-hour later, determined not to be delayed by traffic. They arrived at the chancery parking lot forty-five minutes early.

Emily pulled into a shaded parking space. "Take some deep breaths and relax," she said. "Let's just sit here a minute or two."

Although they were early, the receptionist said the bishop's previous appointment was shorter than expected, so he was ready for them. She knocked quietly on his office door, then opened it for them to enter.

Gerrit and Ida followed her in. She introduced them to His Excellency, then turned and left, closing the door silently behind her. The bishop was standing. He nodded to them, then extended his hand in greeting. Ida wasn't sure if it was appropriate, but she also held out her hand to shake it. She had a momentary panic, wondering if she was supposed to shake his hand or bend over to kiss his ring. She thought she remembered seeing Catholics do that when they greeted a bishop. But then, maybe non-Catholics weren't expected to.

Gerrit and Ida sat facing the bishop from across the large mahogany desk that was clear except for a phone, calendar, and writing blotter. It looked so bare and perfect, Ida thought it couldn't possibly be used for anything as mundane as writing lists or letters. She tried to take her cues from him as they sat quietly. Was he waiting for them to say something, or would he eventually start the conversation? Since it was his office, she figured they were supposed to wait for him to begin.

He did. He thanked them for making the long trip and hoped it was a safe journey. He then inquired about Kate and Annalise.

"They're both in the hospital," Gerrit said quietly. "Annalise had a scare with her pregnancy, and my wife had a small stroke. She lost her ability to speak."

There was quiet for a moment. "Ida, here, is my wife's sister," Gerrit explained.

"I know," the bishop said. "When I talked to Cleary Nolan, he said he often had Sunday evening supper at Ida's house. He said they liked to compare notes on their respective faith traditions." He paused and then nodded to Ida before continuing. "You had a rare childhood growing up in a pastor's rectory. I imagine you absorbed a lot of religious knowledge by osmosis around the dinner table." He smiled slightly.

Ida was relieved that Nolan apparently hadn't told the bishop about her rant in his office a while back. "For shame," she imagined her father would have said about that performance. But the circumstances had called for it at the time.

"We have some serious topics for discussion this morning," the bishop then said quietly. "I thought it best that I have the diocesan attorney sit in on this meeting. He should be arriving any time now, so we will just wait. Would you like some coffee or tea?"

Ida shook her head, then thanked him for the offer.

Gerrit wasn't used to drinking more than his breakfast coffee in the morning. "Thank you, but no," he said.

Ida thought she heard a tap behind her, but she resisted the urge to swivel around to look.

"Morning, Bishop," a voice said. "I see I'm a bit late. Traffic was starting to get a little heavy."

More introductions. Gerrit and Ida both stood up as the attorney made his way around to the bishop's side of the desk.

The attorney was slightly rotund but not very tall. His name was Ryan O'Callahan. Gerrit thought he looked like he'd recently come from the old country. If Gerrit listened closely, he could hear the lilting cadence in his voice.

"Mind if I take a few notes?" O'Callahan asked. The bishop said he assumed he would. Gerrit knew then that this was serious business. Obviously, it was going to be a fact-finding session, not just a friendly discussion. Ida grew more uneasy. The pleasantries suddenly disappeared, and the room grew decidedly serious.

The bishop started, and then Gerrit pulled out a small notebook from his pocket and started writing. The bishop frowned at him.

"I assumed you'd expect me to also take notes," Gerrit explained. "In my job as a county official, I regularly take notes during meetings on points I want to review later."

The bishop nodded reluctantly and then continued. "I've talked at length with Cleary Nolan after your wife came to see me. He vehemently insisted he did not do what he's been accused of. He said he knew that you, Ida, were out of town the day this reportedly occurred, and that your niece was supposed to be at a forensics tournament but stayed home because she had a sore throat and couldn't talk. He said the forensics coach called him when they got back from the competition late that afternoon and he asked that they wait at the school for a few minutes so he could congratulate the team for what had apparently been a very successful competition. He said that was when he learned that your daughter didn't compete because she was ill. He was sad to hear that because he knew how much she practiced and how excited she was to be competing in a real meet."

The bishop continued, reading from typed notes, which he said were from his taped conversation with the priest at this office several months earlier. "He told me that after he talked to the students, he went back to the parsonage and heated up soup the cook left for his supper. He said he sat with Annalise in the kitchen while she ate the soup, then put on his jacket and left, asking her to be sure to lock the door behind him."

"That, your excellency, is not the way Annalise said it happened," Ida interrupted. "and I made arrangements for Anna to spend the night at a friend's house. That didn't happen because Anna was sick. So, Nolan knew she was there alone…and delivering the soup was not appropriate. Even for a clergyman. He said he wanted her to have a few sips of a toddy like his mother used to give him so she would get a good night's sleep. She certainly didn't 'catch' her pregnancy from a cruet of alcohol. But something happened that night, and now she's pregnant, and there is absolutely no one else who could have done it."

She stopped to catch her breath, then continued. "He made sure she got up to her bedroom, and although she admonished him to leave, he stayed. She said he tucked her into bed then took out the cruet filled with a colorless liquid and poured it into a glass on the bedside table. He kept insisting she needed to drink all of it while he sat in the rocker, waiting for her to fall asleep. She told me she didn't remember anything after that, but something obviously happened because her bed was all askew when she woke up in the morning. And her pajama bottoms were on the floor, half under the bed."

At that, she sensed Gerrit tensing up. Although Ida had wanted Gerrit to do all the talking, she had been one of the first to hear the story of that night once Anna was confirmed three-months pregnant. Knowing the exact day of that forensics event pinpointed the date exactly three months earlier.

Gerrit joined in. "Ida called my wife and invited her to come for lunch the next day. She didn't tell her why because she didn't want to alarm Kate with the news over the phone. Since the next day was Saturday, Anna wasn't in school. She was surprised when her mother arrived, but she knew immediately why she was there. Kate said Annalise couldn't stop crying when she saw the horror on her mother's face when she realized why she was invited for lunch."

Gerrit's eyes filled with tears. "Now she's pregnant and confined to bed for months until she delivers. We are horrified by how this happened, but we are proud of her because she is determined to let this baby live. She doesn't plan to give it up for adoption."

Gerrit collected himself before continuing. "Anna had to drop out from not only Saint Michael's, but also from her most recent school because of serious pregnancy problems. Our doctor has been driving out to our place every Saturday morning to check on her so she wouldn't have to ride into town to see him. He's been very worried she'd lose the baby. This, I remind you, is a young lady who is only fourteen. Sadly, she's missed most of her freshman year of high school."

Both the bishop and attorney nodded for him to continue.

"My wife has been caring for her at home," Gerrit said evenly. "The doctor originally wanted to keep Anna in the hospital, but Kate was determined to hire help with the household chores so she could have extra time to work with her on her schoolwork. Anna's brother, our son, just graduated from high school and is enrolled at a college in Green Bay. Throughout the remainder of the school year, Fletcher brought her assignments home every night and carried Anna's finished work back to school the next morning."

"Some of her classmates keep asking her brother why she can't come back to school. He just tells them the doctor has her on bed rest," Gerrit said sadly.

"The pregnancy then reached a crisis," Ida took over for Gerrit. "The doctor immediately admitted Annalise to the maternity department. She nearly did lose the baby that day."

"Due to the strain all this put on my wife, I asked the doctor to check her to make sure her heart was not giving out…." Gerrit started.

"Heart disease runs in our family," Ida added.

"Instead of my wife sitting by her daughter's bedside on the second floor, she ended up having a stroke. So now I have two members of my family experiencing grave physical difficulties because of what the headmaster at the Catholic school set in tragic motion."

The attorney interrupted. "We have to consider that there is another explanation for your daughter's pregnancy. A boyfriend from school or town. There's no evidence to prove that the rector is responsible for this. We have only your word that that's what happened."

"Annalise does not go out with boys. Nor does she hang around with boys at school. I ought to know," Ida said, her voice rising. She took a deep breath, then continued, "As the guardian of my sister's daughter, I watched the clock when school let out and knew exactly when she should be walking through the door. If she stayed after for forensics or something else, she always let me know in advance. If she wasn't home when I expected her, you better believe I'd have been at that school to find out the reason why."

Ida hadn't finished, whether the bishop wanted her to stop or not. "For one thing, her classwork was too important for distraction. She had no time for boys, so that's not how this happened. Her dream was to get the best high school education she could because she wanted to go to a good college and earn a degree. Now look what's happened!" Ida realized her hands were shaking and she detected a noticeable tremor in her voice.

Gerrit didn't say anything. He was curious what the bishop had to say.

The bishop shuffled uneasily in his chair. The attorney, sensing his reluctance to comment, filled the silence. "Why did the family let their young daughter go to a city several hours from their home to go to high school?"

"Because," Gerrit quickly answered, "she raised her own tuition money so she could attend that school. One of her friends had gone there the year before and told her it was a wonderful school. Anna made and sold dried apple rings and banked all that money so she could go for the entire four years. A girl that's driven doesn't fool around and jeopardize her dreams."

The room was quiet for what seemed like forever. Then the bishop asked if they had anything else to add.

"No," Gerrit said. "Our daughter's life is compromised because of what your priest did, and that problem is multiplied now by the medical problems my wife is having."

"I have something else to add," Ida interrupted. "Annalise didn't say anything about that night until she realized what had happened to her. In the morning when she got up, she said she folded the pajama bottom and put it in a gift box she found on the closet shelf. When my sister came down to pack up Annalise and take her home, they left the box and pajamas on the closet shelf, where it still is. I don't know what tests they can do on those soiled pajamas, but the stains left behind should prove who did it. I don't know if science can yet find that out, but we're going to hold onto this evidence until it can."

By the look on Gerrit's face, Ida figured Kate hadn't told him about the soiled pajamas. The bishop and attorney didn't say anything. Thinking what? That they'd have to call Cleary Nolan in for another little chat?

Gerrit spoke again. "I have talked with the district attorney in our county. He advised me that the paternity of the baby could be established with blood work. That will be done once the baby is born. I'm sure you already are aware of that. If the priest's blood type matches the baby's, we'll have to go to court to legally establish paternity and settle on his financial liability. The father of that child has financial obligations to pay for care and costs associated with raising it. That's where we are going with this." Gerrit tapped his fingers on the edge of the large desk.

"We're a long way from knowing the truth here," the attorney piped up. He'd continued taking notes. "There's a lot of proof needed to make such blatant accusations—or a story made up by a young, hysterical girl caught in a compromised situation."

"It's her word against that of a well-known, respected clergyman," the bishop said. "I don't believe one iota of this story," he added curtly.

The bishop's chair scraped across the floor. He stood and faced them. The attorney also stood up, waiting for Gerrit and his sister-in-law to stand. But Ida knew the signals for ending a meeting and wasn't having it. She laid her hand on Gerrit's knee, signaling him to stay seated. She nodded at him, urging him to continue speaking.

"We haven't decided when to meet again," Gerrit said. "As I said before, I've consulted with our DA. He said he's anxious to hear how things went with this meeting. At first it was almost an embarrassment to have to come here and make such awful accusations. But there is no denying that someone made my daughter pregnant and someone is going to have to own up to it and make appropriate contributions toward the expenses. Not to mention take responsibility for how the horrible stigma of a rape and resulting pregnancy can mark a child."

The bishop and attorney remained still, but Gerrit didn't stop. "Solving these issues when you have a DA and the courts involved can be nasty business for a church-run school and the religious affiliation of the perpetrator.

"I would think that a religious organization like the Roman Catholic Church would do more than just deny that it could possibly have been a churchman's doing, especially when their reputation is on the line. You, bishop, may not believe a word of this informal testimony, but the pregnancy is real, the victim is very young, and her entire life has been turned upside down. All because of a man's inability to control himself. Aside from all the financial obligations this situation has caused, the church has not even had the courtesy of acknowledging what my daughter has said or experienced. It's easy to just sit behind a desk with an attorney and pronounce that my daughter is lying and that we, also, are liars."

"Again, there is no evidence that Cleary Nolan had anything to do with this," the bishop retorted. "I don't know how you expect to prove it. Sadly, the headlines and gossip will hurt your daughter much more than it will hurt the person who is ultimately found responsible for this situation. I caution you to consider the harm to your daughter and to you financially if you undertake a campaign to spread false accusations against this priest and our diocese."

Gerrit and Ida stared hard at the bishop.

The attorney continued evenly, "May I remind you that bringing untrue and scurrilous charges will lead to more problems than you bargained for. It may well be that a young student caused this situation and those are not deep pockets you can dip into. The bishop and I will consider your complaint, and we'll prepare a report to advise you of our legal conclusions." That said, the attorney started moving around the desk toward the doorway.

This time the bishop did not extend his hand for a farewell handshake, but neither Gerrit nor Ida were interested in any such civility. Now they stood and stepped away from the desk.

"We will expect your report in the next couple of weeks," Gerrit said. "This is not going to be slipped under the table. There is a baby about to be born, and that baby deserves to know who its father is. And its mother is suffering, has suffered, and will continue to unjustly suffer, should you avoid doing what's right."

"Someone did this," Ida said, bending down to pick up her purse from the floor next to her chair. "And we know who. We won't forget."

Gerrit had the manners to thank the bishop and attorney for making time to meet with them. When they walked through the outer office, there were no other appointments waiting. The office secretary, who had been standing next to her desk in anticipation of their leaving, didn't say anything or even acknowledge them when they passed her desk.

"The temperature really got chilly in there when I mentioned my meeting with our district attorney," Gerrit said as they headed toward the car. "It would be nice for them if an accusation like this was just a figment of a young girl's imagination. But Anna is no liar. I only hope they don't think we're going to get discouraged and walk away from this. Let's go to your house, gather up our things, and head back. I'd like to call the hospital before we go to find out how things are going with my girls."

Emily had moved the car from the now-sunny spot to one with a good shelter of trees in a far corner of the lot. As they walked across the crunchy gravel toward the car, Gerrit and Ida tried to put on happy faces, but they didn't fool Emily.

"That good?" she asked sarcastically, when they got close enough to avoid being overheard.

"Worse," Ida replied. She felt like curling up in the backseat and crying. They had carefully made their points of what had happened to Annalise, but she knew the bishop wasn't buying it. "He made no bones about it," she said softly. "He said, verbatim, that he didn't believe one iota of Anna's story. And, obviously, neither did the attorney." Ida wondered if they'd actually ever get a report from them. Their minds had been made up before anyone from Annalise's family had said one word.

Gerrit leaned against the side of the car before opening the door. "You know, this wasn't the first time that guy did this. Think of how perfectly everything was planned. It certainly wasn't a spur-of-the-moment temptation. He came prepared with the soup and liquor. Toddy, my eye!"

"I think he must've taken one of our spare housekeys from the rack on his way out in order to lock the door behind him. Disgusting," Ida said, rubbing her temples. "We'll check the key rack when we get to your house," Gerrit said as he opened the front door of the car and slid into the passenger seat. Ida spotted the attorney heading toward them. Obviously, the black Buick parked only a few spaces from where they were, was his. Ida hurriedly slipped into the back seat and closed the door. Emily, not realizing who the man was, nodded toward him as he pulled keys from his pocket. She'd said hello when he arrived shortly after her mom and uncle went in. He ignored her nod, opened his car door, tossed his briefcase onto the passenger seat, and got in. He quickly started the car and pulled away.

Just as well, Emily thought.

The drive home was quiet. Even though they knew Emily would have been happy to hear what had happened, she didn't ask. She knew the details of that night and didn't need to have her mom repeat it all again.

Ida could hardly wait to unlock the front door when they got to her house. She only used the front door to bring in the mail or sweep the steps after a snowfall. And, of course, to let Cleary Nolan in and out when he'd come over for sandwiches and tea on a Sunday night. But the key was there, hanging on a hook. She was unsure if it was on the same hook it had been in the months before.

She thought of how easy it must have been for him to scope out the keys there and pick out the one belonging to this house. She'd have to remember that if or when they ever had another meeting with the bishop.

Emily brought out chicken salad and a loaf of fresh-baked bread so they could have lunch when they got back from their meeting. The table was already set and all she had to do was slice the bread. The lettuce from her garden was already washed. She lit the burner under the kettle to heat water for tea.

The three didn't talk much as they ate. Instead, they replayed the forty-five minutes in the bishop's office over and over in their minds. Had they forgotten something important that should have been said?

Nolan's plan, Ida thought sadly, was probably carefully orchestrated down to copying and depositing a new key for locking the front door on his way out. The only thing he hadn't thought about was the incriminating evidence left behind—a pregnant teenage girl who could point the finger directly at him, with his jar of chicken noodle soup and alcohol.

Gerrit put in a call to the hospital. He identified himself and asked to speak to the nurse in charge of Kate and Annalise. While the nurse was not available just then, the receptionist said she could ring the room and Annalise undoubtedly would answer.

She did. She was excited to hear from her Poppa about what happened. But he did not want to recount all those details on the hospital phone. "We'll talk about it when we get you home. How are you, and how is your mom?"

She gave him a quick rundown of her mother's condition. He asked if she could put the phone up to Kate's ear so he could speak to her, but that wouldn't work unless someone came in to deliver the phone across the room.

"I will tell her you called and that you are on your way back." Annalise knew her Momma knew who was on the phone because she tried to smile, but this time, it was more like a smile than a grimace. Progress!

"Tell your mother we are having a sandwich at Aunt Ida's and will be on our way in about a half hour. We will stop at the hospital when we go through town." Gerrit heard the phone click and a nurse's voice came on the line.

Annalise did not listen in on her father's conversation with the nurse. She knew that Momma seemed a little better. It had been a busy couple of days being in the same room with her, but she thought Kate rested easier knowing her daughter was in the other bed.

Gerrit smiled into the phone as he chatted with the nurse about Kate's condition. He could tell Anna was feeling pretty good. He knew letting her stay in her mom's room was a good idea—for both mother and daughter. The nurse relayed that Dr. Wetzel was satisfied with Kate's improvement so far, but they had not pushed her into doing much. Kate was still very fragile, but the doctors were anxious to have her exercise her limbs. The exercise routine to try to re-stimulate the right side that was most affected by the stroke would maybe start tomorrow.

Anna said words to Kate and Kate tried to say them back. It was slow for Kate, whose mind was going faster than her mouth. But each day was better.

"That's very good news," he said, thanking the nurse and hanging up the phone.

Their overnight bags sat near the front door, waiting to be carried out. At the last minute, Emily ran upstairs for something she wanted her mother and uncle to take with them. It was the Christmas box that had been left on the closet shelf in Anna's room.

"Mom, I think these would be safer at the farm. As long as you're going to be up there with Aunt Kate and Anna, I think you should put them somewhere out of sight. No one's going to be in your house here for a while."

"Wonderful suggestion," Gerrit said. "Would you have a large paper bag we could slide this into? Also, maybe some tape to hold the box shut so it is not accidentally disturbed? We have shelves built into the space under the steps; we can hide this there. Maybe we should find a metal box with a lid so no creatures get into it."

He took the gift box from Emily and slid it into the grocery sack Ida had taken out of the broom closet. "Now we're ready," he announced.

After hugs and goodbyes, Gerrit carried out the overnight bags and Ida carried the gift box in the bag. While she had gone hunting for a large enough bag to carry it in, Emily found a big bow that she taped to the top of the box as a last-minute disguise.

The visitor parking lot at the hospital was almost empty by the time they got there. Gerrit spotted a familiar car parked at the outer row—Helen's. His immediate reaction was panic. If something unexpected had happened to either Kate or Anna, the hospital would have called her. Without realizing he was doing it, Gerrit started reciting the "Our Father" as he hurried inside.

When he got to the open doorway of his wife's room, he saw Anna looking at a magazine and Kate sound asleep. By the time Ida came hurrying along after him, Anna spotted them in the doorway and waved.

"Shh! Mom just fell asleep. She was awake most of the afternoon, waiting for you. I know she was anxious to hear about the meeting. You can tell me all about it when I get home. I don't want anyone else to know that story except us."

Aunt Ida gave Anna a big hug. "I missed you."

A nurse came in. Almost time for supper trays.

"Anything good on the menu?" Ida asked.

"I forgot what I ordered for myself, but Momma is having beef broth, a soft-boiled egg, pudding. Doesn't sound too interesting," Anna said, "but those are Momma's new favorite foods. She drinks soup out of a cup she holds in her left hand. She always gets gelatin. Sometimes her hand shook and it tipped out. But pudding is the best. She eats it with a spoon in her left hand. What I don't understand is why she always wants soft-boiled eggs." Anna punctuated that with a grimace.

The nurse disconnected the bag of fluid dripping into Kate's arm and hung another on the steel pole. With the new drip connected, she straightened the sheet and took Kate's pulse.

"The delivery cart is just down the hall," the nurse told Anna. "We have two new patients who came in early today, so they'll be served first. You won't be our star boarders tonight."

Suddenly the door opened. With the late afternoon sun illuminating the doorway, it was hard to make out who was coming in. Once he spoke, they didn't have to see Dr. Chandler's face. He motioned for Gerrit to follow him out to the hallway where they disappeared into one of the open rooms. By the time they returned, Kate was awake and had spotted Ida. She moved her lips to say something. She knew her sister was there.

When her tray arrived, Anna didn't waste time lifting the lid to see what she ordered. They had a main meal at noon, so supper was a sandwich and bowl of soup.

Ida wasn't sure if she should help Kate eat or if the nurse needed to be in the room. Would she choke trying to swallow? As if on cue, the nurse came back with a white paper cup that undoubtedly had at least one pill in it. She cranked the handle at the end of the bed to elevate Kate's head. Then she put one arm behind Kate's head, placed the pill on her tongue, and held the glass so she could suck water through a straw and swallow it. Every time Anna watched her do it, she worried that she might choke, but she didn't.

Anna told Ida, "You can help her eat. You probably would do a better job than Poppa," She laughed.

Sip by sip, bite by bite, Kate ate what had come on her tray—maybe not all of it, but enough that the nurse was satisfied. She didn't sputter. Kate settled back on her pillow, happy that she finished her meal.

When Dr. Chandler came back, he stood next to Anna's bed and told her he was thinking she could probably go home the next morning—Saturday. "If things still look good, your dad will drive in late in the morning. Your mom needs to stay. She's doing well. I was watching her eat. That's a huge milestone for some stroke patients. So, get a good night's sleep."

Gerrit came hurrying into the room to kiss his wife and daughter goodnight. "I'd like to stay awhile and talk, but the doctor thinks Mom and you need to rest. So, little girl, I'll be back in the morning."

Ida and Gerrit walked toward the front reception area when they spotted Helen. She must have been at the chapel or having a sandwich in the lunchroom. She waved when she saw them, hurrying along the quiet hallway, anxious to find out how the trip had gone.

"You made good time. I hope you didn't hear sirens chasing after you," Helen said, then added, "that's what Harald always said when I was late for something. I never did come home with a ticket."

"Were you in the chapel?" Gerrit asked.

"Yes," Helen said. "It's such a peaceful place, even in a hospital. There are so many reasons to set aside time to talk to God. Also, I miss Harald, and it's easier to talk with him when I'm in there."

"I thought maybe we should get something to eat before we head out to the farm. We're bushed from the stress of our unsuccessful appointment. Want to join us? If we go now, we'll be ahead of the Friday night supper crowd. How about some fish at Wally's?" Gerrit asked.

It didn't take much convincing, so they headed out. Ida slept in the bed Annalise had been using for the past several months. She muttered her nighttime litany of prayers for Kate and Anna. She was barely awake when Fletcher got home.

Gerrit slept in Anna's old bedroom upstairs.

The phone hanging on the wall over Gerrit's desk woke Ida in the middle of a dream that she didn't recall but left her shaken. She hurried to answer it, not stopping to even put on her robe. She peered at the clock on the wall. Three-thirty AM!

"Hello?"

"Mom, it's Emily. Something terrible just happened," her voice whispered hurriedly over the line. "I'm sleeping at your house, and I heard someone trying to open the front door downstairs. Someone was jiggling the doorknob. I had my car in your garage, so they must have thought no one was in the house, because they certainly weren't quiet. At first I thought about turning on a light to scare them off. But then I decided to call the police and have them drive by to see who was out there. I could hear their cars coming slowly down the street. They didn't use a siren or lights or anything. But whoever was trying to get in must have seen them, and by the time the squads got to the front of the house, they disappeared."

Emily exhaled and continued before Ida could respond. "The police looked all around the yard, behind the bushes, in the garage, but didn't find anyone. He must have been on foot because they didn't hear a car start up or see any vehicles parked nearby. They asked if this had happened before, you've never said anything about someone trying to break in."

Emily paused to catch her breath. "Still, I was scared. So, I turned on a few inside lights, left the front porch light on, and had a cup of tea to settle my nerves. Then I remembered you mentioning Father Nolan maybe having a key. But I couldn't tell the police about that."

Ida plopped down in Gerrit's desk chair. Her hands were shaking so badly she had trouble holding the receiver up to her ear. Suddenly, she saw someone coming across the room toward her. Gerrit, followed by Fletcher.

"I have a sick feeling that word spread about the gift box on the shelf... and someone came to get it," Ida said. "There are a couple possible suspects. Maybe Father Nolan was warned about the evidence in the closet, or perhaps the attorney sent someone to collect it for them. But if the priest does have a key...he'd be more likely to attempt getting in."

Gerrit lamented, "The evidence is beginning to add up, but I think it will all be dismissed just as everything else has been—as lies. We can't say anything to the police about who might have been trying to break in and why, because that would just start an investigation that we'd have no way of controlling."

"Thank goodness it's Saturday," Fletcher said as he turned to go back up to bed. "See you in the morning."

Gerrit put the kettle on the little electric stove that stood in the corner next to the cookstove. "This is definitely all connected. Ida, do you really think the bishop or the attorney would have sent someone to break in and get that box? They probably called the priest himself and told him to get over to your house when no one was home and retrieve the evidence he stupidly left behind."

"No way," Ida said. "How could a bishop lower himself to that level? But what worries me is that this guy will try again, and I don't want Emily, or anyone else there when he does."

"It will be bad enough if he eventually does get into your house and finds out the evidence isn't there. Then he'll come up here to the farm to look for it. He's been up here before." Gerrit stopped talking long enough to pour their tea.

"This is terrifying. I fear this is only the beginning," Ida said.

"Even if we don't pursue it," Gerrit said, "we'll always have to be looking over our shoulders. Honestly, who else could have done this?"

"It's not a fancy neighborhood," Ida said. "It's an ordinary little house with ordinary things, not expensive stuff that someone could steal and sell. A random robbery is highly unlikely." She tried to settle her nerves. "A phone call in the middle of the night is always scary, and when it's your daughter, sleeping in your bed, hearing someone trying to break into your house, well, it's terrible."

They sat at the dining room table. The darkness outside was intimidating. There was no way to see if anyone was lurking around. Ida tried not to look toward the window, frightened of what she might see. Or think she was seeing. "Gerrit?" she asked, her voice still a little wobbly. "We have to find a very secure place to put those pajamas, and this house isn't it. I assume the Treasurer's office has a safe where things are locked up overnight. Would it be possible to get permission to put the box in that safe?"

Gerrit didn't answer for a while. He finally said, "I could call the sheriff in the morning and ask him what he'd recommend. I know we haven't seen the last of this. If he tried it once, he'll be back. I also worry he might think the box was moved to Emily's, which would put her in harm's way. I'm sure the police will be canvassing that area all night, so he won't try tonight. Or maybe not even for a week or so until things seem back to normal."

They sat in silence before Gerrit spoke up: "Thank God Emily thought to send the box up here. It's the weekend, so he could try and come back up here if he thinks we have it. Yes, I'll put the box in my office safe through this weekend, then decide on a more permanent arrangement. We know how desperate he is."

After they finished their tea, Gerrit went into the storage closet under the stairs, dug out the box from the back corner, and carried it upstairs. There was a tiny crawlspace under the eave in the hallway. With boxes and blankets stacked in front of the opening, no one would ever find it, at least for the rest of that night. Tomorrow he'd take it to his office. A few minutes later, Gerrit was back upstairs in bed.

Ida prayed silently that nothing would happen to Emily while she was alone. She prayed that Anna and Kate would stay safe and that she'd find the courage to not show her fear. Out here, miles from town and with only one neighbor close by, another widow like herself, she felt very vulnerable. When they lived on their farm, they always had a shotgun leaning against the hutch in the kitchen. All those years, they never had to use it. Maybe it was time she learned to shoot. But what if whoever was prowling around her house and scaring Emily was also carrying a gun? And knew how to use it?

Finally, she fell asleep, but when she woke up a few hours later, she didn't feel rested. Gerrit and Fletcher were both up. Gerrit, she knew, was getting ready to go into town to bring Annalise home. She wondered if she should go with him. She certainly didn't want to stay at the farm alone. Then she remembered that on Monday morning, Gerrit would drive into town with Fletcher. Ida would be left home to watch Anna. And Helen, down the road, had no notion of what had happened at Ida's house.

Gerrit stuck his head in the doorway to check if Ida had opened her eyes.

"I'm awake," she said. "Do you want me to go along to help with Annalise?"

"You don't have to," he said. "Unless you'd like to."

"I think I would. Give me a few minutes to splash some water on my face and get dressed."

When she went out to Gerrit's car, she carried the white box with the big red bow on top. She slid it next to Gerrit on the front seat.

Ψ

With Annalise safely back in her temporary bedroom downstairs, the house seemed almost back to normal. Meals were prepared in the kitchen and the menfolk went off to work in the morning, coming back in time for supper at five-thirty. Ida was nothing except organized. She always knew early in the morning what she'd be serving at each of the day's three meals, and she was unconventional enough to not write out a weekly meal schedule a week in advance. She always had time to make sure she had the right ingredients for whatever she was going to make and what time the evening meal needed to be started.

Aunt Ida always saved a good chunk of time to spend with her niece. They played Monopoly and Checkers. Ida thought she'd have enjoyed a houseful of daughters, but Emily was her only one.

Emily and Tom met in college. After graduation and getting married, they both got jobs at the same high school in a small town on the outskirts of Milwaukee. Life was good. Being an only child on a farm miles from her friends in town, Emily was anxious to have children. When she finally became pregnant, she and Tom decided she'd take a leave of absence from teaching until after the baby was born.

Tom played basketball when he was in high school. It was still his favorite thing to do on a Friday night in winter. Usually Emily went with him when he followed the school's basketball team to out-of-town games, but this Friday night she decided she'd rather address their Christmas cards. When the phone rang, she was getting ready for bed. Halfway through the call, she collapsed on the bed, unable to comprehend what she was hearing.

She couldn't even understand who called her. Then she heard someone at the front door. She stumbled across the bedroom and tried to find her bathrobe. The pounding continued until she got down the steps and turned on the porch light. There was a police car in the driveway and other cars in front of the house. She managed to get the door open, then reached for the door jamb to keep her knees from buckling.

She recognized the two officers.

"Is there a family member we can call for you?" one asked. "Maybe a neighbor?" She shook her head.

The people parked on the street in front of her house got out of their cars and hurried across the yard. Teachers from school. Their faces were stricken.

Emily kept asking: "Where's Tom?"

Her friends helped her inside and got her to sit down. The two cops delivered their awful message. He'd hit a stretch of black ice south of town and slid into a gasoline delivery truck. The truck exploded in flames from the impact, and the fire department had a hard time extinguishing the blaze. Tom died instantly, the medical doctor at the scene concluded. Miraculously, the truck driver survived.

There was no way she could absorb that kind of horrific news. It would be days before she could make any sense of any of it. By then, funeral arrangements were made and services held. Ida and Jake stayed with their daughter while relatives in Iowa took care of their farm chores for several days. Emily hadn't told her mom the news about the baby until she miscarried the night of the funeral.

Months afterward, raw memories of those days haunted her. It seemed she'd never stitch her life together again. Then, when her father started exhibiting signs of dementia and her mom had to take over running the farm and caring for him, Emily closed up her little house in Wisconsin and went to Iowa to help her mom. Mostly she sat with her dad, day after day, talking to him, showing him pictures from scrapbooks, singing happy songs, and trying to encourage him to sing along. She even went up to the attic to look for his old banjo. She remembered how she always wanted to learn to play it, but that never happened. Now it needed new strings and he was no longer able to play. He'd pick up the banjo and look at it sometimes; then put it back on the table and walk away, looking sad. Perplexed.

The nightmare never seemed to end. Emily and her father had spent many Sunday afternoons playing chess—Emily learning the rules and Poppa teaching her the finer points. Now, when she set up the chessboard, he'd simply sit and stare at the figures standing in squares on the board.

She remembered a piece of poem she'd written a long time ago about an elderly relative who had lost most of his sight and much of his grasp on reality:

"Alone he sits in dreamtime's flick'ring light

And stares with sightless eyes at men of old."

Eventually, Poppa died, and Momma sold the farm to a neighbor just down the road. Ida and Emily cleared out their family's longtime home and found a house for sale not far from Emily's. They moved Ida and the few pieces of furniture she decided to keep. Locking the door for the final time and driving away behind a moving van with Ida's things was the worst part of all. Everything that had been part of their happy lives together on the farm was gone, memories laid to rest in the cemetery. Farm equipment, tools, buildings now belonged to someone else. Emily knew they were good people and would take care of Jake's farmyard treasures, but their family would have no more stories about cutting hay or shocking bales of oats in the warm summer fields. The cows would still find their way to their own stanchions, but the person stripping the last drops of milk from the cow would not be Emily.

Wallowing in self-pity would make their future a grim place, indeed. Both women decided they'd tuck their favorite memories away and put one foot in front of the other in order to have any chance of moving forward. Surviving.

And so, the two women found comfort in their silent grief as they followed the moving van toward Wisconsin.

CHAPTER FOURTEEN

While Anna had been home from the hospital for a couple of weeks, Kate was still there, undergoing the rigors of therapy, trying to undo the debilitating effects of her stroke. Ida called Kate every morning to give her an update on things at home. Sometimes, when Poppa or Fletcher were around to help her to the phone, Anna also talked to Momma. Kate was slowly relearning to talk, so she mostly listened to Anna's chatter and sometimes tried to laugh. As hard as she tried, Kate still couldn't seem to remember how to pronounce words. Yet. But the doctors were optimistic that she'd not only learn to talk again, but also read and do all the things that were important to her life on the farm.

Ida only rarely was able to drive into town to visit her sister. Anna could not be left alone. Gerrit had missed so many hours of work that he tried to make up for the lost time by spending part of his weekends at the courthouse. Always constant with Kate was Helen, who made daily trips into town to sit with her and help with her therapy routines.

Gerrit and Fletcher were usually early-morning visitors at the hospital on their way to work. Fletcher often walked to the hospital to help his mom eat lunch. Her food was a little more robust these days. She could chew just about any food, and swallowing was no longer a scary exercise. The daily improvements were easy to recognize. Friends from the church Ladies' Guild came to visit, usually in pairs. They'd keep her posted on events at church and deliver messages from friends who weren't able to travel. The Guild took up a collection and bought her a bed jacket to wear like a sweater for when visitors were there. When that happened, Helen reported to Ida, Kate smiled.

She was still trying to read words from some of the children's books in the waiting room. For someone who read books all her life, sitting in bed looking at letters that didn't make any sense was frustrating. Thankfully, her nurse helping with her therapy was extremely patient. She assured Kate that she would read again. And talk, just like she had before.

And little by little she did. The first words she read from a child's book embarrassed her. But it was a milestone they all cheered. The next time she had a book in her hand, she sounded out even more words, and, in fact, learned to pronounce the letters correctly. The more success she had, the more she accomplished.

When Gerrit came by, he always urged her to read for him. More words were being strung together into sentences, even though she still struggled with some pronunciations. Dr. Wetzel promised that she could go home the following Saturday. In the coming days, she not only read more words from a book, but even from the newspaper when it was delivered to her room on Wednesday afternoon. Fletcher began stopping at the newspaper office to pick up one of the first of the day's printings. He'd enter his mom's room waving the paper and say, "Read all about it. Hot off the press." In time, she was beginning to even laugh out loud.

But she longed to go home and couldn't wait until Saturday. Ida had driven into town with Gerrit to help get her home. Helen would stay with Anna. Fletcher cut a little bunch of roses from the bush covered top to bottom with deep red blooms. The smell was heavenly when the flowers were outside, but when he brought them in, the scent permeated every corner of the farmhouse main floor.

Gerrit helped Anna out to the daybed so she could watch for the car when it turned the corner by the mailbox. Helen brought a big kettle of homemade chicken noodle soup—Grammy Iversen's recipe.

Upstairs the bedrooms were rearranged. Gerrit and Fletcher would share the large room at the front of the house. Gerrit would sleep in Fletcher's bed, and Fletcher would sleep on the daybed from the front porch. Ida would have the small upstairs bedroom that had been Anna's. Both Kate and Anna had to bunk downstairs. With Fletcher's help, Helen brought Grammy's old bed over for Kate. The downstairs bedroom was never intended for a bedroom and was overly large. Even with a second double bed in it, there was still plenty of space.

The daybed couldn't be moved until Kate arrived home, so Anna lounged there, watching for the car. Anna was excited to see that Momma had learned to walk some, including the stairs up to the porch door. But it was a worry watching how slowly she moved. She was determined to do it on her own. And she did. When she spotted Anna on the daybed, she tried to hurry her steps to get to her. Gerrit, who was holding her arm, grabbed her just in time to stop her fall.

"Absolutely no running!" he scolded, then laughed.

After the chicken noodle soup, the two 'invalids' were hustled off to their separate beds. Kate recognized Grammy Iversen's feather bed and was grateful to sink into its warm embrace, even if it was a hot summer day. A sheet was adequate during the day, but a blanket at night was always welcome. The excitement of the trip home tired Kate, and the thrill of watching for her mom's return to the farm left Anna in need of a long nap.

Ida hurried to answer the phone before it woke Kate and Annalise.

"Hello," she said in a quiet voice.

"Mom?" was the frantic response on the other end. "Mom, I'm at your house and…" Emily started sobbing.

"Emily, what happened? What's the matter? Are you hurt?"

It took a few seconds for Emily to settle enough so she could tell her mother what had happened. "Mom, somebody broke into your house, and it's absolutely trashed! Stuff is jumbled all over, drawers pulled out. Closets ransacked, especially the one Annalise used. You had boxes and packages on the shelves in there and some clothes stored way back at the far end. All that was pulled out and dumped on the floor. It's terrible. I haven't called the police yet. I don't know when this happened, but someone got into the house without breaking in, because there are no broken or open windows. The house was locked like it always is." She paused to catch her breath.

"Emmy, you and I know who did that. Or, rather, we've got a pretty good idea," Ida said, trying to stay calm. "You must call the police and get a report filed so we can submit the damage estimate to the insurance company. That's the first thing, but under no circumstance can you tell the police who you think did this. Besides, they'll do their own investigation."

"I wish you were here to help," Emily said. "I've never had to do anything like this before. To call the police and know that someone was in this house, tearing it apart. I forgot to check, but I'll bet they were even in the attic. Probably the basement, too…."

"I can't leave here right now. We just got Aunt Kate home from the hospital. She's sleeping. The trip home was very tiring for her. And Anna also is napping. Uncle Gerrit went to work this morning and won't be back until five or so. Fletcher's at work. What made you decide to go to my house?"

"I just thought with everything that's going on, perhaps it would be a good idea to check it occasionally. I never expected to find it totally ripped apart."

"Don't touch anything. Don't pick up or move anything. Just call the police and they'll come to check it out. If they need to verify that you have the right to be there, have them call me. Even though I can't leave here now and come home, I'll make arrangements to get there tomorrow or the next day. This couldn't have happened at a more inconvenient time."

"Mom, I'm so happy you…"

"We'll deal with all that when I get there. In the meantime, don't fret. It's scary, I know. But we expected that whoever tried to break in the other week would probably try again. Why don't you call the police right now, and after they have been there, call me back."

The two women breathed into the phone, collecting their thoughts.

"I almost forgot to ask," Ida said. "Does it look like they took anything valuable? Look around. See if anything appears missing. I wouldn't think there was anything in that house worth breaking in for. Our things are a treasure to us, but they aren't of any real value. Be sure to tell the police that."

"Oh, Mom. I'm so scared to even be in this house right now. When you are here again, I think we should talk about sharing a house rather than each of us living on our own. I was never afraid before, even after Tom died and I was all alone. When you sold the farm and moved here, it was always comforting to know you were close by. I guess that doesn't sound too grown up, does it?"

"Hang up now and make that call. I'll call Gerrit and tell him what's happened. We'll talk later."

Ida sat in the chair Gerrit used when he worked at his rolltop desk. It was on wheels, but the seat could rock back and forth. She didn't know how long she sat there, staring out the window at the clouds gathering up in the west. Then lightning lit up the sky and thunder grumbled.

How could this happen? First someone tried to break in while Emmy was sleeping there overnight. Fortunately, the key they were trying to use to open the front door didn't work because the dead bolt lock needed a different key to open. After the terror of that night, to have this happen, it's no wonder Emmy was scared.

The sky turned so dark that Ida flipped on the overhead light in the front room. She sat down again at the desk and tried to quell the fear that was consuming her. This person, whoever they were, knew exactly what they wanted in that house and exactly where to find it in Anna's old room. Now they knew it was no longer there. She prayed for the importance of Emily not telling the police who or why someone had come again to try to get in.

Then it dawned on Ida—Emmy must have forgotten to set the deadbolt lock when she left the last time. She would have gone out the back door to get her car out of the garage when she went home the morning after that first attempted break-in. She must not have given any thought to setting that extra lock on the front door.

Now what? Would he try breaking into Emmy's house, thinking he'd find what he was after over there? Or drive up to the farmhouse? But how could he hope to get into the farmhouse undetected? Knowing that his semen was on those pajama bottoms made it a serious liability for him. Who told him about the gift box on the shelf in Anna's old bedroom? The bishop?

Probably not. The attorney? Most likely. And he also knew from that last meeting with the bishop that the person responsible for the rape didn't have to break into Ida's house. He already had his own key.

Ida couldn't resist a little smirk. She deliberately dropped the hint about the pajama evidence when she and Gerrit were at the diocese a few weeks earlier, testing to see if the information would be passed along to the priest. Obviously, it was, since he never made any effort to look for the pajama bottom until now.

The way he savaged Ida's house would be nothing compared to what he'd want to do at the farm. But with two people confined to bed, the house was never empty. *Obviously he's getting desperate, she said to herself.*

Ida closed the window over the sink. The downpour was pelting the house, making a terrible racket on the porch roof. When she walked out there, she was surprised to see how much rain had already fallen.

After closing the front door and checking that all the other windows were closed, she picked up the phone and started to dial Gerrit's number at the courthouse. A loud crack of thunder made her hang up. So instead, she paced. Storms always frightened her. She pulled the heavy green shade in the bay window over Gerrit's desk. The shades were already pulled in the bedroom where Kate and Anna were sleeping.

She went back to the porch and found the door key in the flour sifter in Kate's Hoosier cupboard. Kate figured no one would ever think to look for a house key in a flour canister. Ida wanted to make sure she knew where it was.

Looking down the road, she could see lights from the Iversen's back porch windows. Usually they weren't visible, but with the darkened sky, the kitchen lights were a beacon. Maybe she'd call Helen to see if she would drive over after the storm. Having a friend to talk to about current events would help.

Finally, the storm moved east, and the darkened sky showed patches of blue. A rainbow? A good omen?

She had a car in the garage, but there was no way she could get her sister and niece out of the house by herself. And where could she go besides the Iversen farm?

I'm not making any sense even to myself.

When the sun started peeking through the clouds, she called Gerrit. The secretary who answered had a pleasant, calming voice. She said Gerrit was meeting with the County Clerk but expected to be back in his office by four. That's when those who worked there folded up their papers, locked their desks, and headed home. Regardless, Gerrit was always the last one out. His secretary, Rosemarie, promised that if she was gone before he got back, he'd see the big sign she'd leave propped on his desk. "If it's an emergency, I can go in and get him right away," she said.

"It's important but not an emergency. I just need to talk with him before he heads home." Ida wondered if her voice sounded calm. She didn't feel calm.

She started putting supper together when the phone rang again.

"Gerrit?" she answered.

"What's up?" he said. "Everything okay?"

"Not exactly," she said. "Emmy called earlier. She'd gone over to check on my house, and when she walked in the back door, she found the entire place trashed. Stuff pulled out of closets and dumped all over. Beds were disheveled and dresser drawers ransacked."

"Oh, dear God," he breathed. "I hope you told her not to tell the police who might be responsible."

"Obviously, he didn't find what he was after. He just left the mess and went out, locking the door with his key. Now I'm worried that he will assume we have what he wants here at the farm. I've locked the front door and closed and locked all the windows on the main floor. There's no way of knowing when he broke into my house and when he would be likely to break in here." Ida paused, then sighed heavily. "I'm afraid I'll have to go down there and get this straightened out. How can we handle that? I'm sure Helen would help, but that's a lot to expect from someone who is about to move, now that she's found a new home near her church."

"I have to swing by and pick up Fletcher, then we'll be on our way as fast as we can. Do you need anything for supper? I could stop."

"We're not having anything fancy, but it's already started. I'll see you soon."

After she hung up, she looked in the drawer for the book of phone numbers, then thought better of calling Helen. It was better for Gerrit to call.

Ida left for home the following morning. Rebekkah, an Amish neighbor whose children were all grown, had agreed to help Helen with Kate and Anna. Kate was getting better at being up and about. Gerrit had asked Aaron Mellen if he could make a rolling cart that Kate could walk behind so she wouldn't fall. Aaron knew exactly how to make it. He measured Kate so the walker was the right height. Being able to walk to the bathroom and the table for meals was helping Kate get her strength back.

Anna still couldn't use a walker. Dr. Chandler was adamant: she could only walk with supervision. Even though her wings were clipped, Anna was excited to see her mother moving on her own, even with some help.

Helen teased Anna that while she couldn't wait to be up and about on her own, in a few weeks she'd be wishing for a nap after the baby arrived.

Anna assumed a big role in her mom's therapy, working on reading, speaking, and writing every morning and afternoon. Helen had brought schoolbooks for the lessons. She'd been regressed to the beginning, but now it reminded Kate of being in first grade. But words got easier and easier the more she studied them. In time, she'd be back reading adult books from her father's library.

After Kate had fallen asleep that night, Gerrit and Ida sat with Helen on the front porch so Kate would not overhear their worried conversation. Helen needed to know that there was a possibility someone might drive up and ransack the farmhouse.

Ida didn't ask nor did Gerrit divulge what he'd done with the box. She knew he planned to put it in the county safe until he could find a more permanent place. She didn't want to know where it was. Now, Helen wasn't going to know either. The secret was best kept quiet.

Ψ

The mess in her house was enough to start Ida crying. She and Emily sat at the kitchen table, wondering where to start.

The police said they should hire someone to clean up the mess, but how would a stranger even know where to put things? So, they rolled up their sleeves, and, except for tea and a quick apple-butter sandwich now and then, they didn't stop working all day. At day's end, they barely finished the downstairs. The next day, they'd work upstairs, which was far worse.

Facing a problem of another kind, Gerrit was in over his head with caring for his wife and daughter. Helen had made a hot dish casserole and put it in the ice box. She said she'd try to come by in the late afternoon to help him get supper together. Although Helen was anxious to move out and leave her son and his family to settle in and start enjoying their new home, neighbors like Gerrit and Kate, who had been so helpful when Harald died, deserved at least a return favor.

After lunch, Gerrit encouraged his girls to take naps. He also needed a nap. When he was sure Kate and Anna had fallen asleep, he pulled the green shade over the living room window so the room was dark and quiet. There were no shades on the narrow windows that framed the large bay, so he could keep an eye on what was happening outside.

He dozed briefly but woke with a start when he thought he heard a car slowing down as it passed the front yard. He had reclined the Morris chair back to the rest position. He could see outside, but no one, unless they were right outside the window, could see in. The car noise drifted off into the distance, but suddenly, he heard it again, this time heading from west to east. The vehicle had gone down to the mailbox corner then turned around and come back, slowing down again as he drove past the house. He continued up the hill to where the little schoolhouse stood. The driver repeated that routine several more times. Gerrit slid out of his chair when the car was well past the front of the house and quickly headed toward the porch door.

He had a plan. He hurried out toward the grove of apple trees and followed the line out toward the ditch. That would give him a better, undetected vantage point for copying the license plate number on the piece of paper he had in his pocket. He watched the car travel down to the mailbox corner, turn around, and head back up the hill. When he heard the car head east again, he sauntered out into the yard, carrying a hoe. When the car reached his property, he stepped out closer to the road. The man driving the car looked a little startled, believing that no one had noticed his scouting journey. He slowed when he saw Gerrit. Neither man had ever seen the other. At least Gerrit hoped that was the case. The driver rolled his window halfway down. He didn't turn off the engine but waited to hear what the man on the lawn wanted.

Gerrit feigned manners. "I saw you heading back and forth up this road, and I thought you might be looking for something or someone. I was wondering if I could help you find it."

The man was momentarily flustered. "Someone told me there was some property for sale along here, but I've looked and haven't spotted any signs. Do you know, is there any property for sale nearby, or am I lost?"

"Haven't heard of any coming up for sale," Gerrit said. "Was something advertised in a paper, or was this just someone passing information along?"

"Don't rightly know where this man got word of it, but I tried to remember the directions he gave me so I could look things over on my own without some real-estate person. I'm not sure if this is where I want to settle. Sorry if I troubled you. I think I'd better ask my acquaintance for better directions." The man nodded to Gerrit, rolled up his window, eased off the brake, and headed east toward the mailbox corner, only this time, he turned right.

Well, Gerrit thought, *I handled that pretty well…if that was who I think it might've been.* Gerrit leaned on the hoe handle and watched the car's trail of dust. He didn't rush as he made his way back toward the highway.

Gerrit headed back toward the house and leaned the hoe up against the porch wall alongside the handrail. He didn't feel like walking those few steps farther to put it back in the woodshed.

Gerrit eased the door shut so he wouldn't disturb his sleeping ladies. When he'd seen the car and had a hunch about its driver's identity, his immediate thought had been to call the sheriff—not to pull him over, but just to patrol by and give the guy a good looking-over. Gerrit's impromptu act looked perfectly natural for a guy out hoeing his wife's vegetable garden, anxious to help a passerby find what he was looking for. That was a better idea than bringing the sheriff into a situation that would lead to a lot of questions and some answers they weren't prepared to give.

The temptation to take a nap passed. Gerrit was too charged up to even put his feet on the footstool. The audacity of that man, driving up there—to break into someone's house to cover his own tracks. Gerrit knew they'd have to keep that box hidden if they were ever going to have evidence of what had been done to their daughter. His thoughts drifted back over everything that happened and what was to come.

Kate and Gerrit talked often about how Anna could go to school and still have the primary responsibility for the baby. Gerrit worried about only one thing—what would happen when Annalise and the baby left the farm to go wherever Anna found a job after college? Somehow, neither of them ever saw Anna getting married. She just never seemed interested in boys and still didn't, even though recent events forced her to mature.

Gerrit was hopeful Kate would be well enough to be up and around when the baby came. They would have to hire someone to help Kate when Anna started school in fall. Before the stroke, that wasn't even a consideration. Now, they'd have to work their days around her therapy and needed rest. Who could ever have imagined how much their well-ordered lives would be turned upside down?

He tried not to hate this man who had done this. "People have feet of clay," Kate's father used to say when his parishioners did something ill-advised. "Even Our Lord had earthly feet made of clay. Jesus blew his stack at the money changers working in the holy temple. His response was righteous anger." That was a phrase Gerrit called on when he thought of the horrible things his young daughter endured. It was a tough concept. He preferred a little hate mixed in with that righteous anger.

Gerrit sat down and leaned back in his chair. It had been anything but a quiet Sunday afternoon. It was time for the Amish to head home for chores. Cows would need to be fed, milked, and put out to overnight pasture. Children needed to be fed and put to bed. But since it was still the Lord's day, they had to do as little work as possible for evening chores.

The phone rang. Gerrit jumped and reached across the desk to grab it from where it hung on the wall. It was Ida, wondering how her sister and Anna were. She said her plans were to drive up in the morning. She'd be there by noon. If Helen was coming to be with Kate and Anna, Ida could get a few last-minute things done there. Her house, she said, was such a disaster she wound up throwing a lot of things away.

"After your things have been rifled through by some disgusting criminal, they're not private anymore," she said. "And," she added, "Emily and I might be moving in together. After this episode, I don't think either of us has the courage to handle living alone. Is everything all right there?"

"Nothing major, just interesting. I'll tell you about it when you're here. I talked to Helen earlier. She's busy today with farm-selling stuff, but she'll be here in the morning before Fletch and I leave for work. I think she doesn't have anywhere to go tomorrow, so there will be someone with them all day. Aaron's wife Nellie and a granddaughter are also coming in the morning."

"Okay. Emily will finish with the clean-up duties, so I don't really need to be here. She knows what's important to keep and what we can do without when we share a house. I don't think I want to stay in this house. It's close to a lot of things, so I'm sure we can find a buyer and maybe we'll get something new, a little larger. Maybe a ranch so I wouldn't have to traipse up and down stairs. I'll tell you more tomorrow at supper. Tell my girls I'll be back."

They hung up. Gerrit felt he needed to take a deep breath. Ida was such a fast talker, yet he was the one who needed to inhale when she finished.

The next morning, Gerrit hurried back into the house to get the piece of paper he'd left tucked in his Sunday shirt pocket. He blew a kiss to his girls as he hurried back toward the door and off to work. Helen had come early and was already serving them breakfast.

As he and Fletcher drove toward town, he wondered how he'd ever repay everyone who'd helped them those last few months. The baby was due in a couple weeks, which would mean Anna could be up and around again. Kate was still a question mark. Her progress was slow. Words were coming a little easier and her pauses when reading grew shorter. Moving was easier, too, now that she had her wooden walker to stabilize her strolls around the house. But she still needed a steady hand when she had to let go of the walker in the bathroom or sitting down at the table for a meal. Her smile was back. That was the most important part of her recovery, her thankful husband felt. It meant Kate was really back from the shell that swallowed her when something went wrong inside her head.

Fletcher was antsy to talk with his father about something. Gerrit knew that fidgety business with his hands when he had something important to say.

"What's up, Fletch?"

"Well, it's almost time for me to leave for school, and I haven't gotten any of my stuff ready. I don't even know what I'm supposed to take. I can't find the letter from the school giving me my dorm room number and the name of the kid I'll room with. Have you seen it? I think Mom must have put it somewhere for safekeeping, but I don't know where to start looking. The letter included a list of things I should bring for my room and things that aren't allowed. Food is one of the things not allowed."

Gerrit chuckled to himself. "Fletch, we can't solve all of these issues when we're in the car driving to work. Let's work on that when we get home tonight. We should ask Mom first if she remembers where she might have put that letter. That would give her something to think about for a few minutes. After supper, we'll dig through cupboards and drawers. Do you remember the day you are supposed to report to school? With all the turmoil we've had these last few months, it's a wonder we remember our own names. If we can't find the paper, I suppose that means we won't have the phone number, either. Do you have any other papers from the school that might have that on it somewhere?" Gerrit glanced over at his anxious son. "Don't fret about it. We can call information and get the number for the admissions office."

Fletcher bit his lip as he retraced his memory. "I know I need bedding supplies and towels. A duffel bag or laundry case to keep my dirty clothes in until I can walk them to the laundry. Or send them home!" He stopped to laugh at his own joke. "I also need change and soap to run the laundry machines. Too bad Anna wasn't the oldest one. She'd be experienced and could teach me the ropes about living away from home. She really has had experience living away from home, even if it was just at Aunt Ida's."

Gerrit suggested Fletcher not schedule anything on Saturday unless he had to work. They'd have to go shopping. He'd need his own toiletry bag to carry his stuff back and forth from the shared bathroom. Did he need hangers? Where could they find a duffel bag? Gerrit remembered hauling his laundry to a laundromat down the street from the college in Chicago.

He dropped Fletcher off at his corner and drove on to the side of the building where the sheriff's office was. He parked the car nearby and hurried in. He was already behind schedule for getting up to his own office.

"Hey, Sheriff," Gerrit called as he walked in. He closed the door after he entered Sheriff Dudley's office. "I've got a favor to ask. If I have a license plate number, can you find out who the car belongs to?"

"Sure. We have a record of all motor vehicles operating in the state because they all must be licensed. Why do you ask?"

"I'm investigating an 'or-something' situation. But I need your word that this favor and the answer will be confidential."

Gerrit and Dudley had been friends since the first day he was sworn in as County Treasurer. At the time, Dudley was only a deputy. He lived not far from Gerrit's farm and they often took their fishing poles to Turtle Lake. They sometimes caught a fish or two, but it was more of an excuse to lean back against a tree trunk, relax, and hope the fish didn't notice your line in the water.

"Let's see it," Dudley said, his hand reaching for the scrap of paper Gerrit held.

Dudley dialed the state Department of Motor Vehicles and read off the numbers on the rumpled-up piece of envelope.

The voice on the other end suggested that it might take a few minutes. She promised to call back as soon as someone had a few minutes to check their records.

"Good enough," Dudley said and hung up. He assured Gerrit that he'd call him at his desk whenever he received the information. He could tell his friend was anxious.

"If they say I'm in a meeting, tell them I asked you to call me out of it."

"I sure hope you're not starting a detective business."

Gerrit was still chuckling when he got upstairs to his own office. His was not an office where the public was always stopping in. It could get lonely on the third floor, but he always had figures needing balancing, budgets requiring preparation, taxes to be recorded, or deposits to be made.

He had just turned the lights on when his phone rang.

"That certainly didn't take long," he told Dudley through the receiver.

He was thankful Dudley couldn't see his face when he heard the name of the license plate's owner.

"Number belongs to a clergyman," he said. "A Reverend Cleary Nolan. Car is registered in Davis County. My goodness, what did he do that you had to copy his plate number and have me check on it? Actually, I don't think I want to know the answer. At least not yet. I forgot to ask, how's Kate?"

Dudley sounded pleased to hear the extent of Kate's progress. "Molly and I send our love. You know, when she's feeling up to it, maybe we could all go fishing. Molly isn't much for the sport, but she and Kate could sit in the shade. When the weather gets a little cooler. I don't like this humidity." They finished their conversation and hung up.

Gerrit heaved a big sigh. "The Reverend Father, indeed," he muttered. *He wouldn't still be up here, pretending like he was on vacation or something, would he? Maybe I should call Helen and alert her to keep an eye out for a car driving back and forth in front of the house.* Then he remembered— Helen had met him last June.

Gerrit went into the room attached to his office where all the confidential records were kept under lock and key. He needed figures to start calculating next year's budget. But he kept seeing that man driving back and forth down his road, past his house, past his sleeping daughter.

Although hiding the box with Anna's pajamas in his county safe was supposed to be only a stop-gap solution, it was still there, behind the stack of old records. He grabbed the box and took it out of the bag to make sure it was the same as when he put it in there last winter. Only then could he settle down to work on the county's next budget.

Three hours later, it was almost lunchtime, so he called home to see if Helen noticed a black car driving by their house. But it was Ida who answered.

"Ida. It's Gerrit. Is Helen still there?"

"She left right after I got here. Said she had property figures they worked on yesterday and she was anxious to review them. She'll be back mid-afternoon."

"I'm just eating lunch, so I'll give her a call."

"I brought along the ingredients for supper, so you don't need to stop. See you later."

Helen answered Gerrit's call on the first ring. They chatted a minute before he asked if she saw a car going back and forth in front of their house that morning.

"Hadn't noticed anything," she said. "We were busy putting on clean linens. Ida helped with that when she got here. Was there something I need to worry about?"

"No, don't think so. It was just curious. I noticed a black car driving slowly past our house several times yesterday. I went out and asked if I could help him find whatever or whoever he was looking for. Said he'd been told there was property for sale along our road but didn't have an address. Then he drove off."

"Do you think someone told him about our property? Maybe a neighbor figured I might be selling land since Harald died. You know how stories lose something in the repeating."

"I thought about that, but I knew where your land was going, and I didn't want him to pester you. But if he shows up again, call me right away if he pulls into the driveway. We can't stop him from looking, but we can keep him off our property. Also, plan on eating supper with us tonight. You know Ida always cooks way too much food."

Gerrit looked forward to getting back home that evening, despite his worries about the black car and its driver. All of Kate's long naps and rest had given her face a new glow. She looked like she did when they were first married. He looked forward to seeing her smile.

Ψ

Fletcher was seriously considering not starting college in the fall so he could help with his mom, sister, and the baby. He knew he would lose the scholarship he'd received at graduation. He couldn't talk it over with his mom, and he didn't know how to broach the subject with Pops. Perhaps he could delay starting until second semester.

Annalise was sinking into depression from watching her mom struggle so hard to recover from her stroke. Anna would have to stay out of school until Momma was well enough to handle the baby—carry, change, and feed it during the day when Anna was at school. Leaving Kate alone with a baby for five days every week would be too exhausting for her and she might have another stroke. If that happened, no one would be there to help her or the infant.

Anna heard Aunt Ida on the phone near Poppa's desk. From the sound of Ida's voice, it was a happy conversation between mother and daughter.

Anna was happy to have a few minutes to herself. Kate was asleep, her breathing slow, steady. Sharing a room with her at the hospital started her thinking how she, with Aunt Ida's help, could get Momma to talk more, not just one-word answers. Annalise often wondered about her mom's early days on the farm before she was born. And what life was like in Iowa. What her grandparents were like.

Poppa never talked about his family. He just brushed questions aside, saying he didn't have a childhood worth talking about. Sometimes he'd tell stories about his days at the business college in Chicago. He also talked about his job at the Chicago bank after he and Kate were married. Maybe if she could get Momma to talk more about her family, she'd share stories about Poppa's.

Anna leaned back on her pillow. She wanted her child to know the Conner family history. When teachers wanted to know the nationality of each child in the school, Poppa told her to always say they were American. And they were, but she, like school records, wanted to know more about her ancestors. She knew Ida and Kate grew up as sisters and best friends. Ida married a farmer, and when he got sick and she had to run the farm by herself, she knew she had to sell the livestock and the farm. When Jake died, she sold the farm and moved to Wisconsin to be near Emily, whose husband had died years earlier in a bad car accident.

Anna paused. Her mom's breathing had become ragged, irregular. *Dear God, please take care of her. Don't let her have another stroke. Please, God.*

She lay very still, timing her mother's breathing. Maybe she couldn't help her learn to talk again. Or maybe she could. There was no harm trying.

She watched as Momma struggled to roll over on her side, but when she instead rolled on her back, her breathing eased into a steady pattern. The cadence lulled Kate back to sleep.

By the time Ida came to wake her, the afternoon sun had gone behind clouds. The muggy weather made it hard for Anna to breathe. Ida closed the bedroom windows. The sound of distant thunder grew more insistent and lightning flashed. Kate slept through it all. Ida pulled the shades before helping Anna get up.

Ida and Anna talked in whispers while they were in the bathroom. Anna told her about her plan to get Kate talking more. Those conversations would not only help Anna learn about her mom's childhood but also teach her about the years her mother lived on that farm alone, with only neighbors and little Fletcher for company.

Ida leaned against the doorframe, pondering Anna's idea. She also knew she'd better talk with Dr. Chandler. But that made it seem like an "assignment" she had to get done for school. If they could just sit around, casually asking questions and lightly conversing, it might work. Ida offered to help encourage her sister's conversation, too. The words had to be Kate's. If she hit a roadblock, Ida could help Kate find them.

The next morning, Dr. Chandler came to check on his two patients, and Anna broached the subject of pushing Kate to tell stories. At first, he just had a puzzled look on his face. Then he spoke.

"Well, kid," he said, "I think it wouldn't hurt to try. As long as you don't push her too hard. Take it slow. If she struggles with a word, help her out, and she could then go on a little more." The doctor leaned back, considering Anna. "You know," he continued, "I like that idea. Language skills won't come back unless she uses them regularly. Talking about her past would be a lot easier than trying to sound out words on a page. That'll also keep you busy until the baby comes."

Anna wanted to try it out that very day, since she only had another week or two before she had the baby.

The doctor wanted her to have the baby at the hospital, but that wasn't Anna's plan. If the baby was born at the hospital, the weekly news would find out and put it in the paper. That definitely wouldn't work.

Dr. Chandler agreed that delivering the baby at home would shield Anna from prying questions, but it was risky. He said he'd figure out another way. There were people trained in home deliveries, providing there were no unexpected emergencies. He said he'd talk to Gerrit about it.

Once Dr. Chandler had said his goodbyes, Ida went to the kitchen for a glass of iced tea. Kate and Anna both asked her to make some for them, too.

While Ida was gone, Anna tested the waters with her mother. "I want my baby to know where her family came from and who they were. I was thinking that during these last weeks of waiting, I could write down some of these things and keep them in a special notebook to give to the baby when it's older. I know about our family, but I don't know much about my grandparents. Would you help me?"

Kate didn't answer. Anna wasn't sure if she'd even heard her. Ida came around the corner, balancing a tray with three glasses and a pitcher. The tea looked so pretty with the orange and yellow stripes circling the tall glasses. Ida even found sprigs of mint from Kate's herb garden near the front door.

Still, Kate didn't answer, although she did look thoughtful as she sipped the tea from the frosty glass. Then, finally...

"That's a good idea," she said. "We could talk about it over tea, and Ida, you could help me get it all right."

Both Ida and Anna were pleased and excited to see the broad smile on Kate's face.

"Kate, I think this is a great idea. It will be fun for us to help her write stories about us growing up in the parsonage with Poppa and Momma."

"You might have to help me say words," Kate told Ida, smiling again.

They sipped their tea.

Suddenly, Kate started telling them about how she had listened outside the open window in her dad's study when Mr. James, one of the parish trustees, came to talk about the church council meeting the night before. She and Ida both laughed.

"I was there with you, remember?" Ida said. "And Poppa heard us giggling outside, and we got into trouble for eavesdropping."

Then Kate picked up the thread of the story and, word by word, pieced together the tale of how they had to apologize to the trustee. "We never did that again."

Anna started writing Kate's story in one of the notebooks left from last school year.

It was a good beginning. Struggling for her words was difficult and sometimes frustrating for Kate, but Anna and her aunt were patient, always helping find the right ones. If they waited too long to jump in, she'd shake her hands in frustration.

One afternoon, after they all thought the stories had run their course for the day, Kate remembered one she was specifically eager to tell. "Ida. Remember the principal at our school? He had a stroke and couldn't come back to school for a long time. Everyone liked Mr. Carlson. The teachers said we should pray that Mr. Carlson would get better. We all felt sad because they said he forgot how to read. He couldn't recognize letters, much less the words they spelled, just like I couldn't at first. But Mr. Carlson was determined to re-learn what he once knew. It took months, but he did it."

"How could I have forgotten that?" Ida asked. "They told us he couldn't even read at a first-grade level. It was the most awful thing we could imagine. Sometimes he'd come to school to visit and read to the kindergarten and first-grade classes from their little library books. The children didn't have any idea what an accomplishment that was."

When she was tired of thinking and talking, Kate lay back on her pillow to rest. But her mind hadn't stopped thinking about growing up with Ida in a church parsonage. There were so many stories. And Momma was re-learning how to say words and read, just like Mr. Carlson.

As the days of Anna's pregnancy inched toward her due date, Fletcher still worried about leaving for college. Anna couldn't possibly handle the new baby and Momma, and it certainly wasn't fair to expect Aunt Ida to continue living there, month after month, taking care of their family. But how could he be much help with a new baby when Anna went back to school? It was a workable plan when Momma was well, but she wasn't up to managing anything yet, not even herself. Postponing his plans to start college this fall was a logical conclusion.

Fletcher knew he had to talk to Pops about the coming reality of a new baby in the house. It was a conversation he didn't relish. But someone had to face it. A decision couldn't be pushed off much longer. If they wouldn't honor his scholarship for second semester, or even next year, then he'd have to find another way to finance school.

Now that he'd made up his mind, how was he going to broach the subject with Pops? With the family? The best time would be on the drive home from work, but Pops wasn't always much for talking at the end of the day. Still…

They'd already turned off the highway and onto the country road heading toward the farm before Fletcher had the courage to start.

"I've got something I'd like to talk over with you," he started. "It's about college this fall. I don't think I can go. I think I need to delay starting, at least until the winter term. That would allow Anna to start back to school. I don't think Aunt Ida should have to take care of both a newborn and Mom. Besides, she's older than Mom, and that's not fair to her. She had to run their farm by herself after Uncle Jake got sick. She's earned the right to take it easy. So, if I don't start school in September, I could help with Mom, and Aunt Ida could take care of the baby. But about the baby—why is Annalise so determined to keep it? Especially now that Mom is unwell?"

Silence filled the car. Fletcher turned to look at his dad but couldn't tell if he'd even been paying attention. "Pops?"

"I'm listening, but I don't know what the answer is. We can't force Anna to give that baby up for adoption. Besides, your mother was so looking forward to having a little one around. We haven't been able to talk about any of this since her time in the hospital. You're right. We do need to reevaluate and make some decisions. I agree, taking on all that responsibility is not fair to Ida. And Anna is not going to be much help when school starts. She can't possibly be up with a baby during the night. She has to go to school. I've thought about hiring a nanny to come in, at least during the day, to tend to the baby. I don't know if we can afford that."

They then drove in silence until they made the turn at the mailbox. "We'll continue our talk on the way to work tomorrow," Gerrit told his son. "I don't want to talk about this where your mom and Anna can overhear. We need to figure things out before we talk to them about how we can manage everything. Your mom won't be happy if you don't start school this fall, but I'm sure the school would understand if you delayed your start by a couple of months. You can't give up going, but it might be necessary to have you around until the baby is a little older and your mother is a little stronger. We came pretty close to losing her this summer. We can't risk that again."

Fletcher jumped out to open the garage doors. Gerrit pulled into the garage and seemed distracted as he headed toward the house. Still, the conversation had been a good start, but Fletcher knew time was running out. Everything seemed possible in the beginning, but Mom's stroke changed all that.

Suddenly, Fletcher heard a car racing up the road toward their place. As the car got closer to their driveway, he could see the driver waving at him, then heard her honking as she went flying by.

Gerrit hesitated on the top step and turned to look, surprised at seeing Helen waving as she passed their driveway. "What in the world?" he muttered. The racket of her speeding by faded away, replaced by some obvious trouble inside the house. He hurried in as Ida rushed through the kitchen toward him.

"It's Anna," she said. "She's starting to have the baby. Helen went off to get Nellie—she's the closest midwife in the Amish community. I called Dr. Chandler. He's on his way. I can handle Anna until one or the other of them gets here, but I'm worried about Kate."

Gerrit pushed past Ida and hurried through the kitchen to the living room where he found Kate rocking in the kitchen rocker. She was crying. When she saw him coming toward her, she held out her hands to him.

"My goodness," he said. "Fletcher and I come home from a hard day at work, and big things are happening here. It looks like we are going to be grandparents. Soon!" He tried to laugh but instead he put his arms around Kate and patted her shoulder. "It's no time to cry. This should be a happy day." He helped Kate to her feet and held her close.

He approached the bed where Anna looked in great distress. "Hey, little girl," he said, "you're about to be a mommy. Aunt Ida said Mrs. Iversen is on her way to pick up Nellie, who will help you through this. And Dr. Chandler is also on his way. I'm certainly not going to be any help in here, and neither will your mom. We'll come back when baby arrives."

Gerrit kissed his fingers and touched them to his daughter's cheek. Kate was not happy at being hurried out of the bedroom.

Gerrit eased Kate down into the rocker that stood at the far end of the porch in front of the windows overlooking the front lawn. He sat on the daybed facing her, holding both her hands in his. "I know you'd rather be in there with our little girl, but you don't need to be in the middle of all that excitement."

Then he saw Fletcher, pacing back and forth beneath the windows, obviously watching for Helen to come back. Before she got there, Chandler's Buick pulled into the driveway, circling the rosebush garden and parking right in front of the steps. He nodded at them as he hurried through the porch and on into the bedroom. Then, parking right behind him was Helen. Nellie didn't wait until the car stopped before she opened the door and jumped out, rushing into the house after Dr. Chandler.

Gerrit thought about taking Kate for a drive, but he figured that would only increase her anxiety. Ida came out to the porch, closing the kitchen door firmly behind her. Gerrit still held Kate's trembling hands. Ida pulled the bench out from behind the big table so she could sit close to her sister. She eased the rocker slightly, hoping the gentle swaying would help keep Kate calm. Gerrit nodded to Fletcher. He knew Fletcher didn't want to be in the middle of the huddle on the porch. Instead, he waved as he headed toward the barn where the milking would already be underway. That was a much better place for him for the next couple of hours.

The bedroom was far enough away that only an occasional sound carried through to the porch. Gerrit felt the tension in his wife's hands, but at least she'd stopped crying. Gerrit had dreaded this day. The turmoil of emotions that had festered all those long months boiled inside him. He knew now how much he hated the man who had done this to his daughter, to their family, but most of all to his wife, crippled by the stroke brought on by all of this. Would she ever recover? What about their young daughter? Her future was in shambles.

He tried to quiet his emotions. His hands were sweating. He lifted them carefully from Kate's lap and rubbed them against his trousers. They were radiating his anger, his fear and disgust at what had been set in motion nine months ago. If that man drove by their house now, he knew he'd have chased him.

As the minutes stretched into what seemed like hours, he was fearful things weren't going well in the bedroom. He saw Kate was worried about something. "Deh-per," she whispered.

For goodness sakes, he thought. What were they going to wrap this baby in? But Helen had the same thought in mind as she got up and went into the house, again shutting the door behind her. When she came back, she leaned over to Kate and smiled. "All taken care of."

Looking at Gerrit, she explained that Kate and Anna had all these things ready for months. The tiny wardrobe had been washed, folded, and put in the bottom drawers in Kate's dresser. The diapers were hemmed earlier in the summer and stacked on a shelf in the closet. Little pink flannel receiving blankets were ready to bundle the baby.

Gerrit had to chuckle at himself. It never occurred to him that this baby might need something to wear when it arrived. He should have known Kate would have it ready months ago. She probably even had a pin cushion full of diaper pins.

When Chandler finally opened the door to the porch and motioned Gerrit and Kate to come in, it seemed like it should be almost bedtime. Instead, the sun had barely dipped below the horizon. In the background they could hear the little arrival making her presence known.

"It's a girl, just like Anna thought!" Chandler said with a big grin. "She's beautiful, just like her Momma and Grandma. And Auntie."

Gerrit felt tears welling up in his eyes. He swallowed hard, then leaned over to give Kate a kiss. "Well, Grandma, let's go meet our new little girl."

"Annalise came through in great shape," Chandler said as they walked through to the bedroom.

Suddenly, Fletcher materialized. How could he have known to come in? "Can I come, too?" he asked as he hurried after them.

"Why not?" Chandler said. "You're officially an uncle."

Kate and Gerrit couldn't take their eyes off the little face peeking out from under the blanket. She'd finally stopped yowling. Gerrit felt the anger and angst drain away as he stood there admiring the newest member of their family.

"What about me?" Anna laughed. "I did all the work."

"She's beautiful," her dad whispered as he bent down to give her a kiss.

It had been a family decision to keep a positive attitude all these months as they waited for this little one's arrival. But it was especially tough watching Anna during those long hot days when she was confined to bed. They knew they all had to overcome the anger they felt during those early days when they faced the reality of what had been done to Anna. But anger was no way to welcome a new life. Even through these hardships, God had provided.

Anna motioned for her dad to lean closer. She had something to tell him, something Kate probably already knew. He bent down so she could whisper what she wanted to say.

Nellie brought a chair from the dining room for Kate, who eased into it, never taking her eyes off her two girls.

"Ready for the baby to meet Aunt Ida and Helen?" Chandler asked when Gerrit straightened up after his whispered conversation with Anna.

Anna nodded. Without a word, Gerrit bent to give his daughter a kiss on her forehead, felt the baby's wrinkled red cheek, and left the room. Ida and Helen went to Anna's side as Gerrit, Fletcher, and Chandler left the room. Kate stayed with Anna and the baby.

"It's a little crowded in there," Chandler laughed.

"Too much for me," Fletcher added. Gerrit seemed lost somewhere else as he went through to the porch then outside. He needed time to sort through things.

Helen and Ida introduced themselves to the new baby and congratulated Anna on her little girl. But then they had another job to do—feed everyone.

They disappeared into the kitchen, where they retrieved food from the icebox and carried it out to the porch. Kate remained with Anna and the baby, who lay snuggled beside Anna in the bed. It was only a couple of minutes before Anna's eyes blinked, then closed. Both were immediately asleep.

Ida came in to get Kate. The others started filling their plates from the array of food spread out on the long table. Chilled potato salad, cold beef sandwiches, and a tray of garden veggies—sliced tomatoes, green beans, and carrots. They'd found a jar of applesauce in the fruit cellar downstairs. They also shared oatmeal cookies Helen brought and pitchers of cold milk and tea. A well-deserved feast. Ida fixed a small plate of applesauce and potato salad for Anna, but quickly brought it back to the porch when she found her sleeping.

Before he left for home, Dr. Chandler looked in at his patients snoozing away. Nellie said she would stay awhile before going home herself. Ida and Helen knew it would be a long night for them. Who could sleep when there was a new baby to watch over?

"I think my work here is finished," Chandler told Gerrit as he walked down the steps, heading for his car. "You'd better get in there and get some food. I'll be back in the morning to check on things. If you need anything tonight, call me. Nellie will stay a bit longer. Helen is a pro at home deliveries. Besides her own boys, I don't even know how many grandchildren she helped into this world. I think she and Ida can handle things for tonight."

A bit later, when Fletcher left to take Nellie home, Helen and Ida checked on Anna, then went for a stroll around the yard.

Gerrit pulled a chair closer to Kate and reached for her hand. He needed to talk to Kate about what she and Anna had decided. At first Gerrit was shocked—maybe a little miffed—at what his daughter had whispered to him.

How could they not have talked it over with him months ago, rather than leaving it until now? He felt a little betrayed by being left out of something so important. Anger boiled up inside him as he tried to figure out how they intended to make all these things happen. Was it even possible?

Did Anna really understand what she was doing? This had to be a family decision, not just an idea hatched by the two of them. But what was he worried about? It was an amazing idea. It could work—couldn't it? It would give Anna time to grow up and it would give Kate what she'd always dreamed of...

"Kate?" he said. "We need to talk—just you and me. You and Anna have cooked up some pretty fancy ideas for that tiny person in the pink blanket. But you know what? I think it just might be the perfect answer."

Kate, all smiles, nodded.

Ida and Helen came back inside. "We've decided to take turns staying up with Anna through the night," Helen announced. "For starters, I think we'd better see to getting you ready for the night," she said to Kate, helping her to her feet.

Then the phone rang. Gerrit hurried to his desk to answer it. "Hello," he said, then froze as a stricken look came over his face. He slammed the receiver down and told Helen and Ida not to answer it if it rang again.

Despite his earlier bravado about his wife and daughter's decision about the baby, the unexpected phone call had unnerved him terribly. He needed quiet. The whispered conversation with Anna also unnerved Gerrit. At times it seemed like the most logical conclusion. But when he added in the unwelcome phone call, he could hardly hold his hands still.

Whenever things started piling up too fast, he could always pull himself back and start over at the beginning. Logically, step by step, he could figure it out. But he'd never had to contend with something—no, someone—he couldn't control. He had no way to predict what that man would do and when he would do it. Was he back up there, snooping around? Had he been parked down the road, watching traffic in and out of our driveway? Without knowing what to expect of this man, how could he and Kate make any decisions?

Gerrit poked his head into the bedroom to make sure Kate was still asleep. Anna looked so peaceful, the hint of a smile on her face. The baby had been snuggled into a tiny crib beside Anna's bed. Helen had brought the rocker from the porch into the bedroom. Helen, who never seemed to be without a bag of knitting, had one hanging on the arm of the rocker. Her eyes were shut, but she didn't fool anyone. Ida had already gone to bed in

Anna's bedroom upstairs. Later, she would come down and Helen would go upstairs to sleep.

Gerrit went out to the porch and stretched out on the daybed. Earlier, he'd heard faraway rumbling and saw a flash or two of distant lightning, but they'd passed without even a drop of rain wetting the thirsty garden and lawn. Now the moon cast a bright glow over everything. Still, he was uneasy. Fletcher had gone up to his room after he got back from driving Nellie home.

If he'd known earlier what Anna and her mother had in mind, he could have talked to his colleagues at the courthouse to find out what the procedure was for adopting a baby. But why was it even necessary to have them adopt the baby? It had been decided that Kate would care for the baby when Anna went to school and they would both share responsibility when Anna was at home. And then, he knew, Kate was determined Anna would go to college. She couldn't take the baby along, so Kate would just continue taking care of her.

But how was that going to work with Kate still struggling to recover? They could hire someone to come in to help, but that would only complicate things. The poor baby wouldn't know who her mother was.

He didn't think about the alternative—giving the baby up for adoption. He knew neither Kate nor Anna would hear of that. But how could they manage? Then he remembered Fletcher's suggestion that he would delay going to college. He knew Fletcher would try to make the best of it, but he couldn't picture him helping raise his sister's baby and caring for his invalid mother.

He tried to shove all those thoughts aside, especially the whole ugly specter of Anna's rapist. How could Nolan possibly have known the baby was born that day? Had he marked his calendar and kept track of the expected due date? It was uncanny that he'd called that night.

Regardless, Nolan knew. And he was there, somewhere. Whenever the farmhouse got a long-distance phone call, the local operator would connect the call. It didn't automatically go through to the number that was being dialed like a local call.

With all those still-unanswered questions, Gerrit knew they should have arranged to give the baby up. But after all this time imagining it going one way, it seemed utterly impossible to suddenly start looking for adoptive parents. Besides, it wasn't their decision to make. It was Anna's. He could argue that adoption would be the best and most stable home life for this beautiful baby, but it would be the worst possible decision for Anna and Kate. Anna had been so firm in her decision.

Finally, Gerrit closed his eyes and tried to sleep before the baby woke Anna and Helen. It seemed only a few minutes later when the early morning sunshine woke him up. He heard Helen and Ida in the other room and smelled coffee brewing on the electric stove.

He sat up just as Ida came out carrying the baby. Helen followed with Anna in tow. It was good to see her on her feet, but he wondered if she was ready to be up and about without the doctor's approval. She seemed perfectly fine as she walked over to the rocking chair. Ida gave her the baby to hold and the two sat in the rocker.

Everyone settled on scrambled eggs and toast for breakfast. The butter and apple jelly were already on the porch table. Gerrit got up to pour himself a cup of coffee. Anna thought all she wanted was a little toast, but when the eggs arrived, she put a spoonful on her plate and ate it all. Kate had walked all the way out to the porch on her own, but she gladly accepted help getting settled in a chair. Gerrit filled her plate with eggs and toast and poured coffee into a cup, filling it nearly halfway up with cream. Gerrit looked around the table. How could he ever have thought the right answer was to give the baby up for adoption? They had to find a way to keep this baby with them. Somehow it had to work. Keeping the baby would give Kate a reason to work harder on her therapy. And Anna, who devoted those long months to keeping the baby safe until she was developed enough to survive on the outside, would never forgive herself, or them, if she had to give up the baby. It would take more than a few extra hands to make it work, but they could do it. Gerrit knew it was the only answer.

"Why are you smiling?" Anna asked her dad.

"Oh, just happy to see all of us around the table with someone new," he replied.

The phone rang and Gerrit hurried away to answer it. "Probably Chandler wondering if we're up and ready for him," he said as he went around the corner toward his desk and the phone. But it wasn't Chandler. He recognized the voice even though the "hello" was quiet. Gerrit quickly replaced the receiver on the cradle and went back to the porch. "Wrong number," he said.

He pushed the table away from the back wall a bit and slid down on the old bench where Fletcher and his sister always sat when they ate meals there in warm weather. It gave him a good view of the occasional car or Amish buggy driving by. Off in the distance, he saw a car approaching. The dust that settled around the coming car disguised its color and shape until it was nearly up to the driveway. Chandler's Buick slowed and turned into their driveway.

"Oh, boy," Ida said to Anna with a grin. "We're all going to be in trouble for letting you get out of bed."

But that didn't happen. He was pleased to see Anna up and at the table, eating a good breakfast. When Kate moved out of the rocker to a chair at the table, Helen took the baby and rocked her. Ida dished up eggs and made more toast for Chandler. Fletcher returned from his morning chores and was ready for a full breakfast. Ida had it ready by the time he reached the top step onto the porch.

New baby bottles stood upside down in a pan of water on the stove, cooling after a good sanitizing bath in boiling water. In another pan, sterilized water for making formula cooled.

"You know, this is an awful lot of work for Miss Watchamacallit, here," Fletcher grinned at the baby between bites of toast. "What are you going to name her?"

"I haven't made a final choice," Anna said. "I suppose we have to come up with something pretty soon."

Dr. Chandler suggested a couple with a joking smile. "Suzy Q. That's kind of nice. Or Hortense. Maybe not. Annalise? Oh, that's taken, isn't it?"

Anna peeked over at the baby in Kate's arms. "I've been thinking for a long time that I'd like to call her Katherine. Momma named me Annalise after her mother, and I'd like to name my little girl Katherine after my mother. It wouldn't work to call her Kate, but we could call her Kassy...or Kitty, or Katie. No one ever calls Mom anything but Kate, so we wouldn't get the two mixed up."

Kate seemed to follow the conversation because when Anna mentioned naming her Katherine, she broke out into a wide smile. Tears welled up in the corner of her eyes and Gerrit reached over to give her a hug. "I like that choice," he said. "So, what will it be? Kitty? Katie? Kassy?"

"Kath-er-ine," Kate sounded out.

"All of the nicknames can come later," Fletcher chimed in. "Katherine is a beautiful name."

"On your word, that's what we will list as her name at the courthouse," Chandler said. "Oh, she needs a middle name, too."

"Anna," Kate piped up. "Kath-er-ine An-na."

"Katherine Anne might be easier to say," Gerrit added.

"No, Anna." Kate said insistently. "Like Anna-lise, only just Anna."

They talked a while longer before Chandler interrupted and said he had to examine Anna and then get back to the hospital. When he and Helen came back out of the bedroom, Anna wasn't with them.

"She's done enough dancing around for one morning," Chandler said. "I want her to stay in bed as much as possible today. She's young and in good health but still needs rest. And I know this little Katherine Anna has enough caregivers. Anna is not going to nurse this baby. We will get her started on a bottle for her milk, that way it won't matter who is available to feed her. I'll be out again tomorrow morning early so I can get back to town for Mass and communion. Call either the hospital or my house later if you need me."

After Chandler left, Gerrit went up to change into outdoor clothes. While he and Fletcher worked in the garden, they could talk more about delaying his departure for college.

Helen put the baby back in the crib in the bedroom. Ida cleared the table and had the dishpan filled with warm, soapy water for the dishes.

August 1, 1944

Dear Days,

Good news!

My baby was born this afternoon at 6:47 PM. She is beautiful. Momma told me it would hurt and take a long time. She was right. She also told me that I wouldn't even remember how much it hurt. And I don't. Dr. Chandler weighed her on the little scale Nellie brought. She was six pounds and seven ounces. Dr. Chandler said that was a respectable size.

We've decided she will be named Katherine Anna. Momma picked the name and insisted that her middle name should be Anna, like mine. I think it's a perfect name. Everyone always calls me 'Annalise,' and only when they are in a hurry do they say 'Anna.' So, my little girl's name should be Katherine, not Katie, Kittie, or Kassie. Katherine Anna. Welcome!

Annalise

Gerrit and Fletcher had been wandering the acreage, so engrossed in conversation that they walked out the driveway then up the road toward the old schoolhouse.

Fletcher was adamant. He insisted he would delay starting college until after Christmas. There were too many things he had to help with at home. School, he insisted, could wait a few months. But there was one thing he was even more determined about. Annalise had to go to school in September. With Aunt Ida and Helen close at hand, there was no reason for her to stay home. Katherine would be fine with two aunties and a grandmother to dote on her.

When Fletcher finally stopped for breath, Gerrit piped up. "I'm glad to hear your final decision on school, but that's not what I really wanted to talk to you about."

"What's that?"

"Did you know your mother and Annalise had talked about us adopting the baby so that she would be your sister, not your niece? I didn't know that until yesterday."

Gerrit continued. "At first, I thought it might be a good idea, but the more I mulled it over, the more I knew that wouldn't work. It was a nice idea, but the baby is Anna's, and it is important, legally, that she remain Anna's. There can be no formal adoption. We have such a conundrum with the legal situation as it is. If we change the baby's parental status, it could affect your sister's potential legal claim against the diocese. If they were thinking this would be a way to shield Annalise from any gossip about the baby, it wouldn't work anyway. There is no stopping people from talking, but we know what happened, and we know what Anna's motive was for keeping the baby in our family."

Gerrit took in a breath and then clenched his fists. "Did you know that that priest called here last night right after Anna delivered the baby? It was a local call, so he was up here again. How did he know? I hung up on him. Or rather, I slammed the receiver down in his ear. How dare he? And he called again this morning. He never identifies himself, but I know his voice."

Fletcher stopped in the middle of the road and stared at his dad. "I suppose until school is back in session he has the time to drive up here anytime he wants. But the timing?"

Gerrit said, "I think it's a little more than coincidence."

The pair turned and headed back toward the farm. Fletcher tried to sort out his dad's litany of issues surrounding Anna and the baby. When she first came home after the rape, Anna talked with him about possibly having their parents adopt the baby so it would officially be theirs, not hers. But that was the only time she'd mentioned it.

"Has anything been settled with the priest and diocese?" Fletcher asked. "The last I heard anything was at least six weeks ago when you and Aunt Ida went down to see the bishop."

"I expected a call from the bishop's attorney, but so far nothing," Gerrit said. "I thought of calling there after the priest came up here, but I didn't do it."

That ended their conversation for the time being. Fletcher knew he'd have to talk to Pops again that night during chores or on the way into town on Monday. Fletcher would have to take a day off from work so he could drive over to the college to cancel his plans for the fall semester. Their conversation put a lot of things into better perspective.

Later that day, Anna and her dad were deep in conversation when Fletcher came down from his afternoon snooze.

With Annalise's business papers spread all over the bed, he assumed it was time for the start of her apple business season. Their dad was studying the receipt book from last fall. A basket of fresh-picked apples sat in the middle of the paper turmoil. Fletcher remembered the drill: calculating which apples were ready for picking, how many bushels would this crop produce, and how many packages of dried apples would they have to sell.

"Looks like you're ready to start picking and drying," he told his sister. "The season has been so good for growing this year. Looks like it'll be a bumper crop...providing we don't get one of those high-wind storms."

Orders had already started coming in. Kids ready to start school in a couple of weeks would need apple slices in their lunch pails.

Anna lifted stacks of reports, looking for something. "I have a new apple slicer in here somewhere," she said. "It cuts curly edges. I think the kids will love them." When she finally found it, she tried it on one of the apples from the basket. "I'm anxious to see how they shape up after they're dried. We'll have a little more loss of the fruit since the cutter just cuts straight down, but we can use all the leftover peelings and pulp to make apple butter. No waste and a better apple butter to boot." She picked up the raw slices to munch. "Aunt Ida found the cutter in a catalog and thought they'd look so pretty in our bags. I'm going to have to play around with how to use this for the best slices. If we core the apples carefully, we might get slices from each that still have the colored peel on them. That would look nice."

The business meeting was briefly interrupted by Katherine. She barely let out a peep when Ida came around the corner to pick her up.

"Probably needs changing," Ida said, picking up a diaper from the stack on the dresser. "I made up the first batch of formula from Chandler so all I have to do is warm it up."

A few minutes later, Ida was back with a baby who was trying to figure out how to get food from the bottle into her tummy. "You can work with her a little bit and see how she does. She doesn't seem too pleased with her rations of warm water. There's not much nourishment in that, even if it's good for her."

Anna leaned back against a stack of pillows so she could feed Katherine. She looked so contented and happy teaching her little girl how to suck from the bottle.

"Your Momma used to push on the nipple just a little bit so some of the milk would drop out into your mouth," Gerrit explained. "It didn't take you long to figure it out."

Annalise was a little worried about how much to press on the side of the nipple for fear the baby would choke.

Fletcher leaned down to check the baby's progress. "Hey, she swallowed the milk," he said.

This was a far more interesting project for the afternoon than trying to figure out how many apples they'd have and how many bags of dried apple slices they'd have to sell.

The three leaned over to watch Katherine work on the bottle. "She seems too little to work so hard," her grandpa said.

"Is she sucking?" the elder Katherine asked, trying to watch from her day bed across the room.

"She's really starting to eat," Anna said. "Look at her go!"

CHAPTER FIFTEEN

The afternoon sun drifted lower, but the family still sat in the downstairs bedroom watching the baby and talking about her, the apples, and the future with their newest members—Baby Katherine and, of course, Ida.

Ida had cut some of the leftover chicken in the icebox and made a summer salad for their supper. Annalise joined them at the table on the front porch. The windows with screens were open to let in the soft, late-summer breezes. Anna looked over at her mom sitting opposite her. She looked relaxed as she carefully chewed the small chicken chunks with macaroni and fresh lettuce.

Katherine was sound asleep in a thin blanket on the day bed at the far end of the porch. Fletcher turned to look at her. He remembered his earlier thoughts of how much turmoil a tiny baby could cause. What turmoil? The baby had a full tummy and was sound asleep. Not much bother at all.

Fletcher had asked about the possibility of cutting back on his hours at the Ben Franklin store, but he wasn't expecting he would need to terribly soon. It hadn't occurred to him that Baby Katherine would arrive Friday night. On the outside chance he could take at least mornings off for the next few days, he and his dad drove into town in separate cars. Mom, he knew, would not be driving, and Aunt Ida's car was parked alongside the garage, handy for errands.

Even if he had to work all day, he wanted to set up a time when he could meet with Dr. Chandler. He didn't want anyone at home to know he planned to talk with Annalise's doctor.

He knew Doc would be making rounds at the hospital until about nine thirty. He hoped to get a chance to talk with him before he started seeing patients at ten o'clock in his office. Fletcher decided to call the doctor's office over the lunch hour. As it turned out, he didn't need to, because Chandler stopped at the store to do a little shopping before going to his office. He was as surprised to see Fletcher at the cash register as Fletcher was surprised to see him waiting to check out.

"Hey, Fletcher," he said. "I thought maybe you wouldn't be here today."

"I got so wrapped up in all the excitement at home I forgot about calling the store to see if they needed me today, but they only need me this morning. Everything seemed to be going okay when I left home. You saved me a phone call. I wanted to talk with you about something that I didn't want anyone to overhear. I wanted your advice about changing my college plans and some other stuff. Any suggestions on when we could talk somewhere for a few minutes?"

They settled on eleven thirty at Chandler's office.

Fletcher hadn't expected to get to see him today, but he was happy for the appointment. He waited in the doctor's small waiting room, but he wasn't there long before Chandler came out.

"I think I have some idea what you needed to talk about," the doctor said as they walked toward his office. With the door shut, Fletcher didn't waste time explaining his need to get a Catholic person's viewpoint on the issues his family struggled with for so many months. He would have talked to him a long time ago, but he didn't have any idea the doctor was Catholic until he'd mentioned attending Sunday Mass and communion.

Fletcher told the doctor that he could hear the frustration in their voices whenever one or the other of his parents talked about their dealings with the bishop or priest. "I have no idea how this kind of situation should be handled in the Catholic Church. Have you ever heard of a priest raping a student? I need to know the right way to handle this. This is something our family will have to deal with for years. No one ever gets back to my parents, now just my dad. He did meet with the bishop right after Mom had the stroke and was still in the hospital. He said they didn't get any satisfaction from either the bishop or the diocesan attorney on what the next step would be in resolving this problem. No one will even admit this even happened to Anna, and they certainly aren't going to commit to doing anything about their liability. They just keep saying Annalise must be lying to cover up her own bad behavior."

Fletcher sighed, and Chandler nodded for him to continue. "My mother's father was a Methodist minister, so my mom and her sister have experience with how a clergyman deals with problems. But a rape by a clergyman was not something they'd ever heard about. From what they knew, such a thing never occurred. I don't expect answers to all my questions today, but I would like to set up a time when we could go over what you know about handling rape-caused pregnancies and child-support responsibilities. I could talk with the county lawyer, but I don't want my dad to know I'm doing some investigating on my own. We don't have to set up a time today, but maybe you could let me know when we could meet for an hour or so in the future."

Then, before Chandler could respond, Fletcher asked, "Did you go to Marquette University?"

If the question surprised Chandler, he didn't show it. "Yes," he replied, "but only for medical school."

"I'm seriously thinking about going into law due to all this stuff with Annalise. I have a feeling they will just sweep it under the rug and hope we just go away. I want to learn how to use the law to protect people from stuff like this. They can deny it as much as they want, but my sister is telling the truth. Her whole life has been messed up due to what this priest did. As you know, Anna couldn't go into town for my graduation. My parents made arrangements for Sarah Mellen from the Amish farm up the road to stay with her. The priest drove into our yard, came to the door, and pushed his way into the house. He demanded Anna 'stop telling lies about him.' But Helen Iversen saw his car and came into the house and then he left."

Fletcher rubbed his temple and then continued, his voice heavy with worry. "Dad said he saw the priest one Sunday afternoon a few weeks back, driving back and forth past our house. And someone tried to break into Ida's house when she was up here with us. Ida's daughter was sleeping upstairs when she heard someone trying to get a key into the front door lock. We think they were looking for Anna's soiled pajamas the priest had taken off her and left on the floor next to her bed. Anna packed them in a box. Whoever it was trashed the entire house looking for that box. What the person didn't know was that Ida brought the box and pajamas back here. They are now safely hidden somewhere. Poppa won't say where. So, now we have to worry that he will break into the farmhouse looking for them. It's scary. The nightmare just doesn't end."

"How about Friday afternoon when you're through work?" Dr. Chandler proposed. "We could meet at the park near the bandshell. Counting on delays, I should be there by five."

As Chandler walked Fletcher to the door, he set a hand on his shoulder and asked, "Annalise doing okay? I'd like her to bring the baby in for an appointment soon. Tell Anna you saw me at the store this morning and I suggested she make an appointment for the baby. In the meantime, I'll try to get my thoughts organized on all your questions before Friday."

Fletcher was awake early Saturday morning. He and his dad wanted to get another bucket or two of apples gathered before it got too hot. Fletch had more in mind for the apple gathering than just picking the ripest from the tree.

Gerrit already had his coffee and two slices of toast and was outside with the apple picker. He was starting on a second pail when Fletcher came around the corner. They worked together for a while, then stood leaning against a tree, munching apples. Between bites, Fletcher filled his dad in on what he'd learned from Doc Chandler the day before. As Fletcher expected, the doctor said he'd never heard of any such scandal. Of course, he didn't know if they had such problems down in the big cities and he hadn't gotten in touch yet with doctors he knew from medical school who were in practice there. He said he'd try again over the weekend.

"I also talked to him about law school at Marquette," Fletcher said between chewing. "Due to the problems Annalise has been dealing with, I've been thinking about the need for someone in our family to have some law experience. I've often thought about going into law, but I figured I'd have four years before I had to decide. But why not check it out before I invest a lot of time in other studies? I think I'd like to just start my degree at Marquette and line up my classes so they would lead into law school. I haven't really spent much of my summer paychecks, so if the fees aren't too high, maybe I can cover most of the costs myself. I know some students work while they are in college. What do you think?"

"I'm speechless!" his father exclaimed. Then Gerrit, who was never without words to say, laughed. "We'll need to talk to your mom and Annalise about the law school stuff, probably without identifying your main reason for wanting to go into law. I've always thought you'd make a good lawyer. You're great at questioning and getting to the bottom of things. Those are skills lawyers need. And you have no shortage of brains. You certainly could be a teacher or run a business, too. I think your mom will be pleased with what you are contemplating. Let's bring her out to the orchard later this afternoon. It would be a good place for her to sit a spell and talk things over."

Gerrit and Fletcher each carried a bucket of apples into the house where they knew Anna was waiting to admire their selection.

Later, Fletcher set out to find the lawn chair he'd made for his mom in woodworking class his junior year. He found it in the granary. Summer was winding down and she still had not enjoyed the chair he made for her. That day, she would!

Too bad he hadn't made a second chair for his Pops. He carried out several other porch chairs so they could all sit in the orchard together. It was such a nice day that Anna wrapped Katherine in a blanket and put her in the wicker buggy Kate used when Anna and Fletcher were babies.

Ida carried out a frosty pitcher of iced tea, followed by Helen with a basket of glasses. Gerrit wondered why they'd never found an occasion to sit in the shade of the apple trees before.

Everyone marveled at Fletcher's craftsmanship. The chair fit his mom perfectly, and it was more important now than it ever would have been before. They all agreed that life was much better sitting in the shade of their own apple trees, just enjoying each other's company and the peace and quiet of their corner of the world. Then Katherine's yowls reminded them that their lives were far from trouble-free.

Annalise was anxious to start slicing and drying apple rings, but tomorrow was another day to start that. She picked up the baby and handed her to Kate.

Ida had plans for the baskets of apples Gerrit and Fletcher had picked earlier. When the kitchen cooled down, she would bake an apple crisp. And maybe make the rest into applesauce.

Helen was lost in her own thoughts about her conversation with Nellie. Nellie had told Helen about their plans for a surprise baby shower for Baby Katherine and Anna. If the weather cooperated, the Amish neighbors would be going home early from their Sunday church services, and they'd bring their baskets of food to Helen's place to have a picnic.

Helen didn't remember ever seeing Nellie so excited, nor did she remember ever having done anything like that in all the years she'd lived there. Nellie had said they'd arrange everything so Helen would merely be the host. Helen wasn't sure she could keep such exciting plans a secret.

During a lull in the lazy afternoon conversation, Fletcher brought up his college dilemmas. He talked about going to Marquette for law and told them that Dr. Chandler had gone to medical school there. He hesitated but finally got up the courage to also admit that he wouldn't start college that coming September. When he finally took a breath and looked up, he saw five faces staring intently in his direction. Kate looked like she was going to cry. Then she broke out in a big grin and clapped her hands together. Fletcher got up and went over to put his arms around his Mom's shoulders. When he leaned over to see if the tears had stopped, he pulled out his handkerchief and wiped her eyes.

"I hope those aren't tears of sadness," he said. "I hope you think this might be a good idea for my future."

Fletcher admitted he knew being a lawyer would be a challenge, but he wasn't afraid of that. He assured them he had a suitable plan for easing his way into school and beyond. If Fletcher was anything, he was organized.

Finally, the afternoon sun faded to dusk, and the breeze took on a brisk chill. They packed up and went inside. Kate's hand-crafted lawn chair looked so nice under the apple trees that they left it there so she could sit there whenever she pleased, while summer lasted.

Katherine obviously was comfortable in the old buggy where she'd been snoozing since her Grammy cuddled her to sleep, but Anna could tell it was time for a change and a bottle.

Before Helen left for the evening, she invited the entire family to her house next Sunday for dinner, explaining that her children wanted to meet Baby Katherine. "I will not take 'no' for an answer! And I told my kids you'd probably bring an apple crisp or a pie or two."

Saturday afternoon, with the baby and Grandma Kate napping, Ida and Annalise rolled out four pie crusts and filled the pans with apple slices. Ida sprinkled each with a Dutch crumble topping. "My dad's favorite," she said.

Sunday morning, Gerrit drove Ida and Kate to the Lutheran church up the road. It was the first time Kate had been there in weeks. On the drive home, Gerrit noticed the long tables and benches lined up under the big shade trees on the side lawn of Helen's farmstead. "Looks like more than just Helen's kids are coming this afternoon," he said.

Annalise was waiting on the front porch. It was the first time she'd been alone with Katherine, and she was anxious to find out who was at church.

An hour later, with the four pies safely placed in the car's trunk, they headed down the road toward the Iversen's. Fletcher, who had gone to church with Cynthia, was already there. They were surprised to see the whole yard filled with Amish buggies, but no one was around. Not even the dogs. But as soon as their car door opened, the yard flooded with Amish neighbors and the Iversen clan.

"Surprise!" they called out in unison.

What's going on? Anna wondered. *The old order Amish are supposed to be at Sunday services, not here at an Englisher's farmhouse.*

The usually reserved Amish women were anything but reserved that afternon. Their smiles beamed with excitement.

"It's a baby shower for Katherine," Helen explained excitedly. "It was their idea. They had church a little early this morning so they could come. They so wanted to see your baby."

Annalise undid the little blanket and invited them all to come and see her new daughter. Katherine had been sleeping, but her eyes fluttered open as the women moved forward, encircling the young mother and her infant. The young girls in the group held back but still tried to get a peek, standing on tiptoe. The boys weren't so anxious.

"Now, let's all eat," Helen announced. "Gerrit, Ida, please put the pies on the dessert table underneath the netting so the flies don't get at them." she said. The table groaned from the weight of all the sweets, including special cookies for the children.

After spending most of the morning in prayer at their services, the Amish stood around the tables, waiting to ask for blessings on the food they brought to share, including more fruit pies and apple kuchen.

It was a memorable meal for both the Englishers and the Amish Mennonites. Their prayer was one of thanksgiving, not only for the food, but also for the young lady who had brought a new life into the world. The bishop led the prayer: "Little Katherine, conceived in such adversity, is truly a gift from God. While others of less faith might have taken a different path, young Annalise looked upon this coming child as someone who was meant to be in their family. And in our community."

Anna noticed that several of the women sitting across from her had tears in their smiling eyes.

Helen's daughters-in-law carried out platters of chilled fried chicken, sliced potatoes, and garden vegetables that had been baked in their ovens early that morning. There were baskets heaped with bread and rolls placed alongside the plates of sliced tomatoes. At the end, they decided to have their pie a little later. It was time for a surprise for the little one.

The bishop stood again to address the group. "We are old-order Amish Mennonites," he proclaimed. "We believe we are called to live separate from our neighbors. This is the first time I can ever remember sharing a meal with neighbors who are not Amish. Why? Because we wanted to celebrate this miracle with you. And we are so proud of this new mother that we decided we had to break with our traditions to let her know how blessed we all are to know someone who has such convictions. And now, we have a present for this little angel of God."

Around the corner of the house, carrying something covered by a large quilt, came the two oldest Mellen brothers. When they set it down in front of the group, they asked Annalise and her baby to uncover the surprise. Anna was a little nervous at standing in front of all these neighbors, but she approached the gift. The bishop asked if he could hold the baby while she undid the coverlet.

Underneath was the most beautiful baby bed Annalise could ever have imagined. Covering the mattress was a hand-made quilt of squares embroidered with the names of the women and children who hand-stitched it. The men and boys who'd worked on the bed painted their names on the backside of the headboard.

Now it was Annalise's turn to cry. She wiped her cheeks before thanking everyone for the wonderful surprise party and gifts for Baby Katherine, but the tears kept coming.

The bishop handed Katherine back to Anna and once more blessed the afternoon's gathering. Then Nellie hurried over to him and whispered something in his ear.

"Oh, dear," he said sheepishly. "We've been offering our thanks for many things, but we forgot the pie."

They all found a place to sit as Helen and her sons' wives handed plates of pie around the tables.

Finally, the children were excused to run and play—"Quietly, please, so the baby can sleep!" Their parents watched the tiny baby asleep in her new bed parked under a giant maple tree. Gerrit, still dressed in his Sunday suit, talked crops and weather with the Amish farmers. The Mennonite sisters with their Englisher neighbors carried benches to set up a large square circle so they could talk. They had much to share as the precious minutes of the rare occasion ticked away.

All too soon, it was time for the men to gather their families and head home for evening chores. Anna walked out to the road so she could wave to each of the departing buggies as they drove away. Annalise's smile faded after the last one passed by. It had been such a memorable and wonderful day. If only that rare gathering of neighbors happened more often.

Helen walked over to whisper a secret to Annalise. "I took some pictures of the tables after we set them up," she said. "You know, we don't photograph their faces, but I asked the bishop if I could have permission to take some pictures of the picnic. While he was saying the blessing before the meal, I stood in the back so I could take their picture without breaking their rule. When the bishop saw me ready to take the picture, even he looked away just before I clicked the shutter. And when the women were all gathered around the crib with Katherine in it, I got another picture. They were all bending over the crib. I wanted Katherine to see how much she was loved by the people who planned this special occasion to welcome her into the world."

The Iversen clan cleaned off the tables and benches, then piled them on the wagon that stood near the machine shed. The farm equipment had been moved out for the day, but the weather had been so ideal they didn't need to take cover. Shadows gathered in the yard. Helen's crew had their own chores to tend to and loaded up their families to head home. Ronald, the youngest, said he would be back mid-morning the next day to pick up and return the wagonload of tables and benches.

Before they all left for the evening, Helen got her camera for a final shot of the beautiful baby crib surrounded by Kate and Gerrit's family.

CHAPTER SIXTEEN

The roadside café looked like a good place to get a cup of coffee. It would be an easy, in-and-out routine, as if that was anything to worry about. There were no cars parked in the spaces along the front of the building. He thought maybe they were closed. Then the door opened, and an older couple came out and walked toward the row of houses in the residential section just beyond. Even better. If the locals walked to a neighborhood restaurant on a Sunday, that meant the food is good.

The inside looked more like a diner than a café. Still, based on the smells coming from the kitchen, it would definitely do.

Rather than donning his Roman collar and dark shirt, the priest was wearing a light green shirt and khaki trousers. He considered settling for a seat at the counter, then thought better of it. He needed to do some serious thinking and couldn't waste time getting involved in chit-chat with the counter help, wherever they were. When the scruffy man with a white towel tied to his apron came out from the kitchen, he grabbed a menu and hurried over to the priest's booth.

"Welcome," he said, handing the clergyman the single sheet. "Special today is baked chicken with gravy over noodles and a side of green beans. We don't have a big menu, but whatever is on there is guaranteed to be good."

"I think I'll try your chicken," the priest said, handing the menu back. "Also, a glass of cold water and later some coffee."

The man dropped the menu off on the counter and went back to the kitchen. It couldn't have been two minutes before he was back with a steaming plate of noodles and baked chicken. There were green beans that looked like they'd come from a local garden. So did the slices of tomato.

He'd initially thought all he wanted was a cup of coffee and a break from driving in the hot sun. But it had been a long time since he'd eaten the slices of toast after he finished saying his second Mass earlier that morning. Couldn't have been a better choice than this chicken dinner. It tasted like the Sunday dinners his mother used to make. Stella, his housekeeper at the rectory, never mastered the art of preparing chicken. She did alright with hot dishes of noodles and ground meat, but baking a chicken so it didn't taste limp was a skill she hadn't gotten quite right.

"Is there a pay telephone around here somewhere?" he asked when the server came to clear the empty dishes.

"There's one on the outside of the post office just a way down the road, still on this side of the street. Not much privacy, but there's usually no one walking around town, especially on a hot Sunday afternoon. I expect most folks are snoozing in their chairs."

Father thanked him for the good meal and told him how much the chicken reminded him of his mother's cooking. He left the money on the table, including a little extra for a tip.

"I come this way occasionally, and this will be a good place to stop when I'm passing by again," the priest said before stepping out the door.

When he opened his car door, the heat nearly bowled him over. He rolled down the window, started the car, and continued up the road, looking for a post office. If he hadn't been told there was one just a few doors down, he never would have noticed the plain little wooden building with clapboard siding that needed a good coat of paint. But sure enough, there was a phone.

He deposited the coins and dialed the number of the Catholic parish rectory. A man answered on the second ring.

"You must have been sitting right next to the phone," the priest said, blinking in the bright sunlight. "Anyway. Hello," he then added belatedly. "I don't know if you remember me. I'm Cleary Nolan, rector of the Catholic high school in Milwaukee. I met you at a retreat a couple years back. I'm here in your neck of the woods, and thought I'd just stop in, if that's okay."

"I do remember you," the voice on the other end said. "There was a story about your school in our little diocesan paper a couple weeks ago. Said you've added girls to your all-boys school. Article said it was working out just fine."

"I hope my stopping for a few minutes won't be an imposition on your time. I'm looking forward to seeing you, and I'm also looking for a little information about someone we had in our school for a few months. I was through here earlier this summer, and I saw a sign directing traffic to your church. I presume your rectory is right by the church?"

"Yes, and yes," the priest on the other end replied, laughing. "Just follow the signs, and I'll be waiting at the door for you. My housekeeper made some lemonade, and I'd be happy to have someone to talk with while I drink it."

Cleary Nolan found the rectory and looked for a tree-shaded spot in front of the church. The rectory was a very plain building. It looked more like a garage than a house. It was trimmed out nicely but certainly not big enough to hold a meal for a bishop. There were well-trimmed shrubs along the foundation.

"We'll just go through," Father Andrews said. "I have a little sitting area out back. It's shady there and a lot cooler than the house."

"I haven't had lemonade in years," Father Nolan said after taking a long and appreciative swallow of the icy drink. The clinking ice cubes made the glass almost too cold to hold. Father Andrews set his glass on the little table between their two chairs.

"Now, you said you needed some information. Let's see if I can get answers for you."

"You mentioned my school," Nolan began. "This past year was the second year we've had female students. Some come from somewhere else and have to stay with a relative or rent a room. We had a freshman from somewhere up here for most of last year, but she dropped out and went home rather unexpectedly. We were sorry to lose her because she was a very good student and seemed to fit in very well with our local students. I believe she was staying with a relative."

"So, what's the question?"

"She really gave no reason for withdrawing from our school, and I didn't want to pry. If she was homesick, well, then she needed to go home. But I've heard bits and pieces since then that she might have been pregnant and didn't want to stay at the school under those circumstances. The other day, I heard from someone who had been close to her while she was with us that she was having a difficult pregnancy. I've been concerned. We try to provide good grounding in morals, but things don't always work out that way. I just wonder if the family perhaps belongs to your congregation. I was never quite sure if she was Catholic, as we don't require that they be Catholic to enroll. She was very young, seemed a lot more immature than most of her classmates. Perhaps growing up in the country, she didn't have many friends. I just wondered if perhaps you'd heard something about a young high school girl being in the hospital?"

The local priest didn't answer right away. He took another sip of his lemonade and bit into one of the chocolate chip cookies he'd brought out on a plate. Cleary Nolan figured he either had limited information to give or none at all. Finally, he set his glass on the little table.

"A couple weeks ago, one of my parishioners asked me to pray for a young lady who was pregnant and not doing well. I said I would pray that everything would work out okay. You know, God doesn't expect us to list names and addresses in the prayers we take to Him. So, I prayed for a special intention. Not long after that, the person thanked me for my prayers and said things seemed to be getting better. That's all I know." Father Andrews took another small sip of his lemonade before continuing. "I think she'd been in the hospital for some time. I don't know when she was due. Our paper here comes out only once a week, but I don't think I saw any birth announcements from anyone outside my own parish. Besides, I don't think the paper runs announcements in situations like that unless it's requested. I think the young person usually prefers privacy. Enough stories circulate and cause a lot of harm. So, I prayed for someone who had some difficulties, and I found out later that she apparently was doing much better. Does that help?"

"I don't expect she will ever return to our program, especially if she decides to keep the baby. But if it is adopted into a family, maybe she will come back. When I heard the scuttlebutt about her predicament and how things weren't going well, I added her to my daily prayer list. So, I think I'll just keep praying for her and that the baby is well and goes to a good home."

"Well, I'm not sure about any of that. The person who asked for my prayers was not forthcoming with any extra information, and it wasn't any of my concern to be asking questions. I just pray that she and the baby are well."

At that point, Father Andrews once more reached over and picked up his glass, anxious to leave that subject behind. It was awkward to have a fellow priest prying for information about a student who left his school. He couldn't help but wonder about the father of that baby. If it was someone from the school, was that person still enrolled? It didn't say much for the care or concern the administration had for its students. If Nolan was so worried, why didn't he just call the girl's parents to inquire if she was okay?

"By the way," Father Nolan added, "I stopped at the little café down the street. I had a wonderful chicken and noodle dinner. It was like being back at my mother's for Sunday dinner. She has since passed on, so it was a treat to eat such a fine lunch."

As the two priests walked through the parsonage out to the front sidewalk, Father Andrews had the uneasy feeling in his stomach that his visitor knew a lot more than he'd shared.

When they got to his car, Father Nolan thanked Andrews again for his hospitality, lemonade, and information. "You get so attached to the kids; it's like a big family. A little rambunctious sometimes, but always interesting. I can't thank you enough; it was very nice of you to invite me to sit in the shade."

Nolan waved out the window as he drove away. As he turned the corner, he saw Father Andrews still standing at the curb.

"Well," Nolan muttered to himself, "maybe I'll take another little drive out in the country myself." His eyes narrowed on the road as he drove, his thoughts sharp. *I won't linger this time. Don't need any more run-ins with her family. Her father probably thought he was pretty clever.*

This time, he took a different road to the Jansz farm. Instead of turning at the corner with the mailboxes, he took the road two miles beyond the mailbox corner. That way round would make it possible for him to go straight past their place. When he was almost to the mailbox corner, he noticed Amish buggies in a nearby barnyard, along with a half-dozen or so cars. Kids were running around, and a group of men stood off to the side, no doubt discussing farm crops. He didn't see the women until he was past the house. They were sitting on benches in sort of a circle, talking. *Could they have had church there? Not likely,* he thought. No plain blue curtains at the windows. *Amish and Englishers having what looks like a party?* Long tables were scattered around on the lawn. *A Sunday picnic lunch at an Englisher's farm? With the Amish?* Ahead, he didn't see any activity around Annalise's house. *Probably at the same neighborhood gathering.*

So, instead of driving up the little hill and past the farmhouse, he turned left at the corner and headed back to the highway. He wasn't sure where he'd end up, but he'd find his way eventually.

Thinking back to what Father Andrews had said, Nolan wondered if the trip had even been worth it. He couldn't help but wonder if Andrews had been withholding information. Nolan had scoured Ida's house, but never found anything resembling the box with soiled pajama bottoms that the attorney talked about. But he still relished the payback of leaving the squeaky-clean house in disgusting shambles.

He let his mind wander as he drove, suddenly aware that the sun had disappeared and thunderclouds had cast a few warning salvoes of what approached.

Part of Nolan missed Ida and her thoughts on faith traditions. He knew a lot more now than when he'd finished seminary. But this nostalgia merely skirted his mind. There were many other things occupying it. He'd have a lot to mull over when he returned to his rectory. That day was a good excuse to have a couple fingers of Scotch and an early bedtime.

Pulling his car into the garage, Nolan continued fixating on what he still didn't know. "It has to be at the farm," he mumbled to himself. A loud crack of thunder rattled his surroundings as he rushed into the rectory before the storm that had followed him from the north started pelting him. He barely made it.

The telephone was ringing when Father walked into the kitchen. He grabbed the receiver, hoping whoever was calling was still on the line. He barely got a greeting out when the voice on the other end launched into a nonstop tirade. He recognized the voice—Father Raymond, the bishop's chief assistant.

"I've been trying for a couple of hours to reach you. Where have you been? The bishop is really upset about where you went today and what you did. He has guests and asked me to keep trying to reach you. He wants you in his office tomorrow morning by ten. I trust I can tell him you will be here?"

"I don't have anything on my calendar for the morning other than the usual tidying up from the weekend services and Mass at eight. I'll head over immediately after Mass. Any idea what has His Excellency so upset?"

"He got a phone call this afternoon from a priest you apparently visited in another diocese. That's all I know."

"We also have a parishioner in the hospital from a car crash this past weekend, but they're doing well and probably won't require me tomorrow. I'll call if anything comes up. See you in the morning." Nolan calmly hung up the phone.

Although he'd been nonchalant with Raymond, Nolan realized the news had unnerved him. Why would his friendly visit have merited a call to the bishop?

After hours in a hot car, Father Nolan was anxious for a soak in a tepid bath to wash away the day's troubles.

It seemed he'd barely dozed off when his alarm rang. After Mass ended and the church emptied, Nolan knelt at the altar, asking God's help for his meeting with the bishop.

When he pulled into a spot near the chancery office door, he spotted another car parked around back—the attorney's car. Nolan steadied his breathing.

Father Raymond nodded stiffly as Cleary Nolan hurried through the doorway. This, he decided, was not going to be a pleasant meeting. He followed Raymond across the hall to the bishop's office. The door was already ajar, but no voices came from inside. Both the bishop and attorney were seated silently behind the large desk. One chair was set in front of the desk.

The assistant nodded to the bishop as he turned to leave, pulling the door closed as he went out.

The bishop wasted not a single moment on pleasantries or manners. "I had a call yesterday afternoon from Father Lewis Andrews over in Lillehammer. He said you had been there and asked some pretty interesting questions about a former student. At first, he thought your visit and inquiries kindly, but he asked why you hadn't just called the girl's parents instead, had you been so worried about her. Your trolling for information was thinly veiled, Nolan."

The bishop paused only to clear his throat. "You and I have not had a direct conversation about this young lady and the apparent reason for her compromised situation. And I didn't have to read between the lines to know that your Father Andrews had made some accusations about why you would sneak around for information instead of speaking directly to the family. I've already met with the girl's mother, father, and even her aunt. I cannot tell you how upset I am that this diocese must deal with something so shameful and disgusting. I have not yet decided how we will handle the family, but I know how I am going to handle *you* and your transgressions."

The bishop's face, red from anger continued,

"I have already spoken with the staff at a counselling center in West Texas. They admit priests who need to get their lives straightened out and receive counselling," the bishop said, his voice stone. "You are relieved of your pastoral duties at St. Michael's and your station as rector of the high school, both effective immediately. You will probably be in therapy and counselling for at least two months, maybe longer. I pray to God that they will be successful in curing you of these horrible sins of the flesh. You have violated your vow of celibacy. I pray this was a one-time failing, but based on the details I've heard and your cavalier attitude toward what you've done and who you've hurt, I seriously doubt this was the first time you've tried something this evil."

"This girl's mother was here the very day she found out her daughter was pregnant. She was unspeakably angry. Your actions have created a crisis that could easily cause irreparable scandal in our diocese. Due to this potential harm, I cannot assign you to a local counsellor. I am sending Father Raymond with you on the trip out to Texas. While Raymond prepares for the trip, our attorney will go with you to your parish so you can pack. The things you will not be taking with you will be boxed and brought to the chancery for safe-keeping until you return. Obviously, you will not go to that parish or school ever again."

Father Nolan realized he hadn't said a single word since arriving at the bishop's office. Was he not allowed to explain why he visited Andrews? Or defend himself against the girl's accusations?

"Also, I don't know how you found out about the box with the pajamas, or perhaps you just remembered what you'd left behind, but our office learned that someone broke into the home where the girl had lived. The police report we have said person or persons unknown had broken into the house, apparently using a key taken from a rack near the front door. There was no forced entry and the person stole nothing, as they hadn't found what they were looking for. A family member said that several days before that incident, someone tried to unlock the front door while she was spending the night there. The burglar apparently got away before squads pulled up. She was the one who reported the eventual break-in and damage to her mother's house. Do I need to ask who might have been responsible for those two events?"

The bishop was glaring at Nolan by this point. "I also have come to understand that you drove to the girl's family farm and forced your way in and spoke harshly to the girl. The dad told me that you demanded that she stop making false accusations against you. And apparently you've somehow found it appropriate to continue stalking the family's house."

Cleary Nolan was so dumbfounded by the bishop's knowledge that he didn't trust himself to dispute any of it. Nolan didn't remember how many other times he'd had his way with unconscious females, but this was the first time one had gotten pregnant. And the bishop knew all of it and needed no confirmation from Nolan.

The attorney stood up, advising the bishop that he and Father Nolan would have to leave if they were to make the train after packing and picking up Father Raymond.

"I want you to leave your car keys with me," the bishop said to Nolan. "I will have your car brought here and put in a garage until you return. That way there will be no need for you to go back to that parish and school when you return."

The bishop rose to his feet. "I will pray for your safe journey," he said half-heartedly, extending his hand across the desk. "Father Raymond will stay with you for a couple of days until you are settled into treatment. When the doctors are ready to release you after you complete your therapy, Raymond will go out there so he can travel back to Wisconsin with you. They said you were expected to bring your clerical vestments so you could say daily Mass in their chapel. Take your breviary and any other reading material you might find useful. They have a rather extensive library of scriptural readings and therapy-related books to aid their patients. I expect you will treat this assignment as any other you have been given in your vocation. I expect to hear from your doctors and therapists about your cooperation. And I also expect to hear from you at least once a month so I know how you are doing."

"Thank you, Excellency," Father Nolan said quietly as he laid his car keys on the corner of the desk. He held onto the ring of keys for the church, school, and rectory. He promised to leave them on the dresser in his bedroom.

He felt tears well up in his eyes, but he was too embarrassed to even brush them away. He thought of his mother; could the souls in heaven actually see and know what their family and friends did in secret on earth? He could still see the look on his mother's face when he'd offered his first Mass in their home parish. He remembered celebrating the Mass for her funeral. He didn't remember ever straying from his vows while she was still on earth. Could he change his ways? Would God even forgive what he'd done?

The ride out to his parish was long and uncomfortable for both the attorney and his priestly charge. Neither talked until they reached the rectory. The attorney sat on the bed, watching as the priest folded his clothes neatly into a large leather suitcase. He'd forgotten to bring the key for the sacristy, but there was an extra one on the key rack near the back door and another in the top desk drawer.

He took the smaller of his suitcases over to the church when they went to pick up his vestments. He looked around sadly as he went into the sanctuary to kneel and pray. He had used this suitcase whenever he said Mass at other churches or events. He carefully wrapped the chalice in a square of flannel and laid it atop the vestments. There wasn't anything else he needed. Whatever was in his office at the school would just be packed up by someone and stored at the chancery.

"Has someone notified the housekeeper that I won't be here when she comes in this afternoon? She has a key to get into the rectory," Nolan asked the attorney. "And what about morning Mass tomorrow? Do I need to leave a note on the front door that Mass is canceled?"

"The Bishop has all that arranged," the attorney replied curtly. "None of that concerns you any longer."

The reality of that left Nolan devastated. The comfort he'd always felt in his faith, especially when he could kneel before the altar and talk things over with God, had been stripped away in a one short, swift meeting.

If it hadn't been for his visit to Andrews the day before, Father Nolan thought he might have gotten away with it. But his clumsy efforts to get information about the girl and breaking into the aunt's house were too damning to ignore. He could have argued, but he knew he'd never change the bishop's mind. There was no choice but to accept his banishment to the counselling center out in Texas.

The two were already on their way back to the chancery when Nolan realized he didn't have any money in his wallet. He knew the attorney would not detour to the bank so he could make a withdrawal. How was he supposed to get money?

"The Chancery has made arrangements to have an account set up at the center in Texas for you, if needed," the attorney said.

Nolan felt like a disobedient child going to summer camp without money to buy treats. He also knew he was being treated far better than he deserved. He desperately wanted to hide where no one could find him. Then he remembered the blue and yellow afghan his mother had made for him the first year he was at Saint Michael's. He'd left it on the couch in his office at the rectory. "I wish I'd brought my mother's afghan," he said, barely above a whisper. He didn't care if the attorney heard him. But the attorney did hear and made a mental note to tell the bishop to send the afghan to this difficult priest.

Ψ

Annalise wasn't sure how to get the addresses of the Amish families so she could send thank-you notes for the beautiful baby bed and handmade quilt. The crib was big enough that Katherine could use it for several years. She still found it hard to believe they'd arranged such a wonderful surprise for her and the baby.

Annalise hadn't noticed the car that slowed down as it drove past the party, but Gerrit had—and he knew who was behind the wheel. He couldn't imagine what the priest thought he could accomplish by driving up there again. Gerrit didn't tell anyone what he'd seen.

Soon after Gerrit got to his office at the courthouse on Monday, his phone rang.

It was Chandler. "How'd the surprise party for Annalise and the baby go yesterday?"

"Our family was completely surprised," Gerrit chuckled. "We thought we were just going to have a picnic lunch with Helen's family. The party was wonderful. How did you find out?"

"Helen invited us to the gathering, but we had other plans and couldn't change them. We were very sorry to miss such a momentous occasion. Not to detract from that, but I was wondering if you knew who was in the area again yesterday."

"Would you believe I saw his car go by as the Amish were loading up to head home? I don't think he saw me standing at the back corner of Helen's house. He slowed down to see what all the activity was about. How did you know he was here?"

"I had to stop at the rectory to drop off some paperwork for Father Andrews. He mentioned that he'd had a visitor the day before that puzzled—

no—distressed him. He said he'd been so concerned about it that he called the chancery office of the man's diocese and voiced his concerns to the bishop. Seems his visitor was wondering if our pastor knew anything of a young girl who had gone to a Catholic high school in Milwaukee but dropped out to go home. He told our Father Andrews that he'd heard the girl was ill or something and wondered if she was okay. At first, Father said he didn't think much about it, but after the priest left, he thought the whole episode very strange. If a former student had left your school to go home and now you heard she was ill, wouldn't you just pick up the phone and call her family? Father Andrews said he had a troubling suspicion he knew why the priest was digging around."

"When Father told me he'd called the bishop from the Milwaukee diocese, I could tell from his voice that he'd figured out what was behind the situation," Chandler said gravely. "While he sounded distressed that the priest was nosing around asking questions in another diocese, he never let on that he knew the priest had fathered a baby with a young student. Andrews was left with the notion that this priest was in a heap of trouble."

"Do you ever get a lunch break, or do you see patients straight through?"

"I don't have regular hours on Thursday, so maybe this Thursday would be a good time to have lunch and talk some of this over at the back table at the café."

"I'll put it on my calendar. By the way, Kate is just blossoming. She is re-learning a lot of words and phrases and carrying on regular conversations. You should have seen her chatting with the Amish women. She had this beautiful, bright, happy smile. That baby is truly an angel in Kate's life. You've done wonders for getting her on the road to health, but little Katherine is the best medicine Kate could possibly have right now. I owe you more than I can ever repay for helping Annalise carry that baby. Regardless of all the sad details."

"See you Thursday," the doctor said and hung up.

When driving back to the farm that evening, Gerrit and Fletcher were still wondering at the rare occasion they'd been part of on Sunday afternoon. Gerrit was thankful he had something else to focus on besides the unresolved issues with the bishop about the priest's baby. Those unanswered questions still disturbed his sleep. Not that they couldn't cover the bills—they would—but the person responsible for his daughter's pregnancy was still liable.

Annalise was parked in her mom's lawn chair, enjoying the shade under the canopy of the large red maple on the front lawn. She had Katherine, wrapped in a light blanket, snuggled in her arms. Seeing her sitting so contentedly, Gerrit found it hard to remember the months she'd spent trapped in bed. He knew Katherine was Anna's daughter and he was the baby's grandfather, but he had trouble keeping those roles straight in his mind. For now, he thought of himself as a father to both Anna and Katherine. In the days before she was born, Gerrit and Kate regarded themselves as proxy parents of Anna's baby. But Kate's dream of helping Annalise raise her baby was sidetracked when she suffered the stroke. Her therapy had been going well, but she was still a long way from recovered. It would be a long time before she would be able to take over the baby's care so Annalise could go back to school.

Annalise waved as they drove into the yard. Fletcher hurried across the lawn to check out the baby.

"No one even notices me," Anna whined for sympathy and couldn't help laughing at her performance. "She's rested so comfortably out here this afternoon. Momma was napping while Aunt Ida telephoned Emily, but then I think she got supper started. It's such a beautiful day. And, speaking of beautiful, isn't Katherine just too lovely?"

Who could disagree?

"By the way," Gerrit said, pulling a piece of paper out of his suitcoat pocket, "I found the addresses and names for all the families at the party yesterday at the deeds office. You can get your notes written, and if you have them ready by morning, I can mail them in town; otherwise, we'll get them in the mail on Wednesday."

When Annalise got up to walk toward the house, Katherine woke up and made known that she was hungry.

"Thought we could use a pot of vegetable stew for supper," Ida said, setting the Dutch oven on the porch table. Kate found her own way out to the porch and sat next to Annalise so she could watch the baby drink her supper. With everyone around the table, life had found a normal routine again. Fletcher spotted Anna's daybook turned upside down at the end of the table. He pretended to be reading it, then laughed as she snapped it shut and put it down next to her plate.

"I wish I knew what you're always writing about," he said. "Mom tried to get me to keep track of my days, but I always just remember them in my mind."

"Ha!" Annalise scoffed and then laughed. "Katherine will be able to read about my life long after I'm gone," she said happily. "And when she reads my story, she'll also be reading hers."

"And you all will be able to read all about my life—and yours—long after I'm gone," Kate chimed in.

"Did your mother ever tell you why she started her book, or why she called it the Book of Days?" Gerrit asked his children.

Annalise had, but Fletcher had never been curious about the notebooks Kate filled year after year.

Gerrit explained: "When your mother first came to live in this house and I went back to Chicago to work at the bank, she didn't have a calendar. As the days went by, she didn't know if it was Sunday or Tuesday. So, she asked the Iversens to buy her some little notebooks at the shop in town so she could keep track. Of course, she had to have pages to write on. And upstairs in the closet under the eaves are all those books of her life on the farm with Fletcher, and later with you, Anna. I've been trying to keep her current by writing some entries and dates for her. But I think she's soon going to be writing them again."

Ψ

Fletcher and Doctor Chandler arrived at the café at the same time for their appointment.

"I figured if we combined our meeting with lunch, I could turn a half-hour into an hour," Chandler said. "Besides, I had a second invitation for a meeting recently, so I figured I'd combine them into one for today. Hope you don't mind."

They walked through to the far back corner where they'd have some privacy. As they approached the booth, Fletcher caught sight of someone already waiting there. Pops! He was a little taken aback, but then started to laugh. Seems like father and son had some of the same questions to ask.

Before the waitress brought menus and word of the daily special, Fletcher explained to Gerrit that he'd wanted a Catholic's viewpoint on the issues their family had struggled with for so many months, and this meeting would hopefully answer some questions.

The waitress brought three menus to their booth. "Daily special today has two options: a bowl of vegetable soup, or a bowl of vegetable soup with an egg salad sandwich."

Ordering was easy—three specials: soup and egg salad sandwiches, with coffee and water, all around.

When she'd gone back to the kitchen, Gerrit and Chandler leaned in to start their conversation where Fletcher left off.

"I had another chance to talk with Father Andrews about Father Nolan visiting him last Sunday," Chandler said. "The bishop told Father he relieved Nolan of both his rector and parish duties and sent him on a therapy sabbatical to a clinic in West Texas. Our pastor said he got the impression that the bishop expects Nolan won't be back in his diocese any time soon. I know that the reason for the priest's departure was a 'scandalous situation.' Father Nolan traveled with the bishop's assistant. This was not something they deal with very often at the clinic. Still, the counselor reassured him that several therapists had the credentials to work on sexual assault problems."

"Are you telling me Father Nolan has already gone to Texas?" Gerrit asked.

Chandler nodded. "He should be settled in by now. The Milwaukee bishop told Father Andrews he'd had a serious conversation with the priest. I think he went home to pack and then to the train station later that afternoon."

Gerrit seemed puzzled. "If that was his decision on how to deal with the perpetrator, why didn't he have the courtesy to let us know? He told Ida and me he couldn't believe a priest could ever do such a thing. And then he gets a phone call from a priest in another diocese and he ships Cleary Nolan off to an in-house therapy clinic. I was angry before, but now I'm furious. With Father Nolan's forcing his way into our house and stalking us repeatedly in his car…just unbelievable!"

"Well, Father Nolan's been sent away," Chandler said with a nod.

"Puzzles me," Gerrit said. "Do you know whether people with these problems can ever be cured, even with a long course of therapy in a respected clinic?"

"I've been trying to find out what the prognosis is for such treatment. I've talked to several of my medical school colleagues who planned to offer counselling and therapy in their psychiatry practices. They didn't really have any studies to consult on the effectiveness of sexual-assault therapy. One did tell me he had a couple of patients referred to him for counselling.

Over coffee, Gerrit wondered aloud, "Now what? Should I call the bishop again and make another plea for the diocese to provide for Annalise's medical care and Katherine's child support?"

Chandler answered swiftly. "You know I don't expect you to pay for my visits out to the farm and for other expenses related to Annalise. I know the hospital will have to send you a bill or two for both Kate and Annalise's stays, but you are not going to get a bill from me. I'm sure Dr. Wetzel will probably send you some bills. So far as Anna is concerned, you don't need to ask the diocese to reimburse you for my checkups. I'd send the hospital bills to them and let them know you expect that they will provide payment."

"Yes, but how do I approach that? Perhaps I should alert the bishop that those will be coming."

"If there is any hope that you will see even one thin dime for the hospital bills, you'd better advise him you intend to send them to his attention," Chandler said. "It certainly will draw a few raised eyebrows if he puts through a bill for a hospital in another diocese for a pregnant, fourteen-year-old student from a Catholic high school. Of course, the business office is certainly aware a priest has been sent away for counselling and a new rector was assigned to the high school. Tongues always wag."

"That's what I'm worried about—that gossip getting up here and reaching Anna," Gerrit said sadly, picking up his spoon and stirring his empty cup.

"I think we need a second cup, don't you?" Chandler asked lightheartedly.

Gerrit realized the foolishness of stirring an empty cup. "You can see how the stress of this whole situation has played with my brain."

"You've had more than a few stressful situations on your mind for weeks," Chandler observed. Before continuing, he motioned to the waitress to bring another round of coffee.

"Actually, what have you got to lose by contacting the bishop?" Chandler inquired. "You can merely reach out and remind him, although I'm sure he hasn't forgotten, that you are still waiting to hear from him."

They sat quietly for a few minutes. The restaurant's lunch crowd had cleared out. Gerrit told his secretary that he had an important luncheon meeting and might not be back for a good hour or more.

"On another subject," Chandler segued, "Annalise has come through all of this chaos with an excellent attitude. I can't tell you how impressed I was that she refused to have an abortion or consider adoption. She's mentioned more than once to me how important it will be for her mother to have a new little baby to help raise. I think with the way your family works, that plan isn't beyond belief. There is often such a contentious attitude when it comes to these pregnancies outside of marriage. Families often break up over them, and even if they don't, those lingering issues never quite go away."

Gerrit smiled. "Kate has been so much better this week. It's as if she has a new purpose. And she's thrilled about it."

"I thought I'd drive out early Saturday morning to check on them. I know Kate still needs to see the cardiologist, but I want to see how the speech therapy is working."

By the changing expressions on his face, Gerrit seemed to be having an argument with himself. Finally, his scowl fell away, and he smiled. "I think

I need to go home early this afternoon so I can call the bishop in private. I need to let him know, without betraying your confidence, that I'm aware of Nolan's departure. I'll broach the subject of the hospital bills for Annalise. I'm going to tell him I would've appreciated hearing all of this directly from him, but that's neither here nor there."

"You can give me an update on Saturday," Chandler said with a nod.

They finished their coffee, then discussed a possible date for some fishing. With all the complications that summer, they hadn't even dug a can of worms, much less gathered up their fishing gear to spend a whole day cooling their heels alongside a lake.

Anna saw her dad's car make the turn at the mailbox corner. She could hardly wait to tell him what had happened that day. By the time he turned into the driveway, she'd hurried out to tell him the big news.

"Poppa, guess what?" she said, opening his car door before he'd even turned off the engine. "I think I can go to school this fall. We had company this afternoon. Sarah and her mom came over. They drove their little buggy all by themselves."

Anna hurriedly explained, not yet letting Gerrit out of his car: "Mrs. Mellen had an idea all figured out. If Sarah could ride with me and you into town and we brought her back at night, she would repay us by doing our laundry every week. Now here's the best part: if she does the laundry, that will be one less thing Aunt Ida has to worry about. And since Mom is getting better, she can hold the baby and feed her sometimes. She and Aunt Ida think I can go to high school with Sarah because they would only have the baby to take care of. What do you think?"

Gerrit was speechless as they walked to the porch. Kate and Ida had come out, too.

Fletcher, who'd followed them inside, had a lot to say. "How's Sarah's mom going to do all our washing and still get her own work done? And I didn't think Amish kids went to high school. She could ride in with us, but will the Amish bishop and elders allow her to attend high school?"

Finally, Gerrit found his words. "We have chores to oversee and supper to eat. This will take some serious talking before we can decide what's going to happen."

Katherine had a few things of her own to yowl about, too. Even Kate laughed at the baby's inserting herself into the conversation.

Gerrit and Fletcher changed into their barn clothes and headed across the farmyard to check on Sarah's older brother, who was already halfway finished with the milking. Gerrit's nightly job was doing his usual walkabout to check on things. Fletcher had his own assigned routine in the milk house. He was anxious to finish up and get back to the house to find out what Aunt Ida made for supper.

Anna tended the baby, then pulled a rocker over to the end of the table so she could feed her while the others ate. She'd eat later when Fletcher came in. Aunt Ida and Kate had made chicken and dumplings with a plate of fresh tomato slices from the garden. With a little help from Anna, Kate had made a chocolate cake for dessert—a rare treat during the week.

Finally, the conversation worked its way back to the unexpected change in school plans for Anna and Sarah. What days would the family's laundry be done, and how could they possibly keep up with the baby's never-ending pile of soiled diapers, sleepers, and blankets? How would Sarah get to their house early enough so they would all get to where they were going on time? Had the Mellen family already worked out the arrangements with their church to let Sarah go to high school? Could Anna really be able to start school in a couple of weeks, or would Dr. Chandler want her to stay home a while longer?

Gerrit was reminded of Chandler's plan to drive out on Saturday morning. They'd have to see what he had to say about leaving the baby with Aunt Ida and Kate while she was still so little. Laundry was a big problem, especially when winter set in and there was no place to get the clothes dried. Kate used to have clotheslines stretched upstairs in Fletcher's room for drying clothes in winter. That certainly wouldn't work with having Mrs. Mellen come in to do the wash, then traipse through the whole house to get upstairs where it could be hung up to dry.

They still hadn't come to a decision on school, laundry, and the baby after they'd finished eating and clearing up.

"I never realized how much bother a baby could cause when it comes to laundry," Anna lamented.

Gerrit had completely forgotten about his lunch with Chandler earlier that day. He'd been so anxious to tell them what he'd found out about the priest. Now, he knew, wasn't a good time to start that conversation. They'd be up until ten o'clock. That update would have to wait until later.

Anna carried Katherine upstairs to put her in the new crib. She was so exhausted from the excitement that filled their day that she called down the stairs to let them know she was going to pull her shade and crawl into bed. But she would obviously be down again a little later to get a fresh bottle from the icebox when the baby woke for her midnight snack.

Later, Poppa came upstairs to wake her after the phone had rung. Anna looked around groggily. Then he said he had something important to tell her and wanted her to come downstairs so they could talk without waking Katherine. Still only half awake, she checked the baby, then followed her dad downstairs. Waiting there were Kate, Ida, and Fletcher. She looked around at each but couldn't figure out whether their facial expressions were happy or distressed.

Gerrit's desk chair squeaked and groaned as he sat down. Anna switched off the overhead light that cast a hard shadow around the room and turned on the lamps on the sideboard and Gerrit's desk. She pulled out a chair from those lined up around the oval dining room table and sat down.

"We just received a call from Emily," he said in Ida's direction. "She wanted to tell me first, knowing I could explain it to all of you. As it turns out, it was the same information I found out earlier today when Fletcher and I had lunch at the diner with Chandler. This conversation needs to stay in this room. At some point, we will need to let Helen know what has happened, since she has been so involved in helping us deal with all this. But Emily's call moved up my plan by a few hours, as you'd all be wondering what she needed."

Gerrit cleared his throat and laced his fingers in his lap. "Some things were apparently underway last Sunday while we were at Helen's for the baby shower. I'd seen a car slowly drive past her house while the Amish were getting ready to leave. I know I don't have to tell you whose car it was."

The family exchanged solemn glances.

Gerrit continued. "Chandler said that Nolan stopped at the parish rectory here and saw Father Andrews last Sunday. As I think you know, the Catholic church here is part of another diocese, not the one where the Catholic high school is. So, he really had no reason to be going to that parish office. This wasn't a social call, although Nolan tried to pretend it was. He was fishing for information about a former student from here who had attended Nolan's Catholic high school. He was worried about her, but we know that's not the case."

"Father Andrews told Chandler he couldn't figure out why the priest didn't call the girl's family to inquire about her health. Unless there was some connection between the girl's 'illness' and the priest. Then it all came into focus."

Gerrit exhaled heavily. "That visit had been so odd that Father called Milwaukee to let the bishop know what had just happened. Chandler said Father Andrews didn't have to explain why the visit was so upsetting. He said he could tell it was no surprise to the bishop."

Anna found herself balling her hands into fists so tight her nails dug into the palms of her hands. To keep from doing it again, she slid them under her legs. Aunt Ida reached over to hold her sister's hands in her own. Fletcher fidgeted.

Gerrit looked around. While they were discomfited by his news, no one dared look away. "

"He said the bishop was very quiet at first as Andrews talked and didn't say much in response. But later, the bishop called Andrews back, asking that the matter be kept in strictest confidence. Without admitting to anything, he said he'd talked with Nolan and had a meeting with him scheduled for early Monday morning to deal with issues about unauthorized calls looking for information from a pastor in another diocese. In clergy-speak, that seemed to be an admission that Father Andrews assumption was, in fact, right on the mark."

After a brief quiet, Gerrit unfolded his hands. "When I got home tonight, I fully intended to have this conversation with you, but you all had important news to share about Anna and Sarah. So, I thought I'd wait until morning to tell you all of this. But then Emily called. She'd played cards with a neighbor, and that neighbor passed along some very interesting information. Seems she's a member of that parish and has had children attending that high school. So, the word obviously has gotten around that the principal had been relieved of his duties because of illness and is now undergoing treatment. Of course, the families are all speculating what the illness is and asking if they can go to the hospital to visit him. They've heard that the bishop intends to visit their parish this coming Sunday to talk about Father Nolan's replacement principal and parish priest. Emily's neighbor seemed very distressed about it all and wondered what could have made the priest so sick in just a few days that he'd have to go away for treatment. Emily's neighbor speculated that Nolan had gotten too used to drinking the communion wine. She said she heard there was a clinic somewhere where they treated priests and other clergy who had drinking problems. Obviously, we know the truth. And it's not a very comforting bedtime story, but at least we know the bishop has acted on what he has determined to be true. And whether they ever decide to pay Katherine's delivery bills or any child support is still a huge unknown. Also, I doubt an apology to Annalise will ever come."

The room's silence weighed heavily. No one spoke, and their faces reflected the contrasting sadness, relief, and anger inside them.

Gerrit admitted that he wasn't usually one to pray, but he encouraged everyone to join hands and talk to God in response to everything they'd suffered those past nine months. Kate squeezed his hand tightly. He led his family: "Heavenly Father. We tried desperately to cope with the rape of our daughter. Our Annalise would not hear of having the unborn baby destroyed, nor even given up for adoption. That we regard as a blessing for her and for our family. Thank you for Katherine's safe delivery and for the news that the person responsible for all our anguish and worry is now undergoing treatment. We ask your blessings that his treatment will be successful and that he will never do this terrible thing to anyone else. We ask for your blessings on us, especially for the recovery of our Kate, and in deep appreciation for her sister, Ida, who has come to help us as we move into a new and expanded family. We also beg your help in the newest plan with getting Anna back to school and Nellie's efforts to help us here on the farm. Amen."

The sun had barely poked its head above the horizon when Anna got her wakeup call from Katherine. She was not to be trifled with this morning. She was hungry. Wet. And not at all interested in letting her mother sleep for just a few more minutes.

Anna tiptoed down the stairs with Katherine in her arms and went to the kitchen. She was relieved to see there was one bottle of formula left in the icebox. Warming it took longer than the baby was willing to wait. She waltzed the baby around the kitchen until the milk was warm, then tossed a clean dishtowel over her shoulder and headed out to the porch. She and Katherine settled in the rocker, and while the baby worked on emptying the bottle, Anna watched the sun come up. It was going to be a beautiful day.

Suddenly Anna realized she didn't know what day of the week it was. When she'd spent those long days in bed, she always had her notebook close by so she could compile daily records, her thoughts, her dreams about their future, and her worries about what had happened to her. Now that the baby was here, she tried to focus on her, not on that awful night back in Milwaukee.

She often wondered what Momma had written about during the early years on the farm. Did she revisit the childhood dreams she left behind when she and little Fletcher moved to the farm? Did she have regrets about how her life turned out? That she hadn't gone to college? That she lived so far from the sheltered life of the parsonage that she couldn't go there for a Sunday dinner after church?

Katherine, finished with her bottle, had fallen asleep. Anna could hardly believe the changes she saw in her since that Friday night three weeks ago when she'd first held her. Even her head felt heavier in the crook of her arm.

Was this Friday or Saturday? If it was Friday, Poppa would be going into town for work. He'd be getting up soon. If it was Saturday, they should all be getting up because Dr. Chandler would be coming to check on the baby and her Grandma Kate. But, regardless of the day, she didn't have the energy to get up out of the rocker and carry the baby back to bed.

When Gerrit came through to the porch, he was surprised to see Anna and the baby in the rocker. Ida, busy in the kitchen making coffee and toast, poked her head out and waved good morning. Fletcher straggled to the porch, waving a slice of toast in Anna's direction as a greeting. It was Friday, since Fletcher was on his feet and downstairs. Finally, Kate came out, excited to see the baby but disappointed she was asleep.

When they all sat down to breakfast, Anna asked if they could go into town later to register for school—and if Sarah and Nellie could go with them. After a call to Helen and some organizing, it was determined that Helen would take Nellie, Sarah, Kate, and Annalise into town. Sarah was thrilled.

Helen also called the high school to make sure someone would be in the office after lunch to register incoming students. Ida said she'd have lunch ready at noon so everyone could eat before venturing to town. Even though Anna wanted to look for school supplies, too, that would have to wait for another day.

The high school office staff was a little surprised to see Anna and Sarah together, but when they explained that they were neighbors and would be riding to school together, it seemed an obvious solution. A long buggy ride into town and home again twice a day would be a struggle, the school's vice-principal agreed, especially in winter.

Helen helped Kate fill out Anna's papers and counted out the money for the school fees. The staff's secretary asked if it was okay to put down an emergency telephone number for Sarah. Helen suggested putting her number down since she was almost always available to get in her car and drive up the hill to relay a message to Nellie.

Sarah noticed books piled on the counter. She walked over to those labeled as textbooks for ninth grade. This was old news for Anna, who wondered if they'd be able to take a quick walking tour of the freshman wing so Sarah would know where she was going when they arrived for the first day of school. She needn't have worried, since the school had arranged a welcome party for new students the Friday before school started. Anna, who'd only been there a few days before she'd dropped out when put on bed rest, was also welcome to attend. The vice-principal remembered her and said she looked so much better than she did last winter. She also asked about Fletcher and his college plans.

They spent so much time at the school chatting and filling out papers that Nellie said maybe they should head home so Kate could rest. "You're looking a little tired," she said. Helen agreed.

They were halfway down the steps when Anna remembered the lists of supplies they'd need. She hurried back up to the office where she grabbed the supply lists for herself and Sarah.

"Maybe my dad would drive us into town on a Saturday so we can go shopping for paper and notebooks," she said, handing Sarah her packet.

"That sounds like a good plan," Sarah agreed, looking anxiously at her mother.

"Why not?" Nellie said.

Sarah and Anna sat together in the backseat, whispering while their moms and Helen talked about gardens and flowers and Helen's remaining moving plans. All too soon they were back on Cedar Road. First stop: the Mellen farm, where girls in long blue skirts and bonnets waited with their brothers who wore dark-blue shirts with knickers held up with black suspenders, high-top black shoes, and straw hats. Sarah hesitated before getting out of the car. She took Anna's hand in her own and held it tightly for a few seconds. The girls had been whispering about getting bicycles so they could ride back and forth between their houses when they didn't have chores or schoolwork to do. That would also be a good way for Sarah to get down the hill to Anna's house in the morning and back home late in the afternoon—while the weather was good, of course. Sarah's mom didn't even shake her head in disapproval. Sarah had officially become a high school student. Well, almost.

"We forgot to ask if any other Amish would be attending high school," Anna whispered to Sarah.

"Samuel is for sure," she said. "He even wants to go on to college, just like Fletcher."

"Wow! How interesting," Anna said brightly. "I'm going to ask Poppa about the bikes tonight. Maybe we can find some at the second-hand store in town. I heard him say the other day that companies were having to make war materials like tanks and airplanes and such and would not be making any new bicycles 'for the duration,' whatever that means. I sure hope the war doesn't last a long time. But if we can get used bikes, I know we can get them fixed up, if needed."

"Sarah, Annalise and her mom have to get home. The baby is probably up from her nap. Save something to talk about next time," Nellie chided, laughing. "Girls are girls, whether they're Englishers or Amish," she whispered to Helen and Kate.

Ida had come out to the car to help her sister get into the house. "How did registration go?" she asked.

"Easy," said Kate.

"Sarah was so excited," Annalise added. She spoke excitedly at Ida about the new student orientation.

Annalise heard the baby inside. "I missed you," she called out to her daughter. "I'm coming."

August 25ᵗʰ, 1944

Dear Days,

Sarah and I registered for school today. She's a freshman and will ride with us when Poppa goes to work and home again in the afternoon. Poppa agreed I could get a bike so we can ride between our places and Sarah could ride here in the morning and back home at night so we wouldn't have to drive up there. Poppa doesn't mind, though, and thinks we might enjoy it. Provided we can find a couple used bikes for sale. Dad said he will drive me and Sarah into town tomorrow morning to check the thrift store. Please, let them have two girl's bikes!

Baby Katherine is growing. I think she even smiles sometimes. Mostly, she likes to eat when I rock her. I still can't believe she's here. She's so beautiful. Her hair is dark and looks like it might even be curly. Not like my coarse blond straw.

Love,

Annalise

The next morning, Sarah was finishing her breakfast-time chores when Annalise and her father arrived to take her bike shopping.

Nellie was pleased to see them. "Of course, Sarah can leave as soon as she finishes tidying up. She's been so excited about school, about a bike, about having Anna as her real friend. There aren't any Amish girls her age close by. I don't know how to make arrangements to pay for a bike. Did you find out how much they cost?"

Gerrit shook his head. "Don't worry," he said. "We can settle up later. When I called the store, the clerk said they just came in late yesterday. We must get there soon so they don't get snatched up."

The two girls in the backseat never stopped talking. Gerrit was impressed by their shared ability to find new topics.

Harley Hansen at the second-hand store said the bikes had belonged to twin girls who'd left for college and didn't need them.

Harley helped Gerrit fit the bikes into the car trunk. The lid couldn't close, so he got a piece of heavy binder twine from the shop and tied it down so it wouldn't pop up. Every so often along the drive home, one of the girls would kneel on the backseat so she could peek under the lifted lid at their bikes. The matching bicycles were blue and had baskets for carrying things.

"I can put my books in there when I ride down the hill in the morning," Sarah said.

"We can put your bike in the garage alongside mine while we are gone to school," Anna said. "I don't think Ida will get herself on a bike anytime soon, so it should be left alone." Both girls giggled.

It had been such a long time since Gerrit had heard Anna laugh. Hearing it again reminded him of how down she'd gotten during so many months in bed.

Sarah tried to convince Gerrit that she could ride her new bike home from their house, but Gerrit wouldn't have it. He wanted to make sure Sarah's mom approved of the color.

Nellie not only liked the color—she was very happy with the condition of the bikes. "Girls are usually much more careful with things than the boys," she said. "Now, how much do I owe you?"

Gerrit smiled. "These bikes are a wonderful investment for these two girls. It was my pleasure to buy one for Sarah. Remember the day when she stayed with Anna when that priest pushed his way into our house? Consider the bike a thank-you present for your daughter's courage and kindness."

Nellie nodded with a knowing smile, even though she would again try to repay Gerrit later, regardless. They had barely driven down the hill and into their driveway when they turned to see Sarah flying behind them on two wheels. *When did she learn to ride a bicycle?* Anna wondered. Sarah didn't even wobble on the gravel. Anna knew she'd have to practice riding in the farmyard for a few days before she'd attempt riding on the road.

Sarah followed them all the way home. When they went inside to check on the baby, the girls parked their bikes side-by-side along the porch steps.

"Look how big Katherine is," marveled Sarah, peeking into the day crib in the parlor. "It's only been a few days since the party, and she's already changed so much. I don't remember Momma's babies getting so big so fast. Or maybe my memory isn't the best."

More giggles ensued.

Kate was surprised to see the girls back from town.

Ida came out from the kitchen. "How did you get here so fast?" she asked. "Did you ride your bikes all the way from town?" Then she laughed at that idea.

When Katherine opened her eyes, Sarah leaned over to pick her up. "I've had lots of practice holding and feeding babies. I can even change them, and when they get a little older, Momma lets me help with their bath. Do you have a little wash basin, or will you bathe her in the kitchen sink? I think Momma still has the tub left from Johnny."

Anna pointed at a hook on the back of the door in the bedroom. There was a brand new basin, just the right size for a baby. Still more giggles.

Sarah changed Katherine's diaper, then eased into the rocker next to Gerrit's Morris chair. Katherine was a little annoyed at having to wait for her bottle, but Sarah's soothing voice calmed her until Anna returned. While Sarah rocked and fed the baby, Anna curled up in the Morris chair. Next to the rocker on the porch, this big chair was her favorite spot in the house.

"I have to be home in time to help get lunch on the table," Sarah said as she handed the baby back to Anna for burping. "I think I'd better get going. Thank you for letting me feed your baby, and especially thank your Poppa again for my bicycle." Sarah stopped in the kitchen to say goodbye to Ida, and again on the porch to wave to Kate. She was about to ride away when she caught sight of Anna's dad heading toward the house. "Goodbye," she called. "Thank you so much for my bicycle. I don't know how to tell you how happy I am to be able to ride down the road to visit Anna."

He waved goodbye with a smile as the young girl headed toward the road. He thought of the rather steep incline she would face before she got to her driveway, but with the amount of energy she had, there was no reason to worry.

The next afternoon after the family got home from Sunday service, Sarah was back. "I can stay for one hour," she said. "I told Momma I wanted to help you learn to ride a two-wheeler. She didn't know I'd practiced on Aaron Wolter's bike during recess at school."

The two girls traveled from the porch steps to the road and back. Annalise had asked Ida to let them know when an hour had passed. After Sarah left, Anna tried to ride her bike on her own, but she didn't quite have the knack. She promised herself she'd work on it a little every day. By the following Sunday, she was sure she could ride up the hill to Sarah's.

The following Saturday, Gerrit and Anna again drove up the road to collect Sarah for their trip into town to buy school supplies.

Fletcher used his mom's car to get to work. It would be his last day before heading off to college. He was anxious to leave early the next morning. It was only a two-hour drive, but he wanted to get moved into his dorm room and unpacked before it was time to go to orientation. Kate and Gerrit looked both sad and excited when everything was packed into Gerrit's sedan for the trip. Kate had wanted to make the trip, but by the time everything was packed into the trunk and the backseat, there was no room for a third passenger.

Just as well, thought Gerrit. *It would be too tiring for her.*

"I wish I'd packed a little tighter," Fletcher mumbled to himself. He had hoped his mom could ride along so she would know what his dorm room looked like.

"Poppa will bring me another time," she said. "I'd just be in the way today."

Part of Fletcher still wished he could've delayed his start until next term. Momma was better, but she wasn't entirely back to her old self.

Annalise carried the baby out to the driveway so she could wish him well. "Please write," she begged as she handed her brother a little package. "It's a little booklet so you can start your own Book of Days about college," she explained. "And I'll write you to let you know how Momma is getting along. And, of course, Baby Katherine, too. Good luck, Fletch. Maybe someday you'll have a car and you can come home on weekends. Providing you don't find a girlfriend." Annalise let out a teasing laugh to punctuate her goodbye.

The car left a swirl of dust in its wake as it went down the hill. Fletcher raised his arm out the window and waved one last time before they turned the corner.

"Well, he's finally heading off to school," Ida said, sighing. "I can't believe the day's finally here."

Ida watched the dust fade into the sunny air and then cleared her throat, pulling herself out of her thoughts. "So, since it's so nice outside, I thought we could have bag lunches under the big maple. We've got roast beef and at least three slices of apple pie. Iced tea or lemonade?"

"Lemonade is my vote," Anna said, and Kate nodded in agreement.

"I'll bring the buggy out so Miss Katherine can continue her nap in the shade. We'll probably have just enough time to eat before she'll want her lunch," Ida said and hurried inside to get started on the sandwiches.

The Amish buggies had all gone by before Gerrit returned. The girls had long-since finished lunch.

"We had no trouble getting everything hauled up to his room," he told Kate. "I would have started back right away, but Fletcher said most of the parents were staying around to have some refreshments as the orientation party started. I think he was just needing someone for a little moral support." Gerrit chuckled. "Besides, I wasn't going to turn down a big donut and a cup of coffee."

Annalise changed Katherine while Kate warmed the baby's bottle. They settled into the porch rocker in front of the window. Kate brought out a plate of oatmeal cookies along with the bottle. "I didn't let Fletcher take *all* the cookies with him," she said.

"What time does orientation start at the high school tomorrow?" Gerrit asked.

Annalise ran upstairs to get the list of supplies and other information so they would know when they were supposed to be there and when it would end. "We're finished at two both days," Annalise said as she came back out to the porch. "Wednesday, we'll be there until three thirty. So we can ride home with Poppa."

Annalise thought about her past first days of school. She was always eager to get to bed early the night before because morning would not take so long to arrive. She already had her clothes laid out. Her school supplies were packed. Even her new pencils were sharpened. "I don't think I have to take my book bag tomorrow, do you?" she asked.

"I wouldn't think so," was the consensus.

"You won't be having any classes tomorrow," Ida said. "By the way," she then added, "I've already changed Fletcher's bedding, so I'll be moving into his room tonight. I'll get up with Miss Katherine tonight so you can get a good rest. Your Momma and I will have nothing better to do tomorrow than take naps when baby naps."

The sun had vanished behind some roiling dark clouds.

"I'd better shut the garage door and get out to check on Noah in the barn," Gerrit said. "He'll probably need some help, since this is his first night without Fletcher to do the milk house cleanup."

The wind picked up. Ida pushed the buggy over to the porch steps, then went back to collect the last of the dishes on the picnic table. Annalise laid Katherine on the daybed and hurried back to help Ida lift the buggy into the house. The storm hit just as they got the porch door closed. Annalise had pulled down the windows, but rain had already splattered the sills.

"I think the windows are open upstairs," Annalise said as she hurried up the steps. Kate tried to manage the windows in the downstairs bedroom, but she didn't have the strength to push them down. The faraway thunder got louder and closer. Her mother, Anna noticed, was nervous. She'd never gotten over her fear of storms that had so frightened her when she and Baby Fletcher were alone.

Watching the rain pelt the windowpanes gave Ida the idea to make curtains for the porch that coming winter. That way they could be closed at night and whenever a storm passed over. Maybe they could measure how much yardage they'd need and buy the material when they picked up the girls on Monday or Tuesday afternoon. It would give Kate something to help with so she wouldn't worry about Fletcher being away at school. Kate didn't know if boys got homesick when they went away to college, but she knew she'd be missing her oldest child. She'd never known a day when he wasn't close by.

But the next day when Ida and Kate drove into town to pick up the girls from school, their planned shopping trip for curtain fabric was laid aside. The weather was just too nasty for shopping. And the next day wasn't any better. On Wednesday, the sun managed to poke through, but Sarah's mom was coming in the afternoon to talk about the arrangements for doing the laundry. Fabric could wait until Thursday, maybe. But Friday was the day when Nellie would be back to do the laundry. Unless it rained again.

Well, Ida thought, *we'll just be patient.*

Annalise tucked Katherine into her crib upstairs and came down again to take a bath. There wouldn't be time in the morning. "Could you listen for Katherine?" she asked Ida.

"Of course. I think I'll go upstairs and get ready for bed myself."

"I'll help Momma get ready for bed," Anna said. "Then you won't have to make another trip down."

Kate settled into the Morris chair, waiting for Anna to finish her bath.

By the time Gerrit got back to the house, the rainstorm had subsided. Listening at the bottom of the stairs he didn't hear a peep. *Goodness, even Ida's asleep*, he thought. He poured himself a glass of milk when he came in from the barn, drank it, and locked the door before hurrying off to bed. He thought of Fletcher away at school. What an adventure for him, but he was surprised at the gap that left in their lives. Especially Kate's. Even as a small boy, he always seemed to watch out for his mother. But Gerrit promised Fletcher that if Kate wasn't doing well, he'd call him to consider coming home. He knew Anna was so excited about going back to school, but if her mother needed her, she, too, would drop out to stay home.

Worry about all of that if and when the time comes, he thought to himself, yawning.

Another batch of lightning lit up the sky, but he was too sleepy to worry about it.

Sarah was sitting on the porch steps before anyone in the house seemed to be up and about. She'd gotten up early but only had to get dressed and eat a bite of breakfast. Since her mother was still asleep, she tiptoed through the house and out the front door. Her bike was waiting by the steps. The school had suggested in their note about the orientation that new students should bring a small notepad and pencil so they could write down information. She'd hooked the strap of her satchel onto the basket so it wouldn't bounce out on the bumpy ride down the hill. She'd forgotten to check the time before she left home.

Gerrit opened the door slowly when he started out on his morning trip to the barn where Noah would already be half-finished with chores. If he'd pushed his way out the door, as he usually did when he was behind schedule, he'd have knocked Sarah right off the top step. She jumped up as he hastily pulled the door shut again.

"Oh, my goodness," he said. "I wasn't expecting you already. What time did you get up?"

"I woke up early and dressed in a hurry. I didn't want to be late."

"I think Annalise might be up, but I'm sure she's planning to feed the baby before we go. Just go in and see if you can track her down. I didn't hear Katherine, so maybe neither of them is up."

But Sarah found Annalise in the kitchen testing to make sure the milk had warmed enough.

"I came early to feed the baby for you," Sarah said. "Not really, but I just couldn't wait to get here. And I might as well keep busy while you get ready."

"Be sure you take a towel, so she doesn't spit up on you. Sometimes she's so hungry for that early bottle that she just gulps it down. But I'm not telling you anything you don't already know."

It didn't take Annalise long to get dressed and find something for breakfast. Ida left a plate of cinnamon buns on the porch table. Annalise brought out two plates and scooped a bun onto each one. There was a plate of butter on the table, but neither of them used any. The baby had finished her breakfast and seemed to be watching the light shadows overhead as she lay on the day bed.

"I'm a little nervous about leaving the baby," Annalise confided to her friend. "She gets held by so many people that maybe she won't even notice I'm not here. Ida and Momma will drive in early this afternoon to pick us up."

Gerrit had come back to the house but didn't say anything when he went through to get dressed for work. The girls were so busy jabbering that they didn't even notice. Ida came out, dressed and ready for the day. Kate came a bit later, still in her housecoat and slippers. Ida carried out a cup of coffee for herself and another for Gerrit. Kate had a cup of milk with only a couple splashes of coffee—doctor's orders.

Sarah was so nervous that she'd be conspicuous because she was the only Amish student there. While Sarah stood, timidly watching the morning confusion, she was pleasantly surprised when two Amish buggies pulled up in front of the school and several students she recognized and waved to walked over to where she was standing. Sarah and her friends drifted away, and a slightly dismayed Annalise followed a few steps behind. When the bell rang, the students were directed to line up according to class. All the Amish students were in the first line—freshmen. Annalise had to go with the sophomore class. Alone.

Later, after students found their homerooms and signed in for attendance, they all went to the auditorium for a special welcome session. Before he started, the principal introduced himself, then asked each of the new students to stand and give their name, loud enough so everyone on the bleachers could hear. That worked for everyone else, but he made a special effort and invited the Amish students forward to be introduced. That done, he reminded the others that they were expected to show good manners toward one another. Anna didn't understand why the Amish had to be introduced separately. It must've made them feel like outsiders when the principal had to remind the other students to be nice to them. Englisher students joined the Amish group as they went to the lunchroom, though. They were all pleasantly surprised to see parents handing out paper sacks with sandwiches, apples, and cookies. Some of the older students helped pour milk.

When they went outside afterward, one freshman teacher encouraged them to introduce themselves to other students and get acquainted. The principal suggested they might check off the names of students they'd met so they would become more familiar with one another, even though most of the students had gone to grade school together.

It hadn't turned out quite the way Anna expected, but Sarah and her friends seemed happy. The only ones who crossed the line to be more welcoming seemed to be doing it out of a sense of obligation.

Oh, dearest God, Anna prayed. *Please let them welcome these students who have broken their faith traditions to continue their education beyond the first six grades. These students were anxious to learn more than just their separate lives on the farm.* Anna was determined to make this a wonderful year, not only for Sarah, but for all the Amish who had come into town for school. She wondered how many of the others, like Sarah, wanted an education so they could go on to college. Many, she knew, wanted to be teachers.

September 6, 1944

Dear Days,

Today was the first official day of school. Freshmen and new students already had a getting-acquainted day.

The first day of high school is a really big day for freshmen, but this year, it was really important for Sarah and the other Amish. They rarely go to school beyond eighth grade. But some wanted to go into nursing so they could help those in their community who needed more care when they were injured or sick. The Elders approved Sarah's request to go to high school so she'd qualify for nurses training. What neither she nor I knew was that quite a few other Amish also asked to continue their education for a variety of reasons. A few want to start a business and need more formal business education so they can do well in competition with Englishers. Several want to be teachers. When our Amish neighbors came to a baby shower for Katherine, I heard some moms talking about wanting a better education for their children. They weren't being critical of what was taught in the Amish school. One said that while the Amish still lived apart, they needed to know more than just the barest essentials if they were going to fare better in running a profitable farm or business.

I was excited to see so many taking more classes to make their own lives better. Seeing familiar faces put a big smile on Sarah's face. But not on mine. I know it's selfish, but I was happy to have a friend ride to and from school. I felt so out of place (even though no one except Sarah knew I had a baby at home), so it was nice to have someone to walk with when Poppa dropped us off. But when Sarah saw so many of her old friends, she went to stand with them as we waited for the bell to ring. All the kids I used to know in junior high moved on when I went away to school. When I came back, I was so worried they'd find out I was pregnant. Now that Katherine is here, I worry that they'll find out about her. So now I just stand alone, an outsider who doesn't fit in anywhere. It's as if they don't remember me.

Sarah worried how she'd fit in, but with a built-in group of Amish friends, she couldn't have been happier. The trouble is, I didn't fit in anywhere, with anyone. My dream of being able to continue going to school and feel like just another student during the day came to a screeching halt when Sarah left me standing alone. It was only when I got home that I knew where I belonged, and it wasn't with giggly teenagers who didn't have a little girl waiting for them to get home.

    Annalise

CHAPTER SEVENTEEN

Gerrit reviewed the notes he'd scribbled after his visit with the bishop early last summer. It wasn't the first time he'd referred to the notes he kept in his wallet. When he felt comfortable with his preparation, he put the call through to the bishop's personal number. He would ask for an accounting of the long-distance charges when he'd finished. He was a stickler for reimbursing the county for personal calls he made from his office phone, even those to the farm.

When the bishop's secretary answered, he was sure she'd find some reason why the bishop couldn't take the call. But she didn't. Almost immediately, the bishop picked up. When Gerrit identified himself, the bishop graciously said, "Good morning," and asked his reason for calling so early. He obviously recognized Gerrit's name and knew what he was calling about.

Gerrit reminded him it had been two months since he and his sister-in-law had met with him to discuss the unresolved issue of his daughter's rape and subsequent pregnancy by Father Nolan.

"Although my people have had several conversations, we haven't decided on anything and don't have any more to tell you," the bishop said.

Gerrit took a deep breath to settle his voice into its normal business cadence. "The reason for my call today is that I have learned some rather distressing news since Ida and I were last there. But I'm under the assumption that you already know that Cleary Nolan spent a decent amount of time casing our farmhouse. That leaves for me to mention Nolan's digging for information about our daughter with our local Father Andrews—which I'm also sure you're aware of."

The bishop said nothing in response, so Gerrit continued evenly. "I understand from people we know who live in Milwaukee that Nolan has been relieved of his duties and apparently sent to a West Texas counselling center."

Gerrit stopped, hoping that detail would cause the bishop to at least indicate he'd been listening. He still didn't.

"Given what we've learned," Gerrit pushed on, "it seems rather obvious your office has acknowledged his need for some serious counselling for a major infraction. We've heard that his parishioners and school faculty have been advised that he will not be returning to either serve the parish or school. So. Where does that leave us?"

Still no answer.

Gerrit swallowed and continued. "My wife and I would like to meet with you in the next week or two to discuss this situation, as it now stands. There are some serious financial issues that are still on the table. Could we meet with you and the attorney, perhaps this coming Friday morning? We have other information you need to know about, but I don't want to talk of that over the phone. However, if you choose not to meet with us, we will still be driving down later this week to meet with law enforcement and district attorney." *That* got the bishop's attention.

"I will clear my calendar for an hour-long appointment with you and your wife on Friday," the bishop said. "The exact time depends on when our attorney is available. If you give me your number, I will get back to either confirm a Friday appointment or try to work out something else."

After calling to get the phone charges, Gerrit grinned at his desk. He was almost certain there wouldn't have been any time if he hadn't tipped his hand.

Gerrit had his answer in less than a half hour. The bishop said the diocesan attorney could be at the chancery at ten a.m. Friday. After confirming the time, the bishop was cordial in asking Gerrit to relay his greetings to his wife and said he looked forward to seeing both of them again.

Gerrit already checked with Helen to make sure she could drive Annalise and Sarah to school Friday and pick them up after school. He figured Annalise would argue that she should come along, but he didn't want her missing school, and certainly didn't want to expose her to that situation. But since Kate and Gerrit would take baby Katherine with them to see the bishop, there was no reason for Anna to miss school.

He couldn't help wondering what the bishop would think of the house break-in and attempted break-in. Emily had picked up copies of the police reports on both investigations. Since they had no record of anything being taken, the police were still at a loss of who could have been responsible. But even more interesting would be to watch the bishop's and attorney's reactions when they saw the baby.

Before heading home, Gerrit dropped off an envelope at the bookkeeper's desk to pay the phone charges. He was anxious to get home to hear about the orientation for new students that Anna and Sarah had attended. He hoped Helen was planning to eat supper with them. He was sorry he'd forgotten to invite her when he talked to her that morning.

He stopped at the corner mailbox before turning up their road. Someone had either picked up the mail or they didn't get any. He was in hopes they'd at least get a postcard from Fletcher. He missed his son more than he'd expected.

Good, he thought as he pulled into the yard. *Helen's still here.*

Having company for supper made up for Fletcher's empty place at the table. Ida had outdone herself again with fresh baking powder biscuits, fried chicken, and milk gravy. There were also bright, fresh-sliced tomatoes from the garden and a bowl of cabbage slaw with carrots grated in. He didn't see any evidence of it, but he could tell by the smells from the kitchen that there was a cake somewhere.

Kate looked especially lovely when she came out to greet him at the door. She was getting around so much better these days. Speech was still a little slow, but whenever she had the baby in her arms she just beamed. It was still hard to believe that from the horrible nightmare their daughter had endured something so beautiful and wonderful had come.

Usually they didn't stop for a prayer of thanksgiving for the meal. This night, Gerrit reached out to take his wife's hand on one side and his daughter's on the other. Ida and Helen added their hands to the ring of prayer. Gerrit, head bowed, asked the Lord to bless those around the table, their son away at school, Ida's daughter Emily, and Helen's large family. Then he surprised himself. "And Lord, we ask you to bless Cleary Nolan. We ask you to help him as he faces the reality of what he's done to our daughter and to himself as a priest. We pray that his treatment will make him whole again and that in time he will find it in his heart to do what is right. We ask these things in your name. Amen."

A chorus of "Amen" rose from the group. Ida, looking both surprised and pleased, said, "Pastor Conner couldn't have said it any better. I think you must have been practicing meal prayers in your closet." That brought another chorus of "amen" from around the table.

Before they'd finished their stories and their meal, Katherine put up a fuss.

"Time for a change and a bottle," Annalise said, going to her daughter. She quickly changed her and handed her to Kate while she went to warm a fresh bottle. Helen asked if she could hold the baby for a few minutes before she had to leave.

Kate handed Helen the baby with a grateful smile, and when Anna came back with the bottle, she handed it to Helen who'd settled into the rocker to feed her.

Kate reached into her sweater pocket to retrieve the letter from Fletcher that arrived that afternoon. He'd always been a young man of few words, but school was having an interesting effect on him. Instead of the barest essentials, he rambled on about classes, teachers, kids he'd met, and homework, which was already in high gear.

With the baby settled in her crib upstairs and Anna getting herself ready for bed, the night sounds were calming and restful. Gerrit and Kate were back in their own bed for the first time in months. Ida had taken over Anna's old bedroom upstairs, and Anna and the baby were in Fletcher's room. Her little room was too small for both her bed and baby's crib, plus another dresser for baby's clothes.

Yawning, Anna ran through the day's highlights as she prepared to record them in her Book of Days for September before drifting to sleep.

Anna thought she'd be up and ready to leave long before Sarah arrived, but that didn't happen. Sarah's bicycle was already parked by the porch and she was perched on one of the steps. This time, Gerrit was expecting that she was out there as he quietly opened the door a crack to wish her good morning.

The girls chattered the whole trip into town. Sarah was talking about how they had to go from one classroom to another, not just sit in the same room all day. There were different students in each class, so she only occasionally had another Amish student in any of her classes.

When Gerrit dropped them off, he reminded them that he'd pick them up a little after four. If they were finished earlier, they should walk to the courthouse and wait there.

Sarah waved to one of her Amish friends and walked ahead to meet up with her. Anna looked around but didn't see anyone she recognized. She had a feeling it was going to be a long day of classes and another round of welcoming speeches in the gym. The principal was wearing a big smile and checking a clipboard for students who were lost in the shuffle and didn't know where to go. He directed traffic, pointing students this way and that. She'd been worried when Sarah got too far ahead of her that she might not remember where to go, but she needn't have worried. The principal pointed her to the freshman hallway.

As the crush of students thinned out as they headed toward their homerooms, Anna spotted a couple of familiar faces and hurried to catch up with them. After attendance, it was time to line up for the walk to the gym, where she could hear someone playing a march on the piano.

Suddenly, Anna panicked. If she could've gotten through the chaos, she would have hurried toward the front door. What had come over her? Was it that Sarah was off with her Amish friends? She was glad of that, but it left her feeling…what? She was sad to think Katherine was home without her. It hadn't distressed her the day before. What was different today?

When she felt a little woozy as she tried to climb up the bleachers, she decided she'd find a place on one of the lower rows. When a teacher admonished her to climb up to a higher row, she tried again to make her legs work. Finally, she turned to the teacher and told him she didn't feel well and didn't want to go up there in case she'd have to rush down again. He shook his head and waved her to a seat on the lowest row, next to where he'd sit. She couldn't possibly tell him she struggled to climb steps because she hadn't recovered from having a baby.

The bleachers filled quickly, but Anna found herself without any company. *Please, God, don't let anyone ask me why I can't climb the bleachers.* She looked down as she straightened her skirt. A year ago, she'd been somewhere else, starting a new adventure in a new school with new friends, new challenges. When that dream crashed, she thought her teenage years were behind her. But with Momma's ideas on how they could raise Katherine so Anna could finish her schooling, and with the help of Aunt Ida and Helen Iversen…What was the matter with her?

The principal faced the bleachers and once more welcomed everyone to the new school year. He introduced himself then called all the teachers to stand so he could introduce them. Then there was the information routine— an explanation of how the days would run, followed by a never-ending litany of the rules and regulations for lunch time, the library, and leaving the school campus during the day without office permission. There were rules about serving detentions and about being tardy for class without an excuse. Being late in the morning wasn't an option. If you were, you'd need permission from the office in order to go to your classroom. No one could possibly remember it all.

More band music. Then students and faculty, who served as advisors for special groups and opportunity activities, gave a rundown of what those were and how to get involved. Band, chorus, theater, school newspaper, and yearbook. Debate. And, of course, football and basketball for boys. In fall, there were track events and the same in spring. If enough boys were interested, they even had a parent who was willing to coach a baseball team.

At lunchtime, the freshmen were finishing their lunches as sophomores began arriving. Anna waved to Sarah, who was heading out the far door with Amish friends.

"Hey, Anna, why didn't you come up and sit with us?" her friend Betsy asked as they walked to the same table to eat.

"I felt a little sick and thought I'd better stay at the lower rows so I didn't have so far to go if I…"

Betsy and the others with her laughed knowingly. "Come on, eat with us. Anything in your lunch you'd be willing to trade?"

Lunch with old friends helped Anna push her panic down. She wasn't hungry and offered her food to anyone who was. The girls argued over who would get the dried apple slices.

"Any new flavors this year?" Caroline asked. Her family attended the same Lutheran church down the road from Anna's home and were well-acquainted with her dried apple rings.

After school, Sarah and Anna walked down the steps and along the sidewalk toward courthouse hill. They were in no hurry since Anna's dad wouldn't be done for at least an hour. But when they got to his office, they found him ready to leave.

"Thought I'd head out a little early today," he said, tucking his briefcase under his left arm as he reached into his pocket for the key to lock his door. "You two look bushed. Hard day?"

"It was a wonderful day," Sarah announced. "I just love high school. I love the way you walk from one room to the next and have a different teacher and a different subject in a different room. The only thing I didn't like was all the instructions they rattled off at us first thing this morning. I don't think I can remember even one of the rules."

"You girls are smart. You'll figure it out," Gerrit chuckled. "And if you've forgotten something, you just have to ask someone, a teacher, the secretary in the office, even the principal."

Sarah didn't waste any time getting her satchel out of the car and into her bicycle basket. Anna could see she was anxious to get home so she could share her stories with her mom. "See you tomorrow," she called to Annalise and Gerrit as she pedaled out to the road and toward home.

Annalise also was anxious to get inside—not to talk about school, but to find out how Katherine's day had gone. For the short time she'd been alive, the baby had certainly filled up a big part of Annalise's life. Inside, Annalise found that Kate was so comfortable holding and rocking the sleeping baby that the little one wasn't getting handed over. Annalise tiptoed across the porch, peeked down at Katherine, and kissed her mother. Ida was in the kitchen, stirring something in the roasting pan she pulled out of the oven. It hadn't been overly warm that day, and Anna realized the heat from the stove felt good. For good measure, she went back out to the porch and softly shut the inside door. It was indeed getting to be fall.

Anna saw that someone had gathered a large bucket of apples. With the start of school, she hadn't been keeping up with the apple crop. She saw the fruit drying machine on the laundry bench. It had stopped running; the trays were finished drying and would need packaging. Good thing none of her teachers had assigned homework. She had other work to do.

She went upstairs to change her clothes, but when she got into the quiet, sun-filled room, she was tempted to take a quick nap on Fletcher's big bed. That would only put her farther behind. Walking past her little bedroom that Aunt Ida now used, she realized she wouldn't be able to watch the northern lights shine on cold winter nights. She remembered being frightened of them when she first moved upstairs to that room. But now she thought of them as her own private view of another world.

She grabbed a sweater from the bottom drawer and found a warmer blanket for the baby. The phone rang downstairs. Not for her, though. No one ever called her. Probably Emily. When she got downstairs, she saw her dad with the receiver in hand. Although he hadn't said anything, he motioned her to be quiet. *Suppose it might be something at the courthouse.* Since the baby was still comfortable being rocked, Anna asked what she should use to set the table.

"Soup bowls," Ida said. It seemed like a good day for beef stew. "Stew was a favorite at our house when we were in school." She opened one of the warming doors and pulled out a pan of rolls. Anna hadn't eaten much at lunchtime, but she still wasn't hungry. She set out the crock of butter and filled a smaller dish with a fresh batch of apple butter.

Gerrit finished his phone call, but he just stood there holding the receiver, looking puzzled. Finally, he slipped it back into the cradle and headed for the kitchen. "I'm starving," he announced. "Think I'd like to eat right away, then go out to the barn for chores. Besides being hungry, I have something rather important to talk about with all of you."

Annalise finished setting the table, then took the sleeping baby from her mom and laid her on the daybed.

"Momma, look at you," Anna said. "You stood up without any help! That's wonderful!"

Kate smiled as she eased into the chair at the end of the table. Gerrit hurried to help, but by the time he got there, she was already settled.

Ida, carrying the heavy roaster, said she had a lot of help getting all the stew vegetables ready for their meal. "Kate," she said, "helped scrape carrots and peeling a potato. But then we decided since the potatoes were so pretty, we wouldn't bother peeling them, so she just washed them and cut them into pieces."

After their prayer of thanks for the day's blessings that nourished their souls, they also thanked the Lord for the stew and warm rolls that would nourish their bodies. Gerrit stood to scoop out a serving for Kate, then one for Ida, who sat next to Anna on the bench.

"Not much for me," Annalise said. "I couldn't eat much of my lunch, and I'm still not very hungry."

When he'd finished scooping some into his own bowl, the family was not only anxious to eat but also to hear what Gerrit had on his mind.

Annalise was distressed at what he told them. It was the bishop who called. He was asking Gerrit to bring his daughter to their meeting on Friday. When Annalise heard that, she had to gulp back tears. It never occurred to her that she'd have to go there and see him. It never occurred to her that after everything that had been done to her already, she was now expected to face questions from a bishop. She pushed her soup bowl away. She couldn't stop crying.

Ida put her arm around her shaking shoulders. The tight quarters at the back of the table restricted the others from getting up and coming around to comfort her. Her dad reached across and took her hand, holding it between both of his.

"Nothing to cry about," he said. "The bishop asked if we could bring you, but I told him I didn't think anything would be solved by putting you through that. I told him maybe someday you'd be able to go there and talk with him, but not now. Nothing has been resolved. Really nothing has even been discussed. We went there, told him what happened, but he was still preaching the story that you made it all up to hide what really happened— that you'd just been with some boy from school."

At that, Annalise stopped crying. "How could he say that? He just decided that without any evidence?"

"That's one of the reasons I don't want you along," Gerrit comforted her. "He will also be dismayed with other things that have occurred, like Ida's house broken into and trashed. You need to focus on school, and I'll represent you. You've been through enough. Let's eat our stew before it gets cold."

"We are truly blessed to have such a feast to celebrate having our daughter in school. Our contented baby, sound asleep. Our dear Ida."

"Goodness," Ida said. "I think I hear another prayer coming on."

Earlier, Annalise felt her whole world coming apart. School wasn't what she'd expected. She felt isolated, left out, removed from the rhythm of the day. She was no longer a schoolgirl. She was a mom with a baby and a growing despair. about what had been done to her. She kept her eyes downcast as she stirred the stew. She tried but couldn't swallow. She sipped at the broth and hoped no one noticed. Finally, she laid down the spoon and buttered another roll.

Where was her life going? She spent weeks trying to keep everyone around her reassured that it would all be fine. But it wasn't and never would be. The loss of her childhood consumed her. She knew she had to be careful what she said out loud. If she got too upset, it would only worry her mom, and Kate didn't need any more stress. She swallowed the panic and fears and put on a stoic face. Maybe in time she'd find some peace and understanding of the past year of her life. She swallowed her anger instead of more stew. She'd chosen to keep the baby, and as hard as it was, at least she didn't have to do it alone.

She nibbled her roll a bit more, then slid along the bench to the other end. "I'd like to try some of the apple slices that are finished drying," she said, going to the kitchen for a bowl. No one else was ready for dessert. Instead, there were second helpings and another roll or two before the table could be cleared.

"These apple rings are especially good," she announced. "I wonder if I mixed sugar and cinnamon and just sprinkled it on the apple while it's drying. I just let them soak in a watery bath of sugar and cinnamon. You know," she said, "between school and apples, I really can't afford the time to be gone for a trip. Maybe you could take a bag of apples along for the bishop."

Later that evening, Anna said goodnight before she and Katherine went upstairs. Katherine was asleep before she was tucked under her nighttime blanket. Although exhausted, Anna was too restless to sleep. Instead, she pulled out her daybook to see if writing would settle her mind.

September 6, 1944

Dear Days,
Today was the first full day of my sophomore year, but there was something that just didn't fit right. I've been so looking forward to going to class and the normal routine it would add to

my life. Instead, the more I try to convince myself that everything is going as planned, I can't help feeling I don't fit there anymore. Too much has happened over the past year. Too much has turned my life upside down. When I was in bed, away from everyone except the family, it was a new normal for me. While I carried the evidence of what had been done to me, I was more focused on the baby and what it would take to get her here safely. I never focused on the bad side. I was removed from that place and that person, and while he was mentioned occasionally, I felt far away from him. Even when he forced his way into our house, Sarah was there with me, and then Helen and Sarah's dad left in a hurry. Even the discomfort of his threats didn't last long.

Being in that school is uncomfortable. Actually, it makes me afraid. I feel like I am always on the verge of tears. I couldn't eat lunch. I'm so excited for Sarah and her Amish friends who are so happy to be getting a high school education. But the dreams I had for a good preparation are now out of reach. for me. The central focus of my life now is Katherine and Momma's care.

Even my dried apple rings don't interest me. I need to continue making money so I can provide for my little girl, the only way I can do that is my apple business. Momma and Poppa think they can convince someone that the priest should pay for the baby's medical bills and child support. But I took her on myself. I couldn't just discard her or give her away. So, those obligations are mine.

I wish my homeroom teacher was a woman. Mr. Blount makes me uncomfortable. When he *made a face at me because I couldn't climb the bleachers, I realized I'd changed. The baby changed me. He didn't know that, but that was really the start of all this anxiety.*

I will write more tomorrow. I hope by then I won't feel so depressed, so sad, so lost in what should be a secure place for someone my age. But I'm not a girl anymore. All the other kids in school are just kids, but I've had to skip that age. I'm a mom with responsibilities. I've been through things none of the other kids have. Their happiness makes me feel different from them. Do I look different? Act different? Talk different? Does it show I was raped and now have a baby girl? Is that why my old friends don't want to hang out with me? It makes me unbelievably lonely.

Annalise

Annalise wasn't ready for Katherine's middle-of-the-night complaints. She'd gone downstairs to get a fresh bottle of formula out of the fridge, but that didn't settle the baby down. A dry diaper. Snuggling into a warmer blanket. Nothing worked. Annalise moved Katherine and herself to the rocker, and that seemed to be just what Katherine wanted. In only a few minutes, she'd closed her eyes and was sound asleep.

Before she tucked her daughter back into the crib, Annalise whispered a prayer: "Dearest Jesus…Please help me to get settled in my new life as a mom and a high schooler. I love this little girl who will someday call me Mom, but right now I have other responsibilities. For me to be a good mom to Katherine, I need to get my education so I can provide the things she needs. I know my Momma and Poppa are anxious to take that on themselves, but in time, it will be only my responsibility, and I must prepare for that. I don't think I'm complaining, but I need to get over some of these sad feelings and settle into school and studying to get a good start on being a real adult. Please help me get through the day without tears and without fear. Amen."

The next morning, Annalise gave Katherine a quick kiss on the forehead, told her she'd be back in the afternoon, and asked her to be a good girl for her Grammy and Aunt Ida.

Sarah's bike was propped up next to the front porch, and she was already in the car. Anna's dad was anxious to get an early start—budget meeting with the board chairman and department heads. Ida had packed a lunch for Gerrit to take with him after he said he probably wouldn't have time to go out for lunch. He was planning to get final tallies of what the departments were looking for in their budgets so he could start putting the figures together.

Annalise and Sarah walked from the courthouse to the high school. Although both had worn sweaters, neither seemed warm enough to block the cold breeze blowing the first fallen leaves around their feet. They picked up their pace, then finally made a run for it. There were only a few early students ahead of them, all huddled close to the front entryway to keep out of the wind.

"It's way too early to be so cold," Annalise's voice quivered.

Sarah was more prepared for the cool day with her long skirt and long-sleeved top. She opened her satchel and pulled out a knit shawl, handing it to Annalise. "Mom told me we might be cold and said I should take a shawl. I'm not as cold as you are, so wrap this around you." Annalise didn't argue.

Maybe the cold air had cut through some of her angst, but Annalise forgot how worried she'd been about coming to school that day as she hurried along the corridor to her homeroom. Mr. Blount was standing beside the classroom door, greeting students as they walked into the warm room.

The morning disappeared. Lunch. There were apple slices in her lunch bag. She hadn't packed them, but it was nice to find them there. Because most of the students hadn't dressed appropriately for the temperature, they stayed in. After stops at the restroom, some went to the gym. Others, including Anna, went to the library. For a few minutes, she walked around the room, glancing at titles, picking up a book here and there, flipping through the pages. She was anxious to have library class this week so she could withdraw a book or two. One day soon, she wanted to visit the public library at the other end of Main Street. That was always a favorite part of a trip into town when she was little. She and Fletcher could always pick out a few books to take home, even if they weren't old enough to read. She smiled at that, remembering how Fletcher would practice by reading his little sister's books to her during the week they had them. There was always a new batch the following week.

Anna's schedule included chorus. Their regular practice was Tuesday and Thursday afternoons, but the morning announcement reminded chorus members that they would have after-school practices in preparation for the high school's holiday musical the first week in December. That day was auditions for solo parts. Anna liked to sing, and she thought maybe that would give her a chance to get reacquainted with some of the kids she knew from other years. Or maybe not. Still, she could sing. With the chorus. Not a solo.

They also announced something about an after-school meeting of students interested in forensics. That, Anna decided, would not include her.

By the end of the day, she'd forgotten the fear that had engulfed her earlier. The afternoon choral class had gone well, and most of the students raised their hands when the director asked who would be coming to after-school tryouts. During the regular class, they had auditions to assign vocal range placements. Anna was a soprano. No surprise there.

At four-fifteen, the director dismissed the rehearsal session and suggested they might consider having another session the following night. That was followed by a groan from singers who obviously had other plans for a Friday night. Football. That was not something that interested Anna. Fletcher always went, but she'd never gone along. Didn't mean anything to her, especially not now, when she was already anxious to get home to see the baby. She was concerned about Katherine's cranky spell the night before. Maybe it was nothing, but she wouldn't fully relax until she could see her for herself that evening.

By the time Anna found Sarah, Gerrit was at the curb waiting. The girls grabbed their sweaters and book bags and hurried to the car. Gerrit had turned on the heater so it was already warm in the backseat. It was so warm Anna's eyes couldn't stay open. Sarah was talking about something they'd done in one of her classes, but Anna found herself falling asleep as Sarah's voice drifted away.

Anna was startled awake when Sarah pushed open the backdoor of the car, anxious to get out and head the rest of the way up the road to her own house. Before Anna gathered up her school stuff, Sarah was already on her bike, waving goodbye.

"See you tomorrow," Anna called to her, hurrying up the steps to the warmth inside. "It's *so* cold today," she said to her dad as she pulled open the screen door and pushed the inside door open. The baby, usually on the porch with Grammy Kate in the afternoon, was nowhere in sight. *Too cold to eat supper on the porch*, she thought.

"It smells like chicken and gravy," Gerrit said as Ida came out to check on supper baking in the oven.

Anna warmed her hands over the stove. "I think I'll run up and change into some warmer clothes before I set the table. Where's Katherine?"

Ida milled about the kitchen. "Tucked in with your mom in the bedroom down here. Both your mother and daughter got very tired this afternoon."

Anna peeked into the bedroom and saw Katherine snuggled close to Grammy under the warm blanket.

By the time Anna had changed and come back downstairs, she found a crying baby and wide-awake Grammy. She scooped up the squalling child who needed dry, warmer clothes and a bottle.

"So, tell me what you've been up to today, Katherine," Anna teased as they sat in the rocker near the heater. "I had my first class in chorus this afternoon, and after school, I went to auditions for the holiday musical the school is putting on in December. I just want to sing in the choir, though, no solos. I save those for singing to you." Katherine studied Anna's face as if she understood.

Gerrit was anxious to eat before heading out to the barn. He sure missed Fletcher's help—and company.

Before he went out, he gave the family an update on the planned Friday meeting at the bishop's office. Although he'd told the bishop that Anna would not make the trip because she'd miss school, the bishop either didn't hear or care. "I'd like to meet your daughter and her baby."

Besides not wanting to miss school, Anna didn't want to be around someone who'd accused her of being a liar.

"Does he still expect me there Friday?" Anna asked.

Gerrit simply replied that the bishop was insistent. The second-hand accounts from parents and a relative were one thing, but the bishop wanted a personal account from the young lady making the accusations against one of his priests. Without her personal report of what she claimed happened, he was not interested in anything further from the family.

"I told him I'd call him tomorrow morning," Gerrit said. "He offered to call tonight, here at the house, but I told him that would not give me time to talk with Anna and her mother. I doubt he'll call."

Annalise stared down at the tabletop.

"I think," Gerrit continued, "that knowing Anna was reluctant to tell her story directly to him, he figured that would be the end of it. He saw an out for the diocese because she wouldn't make the accusation in person."

"But," Anna interrupted, "'Father Nolan was sent away for counselling. Why do I have to make a case when the man who's to blame isn't even there? What would I accomplish by just talking to the bishop? If Nolan was sent away, doesn't that mean the bishop believed he'd done it?" Tears started again. She handed Katherine to Ida then laid her head down on the table, trying to think.

"Annalise," Gerrit said, "what do you want to do? Do you want to challenge him with your story? If he's laid this out as a condition of our meeting with him, it seems he's saying there's no responsibility if the claimant won't speak. I think it's a legal game they're playing. If you don't come with us, he's implying that we shouldn't bother to come at all."

"Will it truly make any difference if I do go?"

"I don't know. I know there are things I need to tell him, but that's not going to settle this case at this point. Since he's thrown down the gauntlet about the importance of hearing the story from you, I'm afraid we've come to the end of the easy road. I've already told him that if I didn't get any satisfaction from his office, my next stop would be the police and district attorney. If that happens, you will need to be with us to tell them what happened to you. That will set a whole chain of unpleasantries in motion. So, right now, it looks like he's calling our bluff, and if we don't bring you along, we really have no viable story to take to the DA's office."

Anna shook her head in frustration. "I guess that's my answer. If I don't tell my story, I may as well accept defeat in getting the priest to accept responsibility for what he did. But worse, the bishop will just cross off this little problem from his to-do list. It's like they've been accusing me of being with a boy and things got out of hand, and that boy would have to take some responsibility for providing financial support for the baby. So why should the priest, just because he's a priest, get away with it without acknowledging or being held responsible? I certainly didn't make a baby by myself."

Gerrit reached across the table and held his daughter's hands. "So, do you want to sleep on it and let me know your decision in the morning, or should I call the bishop tonight and tell him we'll all be there on Friday?"

"Call him tonight. Or better yet, I'll get on the phone and tell him myself?"

Gerrit's eyes widened. Kate and Ida looked at each other and smiled at Anna's audacious suggestion.

"If you're absolutely sure, I'll place the call now," Gerrit said, his voice excited. "I hope we interrupt his evening meal. He's certainly wreaked havoc on plenty of ours."

When Gerrit told the operator he wanted to place a long-distance call and gave her the number, Anna stood beside him at the ready. Her dad handed her the receiver after he explained to the housekeeper that the bishop was expecting the call.

Anna was nervous as she waited, but when the bishop came on the line, she put on her most confident voice. "Hello, Excellency. This is Annalise

Jansz. I'm just calling to let you know that I will be coming with my parents and my aunt on Friday morning. I think my dad said the appointment was at ten. Is that right? I've never met a Roman Catholic bishop, and I look forward to meeting you. I'll see you on Friday." And hung up.

Anna exhaled and looked around the room. "Well, that's done. He said he was anxious to meet me. Did I sound scared?"

"Not one bit!" Gerrit said, clapping his hands together. "Too bad your brother wasn't around to hear that."

Later, after she'd tucked Katherine in for the first part of her night, she pulled out her Book of Days.

September 7th, 1944

Dear Days,

I have a lot to write tonight. I took a huge step today. The bishop told Poppa that if I didn't come on Friday, they didn't need to bother coming at all. I knew I had no choice but to go. It might not make the slightest difference, but I wasn't going to back away from something that was clearly a challenge to my story.

I think the bishop was shocked to hear me on the line. But with all the sales calls I've made to place my apple rings in grocery and gift stores, this was actually kind of easy. Especially because of Katherine. She will be growing up without a father. But, of course, Grammy and Grampy will fill those roles in her life. How lucky Katherine is to have so many people anxious to help with her so I can finish high school and maybe even college.

I'm actually excited about deciding to tell my story to the bishop. No sense being afraid to speak the truth out loud to someone who has accused you of lying. I felt so sad these past few days, and you have, as always, quietly listened to my words as I wrote them here. Someday, all

*these entries about this time of my life, will be
used to share this story with others. Or, maybe
only with Katherine, so she will know who all
the special people in her early life were and how
important their love was for both of us.*

Thank you for listening!

Annalise

Anna and her dad stopped at the school office Thursday morning to arrange for her to miss school on Friday. He told the secretary they probably would not be back until Saturday morning. Perhaps she could get some assignments to take with her to do over the weekend. The secretary said Anna should stop at the office at the end of the day and she'd have assignments from the teachers for her. Gerrit thanked her, said goodbye to his daughter, and left.

Anna got a note from the secretary that said she was not to be marked tardy. Her homeroom teacher scowled as he scanned the note, then tossed it on his desk, continuing with roll call.

The round of classes distracted her from the commitment for the next day. It wasn't until she stood on the risers in the choral practice room that she really thought about the appointment with the bishop. She made a quick trip to the front office for her homework assignments and hurried back just in time for the warm-up exercises.

A half hour into practice, Anna had to meet up with Sarah for the trip home with her dad. She stepped down from the riser and nodded to the director. He looked at the clock on the wall and motioned that she could leave.

Sarah was surrounded by her Amish friends outside the school. There were two buggies waiting at the curb. Gerrit was just pulling up when Anna and Sarah got to the front sidewalk.

The two friends had a lot of chatting to do on the ride home. Even though Anna would not be going to school the next day, Helen would drive Sarah into town and pick her up after school. Sarah wondered what the trip was about, but she knew it was not polite to ask. And Anna was not forthcoming.

When they arrived home, suitcases sat on the porch, waiting to be loaded into the trunk of the car. The baby's things were packed in a couple baskets and boxes. The baby had a special bed for the car, which Anna and Ida put between them. Kate seemed reluctant to leave. She hadn't been away in months. Ida would tend the baby while Anna and her parents spoke their case.

Emily was at her mother's house when they pulled into the driveway hours later. She helped them carry their things inside and insisted they at least have a bowl of soup and a sandwich before getting ready for bed. Anna would sleep in the downstairs bedroom off the kitchen where a borrowed baby bed was set up. Kate and Gerrit slept in Anna's old room upstairs, and Ida was happy to be back in her own bed.

Emily was anxious to hear what the bishop would say about the break-in at Ida's house last summer. Emily had gotten two copies of the police report, itemizing the damage to Ida's house—one was for the insurance claim, and the second was to show the bishop what Cleary Nolan had done while looking for evidence he'd left behind. Technically, it wasn't a break-in, since the person had a key and merely unlocked the door. Because the key was newly made, it had rough edges that caused it to stick, making the attempted entrance noisier than Nolan had foreseen.

Annalise and baby Katherine slept most of the way to Aunt Ida's. By the time they carried in the luggage and got settled for a light supper, they were wide awake, but everyone else was ready to turn in for the night. The next day's schedule would start early and, they hoped, end by noon. But that would depend on the result of their conversation with the bishop and attorney.

Emily had blankets and pillows piled at the end of the living room sofa where she planned to spend the night. Before they all headed for their separate bedrooms, Kate suggested a prayer for a successful meeting tomorrow. Ida began the prayer with a question: "Who will get the Lord's attention in prayers for the success of tomorrow's meeting? The bishop? Or Annalise and her family?"

Kate added, "And please, heavenly Father, don't let it become a battle." Baby Katherine added her voice to the prayers, more an appeal for her bottle and a change than a specific request for the outcome of her future.

In the morning, Emily had a scrambled egg casserole baking in the oven and a pile of raisin bread already toasted. There was a glass of orange juice for Anna and brewed coffee ready to pour. But there wasn't time to dawdle over a second cup. With morning traffic, it would take nearly an hour to get to the Chancery office. They could do with some stress-relieving deep breathing in the parking lot if they were too early.

Emily decided she should go along, even though they wouldn't all fit in Gerrit's car. She already had her keys in hand. "I'll lead the way, and you can follow me. I think I might be of some help if Katherine gets a little rambunctious." Ida said she'd ride with Emily so they could talk about their plans to sell one or both of their houses and perhaps buy another one large enough to share.

When they arrived, the attorney was already there, forty-five minutes early.

Since Annalise had never met the bishop or been to his office, she was apprehensive about how things would be conducted. Were they going to question her like in court? Did they expect her to just tell them what happened to her? Gerrit said this was the bishop's office and his meeting, and they would be prepared for however he wanted to conduct it. He reminded her that she should pick up on his cues. If she had something to interject, she could do that, but courteously. They also had to insist that Kate have an opportunity to speak without any pressure.

When it was time to go in, Anna handed the wrapped package she'd been carrying over to her dad so she could carry the baby. While the others chatted as they crossed the blacktop, she took some deep breaths to slow her rapid heartbeat.

The bishop met them at the front door and invited the entourage in. He was especially interested in the little girl wrapped in a pink-and-white, embroidered blanket. Four chairs sat along the front of the bishop's oversized desk. The large window that opened to a broad expanse of gardens was especially beautiful, framed by the reds and yellows of maple and birch trees.

They talked awhile before taking their seats. The bishop was gracious not only to Annalise but also to her mother, who still relied on the security of her walker to maintain her balance. Her speaking ability had improved so much it sometimes was hard to tell she had a problem, save for the occasional word that slipped her mind or was hard to pronounce. Gerrit helped her get seated and the others filled in around her. With Kate and Gerrit in the middle two chairs, Ida claimed the one closest to the outside wall and Annalise and the baby sat on the opposite side.

When the bishop sat down, the attorney flipped the switch to start the tape. All conversation stopped until the attorney signaled that the tape was running.

"We'll start with you, Annalise," the bishop said.

Anna handed the baby to her Poppa.

Before she started, the bishop briefly recounted what had transpired at earlier meetings. Then he signaled to Anna that she could begin.

Silence. He nodded and reminded her it was time to give her statement. "Briefly," he said. She hesitated. The attorney gestured for her to speak. Gerrit, sitting next to her, reached over and squeezed her hand.

"I've never talked into a recorder," Anna said.

Before starting, Anna asked the bishop what title she should call him. When he said "bishop" would be fine, she smiled, straightened her shoulders, and began what her dad said would be something like a deposition.

She explained why she was alone at Aunt Ida's house and asleep upstairs in her room when she was awakened by someone banging on the front door.

"I thought it must be Aunt Ida, but they were going to stay overnight at the farm. I put on my robe and went downstairs. When I unlocked the door, the knob turned, and Father Cleary Nolan was standing there, holding a jar of chicken noodle soup. 'Father,' I said, 'what are you doing here?'"

Annalise said he had an explanation for why he brought the soup, but all she wanted was for him to leave. But he had already gotten a soup bowl out of Ida's cupboard and poured some of the lukewarm broth into the bowl. He kept asking if Ida was home or when she would get home. She finished her bowl of soup and left the table, putting the bowl in the sink to be washed later.

Anna was too tired to listen to the forensics results, suggesting instead that he pack up his stuff and leave so she could go back to bed. She walked over to the front door and opened it, but he stood at the bottom of the stairwell, waiting to help her upstairs. "That made me very, very uncomfortable," she said. After all, she knew him from all of his Sunday night suppers he'd been invited to by Ida. And she never stayed at the table longer than to have a bite of soup or a small sandwich, then she went upstairs. Alone! But not tonight.

"Finally," she said, "he came over to the doorway, put his arm around me and helped me upstairs. I could have walked up there myself!

"I didn't feel like talking, but he didn't stop. He said he'd gotten the forensic results from the coach.

"Father Nolan kept relaying events of that day," Anna said, looking directly at the bishop. He just listened.

"Besides the soup, Father Cleary Nolan had some things in a bag. I tried to tell him I didn't feel good and I didn't really care what the results were. I said I'd call and get them the next day. He had to know I was there alone, because Aunt Ida didn't come to open the door for him."

Anna told him the part where Father insisted on following her upstairs, urging her to get into bed. "He got the chair from across the room and sat next to the bed. He said he'd brought a toddy, like his mother made when he had a sore throat. Then I noticed what he was holding in his hand—a cruet like one he used at Mass in the school chapel. He took out the stopper and poured some into a glass on the nightstand. 'This will help you sleep,' he said, handing me the glass. I didn't want whatever it was. He insisted. Finally, I took a sip. It tasted awful. Then he poured more in the glass before putting the stopper back on the cruet."

Annalise looked over to her dad. She saw his eyes were closed. Anna was especially fearful of how this information would upset her mother. Gerrit did too.

She paused. The bishop looked uncomfortable. The attorney wrote several words on a sheet of paper he had inside a leather folder. Aunt Ida, who had graciously invited this Catholic priest to her home on several late Sunday afternoon suppers, was the most agitated by Anna's report that the priest refused to leave her bedroom until she was sound asleep.

"Father Nolan kept telling me to 'finish it all.' He said, 'It will soothe your throat and help you get a good night's rest.' He said he'd let himself out. I didn't think then that either he was going to leave the front door open or he'd have had a key made. You need a key to lock the door behind you from outside. But I felt woozy and had a hard time keeping my eyes open. It wasn't until the next morning that I remembered about the key."

Annalise swallowed hard and laced her fingers. "When I woke up, I put on my robe and hurried downstairs to check the front and back doors. Both were locked. But I didn't know how. I never paid much attention to the keys hanging on the rack next to the front hall closet. I knew some were keys from the farmhouse where they used to live. Aunt Ida said they'd had all the locks in their old house changed when they sold it and moved.

"I thought maybe I'd dreamt everything from the night before. The empty glass was there, and when I smelled it, thinking I could figure out what he'd put in there, it didn't smell at all. Maybe he rinsed the glass before he left. The bed covers were all jumbled, and my pajama bottoms were on the floor." Anna hesitated. "I started to straighten the bed, then noticed spots of blood on the bottom sheet. Ida wouldn't have known that because I washed those sheets before they came home on Sunday.

"I remembered being angry that he wouldn't leave when I said he'd better," Anna said, steadying her voice. "I didn't put the pajamas in the wash. Instead, I carefully folded them and put them in a gift box on the top shelf in my closet. After I took a bath, I put on clean pajamas, crawled back into bed, and went to sleep. I tried not to think of that night, but details of what happened would intrude. It was a few months later when I figured out something wasn't right. Then Aunt Ida and Emily took me to Emily's doctor. That's when I found out I was pregnant. Aunt Ida called my mom and invited her to come for the weekend. Maybe she can tell you what happened after that."

Poppa patted her hand and Anna wrapped her fingers around his. The attorney raised his hand, a signal that the recorder was turned off. Anna had talked so long the bishop said she could be excused. Annalise shook her head and stayed seated. Katherine was still snoozing, and she didn't want to go out to the parking lot.

The attorney lifted the tape off the machine and put it into a box with Anna's name marked on the cover. Then he fit another tape onto the machine and nodded toward Kate.

"You're next, Mrs. Jansz. Are you up to talking to me?"

Kate sat up straighter and nodded. "I can't talk as fast as I used to, but I will do my best. Some words are still hard to say." Then she nodded and picked up where Anna left off.

Poppa put his arm around Kate's shoulders but didn't look over at her until she finished talking. By then, Katherine was starting to fuss, and Ida came around to get her. Nearby were clean diapers and bottles that had been warmed earlier, and Anna let Aunt Ida handle the hungry baby.

There were no surprises in anything anyone said.

Then it was the bishop's turn. He said what he'd been telling our family since the first interview months ago—that Anna made up a story to cover up for her fooling around with a boy. He insisted everything that Anna said on the tape was a lie.

Annalise looked down at the package in her lap—apple slices from their orchard. She'd intended to hand it to the bishop when they were getting ready to leave. But after his accusation that she was lying, she decided not to leave the package for him. But that would have been a mean thing to do. Instead...

Annalise smiled and handed him her package. "I dried these apples for my little business and used the money to pay my tuition at St. Michael's. I do not tell lies," she said. "And if you don't want my dried apple slices, please give them to someone who might like them. They are very tasty."

She handed him the large package of apple slices, then turned and walked away.

"Then why," Gerrit asked the bishop, "was your priest sent away for counselling and removed from his duties as a pastor and rector of the school? He's never answered the charges our daughter has brought against him. And he came to our house to harass Annalise and cruised past our house many times. Why? If he had nothing to do with this rape and pregnancy, then why did he try to convince us that he had nothing whatever to do with sexually assaulting our 14-year-old daughter, Annalise. Incidentally, that assault took place exactly three months to the day when a doctor's checkup found it to be the date when she was impregnated."

The bishop did not defend his priest, but he did try again to disparage what Anna said had occurred.

Gerrit also noted that Father Nolan stopped at the Lillehammer parish office and spoken with Father Andrews about Annalise and her condition. "If he'd just been a caring rector, why didn't he call our house to ask how Annalise was doing?

"But, of course, that stopover and questions about the reason for that were followed by his removal from the rector's job and as the parish priest. He's been sent to a retreat house for clergy in West Texas, who need some quiet time to get their Holy Orders in order. His parish and parishioners have been advised of Father Nolan's removal from his parish. We pray for him.

"That was immediately followed by Nolan's removal from your diocese."

The bishop signaled the attorney to shut off the tape recorder. End of session.

"Thank you very much for making the effort to bring your daughter and her daughter here for this meeting," the bishop said in a flat voice. "We will continue to investigate this. I trust you will have a nice drive home."

Gerrit asked if he could have a copy of the tapes they'd just recorded, but the attorney shook his head.

"Bishop," Anna said, hoping her voice was not quivering, "I had so looked forward to coming here to go to school. I truly spent so much time trying to raise money just to come here, because I wanted the best pre-college education I could get. I worked very hard. Mom and Dad approved of my plans to go to St. Michael's, and my Aunt Ida said I could live with her during the school year. So, Momma brought me down to enroll, pay my tuition and buy my uniforms. She moved me down to Aunt Ida's just before school started last September. One of the first days was an open house for new students. There were a lot of girls there because that was only the second year that we could enroll. Again, Aunt Ida went with me. That's when she met Cleary Nolan. They got into a big discussion about religion. You see, Aunt Ida and my Mom's dad was a Methodist pastor, and they'd had almost no contact with Roman Catholics. Aunt Ida invited Father over for a Sunday night supper so they could compare notes about their faiths. I usually ate with them when he was there, but always asked to be excused so I could do homework or read. Father would always call upstairs to say goodnight when he left."

Anna felt her eyes stinging. "And when I found out that I was pregnant, I was so upset I couldn't even cry. At first, I couldn't figure out how it could have happened, but then I remembered the night Father came over and gave me that stuff to drink."

Annalise waited, expecting the bishop to thank her for her input. Instead, the room was dead silent. Even the attorney who had been jotting something on his legal notepad stopped. He held his pen poised over the notepaper as if he expected that any moment the narrative would continue.

Annalise hated quiet. It made her uncomfortable—five grown people and one teenager sitting in a room, totally mute. It was so quiet she hoped Katherine would let out a yowl.

Finally, the bishop looked across at Anna. It was hard to read the expression on his face.

Gerrit leaned forward. "Bishop," he said, "would you like me to bring Emily in so you can hear what she has to add to this report? We think it's pretty significant. Any of us could report what it is she dealt with in connection with this incident, but we think it might be better if she told you herself."

"Yes," the bishop said slowly. "Yes, perhaps we should get on with it. If you wouldn't mind asking her to come in now, that way we can hear everything in some sequence."

Walking across the parking lot back to the chancery office entrance, Gerrit tried to give Emily a quick rundown on what had already occurred. Someone had brought in another chair. Annalise moved to the new chair on the end, making room for Emily so she could sit directly across from the bishop. When Gerrit introduced her, she hesitated, then extended her hand and bowed her head slightly as she accepted his welcome.

The scary events of that night alone in her mother's house were difficult for Emmy to retell. "At first, I was too scared to even move. I knew it wasn't Mom coming back; she would have called to let me know that. Mom had a phone on her bedside table, and I reached over to quietly pick up the phone and put it under the covers so I could call the police without being heard by whoever was trying to get in. Whomever it was must have assumed no one was home. Mom's car was at Uncle Gerrit and Aunt Kate's farm. When I got the police on the phone, I explained what was happening and asked them to please not turn on their lights or siren, which would scare the person away. They must have been close by, because I soon heard them coming slowly down the street. He must have spotted the approaching car, because suddenly the noise at the front door stopped. The police didn't come right to the door. Knowing that the person trying to get in had gotten away, I turned on the front light when I went downstairs to wait for them to find out if they caught anyone. Sadly, they had not. They came in to fill out their report and asked me to call them again if anyone came back. They wanted to know who might have keys to the house, but I knew Mom was very cautious about such things. If she was going to be away, she knew I would be the one keeping an eye on her house, not the neighbors."

Emily cleared her throat before continuing. "After the police left, I called to tell her what happened and ask her about someone having a key. We puzzled over it, but it wasn't until much later and another incident that we figured it out. A few days later, when I pulled into my mom's driveway, I saw the back door was ajar. I quietly pushed the door open and looked inside. I could not believe my eyes. Whoever had been in there had totally trashed the house. Cupboard doors were open, drawers pulled out. All the closet doors were open and clothes and other closet items were scattered on the floor. Even the cupboard in the downstairs bathroom was emptied on the floor. Upstairs was even worse. Again, I called the police and my mother. Nothing was stolen. I mentioned nothing to police about our idea who the culprit was."

"May I ask what was hidden in the house that this person was supposedly looking for?" the bishop asked. "Are we to assume you are tying those two incidents into the incident you are here today to discuss?"

"Yes, bishop." Gerrit had a scowl etched on his face. "But it didn't end there. As I said, he then came to our farm and stalked us. We know that all of these incidents tie together, and we know it was Cleary Nolan."

Gerrit took in a breath to calm himself. "As you can see, this unfortunate situation has done nothing but grow and grow and grow. Our daughter was in bed throughout the summer months, creating an unbelievable workload for my wife and her sister. We have come here today to inform you in person, on the record, of everything that has happened and who, obviously, was behind it."

Gerrit leaned back in his chair. Suddenly, his heart started pounding and he found it difficult to swallow. Fortunately, Katherine started complaining, as if on cue.

The bishop suggested a break while Annalise took care of the baby.

Emily asked to be excused. "I'd rather go back outside to wait," she said.

Annalise and Katherine followed Emily. They walked over to the car without saying a word. By the time the baby was changed, Emily had another bottle ready for Katherine.

"Why don't I just sit here in the sunshine with the baby, then put her down for a nap after she finishes her bottle?" Emily suggested.

"Good idea," Anna said as she pulled out a collapsible lawn chair from the car trunk. "If she doesn't settle down, just bring her back inside." Katherine didn't seem the least bit concerned that she was having her mid-morning snack in a sunny parking lot. At least it was warmer than the bishop's office.

Everyone was seated and ready to go by the time Anna came back.

Gerrit explained his sighting of Nolan at Katherine's baby shower and the constant phone calls. Then he added, "And I assure you, bishop, that we heard about Nolan's departure from a reliable source."

"Most stories are just idle gossip," the bishop interjected with more than a hint of displeasure. "And what you believe to be Nolan's reasons for leaving his duties is also unfounded gossip that is not even germane to this fact-finding session. How dare you pass along stories like these without any basis in fact? The principal has been given much-needed vacation time, and I will not listen to these wild tales that you are peddling to add layers to your stories based on unfounded accusations. It is very presumptuous of you to bring such nonsense to this office." The bishop could barely contain his anger. "Your daughter is not of our faith, neither are any of you. We agreed to enroll her in our program, but she will be the last non-Catholic to be given admission to our school. We are not deep pockets that you can dip into based on such unfounded lies. Yes, your daughter was pregnant, but how she got that way is in no way connected with our school principal, nor the diocese. It's just a fanciful story she made up to cover her own lack of morals and the trouble she got into on her own. Find the teenage boy who did it and visit his parents."

Gerrit continued, unfaltering: "I wonder why someone would rummage through Ida's entire house but not take anything. He clearly didn't find what he was looking for—because we had the pajamas with us at our farm. And how did he even know what to look for? How did he find that out, I wonder?"

The bishop pressed his lips together, but Gerrit plunged on. "But since you will not entertain any of this information despite our assurance that it is valid and an outcome of the priest's disgusting behavior against our daughter, we will leave. As I've told you in the past, if the information we are presenting to you is going to be dismissed without due consideration, our next stop will be the district attorney's office. Alongside our charges,

Ida will seek to get charges leveled against the priest for the break-in and his malicious destruction of her property."

Gerrit stood. "Thank you for your time," he added as he and Ida helped Kate out of her chair.

Annalise sat, slightly numbed by the anger filling the room. Neither the bishop or attorney made any move to stand or stop them from leaving. Anna wondered if they didn't understand that if Ida went to the DA's office to report a suspect in the break-in at her home, the police would wonder how they knew who had broken in and why.

The family turned to leave and still no one said anything. Annalise started to walk away, then turned to thank the bishop for his seeing them.

Emily was still burping the baby when she saw the group leave the chancery and head to the car.

Gerrit pulled out a slip of paper from his pocket and showed the name and address of the DA's office to Emily. "Can you help us find the way there?" he asked before sliding into the driver's seat.

"Just follow me," Emily said as she walked to her car. Again, Ida rode with her.

Gerrit just shook his head. "I can't understand why he just dismissed all the evidence. Apparently, the diocese doesn't care if these accusations hit the newspapers."

When they got to the DA's office, he wasn't in. He was on vacation for an entire week. And, no, there were no assistants available for last-minute appointments.

Annalise was so upset she thought she might throw up. She knew her dad couldn't make an appointment to see the DA without explaining his need to meet with him. So, the whole trip was a fiasco. How many times had they met with the bishop and come away empty-handed with not even a half-hearted promise to take a closer look at the charges they were leveling against the priest and the diocese?

A decision to make a second stop at the police department fared no better. The officer assigned to investigate the break-in at Ida's house, had concluded that follow-up investigations led nowhere, and the case was set aside. A couple of people from out of town certainly wouldn't have vital information needing to be shared in person. The officer at the desk took Gerrit's name and number and promised to pass it on to the detective.

As Gerrit headed toward the car, he was almost certain he'd never hear from the investigating officer. He did, however, have a name. The officer taking the information inadvertently mentioned his name in explaining that the file was set aside. Gerrit had a good memory for names and would start making follow-up calls to the detective.

September 9th, 1944

Dear Days,

I didn't forget about you yesterday, but I was too distracted to settle down enough to tell you what's been going on. We had a meeting with the bishop yesterday. We stayed overnight at Aunt Ida's the night before. I was so nervous about meeting the bishop and telling him what happened to me when I was going to St. Michael's High School. I think my voice was shaking when I started talking. We had baby Katherine with us, but Momma held her while I told the bishop what had happened to me. I thought I might be expected to stand up as a courtesy to the bishop, but Poppa said I should just stay seated, otherwise it would seem awkward. He was right. Just before I started talking, I remembered some of my training for forensics, and I settled down and wasn't even nervous. I just looked at the bishop, then at the attorney, then back again. That's a tip Fletcher suggested when he sent a note wishing us luck for our appointment.

Neither the bishop nor attorney asked questions. I couldn't tell if they were even paying attention. I had a sheet of notes so I wouldn't forget anything important. I was sitting next to Poppa and that gave me more courage to just tell him what I remembered about that night and the next morning. When I finished, Poppa told about the priest driving back and forth past our house, and Emily described the attempted break-in and then the one where he trashed Ida's entire house.

When Poppa and Emily finished telling those things, the bishop just sat there. He didn't thank us for coming nor stand up to shake Poppa's hand. It felt like such an insult to invite us there, have us speak, and then just call me a liar. Poppa told him if we didn't get any satisfaction from them about the break-in and what had happened to me that we'd take that story to the police and district attorney. But the bishop didn't seem worried. He didn't say anything about getting back in touch with us or anything. The bishop and attorney just sat behind the desk. Poppa nodded in their direction and walked out.

When we got to the DA's office, there was no one there except the secretary. She said if we were interested in setting up an appointment, we should call on Monday or Tuesday to make one. With that reception, we knew no one was interested in anything we have to say. The secretary certainly acted like she knew why we were there and why the DA and his assistants weren't.

We're back home now, and we didn't even talk much about it on the drive home. At first all I could do was cry. Then I decided that wasn't going to solve anything. So, I told Mom and Poppa that that's where it would have to end. The priest was sent away and punished for what we know, they know, he did. They are not interested in any kind of justice or even an apology. So, the rest of the family can talk about it if they want, but I won't. I have Katherine. We've figured out how we can keep her and I can stay in school, at least until I graduate. I won't have the college prep classes I wanted, but maybe I won't be able to go to college. However, it works out, what's done is done, and I won't revisit it ever again.

I thought when I started school at St. Mike's that I might even be interested in someday becoming a Catholic. I liked going to daily Mass at the school chapel. Those students who did the same were always friendly and welcoming. I know what happened to me wasn't their fault, but I also am sure they would be upset if they knew why I left without saying goodbye.

I have more important things to worry about than a bishop who refuses to have the courtesy of considering that his priest might have been responsible for what happened to me. But he wasn't interested.

So, that's the end of that. If I think of it next year on this day, I'll re-read what I've written here. Perhaps I will just have forgotten the whole thing.

Besides, I have a lot to do. Apples to slice and dry. Packages to put up and deliveries to make. I've been planning to use Christmas ribbons to tie the bags closed for those who might want to give the dried apples as presents. Aunt Ida and I are going to make Dutch apple pies to sell in time for Thanksgiving. We might even make apple coffee cakes for Christmas breakfast. We have such a big apple crop this year. Those little trees Momma and I watered and pruned and worried over for so many years have so many apples hanging on them that the branches look like they might break.

This is really a cash crop this year. Most of it will go into the bank. Eventually, I will need a car so Katherine and I can make our apple deliveries. And, oh, yes, Helen said her son isn't interested in continuing any of his mom's egg routes. They will need more eggs for their family now that the boys are getting bigger and John won't have time to be running all over delivering eggs to stores and the people on Helen's old route. So, looks like Momma's long-ago plan to pick up where Helen left off will happen. I'm thinking that money could go for equipment for the house, the farm, or just save for a rainy day.

So, this is the last you'll hear from me about my troubles. Momma's getting better, Fletcher's away at college. Aunt Ida and I have a lot of plans for the coming months. And Sarah and I still have weeks to go when we can ride our bikes up and down the road. Life is good.

Annalise

CHAPTER EIGHTEEN

Annalise had just finished feeding Katherine when the porch door opened. Sarah was early. Poppa was still pacing with his coffee. He looked at the clock over the kitchen sink. "Heavens," he muttered. "We're going to be late."

He set his cup on the stove and blew Kate a goodbye kiss. "We're going to have to drive fast today," he said as he waved goodbye to Ida, who retrieved the complaining Katherine. "See you tonight," he called. "Katherine, be a good little girl today. Take care of Grammy and Auntie until we get back."

The girls usually talked all the way into town and all the way home, but there wasn't a peep from the back seat. "Goodness," Gerrit said to himself. "I think I forgot the girls this morning. Now I have to go back and pick them up. I will surely be late for work, and they will certainly be late for school and have to sit for a detention for being tardy."

That prompted a few giggles, but nothing more.

When he dropped them off near the front door of the school, they waved goodbye and were quickly absorbed in the confusion of gathering students.

Annalise stood alone on the sidewalk. Nearby, a group of girls she'd gone to school with before were too busy talking to pay any attention to her. Meanwhile, Sarah joined the knot of first-year Amish, all dressed alike in their dark skirts and white tops and caps.

A wave of sadness washed over Annalise as she tried to push back the suffocating feeling that she was walled in.

During lunch period, Anna looked for Sarah, but again she and the Amish cousins and friends had their usual table by the large windows at the back of the room, bent over in eager, quiet conversation. As much as she needed a friend, she knew they weren't excluding her, but she just didn't fit in their circle.

After lunch, Anna stood alone, basking in the fall sunshine. Deep in thought, she didn't notice Sarah until she was standing in front of her by the main entrance to the high school.

"I won't be riding home with you and your dad tonight," Sarah said, unaware that she'd startled her friend. "Our church district has made arrangements for the Amish students to have a bus pick us up in the morning and take us home at night, so I won't be riding my bike down to your house in the morning anymore. Please tell your father I thank him for letting me ride with you to and from school. The church Elders thought this would be a better way. Some of us had rides, many didn't. So, we will all ride on the same bus."

Although Anna tried to smile, she knew it was a poor attempt.

"I hope we can still be friends," Sarah said before heading back down the steps to where the others waited. Anna was speechless. Why hadn't Sarah told her that on the drive into town that morning? Swallowing tears after the curt announcement, Anna wondered if Sarah had only just found out about the new bus arrangement. Or maybe she'd known but didn't know how to tell her.

She raised her hand to brush her hair off her face—and the falling tears from her cheeks.

The bell rang and students re-arranged themselves into class lines. All the Amish students were in the freshmen row, Anna and her sophomore classmates in the second.

As she followed the line down to the sophomore wing, Anna kept replaying Sarah's indifferent announcement that meant an abrupt end to their fun. Another crushing blow to an already fragile period of her life. Heaped on the distress of their recent, ill-fated trip to see the bishop, this was an even heavier burden to carry. She knew it probably made good sense to have a bus transport all the Amish students together. But it also meant Sarah was back with her friends and cousins, leaving her to arrive at school alone every morning. There was no reason to think they had done anything to purposefully cut themselves off from her, but it nevertheless was more than she could deal with.

The Amish bus slammed its door shut on what was, for her, the only normal thing in her life. She could no longer laugh and talk with a friend, just like every other kid arriving at school in the morning. That little trip into town was a dividing line between her obligations as a young mom with an infant daughter and the carefree life of a student.

She knew enough about the Amish lifestyle to know that riding into town with Annalise and her dad was probably something their faith didn't approve of. It put one of their own into too-close a relationship with an English girl. Never mind that their friendship had grown out of a need for Anna to have a trusted friend during her long days of summer as she awaited the birth of her baby.

The day dragged on. Monday was choir day, a class Anna looked forward to, but not that day. She couldn't skip the class since they already started rehearsals for their holiday music program. Choir was the last class of the day, and Anna knew it would run at least another half-hour after the other classes ended. She kept an eye on the clock so she wouldn't be late for Poppa.

Gerrit was puzzled when he saw Anna standing alone. "What happened to Sarah?" he asked.

She hesitated, unsure of how to tell him. And not realizing how his daughter would be affected by Sarah's new ride to school arrangement, he said: "I was expecting that eventually would happen." Then, glancing in the rearview mirror, he realized how sad his daughter looked. "Sarah's been a good friend to you, and I'm sorry she won't be riding with us anymore. Letting so many Amish girls enroll in high school was almost unheard of for their church," he said. "It just made sense for them. It was one thing for her to ride into town with us, but there were many other Amish who had no such easy connections into town. And, of course, if a bus was going to pick up and deliver Amish students from their area, she would be expected to also take the bus."

Annalise knew all the right answers. It was just the personal cost to her self-esteem that troubled her. "I know all that," she whispered.

When her dad didn't say anything else, Anna leaned back and closed her eyes. She knew he wasn't ignoring her, but she also knew he didn't know what to say to help her cope with this unexpected change in her dream of blending the two parts of her young life into a workable routine.

Back at the farm, Anna was out of the car and up the steps before Gerrit pulled into the garage. She found Katherine snuggled under a blanket on Momma's bed. They were both asleep. She picked up Katherine and carried her upstairs to their room. She pushed the door shut until it latched, then put the baby in her crib. She sat in the rocker in front of the window, staring at the cornfield across the road. In the distance, trees in the grove beyond the field were painted with splashes of brilliant red mixed with golden birch leaves dancing in the late-afternoon breeze. The view was mesmerizing.

Her reverie was cut short by Katherine's complaints. Time for another change? A bottle? Getting up from the rocker, she changed the baby and put her in warmer pajamas for the night. Anna was about to go downstairs to warm a bottle when she met Aunt Ida coming up with one.

"We'll eat in a half hour," Ida said. "Your dad hasn't come in from the barn yet, and the meatloaf isn't quite done. It should be by the time the baby finishes her bottle. Come down when you're ready. We'll keep dinner warm until you finish up here."

Annalise took the bottle, nodded thanks, and went to her room. The baby was hungry, but Anna wasn't. It had been such a disastrous day she just wanted to pull the covers over her head and sleep. Maybe tomorrow would be easier.

When Anna didn't come down to eat, her dad went upstairs. "It's time to eat. Ida's got a beautiful meatloaf ready to serve, so if our little girl isn't quite finished, bring her down and we can take turns feeding her."

Annalise didn't argue.

She made a good-faith effort to eat a little of everything on the plate Aunt Ida dished up for her. She finished most of her slice of meatloaf, a few bites of mashed potatoes, and the glass of cold milk Poppa poured for her. Katherine, meanwhile, had a full tummy and a warm spot on the daybed.

Helping carry plates and silverware to the kitchen, Anna noticed an Amish buggy slowing down as it neared their driveway. The buggies all looked so much alike it wasn't until this one parked at the front porch that she realized it was Sarah and her parents.

Gerrit walked to the doorway, pushing the screen door open as the Mellen's got out and walked up the steps. "We were just about to have a little coffee and Ida's fresh-baked apple cake. Won't you join us?"

"A cup of coffee would be good, but we just finished our supper and need to head back soon so we can start evening prayers," Mr. Mellen said. "We wanted to talk with you about the change in Sarah's transport to school. We know the girls had a good time traveling with you, Gerrit. But our church district decided that with so many families having children going to high school this year, it would be better to hire a bus to take all the Amish high schoolers together. While we had a wonderful arrangement with you, the church didn't approve, since there were many others who had no way to get to and from school. The only thing that made sense was to bus them. We have not had this problem before, since most of our children did not go on to high school."

"We hope you understand," Sarah's mother added. "We hope our girls can continue to find ways to spend time together. But it probably won't be after school, with chores, evening meal, prayers and homework."

Anna and Sarah sat quietly while their parents talked. They forgot to giggle.

The Mellen's finished their coffee and conversation and got up to leave. But before they did, Sarah checked on Katherine. "She is so beautiful and getting so big. Do you think she will have curly hair? It certainly looks like there are ringlets winding up around her ears."

"Thank you for the coffee," Mrs. Mellen said. "By the way, Annalise... are you still planning to have dried apple rings for sale? I need to figure out how many packages I'll need for Christmas gifts. If you don't mind, I'll stop by in a few days to place an order."

Sarah's goodbye had an edge of discomfort. Was she mad that she couldn't ride with them, or upset because Anna looked miserable? Both girls looked sad.

"We could still ride our bikes together sometimes," Sarah told Anna, patting her arm as they walked toward the screen door.

Anna picked up the baby and watched as they climbed into the buggy for their trip home. Maybe holding the baby made it easier to look less stressed.

"We truly enjoyed having Sarah ride with us for as many days as she did," Gerrit said as he shook hands with Aaron. "You are such wonderful neighbors, and we are very happy to live so close to you. It was thoughtful of you to interrupt your evening to come over and talk with us."

Anna hadn't noticed that Ida went back in the house and was washing supper dishes. Kate sat quietly while the rest talked about bus arrangements.

Ida came back out to the porch. "Nellie didn't say anything about helping with our laundry. I'm sure she probably isn't planning to do it now, since it had been her way of repaying us for her daughter's rides to school. We'll figure out a way to get the diapers and everything else done."

Anna laid the baby down again on the daybed. Kate reached over to the rocking chair and easily made the switch from the straight-back chair. A rim of darkening clouds signaled the weather was going to get wet and thundery.

"Gerrit?" Kate asked, "could you make sure all the windows are closed before you go out to the milk house? Most are open."

"I'll shut those upstairs when I take Katherine up," Anna said. "I have some reading to do, so I might just stay up there until I finish."

Anna was still curled up in the rocking chair next to Fletcher's bed when her alarm went off. What happened to the night? Frightened, she glanced over at the baby, who was beginning to stir. She remembered setting her alarm for three a.m. but she never heard it. Had Katherine missed her early feeding?

The book Anna was reading for a class assignment the night before still lay in her lap, unfinished. Even if she read while they drove into town and she skipped lunch, there'd be no way to finish the assigned pages. How long did she read before dozing off? She picked up the book and tried to scan down the open page to see if any words looked familiar. None did. She turned back a page, but still didn't recognize any words. What a night for Katherine to sleep straight through. It wasn't bad enough that her whole life seemed upside down, now she'd be in serious trouble with Miss Adams for not reading the assigned chapters.

Anna heard sounds from downstairs. Aunt Ida making breakfast. Or maybe Poppa filling his cup a second time. Rather than waiting for Katherine to open her eyes and let out her call for breakfast, Anna put on her robe and ran downstairs, making a stop in the bathroom before going to the kitchen for a bottle. By the time she finished those errands, Katherine was ready for a change and snack. No time to worry about homework.

Dappled sunlight spread across the lawn, highlighting the golden yellow streaks in the piles of fallen birch leaves. The sun looked warm, but the trees sending leaves flying in all directions spelled a sunny but cool forecast, and warm jammies.

Rather than spend time doing her favorite thing—rocking Katherine while she finished her breakfast—Anna put a blanket under the bottle and let her drink by herself for a few minutes while she changed from yesterday's clothes into a fresh outfit for school. She combed her hair and put on her saddle shoes.

"Come here, little girl," she said, picking up her daughter. Katherine complained a bit when she lost the bottle but quickly settled again when she found it was only a temporary delay. "You know," Anna told her, "you were supposed to wake me up for a midnight diaper change and feeding. Didn't you know I had a chapter to read in that book?"

Katherine didn't care. Soothed by a familiar voice and the rhythmic motion of the rocker, she dozed off. After sucking the last sips, it was burp time.

"Annalise? Breakfast is on the table."

"Down in a minute," she called.

Kate was already at the table when Anna and the baby stepped onto the porch. Ida was dishing up a bowl of steaming oatmeal for Anna. "I figured you'd like a warm treat this morning," she said, reaching for Katherine.

CHAPTER NINETEEN

FATHER CLEARY NOLAN'S STORY

The night orderly noticed Cleary Nolan watching him open the blinds to what would have been a glorious sunrise, if it hadn't been for the swirling dust blocking the sky.

"Looks like we're not going to see the sunrise today," the orderly said, glancing toward the bed where the glum priest still stared at the window. "This time of year, it's not unusual to see New Mexico blowing over into our neighborhood. Looks like it's been blowin' most of the night."

The priest still didn't react.

The orderly smiled, pulling the door partly closed as he stepped back into the hallway.

It had been a very long train ride, most of it wrapped in austere silence. Father's traveling companion had been anything but pleasant. He read his prayers, shuffled paperwork, snoozed and snored—anything but talked. The silence was annoying, but he didn't mind not having to carry on polite conversation with this overseer who had the responsibility of keeping him in check during the long commute.

He never would have believed he'd be relegated to such a low spot on the priestly ladder, but he had no one to blame but himself. That reality kept chewing on his insides. What he'd done, he had done to himself. It was his downfall. The notion that "the devil made him do it" sounded like a little kid in the confessional, trying to explain away how something bad had happened. He'd chosen to do it of his own free will. He'd planned all the details—a long time ago, in fact. The routine was a familiar one for his lustful fantasies. The only difference this time was that there were consequences. There might have been at one of the other dozen or so times he'd played the same game with a young student, but this was the first one that went terribly wrong.

On the long ride, he'd only occasionally shifted in his seat, careful not to disturb his snoring companion. He thought of the girl, new to his school, who'd introduced herself at the reception for new students last September. Her aunt had invited him for a soup and sandwich supper the following Sunday night so they could continue their discussion about the differences between their two faiths.

Father Cleary was always interested in her recollections of the family life of a Methodist preacher and the different traditions and beliefs, but

Ida's niece rarely stayed longer than to finish her sandwich. She always had homework, friends to talk with, letters to write home.

The torment of revisiting those pleasant evenings made him sick to his stomach. He could still picture Ida's stories about growing up in the parish house across from the Iowa church where they lived. Part of the pleasure was that it reminded him of his own mother's little house after his dad died. She would have been alone, except for an elderly retainer who helped with the horses and other chores on the mostly mothballed farm. Even though she didn't want to live there alone, she could not bring herself to sell the estate.

Father Cleary still missed her. Thinking back, he realized his problems started when she died. He was left with a heart-crushing sense of loneliness. He had no one. No one he could share stories with, no one to sit around a kitchen table with and enjoy a cup of tea and a plateful of oatmeal raisin cookies.

Faces and names were long forgotten, but treasured memories of his mother haunted him. Much as he tried, he couldn't erase them. They were alone in the big house on the bluffs overlooking Lake Superior. Nolan's dad had only rarely been there. He'd grown up in that house and was always anxious to get away from it. His mother, Nolan's grandmother, who grew up in a cottage in Galway, Ireland, never liked the manor house. So, after Nolan's grandfather died, she moved out of the big house into a little cottage nearby. "Someday this will be yours," she used to tell him. But he'd felt a calling to the priesthood, and his mother was overjoyed. When he was on vacation from the seminary, she'd move back into the big house so he could spend time there, riding and walking along the Superior shoreline. Even those days were unsettling, because he knew one day she wouldn't be there.

Thinking back now, he must have known from Ida's first invitation how it might eventually end. Not that the aunt would ever have allowed any impropriety, but he could pick a time. He'd planned ahead, slipping a key from the key plaque alongside the front door and had a copy made. It took a couple of times before he was able to replace the original key on its proper hook. Then it was just a matter of waiting for an opportunity.

What a fool he'd been. So smug. He'd never given it much thought all those other times. Usually didn't even bother to confess the sin against his vow of celibacy. Occasionally, he'd think about it, but only to remember the pleasure, not the horror of what he'd done. He couldn't remember ever thinking he should be sorry for what he'd done—raping a young girl after plying her with a cruet of alcohol. His mother used to give him a warm toddy when he'd had bronchitis as a boy, but that toddy only had warm water, lemon juice and lots of honey. The only part of his mother's recipe in *his* toddy was the honey he'd scooped from the jar he always had in his kitchen cupboard.

His reverie was rudely jarred back to the present by the housekeeper's cheerful greeting as she opened the blinds to let in more of the darkened morning sky. "Breakfast is on the way," she said. "Sorry you had to spend the night in our infirmary, but your room in the treatment center wasn't ready. You looked so tired. We're a long way from Wisconsin. But the weather's a bit warmer here, at least." She told him she'd lived there a short time with her grandmother years ago when her mom had been sick.

Before she moved on to the next room, the cart with breakfast trays pulled up outside his door. He wasn't sure how he was supposed to act—a perfectly well person (although not mentally well), getting served breakfast in bed in a hospital. He wondered if his traveling companion had found a hotel room for the night or if he was sitting in the train station waiting for his return ride.

He swung his legs over the side of the bed and pulled the tray up to a comfortable height. He was just starting to remove the covers from the warm food when he heard familiar footsteps getting closer to his room.

"Mornin', Cleary," the voice said as he came around the corner. "See they've got a breakfast tray for you. Hope it's as good as it smells."

He was unbearably cheerful, happy, no doubt, that his babysitting chores were almost over. Father Nolan wasn't sure what he was supposed to say. They hadn't established any rapport on the two days they'd spent together on the train. He wasn't sure he'd ever see him again, anyway. If he'd reached one conclusion during the long trip down the railroad line, it was that he'd undoubtedly never be assigned anywhere in that diocese again. Suited him just fine. Actually, he'd been thinking maybe life would be a whole lot easier if he just slipped off his clerical collar and went on his own way.

"When do you head back?" Father Nolan asked, surprising himself with the question.

"Have to leave in a few minutes for the station. Wouldn't want to miss it. Anxious to get back. I don't like just sitting around, so I guess this is goodbye. I personally want to wish you well in your treatment here. I know the bishop is hopeful it will help you sort through your mistakes and learn how to make better choices in the future. With your counseling, please remember to pray. I know I don't need to tell you how important prayer is. Work hard on your therapy. Those of us who know where you are and what your current assignment is will be praying with you. Know that we care about you and need your considerable talent as a priest. Those you have served have high regard for you. They would be very distressed if they knew where you were and why. We pray this will bring you back to Christ's fold as a priest in his image."

He leaned over and kissed Nolan on both cheeks. "Christ be with you. Christ lead you back to your holy orders. Christ help you to atone for the sins of the flesh you have committed and give you the strength to make amends. Come back to us spiritually refreshed and cleansed."

Cleary Nolan found no words in response to that farewell. His mind was a muddle of anguish, sorrow, agony. Fear.

After his travel companion left, Nolan wondered why he'd never suggested confession. Priests, after all, had as much need for confession and absolution as any of the faithful did. Perhaps he thought Cleary could not make a proper confession without having some therapy sessions to help him cleanse his own soul. Pity. He could've used the counseling of a confessor and, even more so, forgiveness for his sins. He could not forgive himself for what he'd done, not just once, but more times than he remembered.

The first days were a blur. There were other men there, but he had not yet met any of them. They sat together in a large dining room for meals, but only a few shared tables. Most, like Cleary, sat alone. Each day when he walked into that room for breakfast, he thought he could not feel any more depressed. But he knew that he had not yet sunk to the depth of his personal grief and horror at where he was and why. It was a pit he thought he could never climb out of. He knew there was no way to go back to where he'd been before. His life as he'd known it was over. He didn't know how he could possibly survive when there was no daily Mass to be said for students and parishioners looking to him for help and comfort. Those days, he knew, were now closed off. Permanently.

He still had a hard time putting his fingers to his forehead for the first mark of the sign of the cross and even the mundane prayer before meals was impossible to say without the words catching in his throat.

He still read the hours of his daily office, but it would be weeks before he could focus on the words he was whispering. Was anyone anywhere listening to his agonized cry for help?

In the dark of night, he talked to his mom. He tried to tell her how sorry he was for his terrible fall from God's grace. He could sense her chiding him for trying to hide from the one he should be talking to: God. But for all the hours he'd spent on his knees over his lifetime, he couldn't face Him. He could hear her voice reminding him that God was always ready to listen. If only he could find the courage to kneel and beg forgiveness.

And then one day he did. He had just finished shaving when he had the overwhelming desire to pray. He knelt there by the sink, his hands clasped but shaking uncontrollably. There were no words—just sobs. Why now? He'd done this same awful thing before. Faces cycled around and around in his mind, but he couldn't put any of them in focus except for the last one. Annalise.

"Oh, God," he whispered. Or was he shouting? He leaned his forehead against the cold rim of the sink, but all he could think was, *Oh, God!* There were no other words left to say.

Suddenly, he realized someone was tapping on the door. He felt the door push slightly against the soles of his slippers. He heard his name being called, but he couldn't answer. Finally, he roused himself enough to try to stand, but he knew if he could manage it, his sorrow would be visible to the world.

He stayed in the bathroom for a very long time. Eventually, he was able to pray that his evil could be forgiven, if not forgotten. He imagined himself standing at the bottom of Christ's cross of Calvary and knew then that his anguish might just consume him. He knew God was looking down on him, but he didn't dare to look up. At one point during that long morning, someone came to check on him. Eventually he heard his own voice, talking to God, his words caught in sobs. Once he started talking to God, he couldn't stop. At first, he did all the talking, not waiting to hear what God might have to say in return. He knew he needed to confess his sins. But first he had to talk to God about where this sin had taken him. He no longer saw himself as a priest. He resolved to live a life of penance, seeking forgiveness for what he'd done. Was a lifetime long enough?

It was early afternoon before he opened the door and left the bathroom. He thought about getting dressed but realized that would take more energy than he had. A lunch tray had been left on his bedside table, but he had no appetite.

Eventually, he dressed and stood by the window, looking out over the backyard, watching as some of the priests strolled along the walkways, reading their prayers.

The long day ended when he undressed and crawled into bed. The lunch tray was still on the bedside table. Maybe it was a supper tray.

The next morning, he was awake long before the sun came up. He'd left the blinds open the night before so he could watch the dark sky. This time, when he got up and went into the bathroom to get ready for the day, he could look into the mirror and recognize the face of who he used to be. He shaved without falling to his knees. He realized he might even enjoy a little breakfast before the morning sessions began.

The following days were easier to handle, but his world would never, ever look the same. He could see his mother's face, a faint smile on her lips, but without that Irish twinkle in her eyes.

He took walks with the others around the backyard and found snatches of time to drop in at the little chapel to whisper reassuring prayers to himself. Day by day, those prayers grew longer and more fervent. Some days, he just sat in one of the back pews, hoping God would offer a word of encouragement to him. But he hadn't confessed his sin to an earthly confessor priest, and the reassurance that all had been forgiven didn't come.

Then, he finally found the courage to ask to go to confession. Even when he heard the priest's words of forgiveness and penance, he couldn't leave the booth. He heard the priest leave, but he stayed where he was, saying his penitential prayers in the shelter of that box. The door to the priest's cubicle had been left open, and a small ray of sunshine seeped into the other space from one of the windows along the outside wall. Eventually, he finished his prayers and stood up to leave. But he couldn't. He knelt again and continued praying.

Eventually he heard the chapel door open and close, and he sensed someone standing outside the confessional. He tried again to stand but couldn't. The person outside the curtain pulled it back and slipped an arm around him, helping him up. It was the priest who'd heard his confession, probably hours earlier.

"It's time for our evening meal," the priest said as they bowed their heads toward the altar and turned to leave the darkened chapel. "God's heard your prayers and has brought you here to ask for and receive forgiveness for your sin. Now you have to face the rest of your life and pray over how you will begin again."

For the first time since he'd arrived at the center, Nolan shared his small table with the priest from confession. They had a pleasant conversation. Without tears.

That day marked a serious turning point in Father Nolan's therapy. Blessed with the miracle of forgiveness and prayers for strength for his new convictions of celibacy, he couldn't stop thanking God for bringing him this far in his journey to…what? He knew it could not be back to the priesthood. There were too many pitfalls that could trap him again. He'd be a priest in his heart forever, but he could never face a parish or school again. He prayed that he could remain faithful to those vows he'd taken, even if they would no longer be required of him.

A few days later, Nolan spotted his new priest friend seated on a bench down below his window. He hurried out of his room and went outside to join him. He waited for the other priest to finish his prayers. When he looked up, smiling, Father Nolan told him he needed some advice on how to go about being dispensed of his priestly vows. They talked for a long time about whether he was serious or if it was just more of his need to punish himself for what he'd done. Stepping away from vows could not be done on a whim, even if it was a whim fueled by horror and shame at what he'd done. God had forgiven him in confession. But He hadn't forgiven himself. And spending it in a dark confessional wasn't the way to look ahead at what was next.

They both smiled a bit at that.

The days passed, and the two priests continued their conversations about what to do with Nolan's priesthood. One thing Father Nolan knew for certain —living a solitary life as a priest would not guarantee that he'd never fall into the same sin again. Gradually, their conversations turned to the laicizing process. There was no comfort in reaching that decision, but Nolan knew he had to do it if he were to save his own soul.

With his friend's help, Nolan composed a letter to the bishop to explain his decision to leave the priesthood.

Father Nolan tried to think through where he could go, what he could do to support himself. He had a couple of elderly aunts living in warm climates, but he wasn't close enough to any of them to consider living near them. He wanted to settle anonymously somewhere he could do social welfare work that would give him an opportunity to live a life of repentance. He'd prayed enough about that for months, knowing as far back as his first fall into sin that he didn't belong in the priesthood. He couldn't take a chance that he'd bring more shame to the church, but there was no plan to leave the church, either. It had been such a central part of his life since early childhood that he couldn't imagine not having its comforting arms around him.

One thing still bothered him: the inheritance he had received from his mother. Not needing the income at the time, he'd met with people at the bank to get it all safely invested. He had no one to inherit the tidy sum after his death. The aunts in California were so far removed from him he didn't want the money left to them. Besides, they'd undoubtedly be gone long before his inheritance would be an issue. And now, he had more pressing concerns for that money. It would need to remain invested until his death—he was pretty sure of that—but he now had an heir entitled to that money. But how could he add a beneficiary without showing up in the old neighborhood and taking a chance at being found out?

During a phone call to the chancery office, Nolan explained to the bishop his dilemma. Next, he talked to the diocesan attorney, who put him in touch with another attorney who could make the necessary changes to that invested money so it would eventually go to his son or daughter. The attorney explained that the baby was a girl named Katherine.

Father Nolan couldn't breathe for a minute. Katherine. Annalise could never have known that Nolan's mother's name was Katherine, too. "She kept the baby," he said aloud to himself.

"Yes, she did," the lawyer said. "Annalise brought the baby with her to a meeting with the bishop shortly after she was born. The family is raising her as just another child while the girl finishes high school. She's a sophomore now, I believe."

Weeks later, Nolan and the investment lawyer met to review the paperwork for the beneficiary to his will and the invested inheritance. That's when Father Nolan realized he didn't even remember Annalise's last name.

CHAPTER TWENTY

Gerrit stopped tapping on his vintage typewriter and reached for the phone. "Ida, it's Emmy."

Gerrit handed Ida the phone and went to find Kate. The conversation went on a long time. Ida's face reflected the conversation, alternating broad smiles and tears.

What happened? Anna wondered as she carried Katherine upstairs for her nap. She thought about a nap herself, but she wondered what happened to Emily.

"Emily's invited herself here for Thanksgiving, if it's okay with all of you. She's bringing a guest for us to meet. I said I'd call her back later to let her know if they can come."

"Emily is welcome anytime," Gerrit said.

"She wants us to meet the man she plans to marry," Ida said. "They just became engaged." I didn't even know she was dating someone. I'm very happy for her, but she's kept this all a big secret, leading me on to believe we were going to sell both of our houses and buy a bigger one so we could live together. I wonder why? Maybe she didn't believe he was going to ask her."

Ida moved the rocker next to the space heater that was quickly warming the chilly room. "She said we'd have to spend Thanksgiving dinner discussing wedding plans. He taught senior classes at Saint Michael's High School, but he's given his notice to leave at the end of this semester. He's going to be principal of a Catholic high school in Chicago. That's where he's from. In fact, that's where they are going for a second Thanksgiving with his family on Friday. They want me to go with them so I can meet his parents. She said they have a big, beautiful house, so there's plenty of room for guests. I feel like I'm babbling. My Emily will be moving to Chicago. What will I do without my little girl nearby?"

She got up from the rocker and headed for the stairs. "I think I need to sit awhile and let this all sink in. I'll be down later."

After Ida returned from her quiet, the rest of the family found out more about the engagement. Emily had met him when she was subbing for a Saint Michael's teacher on long-term maternity absence.

When Anna heard where Emily met him, she panicked. He might have seen Anna at school last year, and now he'd see her with a baby.

Emily's husband had died in a dreadful car crash on a wintry road. And the man she was about to marry had lost his wife in a bad car crash two years earlier. Like Emily and Tom, they'd only been married a couple years. She said he'd never planned to marry again—until he met Emily. Emily had never talked of looking for a new mate, either.

"She said they talked over lunch in the cafeteria a few times, then went on a formal movie date on a Saturday night. They've been dating ever since," Ida said. Then she sucked in a breath. "Oh, my goodness. We can't have him here for Thanksgiving. He'll recognize Annalise, see the baby, and put two and two together about what happened to the freshman girl who'd left the high school without explanation last year."

She didn't hesitate and quickly walked over to the phone. The long-distance call was quickly connected. "Is your fiancé there now?" Ida asked her daughter.

"Uh huh."

"I didn't think through his connection with Anna's old school," Ida explained. "He would recognize her, see the baby, and realize why she'd left so hurriedly. Although Anna has not kept in contact with anyone at the school, this could become the topic of conversation among the teachers and that would spread to all grade levels."

Anna's biggest worry was that they would connect her new baby to the principal's banishment from the parish. There were plenty of voices trying to put a reason on why Annalise disappeared over a weekend, she was sure of it.

Anna thought Aunt Ida was about to cry. She knew Ida wanted to be with Emily for the holiday, but she couldn't risk the danger to Anna and Katherine. Rather than listen to the ongoing phone conversation, Anna went upstairs, shutting the bedroom door behind her.

However things worked out, it would put a damper on the celebration she'd been so looking forward to. It meant Fletcher would finally come home for a long weekend. She had so much to tell him, so many questions to ask about college and making friends. She was sure Aunt Ida would go home for the holiday weekend to be with Emily in Chicago, which would eliminate any concern about her friend seeing Annalise.

Katherine was still snoozing, so Anna snuggled under the afghan from the bottom of the bed and quickly fell asleep. When Katherine finally woke up, Anna saw by the angle of the light that it was almost time for supper. She quickly changed Katherine, then took her downstairs to get a bottle. But when she went to open the bedroom door, had her hand out, reaching for the knob, Ida surprised her.

"Funny meeting you here," Ida laughed. Ida walked in and settled into the rocking chair that stood near the window. "Emily and I had a long talk about the whole situation. She'd anticipated that if she brought him up here for Thanksgiving, seeing you could be an issue. So, Emmy said she figured she might as well tell Robert exactly what was what. He'd find out about it all soon enough, anyway." Ida stopped, and Anna noticed there were tears in her eyes.

"Oh, Auntie, are you upset?"

"I'm just so happy that I can't even express it. She seems so excited, so pleased with her choice, and so anxious for all of us to meet him. Yes, I could have gone down there and had the holiday in one of our houses, but she wanted him to meet the family, all of you, so it didn't make sense to keep him away then have them drive up another weekend to meet you. He understands the situation, or most of it—but nothing about the priest— although she thinks he probably figured that out already."

"Where is everyone going to sleep?" Annalise asked, surprised that was her first question.

"Oh, that's no problem. They'll drive up early Thursday morning, then drive back to Emily's house late in the afternoon. They plan to have turkey sandwiches and pie at a relative's house in Milwaukee, then drive to his parents' on Friday. Now we not only have to get you through high school, but I've got to plan a wedding and figure out what we're going to do about my house. Apparently, Robert was just hired as top administrator for a Catholic high school in a Chicago suburb, starting with the new semester in January. The person who has the job now recently developed a serious health condition and can no longer work. It's the high school where Robert went when he was a kid. Isn't that exciting? Except it's scary for me, because eventually she will move to Chicago with him. and I will be left up here. Not that that's all bad, because I have all of you to fill my life with such pleasure and happiness. I am so blessed!"

Katherine didn't think much of all the conversation. She had a dry diaper but no bottle. After her long nap, she was hungry.

"I'd better get something for Katherine to eat," Annalise said, wrapping her daughter in an afghan.

Downstairs. Anna found her parents in the living room. Momma, as usual, had chosen the old rocker; Poppa was in his squeaky desk chair, his left leg stretched so his foot could rest on the slide-out writing board. They weren't talking, but Anna knew words were going back and forth without either moving their lips. Kate probably had the decorations already planned for the wedding reception. Her dad would be thinking of a good place to have the ceremony and reception, even though it undoubtedly would not be in their old neighborhood. Maybe Emily would ask him to give her away. Anna had only been to one wedding, and that was for a neighbor who was married in their little church down the road. Then she had an awful thought. If the wedding was in the city, Annalise wouldn't be able to go, because all the teachers from the school would be there—maybe even some students. They'd see her and the baby and...

The complications kept growing. When the bottle was warmed, Kate and Katherine sat with Annalise, quietly trying to sort out this news, then exchanging her grim, pursed lips for a happy smile for Katherine. There'd be plenty of time to get it sorted out. *If Katherine could be my child,* thought Kate, *no one would know the difference if Anna held and fed her. Even if old classmates were there and asking questions.*

The ringing phone shook them all back into focus. It was Fletcher, letting them know he'd drive home Wednesday night.

Gerrit said he had a plan for Fletcher's break next summer. "Fletcher, you're going to build an addition on this house. We're getting a little short on bedrooms. Now that Emily is getting married, I figure she'll visit occasionally. We could fix a bedroom for you in the granary over the garage. It's not very warm up there these days, but it's quiet. Unless a mouse or two stop by."

Ψ

Annalise could hardly wait for Thursday morning. She was so excited for Fletcher to get home too. As Wednesday evening wore on, she didn't even bother to carry Katherine upstairs. She knew her brother would want to see how much she'd grown in the weeks he'd been gone.

Baked apple and pumpkin pies covered the kitchen table. The turkey sat legs-up in the covered roaster on the front porch. It would be ready to go in the oven as soon as the cookstove was fired up in the early morning. But still no Fletcher.

They decided he stopped at the Iversen's to visit his girlfriend, Cynthia.

"You can all go to bed. Katherine and I will wait up for Fletch. I can't wait to see him and hear stories about college. If he wants to sleep in here, I'll help him move the daybed. Otherwise, I'll find blankets to keep him warm on the porch."

Baking pies for all their customers had taken some doing for Anna and Ida. The big table on the porch groaned under the weight of the breads, relishes, and pies. Between their own preparations, friends and neighbors knocked at the door all day. There were breakfast rolls glazed with frosting and nuts. There were fancy dinner rolls and loaves of bread to slice later for turkey sandwiches. Nearly every kitchen towel covered something on the table.

The dinner table's leaves spread it to full size, with the fancy dishes stacked in the center, ready to set after the breakfast of sweet rolls and baked egg casserole.

Anna didn't remember the house ever looking quite so clean and festive.

Dinner preparations were well in hand when the lights in the kitchen clicked off, and Ida excused herself to go upstairs to bed. "I think the rest can wait for morning."

Anna, rocking a restless baby, suggested her parents also go to bed. "I have to stay up awhile for Katherine," she said, "and I might as well just hang around down here until Fletcher gets home." She wondered why he hadn't arrived yet but didn't say anything. If something had happened, he would have let them know. "Perhaps he's still at Cynthia's house," she whispered to Katherine.

"Wake me when he gets here," Gerrit whispered as he bent to kiss the baby goodnight. "But don't wake your mother. Tomorrow will be a long and tiring day for her."

It was a mild night for late November she thought as she carried the blanket-wrapped baby out to the front porch. She thought family arrangements for the holiday would have put more cars and buggies on the road, but deep darkness engulfed the area, leaving her with a sense of uneasiness.

Anna settled a sleeping Katherine on the daybed, and she leaned back in the rocker, watching for Fletcher's car. She'd dozed off before headlights came up over the slight rise in the road, slowed, then turned into the driveway. "At last," she said as she tiptoed across to the doorway. She would have gone to meet him but decided against going outside in bare feet. The ground was covered with frost. Or was it snow?

Fletcher had to know she'd be up, waiting, even if the house was resting in darkness. He must have noticed her in the rocker. Still, he didn't make a move to come inside. Finally, she opened the door just wide enough so she could get out. When he saw her on the steps, he slid out of the vehicle. She expected him to bound over to her, giving her his usual enveloping bear hug. When he didn't, she knew something was wrong.

"Hey, Fletcher," she whispered. "Glad to see you." She moved inside, but he was slow to follow. "What's wrong?"

"Cynthia," was all he could say.

The questions tumbled out, but the words didn't. She just stood there, afraid to ask what happened. Fletcher and Cynthia had been friends for a long time—since they were kids. Anna knew they'd talked about getting married someday after college.

"What happened? Is Cynthia okay? Is she sick?" Anna asked.

"She said she doesn't want to go out with me anymore," Fletcher explained. She's started seeing other guys at school. She says I'm still her best friend, but she can't go out with me. She said I was like a brother, and you don't date your brother."

Fletcher let out a slow breath before continuing. "I left her place and just drove around, but that didn't help me feel any better. Finally, I figured I might as well just come home and go to bed. Am I supposed to sleep out here on the daybed?"

"I brought down a stack of comforters for you. I piled them on the bench. I'll take Katherine up to her crib, then come down so we can talk a bit."

When she came back, Anna found Fletcher sound asleep, buried under a mound of their grandparents' quilts. Anna liked looking at the old quilts Nana had made.

Anna turned off the light over the kitchen sink and got herself to bed. She figured there was no sense waking their dad. She could hear him snoring, and morning would come soon enough. Then he'd find his college student son buried under a small mountain of quilts.

The nighttime rhythms of the house had settled into a peaceful quiet, but Anna was restless. Her brain kept replaying the sad message Fletcher had brought home for the holidays. His dearest friend in the world was looking for someone else. Her brother had loved Cynthia forever. Yet after only one semester apart, she'd dumped him so she could shop for his replacement.

Anna dozed off but woke only a few minutes later to stirrings downstairs. *Thanksgiving*, she thought. Then another pang of sadness for Fletcher struck her.

Baby Katherine had more important concerns than Anna's worries about Fletcher. Time for breakfast.

When she went downstairs for a bottle, she found her dad pacing, steaming cup in hand.

"Why didn't you wake me?" he whispered to Anna.

"Something's happened between Fletcher and Cynthia, and he was so overwrought and tired he was practically asleep before he even crawled under those quilts."

Gerrit, staring down the porch to where his son was still asleep, worked his hands, opening and closing his fists. That tic always showed up when he was worried about Fletcher.

Just then, Kate came into the kitchen. Ida followed her with a plate of buttered toast and steaming coffee waiting for her. "Emily's on her way. They should be here within the hour," she said.

When Anna went back upstairs to feed the baby, her dad followed. "Give me a few hints about Fletcher and Cynthia. Does she have another boyfriend? Did they have an argument?"

"He said Cynthia told him that they were like brother and sister since they'd been friends for so long. She's dating other people at her college. He was so distraught. I think he'd been crying. He always has such an air of confidence...but that was all gone last night. He didn't even take his luggage out of the car. I think he would have slept in the car if I hadn't gone out to greet him on the steps."

"I think that he and Cynthia have been friends for so long she hasn't moved from friendship to love. Or, whatever that stage is called when friendship can grow into love. She still sees him more like a brother than a boyfriend. I think she needs to test the waters a bit to see what else is out there. To decide if he *is* just a 'brother,' or if he could well be a real boyfriend, she might someday think about marrying."

"How'd you get so wise?" Gerrit asked, his face relaxing into a smile.

"Nothing better to do in the middle of a long night than try to make sense of your brother's despair. I think if he can just settle back a bit, he will see that she needs to grow into the idea that he loves her and wants to spend his life with her. She's just not ready to move to that level. Yet!"

After Gerrit pondered his young daughter's conclusions, he picked up Katherine and carried her out the doorway. "Get dressed and come down. Let's get this holiday underway," he said, rounding the hallway to the stairs. Still in her bathrobe, Anna followed. She wanted to see Fletcher's reaction when he saw how Katherine had grown.

Fletcher wore a broad grin when he showed up in the crowded kitchen. It seemed he had spent little time worrying about his conversation with Cynthia on his way home. The despair that had haunted his eyes was gone. Even if the worries were still there, he wouldn't let that put a damper on the holiday weekend.

Now all Anna had to worry about was what would happen when Emily's friend recognized her. But, like Fletcher, worrying wasn't going to solve anything. Anna took Katherine from her dad and handed her over to her brother. "She has your eyes," she said. "Blue eyes to match your blond hair."

November 22, 1944

Dear Days:

Fletcher came home for Thanksgiving last night, but it wasn't the happy time I'd been looking forward to. He was so upset over Cynthia, his best friend forever. But I honestly believe she does love him. I suppose she thinks it's only friendship, not courtship.

I know I haven't had any experience in things like this, but it seems this might just be a phase she's going through. Maybe she's afraid of falling in love. I think she wants their close friendship to continue but not cross over into actual courting. I honestly think eventually it will all sort itself out, but right now, he can't accept that she's seeing other boys at her school. Probably testing whether she might really be falling in love, not just hanging out with a family friend and neighbor.

Poppa thinks that's wise advice from a kid without any experience in the love department. We'll see how it works out.

I thought I heard a car coming up the road. It's probably Emily and her friend. I'm really worried about today. Her fiancé might remember seeing me last year at Saint Michael's, as he is a teacher there. When I left, I thought I would never see any of those teachers or students again. Now, one is here to eat Thanksgiving dinner with us. I wonder if he remembers me and will tell other teachers about me and the baby next week. I shouldn't worry about it, but I am upset, because I can imagine how they will all laugh about me. They wouldn't know what really happened, nor would I ever want them to. Emmy told Aunt Ida that the priest still had not returned to school. She said she overheard some of the teachers talking during lunch period about why he left and if he will ever come back.

Aunt Ida told me not to worry, because Emily told her fiancé a little bit about what happened, and he would never say anything to anyone else. I hope I can believe him. Funny thing, I can't remember if I ever saw him at school. I didn't have him for any classes.

I've got to go. Fletcher's on his way to drag me downstairs to join the family.

Thank you for listening.

Annalise

She slid the little daybook under the mattress, even though it was probably the first place anyone would look.

"I'm coming," she called, closing the door behind her as she hurried toward the steps.

Fletcher, holding Baby Katherine, had almost reached the landing by the time she reached the stairway.

"What's taking you so long? We've got company."

Annalise was a little taken aback at her brother's sudden holiday mood. Gone, but probably not forgotten, were worries about his blossoming love for Cynthia Iversen.

Good, Anna thought. *No time for that when we have company.*

As everyone finished their dinners, Anna looked across at Robert for the first time. She had been hesitant about making eye contact with him, but he had been too busy talking with Gerrit to pay attention to anyone else. She studied him for a few seconds, finally deciding she didn't remember him at all. Of course, he would have been in the upper-class wing, she in the freshman.

The pre-dinner introductions had been painless. She assumed he wouldn't ask about the baby, as he apparently thought Kate was the baby's mother and Annalise her sister.

The main topic of conversation was Emily and Robert's engagement and upcoming wedding. An even bigger topic was that they wanted to get married before he moved to Chicago, even though Emily hadn't told her mother that they'd been dating more than a year. Robert's new school had suggested that Emily sign on as a substitute teacher.

They didn't want a big wedding with a lot of fuss. Since Robert was Catholic, they decided to be married in the Catholic Church. Emily had just finished her instruction classes, so they could be married in late December.

"It's a wonderful school," Robert said enthusiastically. "Emily and I drove down a while ago to look over the area and see what would be close by for apartments. Then, when they called and offered me the job, we knew we'd have to decide if we'd get married before we moved there or next spring. I know Chicago's not terribly far away, but getting married now would've saved us a lot of travel and headaches."

Anna initially was surprised that Emily hadn't told her mother all this wonderful news sooner. They'd always seemed so close.

Even Fletcher became engrossed in the back-and-forth of wedding planning. When someone mentioned getting the dishes washed and the kitchen put to rights, everyone around the table concluded that December was just too soon. Springtime, over Easter break, was a much better choice. Ida also agreed she probably should go with them when they left for Chicago, where they'd have a belated Thanksgiving with Robert's family.

Faced with an early start for the long drive down to Illinois, Ida pushed her chair back from the table and gathered up a stack of empty pie plates and took them to the kitchen. Katherine was fed, snuggled in her warm sleeper, and put in the middle of the coats in the bedroom. Gerrit and Fletcher stacked empty cups and saucers while glasses were washed and dried. Kate picked up the napkins and brushed crumbs from the tablecloth. Emily took over the dishpan job and sent her mother upstairs to pack clothes to take for the weekend. It was decided that Fletcher would collect Ida on Sunday night for her trip back to the farm.

Anna was so revved up by the wedding plans that she wondered how anyone would be able to sleep. Ida and Emily would share the double bed in what used to be the back bedroom. They undoubtedly would be whispering far into the night. Robert would bunk in Ida's bed in Annalisa's old room upstairs. Anna and the baby were settled in Fletcher's old room, and Fletcher was stuck again with the daybed on the porch. Gerrit made the rounds of the sixteen windows that encircled the porch, pulling the heavy green shades to block the cold seeping through the glass.

Once everyone had settled in bed, the house seemed almost too quiet, like everyone was just savoring the joy that had circled the dinner table. Anna, whose past year had been focused on such dire, sad things, was so engrossed in the wonder of a couple so much in love that she almost forgot about Katherine until she started stirring and whimpering in her sleep. She got up and rubbed her back and tucked the woolen blanket tighter around her. Katherine relaxed and began sucking on her fingers.

Anna hadn't closed the shades so she would wake to the sunrise and Ida's trip with Emily and Robert. She'd have to remember to write a long diary entry about Thanksgiving dinner and the wedding plans. When Katherine awoke in the morning, Anna was already dressed, ready to change her and take her downstairs for her bottle and to see their company off.

Robert had packed their overnight bags into the trunk of Emily's car, and Ida was gathering up last-minute treats to take along as gifts for Robert's family—apple slices, to be sure...apple butter and a few apple breads they'd frozen until the next big meal.

Emily and Ida decided they should stop at Ida's house along the way to get an outfit for her second Thanksgiving dinner.

They were in the car, ready to head south when Fletcher came hurrying across the farmyard carrying a jar filled with milk. "Cover is tightly screwed on so it shouldn't leak," he said, handing it in to Ida. "Or would you rather I put it in the trunk?"

"In here on the floor will be fine," she said.

"Wait," Gerrit said as he turned to go back in the house. When he came back, he had a soup kettle partially filled with ice to keep it safely chilled. "It'll be a creamy treat for Thanksgiving coffee. Safe trip." Their car pulled onto the road, then paused for another round of goodbyes. The Jansz family stood waving by the rosebush until the car reached the mailbox corner, turned left and headed toward town and the highway.

Back inside, a long day stretched after the previous one's excitement. Anna laid the baby on the bed with Kate, already under the covers. Without Ida, the kitchen was quiet; no one seemed ready for breakfast.

Thinking back over Thanksgiving dinner, Anna realized that her biggest fear had been unfounded. If Robert did recognize her as a freshman who left the school early last spring, he never gave any indication of it. Nor did he seem puzzled about the daughter having the lead role in the baby's care. Obviously, Kate's stroke was a handicap in caring for a baby.

As lunchtime rolled around, Anna decided to get the leftover turkey out of the fridge and slice bread for sandwiches. She'd made a plateful and set the table before calling them to eat. Kate was just waking up when Anna called her. Anna was surprised to find her dad sleeping on the other half of the bed beside Kate. Katherine was again sucking on her fingers, but not yet awake.

Anna found Fletcher sleeping upstairs on his old bed in the front bedroom, shades closed tightly against a late-fall sun. Still, the room was warm. She noticed the floor register above the heater in the main room downstairs was open. When she saw it, she remembered those nights when they were little, crawling out of their beds to peek downstairs through the floor louvers. They always peered through the slats on Christmas and Easter, when treats were part of the celebration.

"Hey, Fletch," she said, rousing her brother. "I've got a plate of turkey sandwiches and a table full of leftovers. Including pie. Since I did the making, you can do the cleaning up."

He tossed a pillow at her. "Who told you that you could sleep in *my* bed?" A second pillow hit her on the shoulder as she ducked out of the room.

Each of them seemed lost in thought as they filled their plates and ate, relaxing a bit more as they tucked into their pie choices. When they finished, there were still sandwiches and other leftovers for the next meal.

The yowl came from the bedroom. Within minutes, Anna fed Katherine as they rocked next to the heater.

Gerrit listened to the radio as he shuffled papers from his briefcase into stacks on the table. Between the music, the announcer talked about the weather and what was happening in the United States and the world.

The phone rang, and Gerrit absently reached over to pick up the receiver. When he didn't say anything more after a quick "hello," Annalise looked over at his suddenly stricken face. Tears spilled down his cheeks as he swallowed to check a sob. He listened for what seemed forever, then in a shaky voice promised to call back in a few minutes with his plans. Fletcher, who'd gone to the kitchen for another slice of pie, stared at his dad sitting in his chair, still holding the phone.

"Pops?" he whispered. "What is it?"

"Illinois State Patrol. Terrible accident near Chicago. Ida and Robert. Fatal injuries. Emily's in surgery but could survive. A freak icy rain that slicked the roads. A semi swerved trying to keep from sliding into other cars and tipped over. On them."

Kate heard the chatter and came out from the bedroom. "What did you say, Gerrit? Wh-what's the matter with Ida?" she whispered, her face twisted in terrible pain at the fragments she'd overheard. Gerrit tried to keep his anguish under control, but she knew in her gut that something very, very terrible had happened.

Fletcher made a grab for her as her knees buckled, then eased her into the Morris chair.

"The Illinois State Police," Gerrit said again, so softly Anna could hardly hear him. "A terrible accident near Chicago. Ida and Robert are badly injured. Fletcher and I should get there as soon as we can. Police said we should let them know when we can be on the road. He called their injuries fatal. Emily is in surgery and less seriously hurt."

Even Katherine didn't squabble when the bottle was set aside while Anna sobbed into her handkerchief. "Not Aunt Ida," she sobbed. "Oh, God, no…please, God, don't take her."

Gerrit said they would start out as soon as he could notify his work of a family emergency. At first, Gerrit wanted Fletcher to stay home to take care of his mother, who could not make such a dreadful, worrying trip. But after a call to Chandler, Gerrit relented. It would be much more stressful if she was left behind. If there was a chance of being able to see her sister before she died, it was worth the effort. Anna and the baby would go. The police assured Gerrit the icy road conditions that made a skating rink out of the highways had melted in current rising temperatures and rain.

While a flurry of phone calls was placed and arrangements made, Anna rounded up clothes for them for several days and tried her best to fold things neatly enough that they could be worn when they got there. They promised Helen they would stay in touch and she could relay information to and from the farm. Noah arrived early to do his nightly chores so Gerrit could explain the terrible situation to him without driving to the Mellen farm. Gerrit gave him a spare key to the house and suggested he might like to stay there until they came back. Or at least stay overnight.

Robert's parents lived only a short distance from the Chicago hospital where their son was taken after he was seriously injured when a truck rolled over on Emily's little car on the icy highway. Investigating officers told Gerrit the truck initially barely clipped the driver's side of Emily's car. But when the truck ultimately rolled over on top of the small car, both Robert and Ida, who was riding behind Robert, incurred serious brain injuries.

Robert's parents were in Emily's room when the Jansz family first arrived. Robert was their only child and they said they had been very excited at the prospect of their son marrying Emily. Fletcher walked with them down to Aunt Ida's room to introduce them to Kate and Gerrit. Fletcher stayed in the room with Ida while they walked in the hall talking with Robert's parents, who promised to check back in the morning to see how Emily and her mother were doing.

By the time they arrived at the hospital, at nearly midnight, Robert had already died. The Jansz family found themselves pacing the hospital corridor while Ida struggled to stay alive. It was, Anna thought, as if Ida knew her sister, Kate was coming and held on until then.

Gerrit gripped Kate's hand as she held her sister's fingers, leaning over to kiss them from time to time. At one point, he let go of Kate's hand and walked around to the other side of Ida's bed. Leaning over, he whispered into Ida's ear. Kate was so grateful Gerrit had thought to whisper to her sister how much they all loved her and how grateful they were for her helping Annalise and the family. Kate tried to whisper to her sister how much she loved her, but she wasn't sure she was saying the words correctly, and certainly not fast enough.

Emily was in another room down the hall. Although she was unaware of Robert's death and her mother's serious condition, when Fletcher and Annalise saw her, she seemed agitated despite being unconscious. Anna talked to her, telling her Kate and Gerrit were with Ida in another room and she and Fletcher were with her. They didn't know what to say about Robert, except that his parents had arrived and were with him.

There was no way to comprehend how their Thanksgiving celebration could collapse into such a nightmare. Aunt Ida, who had been such a central figure in their lives for so many months, slipped away without ever opening her eyes. Kate remained by her bed, never letting go of her hand, still trying to whisper to her through the bedrails. When doctors and nurses converged on the room, Gerrit tucked a blanket around Kate and wheeled her out into the hall.

"Ida's gone," Gerrit whispered to Kate. "I'm sure your parents were there waiting for her. As was Jake."

Anna and Fletcher were still with Emily. She hadn't moved since they arrived. Doctors told Gerrit, Emily would be lucky to make it until morning. Her head was swathed in blood-soaked gauze that nurses frequently changed. Her age and good health aided her battle to survive, but it was the brain injuries that were most worrisome.

Anna had changed and fed Baby Katherine, who was sound asleep, snuggled in a chair in the corner by the window. The siblings didn't bother to move her when they were sent out of the room when the doctor and nurses came in. The clock over the nurse's station showed quarter to three when they saw their parents heading toward the visitor lounge, bringing news of Ida's death.

For the rest of the night, Gerrit and Fletcher took turns sitting with Emily. She was still in a deep coma, and the doctors weren't sure she'd ever wake up. Anna had gone to the maternity section on second floor to inquire about some formula for Katherine's breakfast. They'd left in such a hurry it never occurred to them they should have brought extra formula along. When the nursery staff heard why she needed milk, they were only too happy to find a bottle of formula for her. They said they'd order extra so Anna could pick up a bottle whenever Katherine was ready for another.

Annalise fed Katherine while taking a shift sitting with Emily. Fletcher went off to find a couch where he could nap. There was a phone in the lounge, but Gerrit found a cafeteria downstairs where he was told there was a bank of phones. He needed to call the courthouse and let them know the latest news. He also put in a call to their doctor at home. Doctor Chandler had gotten to know Ida well since she'd moved to the farm to help. Next, Gerrit felt in his jacket pocket, looking for a scrap of paper he'd scribbled on just before they left. But when he placed the call, the long-distance operator said there was no answer. The next number he tried was answered on the first ring.

"Helen? Gerrit here. News isn't good here. Ida is gone. She was so badly injured. She was still alive when we got here, and Kate spent as much time with her as she could—she held her hand and tried to talk to her. But Ida never woke up.

"Robert's mom and dad live near here, so they were with him when he died. We met them only briefly before they left to go home. They said they'd come back tomorrow."

Gerrit sighed. "The truck that crashed on top of them hit an icy patch and barely clipped them as the driver tried to regain control. But then the truck hit something, maybe a highway marker causing it to jump and then flip—right on top of their car. Robert and Ida never had a chance. Ida lasted several hours. It was like she was waiting for Kate to get here.

"Emily is still unconscious. She has severe head and internal injuries, but doctors are now hopeful she has a chance. Anna and Fletcher stay with her as much as possible."

"When we got here it seemed as if they could survive, but as the hours passed it was less hopeful, especially after Robert died. We had such fun when we were talking about Robert and Emily getting married. How can it all have gone so terribly wrong."

"We have so many things to arrange here, mostly by phone right now. We're not sure when we'll get back. I'm not even sure where Ida planned to have her services. Her Jake was buried in Iowa. Since Emily is still in a coma, I need to make these decisions. I'm thinking I'll call the funeral home in Iowa to pick up Ida's body. I'm sure she'd want to have her service in her dad's old church and then be laid to rest next to Jake, who is buried alongside Pastor Conner and his Annalise. Could you pass this information on to our hired man? We gave him a key to the house and suggested he stay there to keep an eye on things.

"We forgot to bring extra formula for Katherine, but the hospital has provided formula, diapers and clean clothes for Katherine.

"Also, could you see that our mail is picked up from the mailbox? Nothing much ever comes, but Kate's worried about it being left overnight. I think there are a couple of checks coming around the first of December."

When he ran out of details to tell her, Helen started with questions about funeral arrangements. Notifying family in Iowa. Stopping mail delivery for Emily's address. Forwarding Ida's mail to their farm. What about phone numbers? Where's the address book? And Kate's Book of Days journal? Maybe Fletcher could find a stationery store and get a new one for her. Both Kate and Anna could use new journals so they can keep a record of all that's happening now.

"Anything else I can help with from this end?" Helen added. "Would it help if I drove down there? I could bring along whatever you might need. I could help with the baby."

"No, Helen, no need for you to drive down. We can talk by phone, and you can help me keep things under control until we get back. Since Emily is still unconscious, we'll need to wait on setting up Iowa funeral arrangements. Not sure when, or if, she'll come around. I'm thinking if the funeral home came here to pick up Ida's body, perhaps we could delay her services until Emily was able to attend."

Gerrit exhaled heavily. "My head is in such a whirl. I think I might be repeating myself. If so, I'm sorry. Do you still have your key for our house? We'll need an outfit for Ida. Pick out something you know would look especially nice on her. Kate and I will drive over to Iowa tomorrow. We haven't slept since we've been here, other than a few catnaps. Still not sure how to handle Emily's care. Sorry to dump all of this on you. I'll call you either later this afternoon or tomorrow morning. Probably in the morning. If shipping an outfit would not get it there before it's needed for the funeral, we'll just buy a new outfit here. Maybe that's easiest. I know that Emily told Ida to pack a special outfit for the family party here, which was supposed to be today, but we don't know what's happened to their suitcases that were in the trunk...Helen, I'm just in shock. I hope some of this makes sense. It's hard to remember what day or time it is and how long it's been since we got the call and threw things into the car. I'll call the Iowa funeral home this afternoon and get some answers. We also need to notify the newspapers with her obituary. And make church arrangements. I need a place for Kate to sleep.

"And don't even think of driving down here," Gerrit said. "We'll welcome your help if you can come to Iowa—when services will be held and providing the weather isn't wintry. It might be nice to have a memorial service at the church up there. I'll keep in touch. Sorry to rattle on, but with everything crashing around us, it's hard to focus."

Helen tried to find words to comfort her friends. "I'm so sorry this has happened," she whispered. "I'll try to have the information you need when you call later today. I'm staying at our farm, not my new place. It's easier to go to your house for things if I'm only just down the road. And please give my love to Kate and Anna. And Fletcher."

Fletcher had called the main office at his college to let them know his family's situation. With semester exams starting next week, he wasn't sure he could get back in time to take them on schedule. The office secretary reassured him it wouldn't be the first time a student had to delay taking exams. She promised to notify his professors, who would arrange for Fletcher to take his exams when he returned.

"Tragedies around holidays are always harder to cope with," the secretary said. "My sympathy to you and your family."

"Thank you for your help," Fletcher said softly.

Fletcher found his mother sound asleep on a couch in the visitor's lounge. Annalise was nowhere in sight—probably still in Emily's room. His dad, he knew, was using a phone somewhere.

Fletcher went looking for him. He hoped his dad could help him find a bus or train that would get him back to Green Bay. Since Gerrit had worked in Chicago when Fletcher was a baby, he might remember where to find the train station. Bus depots might change over time, but train tracks were permanent. He was anxious to finish his exams so he could get back to Chicago in time for the funeral, or funerals. He prayed Emily would live.

CHAPTER TWENTY-ONE

Helen was waiting on the platform when Fletcher's train pulled into the tiny Lillehammer station. It seemed like he'd been away for weeks—not three days. He was surprised to see deep snowdrifts banking the nearly deserted roadways northwest of town.

"It's been snowing a lot since you left," Helen said. "But not to worry, Noah has plowed the driveway. He's been staying at your house these past few nights. I've been staying at our farm. Made it easier for me to get back and forth to your place."

It felt strange knocking on the kitchen door to his own house, but Fletcher didn't want to startle Noah. The door swung open, and Noah looked surprised at seeing people waiting on the front porch.

"I was so sorry to hear about Aunt Ida's death," he said, reaching over to shake Fletcher's hand. "She was such a nice person. Will her daughter be alright?"

"The doctors aren't sure. So far, prayers seem to be helping, because she's doing better than we expected. We just keep praying."

Fletcher set down his bag on the kitchen table. "I'll take my mom's car to the college. Semester exams start tomorrow, and since Aunt Ida won't be buried for a couple days, in hopes Emily will regain consciousness, I won't be going to Chicago until late in the week. The Iowa funeral director is transporting Ida to Iowa where her funeral will be held at her dad's old church. My mom is the only child left in her family, now that Ida is gone. When Emily realizes she's lost not only her husband-to-be but also her mother, we worry how she'll cope."

"I'll call in the morning to make sure you are up and ready to go," Helen told Fletcher. "You'll need time to study before taking that first exam. Good luck and please, please be careful driving. Some of these roads may be iced over." She excused herself and headed home. Fletcher knew it was time to turn in when he started yawning after sharing coffee with Noah. "Guess I'd better head upstairs." When he got to the second floor, he remembered his sister and her baby had taken over his old room. Aunt Ida had been using Annalise's old room—he couldn't sleep in there. Instead, he went out to the front porch and unfolded a couple of the quilts he'd slept under over Thanksgiving. He didn't even remember falling asleep.

Noah was up and out to the barn by the time Fletcher woke up. He went upstairs to find clothes that would be more suitable for funerals and other memorial gatherings in Chicago and Iowa. And he couldn't forget to fill a bag with baby clothes and all the diapers.

In the kitchen, Fletcher saw a loaf of Ida's bread already sliced for toast, but he didn't think he could swallow even one. Still, it would be a long, tiring day. He slathered his bread with the soft butter Noah left on the table. The heat from the cookstove felt good after his cool night on the porch. For good measure, he poured a half cup of coffee, but only had a few sips before emptying the rest in the sink. He looked around for his coat, then found it hanging on a hook behind the kitchen door, where he figured Noah must have hung it. He pulled on boots and the woolen cap he'd bought to wear home for Thanksgiving. In the jumble of events of the past days, he'd completely forgotten about that night before Thanksgiving when Cynthia, the Iversen's granddaughter, told him she couldn't go out with him anymore. Driving on slick roads was not a time to wallow in self-pity. The accident had put that all into perspective, at least for now. Instead, he tried to focus on some of the work he'd have to sort through for exams. Credits toward his future degree depended on his anchoring himself in his new reality—a new reality that began back when Anna came home from Milwaukee. And how would their household run without Ida?

Kate couldn't take care of her granddaughter so Anna could go to school. She had to go to school. Fletcher didn't have to go to college next semester. Anna could ride into town with Pops, but they couldn't leave Momma alone all day with a baby. Not only couldn't she lift her, but she didn't have the energy to keep up as the infant rapidly grew into a little person, exploring the world she lived in. Kate needed to rest several times a day, and for sure those naps would never coincide with the baby's.

Fletcher needed to pull off the road for a few minutes. He remembered passing a small park along a stretch of highway where he could pull his wits back together. He didn't dare sit too long; the temperature was dropping. Ominous gray snow clouds gathered ahead. He had to keep going.

The next day, he had a sick feeling when he walked into the examination room for his math test. His mind had zeroed out, as he figured he might not have to even worry about not returning to school next semester. He was sure he'd flunk out. He shouldn't have even bothered coming. Then the dull ache of despair eased up as his pencil marked the pages. He had a good feeling about his work as he handed it to the professor. He knew the answers weren't all perfect, but he should've scored a "B" at least. After the previous few days, that would be a gift.

He stopped at the main office to check the posted exam schedule. The secretary handed him some paper so he could write down his test times and wouldn't have to keep coming back to the office. After he copied the information, he thanked her again for her help and started to leave.

"Fletcher? How are things? I was so sorry to hear about the terrible accident last Friday. Your aunt was killed, right? And the man who was to be her son-in-law, also?"

"Right and right," he replied. "My cousin Emily was still unconscious when I caught the train yesterday. Everyone is getting more and more apprehensive since she has not given any sign of regaining consciousness. After exams are finished, I'll head back to Chicago and then to Iowa for my aunt's funeral. The man my cousin was going to marry will be buried tomorrow. We just met him on Thanksgiving."

"I wanted you to know I've been praying for you."

"Thank you," he said, his voice barely a whisper. He was surprised when he started telling her he might not be back next semester. "I can't figure out how I'm going to continue. Maybe something will work out, but so far, I haven't figured out how. I'll stop back before I leave after exams are over."

Ψ

Fletcher and Annalise sat on straight-back chairs in the hallway. Baby Katherine slept in her buggy beside them. They'd left Emily's room when the doctor and two nurses came in. Their cousin was still in a coma, and by reading the doctor's somber expression, they knew the prognosis remained dire. The siblings felt residual pains from their mother's stroke, memories of hospitals, even though they were a state away from their origin, and the current injuries claimed more.

"I'm worried about when Emily wakes up…could she handle knowing she lost her mother and fiancé at the same time?" Fletch whispered. "They were so excited and happy on Thanksgiving. But Aunt Ida was most excited. She and Emily were so close. I can't imagine Emily's loss."

When the doctor came out of Emily's room, he stopped to ask if Gerrit or Kate were somewhere in the building. "No," Fletcher responded. "They went to Iowa when the undertaker came to pick up Ida's body."

"Dad promised to call before they started back," Anna said. "Is there anything we need to tell them when they call?"

"Just tell them Emily doesn't give any indication she'll wake up anytime soon, but her vital organs are functioning just fine for now. I'll talk to them in the morning. If anything happens to Emily tonight, I've left orders for the nurse to call me. If need be, I'll come back. I presume your mom and dad will arrive overnight?"

Fletcher and Anna nodded.

"You two look beat. The only one getting a good rest is that baby. She certainly is good," the doctor concluded, then turned to check with the nurse's desk before heading downstairs.

Baby Katherine had settled in for the night, as Anna covered her eyes from a bright overhead light. "I think we both should get a little sleep," she said to her brother. "The nurses will wake us if there is anything we need to know. Momma will need sleep. A good restful night of sleep."

"Were they going to Robert's funeral tomorrow? At least Pops?"

"I think that was the plan," Anna said. "One or both of us should go, too, since Emily can't."

Gerrit and Kate had only a slice of toast to eat before driving the forty-five miles to the church for Robert's funeral. Anna had dressed Katherine in one of her prettiest outfits, even though the baby seemed a little fretful. Not even cereal with applesauce appealed to her, but she settled down as soon as she had her bottle. At church, she only whimpered a little while Fletcher fixed her another bottle. Halfway through, she dozed off again.

There was a gathering for mourners after the service. A church group had prepared a luncheon, and Robert's mother and father insisted they all stay. It was such a sad day—they had been expecting wedding vows, but instead had funeral rites. Two funerals, one in Illinois, the other in Iowa. Anna was happy Baby Katherine was awake and in good humor. She seemed to coax smiles from the sad faces crowding into the gathering area at the church. The burial was private—only close family and friends.

Many of Robert's students had carpooled to Chicago for the funeral, along with a lot of faculty. Anna hadn't seen the upper-class wing where Robert worked, so she had not met any of his students or teachers. She figured none would have any idea she had even gone to their high school. It was unlikely they'd figure out who she was or wonder about the baby she held. Besides, what would it matter?

Robert's mother told them they were hopeful that Emily would stay in touch with them once she recovered. "We just love her," she said, tears starting again.

"We know you have to get over to Iowa," Robert's dad said. "We plan to stay with Emily until we drive over for Ida's funeral. My sister lives near here. She said she'd welcome the opportunity to stay with Emily, knowing she was the love of Robert's life. She had been Robert's baptismal sponsor. We hope those plans are okay with you. We didn't think Emily should be left alone in between visits from the nursing staff. My sister is quite a talker and reader, so she said she'd read and talk to Emily so she would wake up. She will do what the nurses allow. She remembers all too well what it was like to be in a hospital bed, seriously injured and unconscious for days."

Ψ

Kate hesitantly waited for the door at the parish house to open. The Conner children had played in the backyard and across the street at the parish school playground for years. Her father's replacement was an older man whose children were grown. When the door opened, Kate was surprised to see Elsa, the same housekeeper who'd helped at the parsonage in the later years of her dad's assignment there, especially after their mother died. Pastor Conner could make a pot of coffee or brew afternoon tea, but he wasn't much for cooking.

The current pastor's wife came around the corner into the front hall. Elsa stepped back and waved to them. "We can talk later," she mouthed.

Gerrit and Kate followed her into the house. Kate certainly knew where to find the Pastor's office. For all the times Kate remembered the somber meetings in that office when funeral services had to be arranged, now she was the one sitting there talking about hymns. Those were easy to pick out. Ida was very fussy about the music she liked and often threatened to haunt her sister if they dared play any hymns she didn't approve of. Ida also had a regular routine of Bible passages she thought people should pick for funerals. Now it was up to Kate to remember which ones they were.

Fletcher, Anna and baby Katherine stayed only long enough to be courteous to the pastor, then left to make preparations for Ida's wake and funeral. The siblings were anxious to see the town where their mom had grown up.

Kate carried a small suitcase that held the burial outfit Helen picked out for Ida. She had put it in the trunk of Kate's car that Fletcher drove to college, then back down to Illinois and now to Iowa.

Driving around the small town, Fletcher reminded his sister of Ida's classic story about the day the bells rang. She'd been helping the ladies clean the church by dusting anything that stood still. When she came in from shaking out her dust cloth, she spotted a shelf above a bank of buttons that had not been dusted. To her chagrin, Ida's dusting not only cleaned the shelf but also bumped the bank of buttons, which sent the church bells ringing. It didn't take their Poppa long to get from his office to the church and push another button to stop them. Ida always said Poppa told her it was a good thing she'd hit the funeral tolling bell rather than the full-blast ringing, otherwise the whole town would have come running, thinking there was some emergency.

Their family's next stop was the funeral home to not only deliver Ida's burial outfit but also choose her casket and finalize all the arrangements.

Gerrit and Kate knew there would be a large crowd for Ida's service. Her Poppa had passed on quite a few years ago, but he'd been such a part of the community she was sure no one had forgotten him.

When the music and readings for the funeral were selected and the wake and burial arrangements made with the undertaker and church sexton, the obituary was prepared and delivered to the newspaper. They also decided on the luncheon menu for family and friends in the parish meeting room.

For Kate, it was such a familiar routine, only now she was the one making the decisions. If she thought about it too long, it completely overwhelmed her.

They headed to the motel so Kate and baby Katherine could rest. Fletcher and his dad went to a nearby diner, where Gerrit hoped they still made Kate's favorite, a BLT sandwich. Assured that these sandwiches were as good as ever, they ordered four. They even agreed on hot cocoa.

After Kate fell asleep, Gerrit went next door to use the phone so he wouldn't disturb her. He placed a call to the hospital and spoke with Emily's nurse. She said Robert's parents were both there all day with Emily. There had been no change. Gerrit gave them the phone number for the motel so the family could be reached in an emergency. He also left the number for the parish office, since someone there would know where to find them.

The next day was a long one—an off-day before the funeral. Gerrit and Kate considered asking the mortuary to keep the body in storage until Emily woke up and could attend a burial service, but that, they decided, would never have met Ida's approval. She needed to be laid to rest. Nothing would ever make any of this sadness easier for Emily when, and if, she woke up. Anna asked the undertaker if he could take a couple of good photographs of Ida as she looked in the casket during the wake. If not, she suggested asking a photographer from the newspaper office to take one and have it developed. That way, Emily would at least have a reminder of her mother's funeral. Kate hoped that would not be so macabre that Emily would be offended.

The night before the services, the funeral home was filled with parish members who remembered the Conner kids and still talked about their old pastor. Kids that Ida, Daniel, and Kate grew up with were there, offering condolences and sharing memories. Their children and grandchildren also came to pay respects to Pastor Conner's daughter, who had always been so full of fun and mischief. Annalise didn't know anyone at the wake. She'd been too young to remember from the few times she'd visited previously. Fletcher saw familiar faces, and, like his dad, moved from one group to another, accepting condolences and talking about the tragedy that had taken Ida and left Emily in a precarious situation.

The next morning started with a sleet storm that iced the roads and sidewalks. Then, as if in answer to prayers, the sun came out, and the temperature inched up into the low forties. As the day progressed, Kate was enchanted by the warm glow the sunshine spread through the stained-glass windows and across the weathered wooden pews. The family, the mourners, lost their grim pallor and smiled. It was the type of church gathering Ida would have loved. People laughing, talking, sharing.

Just before the service began, Kate turned to look over the crowd in the gathering area. She spotted Helen, who'd just arrived. Was that Cynthia with her? Fletcher spotted them as well, and immediately headed to the door to welcome them. Kate excused herself from the group she'd been speaking with. "I see someone who has traveled some distance to be here today. Please excuse me while I go to welcome her."

Helen took the baby from Annalise. Fletcher and Cynthia stood talking near the back of the room. They missed their place in line but took the side aisle up to where Helen and Anna were seated. Helen winked at Anna when she noticed Fletcher and Cynthia were holding hands, an *issue that's been straightened out*, Anna thought.

Gerrit and Kate led the mourners into the cemetery. The wind had picked up, and those who hadn't worn hats and gloves shivered. The committal service was blessedly brief. Anna stayed in the car with the baby. Fletcher had his arm around Cynthia as they stood shaking in the nasty wind.

Some of those who'd driven a distance decided to leave before the luncheon was served. Anticipating that, the women in the kitchen had packed hot beef sandwiches for them to eat on their way home. The hot beef might have cooled off, but the sandwiches were much appreciated. So were the homemade cookies church members had made.

True to their word, Robert's parents were there. Many of those attending figured out who the couple was and made sure they offered condolences to them, as a story about the accident had been published on the front page in the local paper with Ida's headshot. Robert's parents brought a message of some hope. Emily's vital signs had been strengthening, and the doctor thought she might wake as early as tomorrow.

As they gathered for a late supper at a restaurant on the west side of town, Gerrit talked about having Emily transported up north where she could be under Dr. Chandler's care and eventually receive therapy. He'd been away from the courthouse for more than a week and mentioned heading back the next day if the weather was safe for travel. The budget hearing was coming up Monday morning, and he needed to be there. With three cars, getting people home was not a problem. Anna thought perhaps she and the baby could go back with her dad, because Katherine had tired of the trip.

Helen said she would stay with Kate until she was ready to go home. Cynthia wanted to stay, but she was due to return to her college in the next week. Fletcher said he was planning to stay and could help arrange moving Emily back to the farm.

In the end, all they decided was that Gerrit had to get home to prepare paperwork for the public hearing on the budget and Annalise had to get the baby home and settled back into her routine. Once the budget hearing was over, Gerrit could take a little more time off. In the meantime, travel plans for the rest were left up in the air.

But all those plans changed by the next morning. Kate put her foot down. Anna would go back to the farm with her dad, but Katherine would stay with her grandmother and uncle. Anna, she announced, needed to get back to school. Final exams for the semester would begin next Monday. There was no other option—Anna had to go home, and the baby would distract from her studies.

The baby was so used to all of them, including Helen, that she probably wouldn't miss Anna for a few days. "We'll manage," Helen said, putting her arm around Anna. "And we'll sort things out in the meantime as to how we'll manage without Ida. We don't have a choice. She was such a helpful presence in our lives through so many hard days, but we have to go on."

"There have to be changes," Gerrit said. "But you and Fletcher have to stay in school. No questions asked."

November 30, 1944

Dear Days,

It was so unbelievably hard to get in the car and drive away with Poppa, leaving Katherine behind. I miss her so much. Momma was right. I had to go so I can study for my exams and go to school to take the semester tests next week. I must do well on those tests.

So many of my plans have backfired. My dream of a good college prep education... no sense rehashing that disaster. I could never have imagined such a mess happening to me and our family.

Momma's stroke! I still can't believe what happened to her and what it took to bring her back this far. Momma is so much better. But she gets so tired. She still can't take care of Katherine like she could have before the stroke. Aunt Ida would have been the difference in making it possible for me to go to high school and keep the baby. Momma thinks it's still possible. We don't have a choice if I'm ever going to grow up into a good mom and raise my Katherine Anna.

I thought what happened with my high school plans was awful, but it was nothing compared to losing Aunt Ida. There is such an empty place in our hearts, in our family. The tears are always right there. But they won't bring her back.

Please, dear God. Let Emily get well and be part of our family.

It's only been a week since we had our happy Thanksgiving party. It was such fun meeting Robert and thinking about their wedding and his new job in Chicago. I never could've imagined that what started as a perfect holiday weekend could turn into total despair. Aunt Ida, who was all smiles when she left with Emily and Robert for a trip to Chicago, is gone. So is Robert. And maybe Emily.

Momma reminded me we have to keep going. Heavens, she certainly has. But a lot of that was due to her sister coming to help us. How will we ever get along without Ida?

I can't keep going over and over these same things. It just pushes me down deeper and deeper into despair. And I can't go there because I have tests to study for, tests to take, and a baby.

"We just have to pick up the pieces," Momma whispered when she and I sat together on the bed in the motel. "We'll work together, and it will work out. I promise. And your plans to do what I didn't do, go on to college, we'll make that happen, too. Helen and I have a lot of things to work out. She helped raise you when you were a baby, now she's going to help you— and me—raise this little girl.

The baby and I come from solid stock.

I just remembered Katherine's middle name: Anna.

Annalise

Helen and Kate tried calling the nurse's station at the hospital to find out how Emily was doing. Helen didn't have much luck, because she was not a family member authorized to be given any information. Although Kate was still uncomfortable talking on the phone, she did it.

"I'm Kate. Emily is my niece. Her mother, who died there at the hospital, was my sister. We are trying to figure out how best to get Emily moved back to Wisconsin, closer to where we live. The rest of my family has gone back to Wisconsin, to jobs and school. We plan to stay here until Emily is well enough to travel. Could I put Helen back on the line? I am still recovering from a stroke last summer."

Kate handed Helen the phone. "The nurse will give you the information about Emily so you can tell me."

Kate and Helen decided to stay at the motel until the baby woke up, but the nurse suggested they go to the hospital and sit with Emily. "She's been restless this morning and might be on the verge of coming out of the coma," Helen explained to Kate after she hung up. "Sounds like they'd like us to come this morning. The nurse said Emily's doctor had been in and wondered if the family was still around and if they could come to sit with her."

Kate was dressed and ready to go. Helen packed a diaper bag for Katherine and bundled her up in a sweater and cap. "It looks windy and cold out there," she said, wrapping the baby in a warm blanket. "I'll get the car closer to our door. You wait in here with the baby, and I'll come back and get you both. We'll have to be careful walking, but they've got sand spread on the sidewalk and driveway."

"I hope we can talk to the doctor today so we have an idea of when we can take Emily home," Kate said softly.

Helen got Kate settled into the backseat of her car, then hurried back in for Katherine. She made another trip for her purse and the baby's things, locked the door, and got into the car.

Getting Kate and Katherine into the hospital was much easier, since there was a doorman with a wheelchair to transport them up to Emily's room. The baby didn't make a peep the entire trip.

Helen knew they'd have to limit the traveling back and forth, especially now that the temperature had dropped to near zero.

A woman volunteer stopped in Emily's room, offering to help the two women get settled. Another volunteer brought a small crib from the children's area so Katherine could be tucked away for a quiet nap. Two cups and a pot of warm coffee arrived, along with a plate of buttered toast. Helen and Kate sat on either side of Emily's bed so they could carry on a conversation and perhaps stimulate Emily into waking up.

Kate leaned back in the rocker, trying not to fall asleep. Helen was gently rubbing Emily's hands.

"Emily, this is Helen from the farm down the road from your Aunt Kate and Uncle Gerrit. We have Baby Katherine with us today. The rest had to go home for a couple of days, but they'll be coming back. We hope you can wake up soon. We want you to know that we are here and that we love you very, very much." When she turned to make sure that Kate had gotten settled in the rocker, she saw that she'd already fallen asleep. This was all too much for Kate. Even a little too much for her. With Katherine and Kate both resting, Helen decided to see if she could find a restroom.

By the time she got back, the baby was complaining loudly in the little crib. It undoubtedly was time for her lunch. Someone had left a warm bottle nearby.

"Come here, little one," Helen said, lifting Katherine out. They settled into the second rocker that had been brought in while she was gone. "They certainly know how to take care of babies around here," she whispered as they rocked.

When Kate and Helen woke up, they were surprised to see Robert's parents in the room with them.

"We thought you'd be more comfortable staying at our house for the next few days," Robert's dad said. "That way you can get a good night's sleep, and we can easily take you back and forth so you won't need to fuss with a motel room."

"Besides," Robert's mother said, "we'd love to do a little babysitting."

Robert's dad went with Helen to close out their motel rooms. Gerrit had left money with Helen. With everything packed up, they drove back to the hospital to collect Kate and the baby. Robert's mother had gone ahead to get supper started.

The next morning, the phone rang in Emily's hospital room. It was Gerrit, looking for Helen. One of her grandchildren had fallen from the haymow and broken his right leg. The family needed Helen home to help with the other children until the boy was home from the hospital. The other families were trying to help, but it was getting to be too much.

Kate thought, *Perhaps I should go home with Helen.* But suddenly, she saw herself trying to manage with the baby in the car while Helen was driving, and she knew that would be a disaster. As if they knew what she was thinking, Jack and Julia looked at her and shook their heads.

"No, that will not work," Julia said. "You can just stay with us, and we'll bring you back and forth to the hospital every day. We can even keep the baby at our house so you don't have to take her out in the cold. She's such a good baby and seems to like Robert's little bed we brought down from the attic."

That settled, Jack took Helen back to the house so she could pack her things and get on the road. It was, thankfully, a sunny day, although cold.

"It'll be a while before I get back," he said. "I think I will have Helen follow me so I can get her out of the city and onto the highway heading north. That would be easier than trying to draw a map for her to follow while she's driving."

At that suggestion, Helen let out a huge sigh of relief. What unbelievably thoughtful people these were.

Julia and Kate sat quietly on either side of the bed watching Emily. "Was it wishful thinking, or did she seem to stir just a bit?" But Emily's eyelids didn't shift. Kate leaned back in her chair. The nightmare of the past week seemed as if it would never end. How could it be that what started out as such a wonderful dream for Ida and Emily had ended in such unbelievable tragedy? Would Emily ever wake up, or would she die, too? That, Kate realized, was the first time she'd lost hope of Emily's survival. Two funerals already. How long had it been? It seemed like weeks had passed. She'd lost track of the days, and like those early days on the farm, alone without Gerrit, she had no idea what month or day of the week it was.

Later that afternoon, Kate heard music coming down the hallway toward the room. Christmas carols. Children's voices. For a few minutes, she was lost in the sound—back at Poppa's church in Iowa where the children's choir would practice for the Christmas service. She and Ida were always in the choir, but it was their brother, Daniel, who'd always sung the solos. At first, most of the voices were little girls. Then, was she dreaming, or did she hear Daniel's voice, too? Couldn't be. She was sitting in a hospital room. Daniel had been dead more than a year.

"Kate? Are you alright?" Julia asked.

Words didn't come, and Kate realized she was crying.

The singing children reached their doorway. There was only one boy with the group, and he wasn't Daniel. But his voice could have been. The jumble of memories was overwhelming. Kate closed her eyes and lost herself. For a few minutes, the horror of those past weeks melted into those now-peaceful memories. She was confident Emily would wake up and eventually recover. Like all the other tragedies they survived that year, they'd pick up the pieces of this new life and go on. Wouldn't they?

Ψ

It had been weeks since Thanksgiving. Sometimes Emily's eyes would open, but she just stared into the distance. Kate reached for her hand, but her niece quickly pulled it away. Then she'd close her eyes again and drift away. The doctors were optimistic that one of these days she'd open her eyes and be there, maybe not talking, but at least recognize those in the room with her. They somberly also noted that she might notice people around her, but they couldn't be sure who, or what, Emily might respond to.

Then unexpectedly, one morning in mid-December, Emily opened her eyes and looked right at her Aunt Kate.

"Where's Mom?"

Kate was so astonished she didn't know what to say. Emily had no recollection of what had happened on the trip to Chicago the day after Thanksgiving. Robert's parents had other appointments that morning, so Kate and baby Katherine were there alone with Emily. The baby napped in the nursery crib. Kate reached over to take Emily's hand in hers. It was all happening so fast. She knew she needed to call a nurse. While still holding

Emily's hand, she reached up to the call button hooked to the sheet above Emily's head. Almost immediately, a nurse hurried down the hall.

"You're awake, Emily," she said, flipping off the call button. "It's so nice to have you here."

"How long have I been sleeping?" Emily asked in a raspy voice, looking first at Aunt Kate, then the nurse.

"A few days," the nurse answered simply, then excused herself and left the room. Kate knew she was retrieving one of Emily's doctors.

"Is my mom here?" Emily asked again, but Kate just shook her head. When Emily asked, "Do you know where she is?" Kate noticed her own hands were shaking. She felt her mouth open, but no words came out.

The head nurse for that floor came hurrying into the room. She was always a little gruff and never, ever smiled, but there was a huge grin spread across her face now. "Welcome back, Emily," she said.

A few seconds later, one of Emily's doctors arrived. Kate moved away from the bed so the doctor and nurses had room. She sank into the rocker in a corner. She was haunted by Emily's worried face. She knew someone was going to have to tell her, but Kate knew she could never get the words out without sobbing.

A second doctor arrived. Kate recognized him as the one who most frequently saw Emily since the day she arrived. Then suddenly, Emily seemed to remember some of the details of the past weeks.

"Where's Robert? Is he here? What's happened? Why am I here? Where's Robert? Where's my mom?" Suddenly she was screaming. "Where's Robert? Where's my mother? Are they all right? Are they dead?"

Kate saw the nurse trying to soothe Emily, but that only infuriated her more. Another nurse came over to help Kate up from the rocker. The baby, distressed by the screaming, had started crying. One of the doctors hurried from the room, coming back a couple of moments later with a syringe and a bottle. They would have to sedate Emily until she was settled enough to cope with what would be a devastating piece of news for her fragile nervous system.

It took a few minutes before Emily stopped shrieking and crying. Kate could only stand in the distance until things settled down. Dr. Warren, her main doctor, was leaning down, talking quietly to her, holding both hands in his. There was no easy way to tell her what had happened during the long weeks she was not awake. One of the nurses moved away from the bed and motioned Kate to stand next to the bed where Emily could see her.

"Do you remember who this is?" the doctor asked. Emily nodded, trying to smile at Kate. "She's my mother's sister."

Very gently, the doctor explained about the accident the day after Thanksgiving. "Your mother was very badly injured, but she didn't die until the next day. Your Aunt Kate was here with her, but your mother never woke up. Robert was driving the car when the truck slid on the ice into your car, just nicking it, but then tipped over on your car. Robert died soon after they got him here. His parents were with him when he died. They have been here visiting you nearly every day since then."

Emily's sobs subsided when Kate leaned over to kiss her on her forehead.

The sedative had set in, and the doctor motioned Kate to move back and let Emily fall asleep. "I'll be right over there in the rocker while you rest," Kate said softly. "Baby Katherine and I will be here overnight with you. And Robert's mom and dad will be back later this afternoon."

The doctor took a moment to set down some rules. "I know you have been asleep for a long time, but it is important that you rest now. You have a lot of information to absorb, and you will need to take it in a little at a time. You've had some serious head injuries, including a concussion, so it's important to not put too much strain on your brain. All in good time." That said, he patted her on the shoulder and left.

When Jack and Julia returned, they were surprised to learn that Emily had been awake. They tried to convince Kate that she and the baby should go back to their house and get a good night's rest, but Kate refused. "I promised Emily I'd spend the night here with her," she insisted. They didn't argue. They, too, needed to stay with her, not knowing how she'd cope with the realization that the two most important people in her life were gone.

Kate found a handful of coins for the phone. Jack walked down the hall with her. He arranged with the hospital switchboard to have any phone charges added to their late son's hospital bill. When Annalise picked up the phone, she was surprised to hear her mom on the line.

"Poppa's not here," Anna told her. "He went over to Helen's for supper after he finished with chores. I had to stay home so I could finish my homework. Is everything all right?" Anna squealed with joy when she heard that Emily had finally opened her eyes but was dismayed that they'd given her something to make her sleep again so she couldn't talk on the phone.

"Just tell Poppa that Emily woke up and the doctors are hopeful she'll continue recovering. For now, they want to keep her as quiet as possible until they are sure her head injuries are healing. I don't think we can bring Emily home with us yet, and the baby and I will try to stay here until then.

I'll tell you more when we can call you from Robert's house tomorrow or the next day. By then, we should know more about what the doctor thinks about Emily's release. I love you, Anna. Study hard."

Back in the room, Kate noticed Emily was still asleep, but it did not seem restful. The nurses took turns coming in to check her. Katherine, it seemed, knew that something had changed. Once she'd been changed out of her day clothes into her warm jammies, she quickly settled down to sleep. Despite her own exhaustion, after hearing Emily's horror, Kate had a hard time going to sleep herself. She knew Emily was well looked after, but she still felt uneasy.

A distressing list of questions kept repeating in her mind. Why had Gerrit left Anna home alone at the farm while he went over to Helen's new house for supper? Why hadn't he called her at the hospital to find out more about the good news? She knew she'd told Anna that she'd try to call from Robert's parent's house in a day or two, but why wouldn't he have called her that night? Unless he wasn't home yet. Or didn't care. She'd been alone in Chicago for more than a week since Helen left, and he hadn't talked to her even one time.

She knew this was all silly. She'd been alone on the farm for all those years and she never worried about him being alone in Chicago. Still! They'd eventually have to discuss Emily's returning to Wisconsin. They had hospital and doctor bills to take care of. How were they going to pay everything? The insurance beneficiary from Ida's policy obviously was Emily. Kate had never even thought about needing to know how much money Ida had. Perhaps, Gerrit had at some time, talked with Ida about how much money she had invested and where it was. Kate wouldn't even know where to start. Emily, no doubt, would have known. There were so many things to find out, to sort through, to make decisions about.

Finally, Kate put her head back in the chair and found herself saying the nighttime prayers she and Ida always said as children while on their knees, facing each other across the double bed they shared. The simple phrases were comforting. Tomorrow would be better now that Emily was awake and possibly going home soon.

The next morning, Robert's parents arrived very early. The hospital room was crowded with doctors coming to check on Emily, nurses taking blood pressure readings and giving meds, housekeepers anxious to change the bedding and dust the floors, and the kitchen crew delivering a breakfast tray and collecting empty dishes.

December 10, 1944

Dear Days,

It's been so many long, sad days since I last wrote to you. We had so many wonderful reasons to celebrate at Thanksgiving. Baby Katherine. Annalise back home and taking classes at the high school in town. Fletcher finished with high school and now away at college. And me, getting over my stroke. And Ida. My dear big sister, who came to help me take care of Anna's little Katherine. She was so happy when Emily and Robert surprised her with their news about getting married and moving to Chicago for his new job as a principal. It was all so exciting that it took my breath away. And then the next day, the phone rang and everything changed.

I don't know how I can go on. Everyone in my family is gone. First Momma, then my father. Daniel had finished his studies and was so excited to get a parish in Chicago. But it must have been too much for his heart to handle. When Ida and I drove to Chicago for his funeral, I don't think I ever stopped crying. We couldn't believe our brother was gone. Ida scolded me for being so distraught. She reminded me that Momma and Pastor Conner were probably waiting at the gates to welcome him home to heaven. It was small comfort when the brother we loved left us so soon.

Then when I had my stroke, I was sure I would never recover. But Gerrit called Ida, and she just got in her car and came to help. She was sure I would get better. She and Annalise figured out a way to get me to talk about the things I remembered from our childhood. I liked doing that, but I didn't understand why they did that until I noticed that I had started to talk like my old self.

I thought Ida and I still had a lot of years to do fun things. I wanted to go through our Momma's Books of Days and write a story that told about our lives in a small town in Iowa, running a parish and raising a family.

Thinking back to memories of our happy childhood at the parsonage always erases the sharp edges of whatever bumps come in our road. But treasured memories will never fix this terrible heartache. Dear Father in heaven. Please help me accept what has happened. Please give me the courage to go on. I pray and pray, but my heart finds no comfort in the words.

I've been writing most of the afternoon. Emily woke up a couple of times and we talked. The doctors are trying to keep her calm so she gets some good rest. She is getting stronger and could be discharged soon, but they want her to stay close by so they can check her progress. She had very bad injuries inside her head. They even had to shave off some of her hair so they could stitch the scalp injuries shut. Jack and Julia said when Emily is dismissed, they will take her to their home. They have a bedroom on the first floor for her. It even has its own bathroom. They said that was how many of the big houses in Chicago were built.

I will stay here until Emily leaves the hospital. The doctors think she should stay for a week or so. I hope she will want to live with us at the farm. We also must figure out what to do with Ida's house and all her things.

I get so lonely. It's better now that Emily is awake more, but I want to go home. Everything *here reminds me of all I've lost. It's hard to remember that we once lived here in Chicago. I'm not sure I could even find my way to our old basement flat and the bank where Gerrit worked all those years ago.*

All of this is making me sad. I thought I would feel better talking things over with you, but I think I need to take a walk down to the visitor's lounge. Even if I never re-read what I've written here, someday someone will open to these pages and know the sorrow that these events brought into my life.

Kate

When Emily woke up from her nap just before her supper tray arrived, she had more questions. It was as if she'd been compiling a list of things she wanted to talk about while she was sleeping.

Kate pulled a chair closer to the bed so they could talk while Emily ate. Kate didn't bother ordering a meal those days, because Julia always had supper ready for her when she got back to their house for the evening. Jack took his turn staying with Emily during the early evening until it was time for lights out. That way, they figured, Kate could spend time with Baby Katherine and help get her ready for bed.

That night, the farm seemed a million miles away. She didn't try to call home again after the first night that Emily was awake. Gerrit hadn't called her to find out how things were going. Neither did Annalise. Perhaps he made phone calls during the day to the doctors and hospital. She couldn't help feeling they'd forgotten her. Anna did send Emily a card she'd made. Ida had always been the artistic one of the Conner children. Daniel was always "on stage," singing, shuffling dance steps across the floor in the attic, and reciting dialogue from plays they'd done in school and for church events. Kate was the writer.

During her summer breaks when the weather cooled and the attic was livable, Kate would sneak up there, pretending she was a famous writer. Eventually, someone would come looking for her, but no one ever seemed interested in what she'd been writing.

She tried writing a novel, but when she re-read her words, it sounded childish and unworthy of the paper she'd used for it. She was at first tempted to hide it in a box for someone to find years later. But in the end, she ripped up the pages and shoved the scraps into a paper sack and dug a hole in the garden near the rhubarb and buried it. She rolled one of the big rocks across the garden to cover the evidence. Funny, she hadn't thought about any of that until then. And the sack of words would long ago have disintegrated. It was too bad she hadn't remembered it when they'd cleaned out the parsonage after Poppa's funeral.

In the years since those writing sessions, Kate's literary creations were recorded in a growing stack of journals. That had been an exercise encouraged by both her parents, but especially her mother. Ida never had much time for that "foolishness," as she called it. Instead of words, she used her creative talent to sketch scenes around their small Iowa town and faces of friends and neighbors that got to be so good you could even recognize who Ida was trying to draw. Kate was always complimentary. When you couldn't draw, you always were in awe of what someone else could do.

Daniel could write, but his words always turned out to be sentences in a sermon. Eventually, he did deliver sermons, but only two in their father's church. He delivered two of the most beautiful sermons Kate ever remembered—tributes to their parents at their funerals. She wondered what happened to them. Did he take them back to his parish in Chicago where they got lost in the shuffle of papers after he died? Even without the papers, Kate could practically recite his tributes word for word, all these years later.

Ψ

Grief-filled days began drifting away as Emily prepared to leave the hospital. Doctors were happy with her progress, but wanted to monitor her longer. Kate wasn't sure she should leave Emily behind and head back north on the train with the baby. Unless Robert's family preferred that, she and the baby would leave. They would, they said, drive Emily at least part-way back to Wisconsin, probably as far as Milwaukee.

Emily liked the idea that in another week she'd be back to her own house. Kate was worried that she wouldn't be ready to function on her own in little more than a week. It wasn't as if she had relatives living close by who could pop in to check on her from time to time. Kate felt they should move Emily up to the farm for a month or two, where they'd have Dr. Chandler in case of an emergency.

One night, Jack came back from the hospital and Kate heard him come into the house and climb the stairs. Instead of going straight to bed, he stopped at her door and knocked quietly in case she was asleep.

Kate pulled her robe on as she padded barefoot to the door, turning on the light with her right hand as she grabbed the knob with the left.

"I talked to Gerrit tonight," Jack said. "I wanted to let you know what his plans were for getting Emily back to Wisconsin."

She held the door open, inviting him to come in. She tried not to look put out that Gerrit had called Robert's dad, not her. After Jack gave her a quick run-down on what they had talked about, she tried to focus on those details.

"I tried Gerrit at work, the farm, and then I finally reached him at Helen's. He said he'd been talking to the business office at the hospital to find out what the unpaid bills amounted to and what arrangements he needed to make to get those paid off. He said he still hadn't figured out Ida's banking arrangements but thought Emily certainly would know. I didn't get a chance to talk with her tonight about that, but when I drive you to the hospital in the morning, I'll try and get that information for him so I can call him later in the day."

Jack said he had an attorney friend who handled a lot of accident cases. He said he'd already talked with him about Robert's last expenses and would do the same for Gerrit about Ida's final expenses. He reassured Kate that he could do some of the leg work for Ida's expenses and the growing expenses for Emily's medical bills.

Kate thought at first those would be her responsibility, but Jack said there was no need for her to use her healing time when he could easily make the phone calls and gather information for Kate.

For the time being, Kate was satisfied that Jack would save her energy by collecting the liability insurance information for Ida and Emily that he could then pass along to Gerrit.

Jack stretched and sighed. "I just wanted to give you a quick update on this and let you know that I'll keep a file so Gerrit won't have to make more trips down here and back that aren't necessary. It's all from the same accident, and we were only a few months shy of having Emily as our daughter-in-law. It's the very least we can do to help get all of this underway. Now, you get back in bed, and we'll talk more in the morning. Since I will be in and out most of the day, would it be alright if Julia didn't go to the hospital with you and stayed here with the baby?"

After the door closed, Kate lifted the corner of the mattress and slid her notebook out. She sat on the edge of the bed and jotted down as much as she could remember from what Jack had told her. What was happening to her? Did she have the same memory thing that Ida's Jake died of? She had the awful feeling she had been shoved aside. Instead of Gerrit talking to her about her sister and her niece's affairs, he was having late-night suppers with her friend, Helen, to arrange for Kate's family. Without any input from Kate.

Had she become irrelevant? Had the stroke caused irreparable damage to her brain? Was she just kidding herself, believing in time she'd be back to her old self? She was too tired, too distressed to make much sense of all this. She would have to struggle through the next weeks, but she could do it. And once Emily was settled either at her house, her mother's house, or the farm, Kate would decide where she would fit in. Sadly, she saw herself as no longer important in the family. What if she moved to Ida's little house? Fletcher and Anna could come to visit her sometime. It all sounded too dramatic, but being overlooked when such important family issues involving her sister and niece were discussed was like getting punched in the stomach.

Jackson decided it best if Emily did stay at their house for a week or so after she was dismissed from the hospital, so doctors could continue to monitor her. And, rather than drive Kate back to Wisconsin, they thought she and baby Katherine should stay another week in Chicago. That way, they'd be available to not only drive Emily to doctor appointments, but also help care for the baby, giving Kate more time to adjust to the loss of her sister. They certainly had more than enough bedrooms.

It was, Kate knew, a way for them to fill up the empty space in their own lives.

Kate and Katherine felt at home at Jack and Julia's, a large Queen Anne with a wraparound porch that opened into an entryway big enough to accommodate a welcome area for the gatherings they frequently held. From there, guests stepped into a grand hall where they always seemed to congregate rather than the huge adjacent living room. At the far end of that hallway was the grandest of all the fireplaces in the house. This one, which backed up to the grand staircase to the second floor, had a large stone sculpture of three whimsical musicians and their instruments parked atop the stone mantel. Kate always found time to pause and admire the fireplace every time she walked through the hallway. That section of the house had no end of treasures to look at and study.

Kate always thought the parsonage where she'd grown up was a rather grand place to live. By comparison with most of the neighbors, it was a large house with a fireplace and a separate study for the pastor and an expansive dining room which, when dressed up for a bishop coming to dinner or parish leaders at holiday parties, was extravagant indeed. But compared to the house where Robert had lived, it was overall very plain.

Patricia G. Raab

December 15, 1944

Dear Days,

I am sitting in the guest bedroom of the unbelievable house where Emily's Robert grew up in Chicago, trying to figure out a way to capture some of this experience in a visual paradise that someone like me would never have even seen without the tragedy I've been living in for the past few weeks.

Every day, Emily seems to grow stronger. At first, she seemed reluctant to move into Robert's bedroom, but once she was settled in, it seemed the most natural place for her to be. And Robert's family was especially pleased that this beautiful lady who would eventually have been their daughter-in-law was sleeping in his bed and under his college-days bedspread. I guess I don't need to worry about how Emily will transition back to her own little house, or to her mother's house where they sometimes talked of living together.

I keep expecting Emmy to break down. After everything she's been through, she just keeps going. It hardly seems possible that she can be so accepting of everything. One of these days, Robert's mom and dad plan to drive us over to Iowa so Emily can visit her mother's grave. That's a day I worry about. We'll also be making a trip to the cemetery near here where Robert was buried. But his parents will be with us when we go there. Or maybe I shouldn't go. Not only would it be too cold for Katherine, but I think it might be better if Emily just went with Robert's mom and dad.

Emmy's had special therapy sessions almost every day. I can tell it.

It's having a positive effect on her. It seems to relax her. I wish I had been able to have some sessions like that. For Emmy, it seems to have put her in a different place. It seems she's ready to go on with her life. I think that's a trait she inherited from Pastor Conner. She told me yesterday that she can do nothing about everything that has happened except accept it all. She told me their months of dating were such a special time that she has only very happy memories of their love. "You know," she said, "you have to accept that this is what God had in mind." At least she has truly wonderful memories of spending time with a very special person.

I think I had best rest awhile. I feel as if I am falling deeper into sadness.

Until next time,

Kate

December 17th, 1944

Dear Days,

After another visit to the hospital for a checkup, Robert's mom and dad took Emily to the cemetery to show her where Robert is buried. They didn't even ask if I wanted to go with them. Of course, I didn't. I felt I would just intrude on their privacy. Katherine and I had our own quiet time to think about all the changes in our lives. All the terrible grief. Sometimes the sadness is so horrible I can hardly breathe.

I thought of calling Gerrit when they went to the cemetery. I wanted to have some time alone so I could tell Gerrit...tell him what? That he seems to have forgotten that I am still here. That I didn't die in that accident. He has not called me for several weeks. When I call the farm, I *only get to talk to Annalise, and we only talk about how the baby is doing. I don't know if she even tells her dad that I've called. When I think about what is happening to me...*

Fletcher called last night. It sounds like he has really settled in. He said he talks to Cynthia now and again, so I guess things are much better between them. He said he was surprised I was still in Chicago. I told him that as soon as the doctors okay the trip, we will take Emily over to Iowa to visit her mother's grave. I worry over how her seeing her mother's grave will affect not only Emily, but me, too. I feel such an incredible loneliness without Ida. She was such a presence in my life. She helped me so much. When I think about our growing up together, I realize she was a second mother in my life. Momma was always busy with our family, with church obligations, with friends and relatives who always seemed in need of her strong shoulder to lean on. Ida was always there for me when Momma couldn't be.

I just heard a car in the driveway. Until next time....

Kate

Emily didn't say much when she came in after the trip to see Robert's grave. As winter days went, it was a pleasant afternoon. The sun shone, and although it was cold, the wind wasn't blowing—a rarity in Chicago, for sure.

Kate had put Katherine down for a late-afternoon snooze. By the time she'd gone back to the living room, Emily was paging through a family scrapbook that held page after page of pictures of Robert—as a baby, a toddler, little boy on a tricycle, and a little guy on his first day of kindergarten. Kate was impressed by the family's careful documentation of their little boy's life. She didn't have a camera until Fletcher was almost grown up, and with infrequent trips into town, a roll of film for the box camera rarely made the shopping list. And even with the film in the camera, she rarely remembered to bring it out, except for special occasions like a birthday or Christmas.

She remembered her own family's scrapbook pages devoted to pictures of Annalise, and only a few with Fletcher. In all, there were hardly enough to fill one album. But on the other hand, Kate's Books of Days were filled with stories about the children and their milestones during their childhoods.

Robert's mother looked over Emily's shoulder as she stared at the photos on the black pages. "This is one of my favorite pictures of Robert," Julia said, pointing to one at the bottom of a page. "He insisted I had to take a picture of him with his new puppy that he got for Christmas when he was five. Of course, the puppy didn't want anything to do with posing for a camera." She laughed to herself. "Robert had to hug him for dear life to keep him somewhat quiet. We were laughing so hard that the camera was out of focus. A few days later, the puppy was more settled, and happy to be held, with or without a camera keeping an eye on him. We had that dog until Robert was a sophomore in high school. It was such a sad day when the dog got so sick, we had to have him put down. Poor Sport. That was what Robert named him. They were inseparable."

The memories of those pictures seemed to upset Julia, even through her laughter. She turned without saying anything more and went back to the kitchen.

It was quite a while later when she came back to call them for supper. "It's not much," she said softly. "Just some soup and sandwiches." What they ate didn't matter. Everyone sat around the table, lost in their own thoughts.

Rather than eat, Emily went to the front bedroom to retrieve a squalling Katherine, who'd smelled the chicken soup and figured it was time to eat. It didn't take the baby long to finish her bottle. After the burping routine, she was content to just sit on Emily's lap and look around the table.

Kate glanced at the baby a couple times. She had such delicate features, and as she stared at the faces around the table, it was with serious concentration. Kate wished Anna was there to see how well adjusted her little girl was. She didn't seem to mind who held or fed her. Her features were so like baby Annalise's. Gerrit never was comfortable holding a baby, and while Fletcher always seemed to adore his baby sister, he didn't adore her enough to want to chance holding her and ending up with a wet leg in case the diaper leaked. Kate smiled at the memories.

"Robert's place in the cemetery is so peaceful," Emily said, half to herself. "There are so many trees around, but it's still open enough that the sun shines down on his grave. I would like to have some pictures of it so when I go home, I can look at them and remember…"

Emily didn't say anything else, and they ate the rest of the meal in silence.

Several days later, after another visit to the doctor, Emily was given the okay to go to Iowa. This time, Kate hoped she would be included in their plans for the day. As a guest in their home, she didn't know how to suggest that she'd appreciate the chance to visit her sister, and maybe they didn't want to be bothered with taking the baby along.

Kate didn't ask. She didn't have to. As they talked about their travel plans, the baby's arrangements were settled first. She'd ride in the backseat between Emily and Kate. Jack checked with the police department to find out what they knew about the Chicagoland weather and over to Iowa. The answer: "Good driving conditions today and tomorrow. No snow. No freezing rain. Even some sunshine." Kate wasn't so sure that would really happen, but she was hopeful.

They bundled the baby into the car, fit everything and everyone else in, and set off. The trip over to Brighton was an hour or so. The trip back would be a little more worrisome. Kate could sense Emily tensing as the sun slid down below the horizon. In the fading light, Kate noticed her clenching her fists. Finally, she reached across the baby, who'd fallen asleep, and took Emily's hands in hers. The day's sad journey to visit Ida's grave had been peaceful. Emily had been relaxed, occasionally talking about some of their mother-daughter trips in recent years. But the darkness shut the door on happy memories, and Emily pulled her hands away and clasped them tightly in her lap.

Most of the drive back to Chicago was quiet. Those in the front seat reviewed a lifetime of memories of their son. Emily, Kate knew, was remembering her days on the farm in Iowa. Kate would've liked to have driven by the farmland Emily knew as a child, but that, apparently, had not occurred to Jack and Julia. Kate was lost in her own memories, most of them unhappy. She replayed the years alone on the farm with only neighbors and chickens for company. There were the bright spots, though, like when Annalise came and Gerrit moved to the farm.

Kate kept seeing Ida's grave in the Iowa cemetery, next to Jake's and down the row from where their parents and brother rested. She thought of the Lutheran church and cemetery east of their farm in Wisconsin, wishing Ida was buried there, waiting for the day when Kate would be laid next to her. And Kate knew that when Emily's time came, she wouldn't be taken to Iowa, but rather to the cemetery a couple miles down the road from where Emily's first husband was waiting. Surely, since she and Robert had never actually married, she wouldn't be buried in Chicago. But that, Kate knew, would not be her decision to make.

Kate didn't remember falling asleep in the backseat of the car until Emily reached over to take her hand. "We're back in Chicago," she said. "You had a good nap. You don't even snore like Mom always did when she fell asleep in the car."

They both laughed as they gathered up the baby's things and carried her into the house. Kate, exhausted, was glad they weren't planning to head north to Wisconsin the next day.

The long trip had tired not only Kate but also Katherine, who snuggled under her warmest blanket in the little crib and didn't utter a peep until morning.

Kate slept late the next morning. "Grammy," Emily said to her aunt as she walked into Kate's bedroom, reaching for Katherine, "I've already changed her twice and fed her once, and she's about to take her mid-morning snooze. So, you can just get up and come down to the kitchen. I think breakfast for adults is ready."

The conversation over scrambled eggs and toast centered around their outing the previous day. Emily, Kate thought, did not seem distressed by talking about seeing her mother's grave.

"I'm glad you didn't wait to do the burial until I came out of the coma," Emily said. "I wouldn't have wanted to keep her at the funeral home in a refrigerator until I woke up. I've been thinking a lot about all of this. Maybe it's my mom's pragmatism, but we all will leave this earth eventually. I know Mom's life was very full when she went up to the farm to help with Katherine and you, Aunt Kate. I know she missed my dad and her life on their farm. And, of course, she always talked about the day when she could see Pastor and Grammy Conner again. We always had a good time visiting one another when we lived in our separate little houses. I miss her terribly and will always miss her, but she used to tell me that she'd heard there was a little front porch in heaven where she'd be able to lean over the railing and keep an eye on me from up there. We used to laugh about it, but now I feel she was watching us visit her at the cemetery from her front porch in heaven."

They all had a good chuckle over that.

"That," Kate said, "was where we were raised. And, yes, Poppa always told us about that front porch…that he'd be able to keep an eye on us from up there, making sure we were behaving. We kids used to wonder how anyone could actually see anyone from that distance. When we asked Momma how anyone could see down to earth from so high up, she'd always say pastors had a special lookout spot where they could watch out for their flocks for eternity. That's just the way it was."

Jack got quite a chuckle out of a Methodist's view of heaven. That, he said, was a subject he'd never heard anything about. People coming back to Earth to wander around was one thing, but sitting up there, scanning the old neighborhood with a telescope, was not something he could envision. He promised to ask the young priest at their parish about that.

Julia had other things on her mind. "I need to do a little shopping today. I was going to send out the thank-you cards for the funeral, but since it's almost Christmas, I think I'd like to do both sets at the same time. Anyone want to come along?"

Kate knew she should think about doing some shopping herself but didn't have the energy that day. Jackson offered to babysit Katherine but cautioned Julia not to overdo it. "While Emily might enjoy getting out, I don't think the doctor wants her running from store to store shopping for holiday gifts."

In the end, Kate decided she'd do a little shopping when they got back to Wisconsin. Emily thought it might be fun to see some of the big Chicago department stores—if she wouldn't have to walk too much. So, Emily went along for an abbreviated shopping excursion. She promised to look for Christmas greeting cards for herself and Kate, since that's what Julia planned to shop for. At the last minute, Jack decided to go along so he could drive Emily back to the house if she got tired.

Kate decided she'd spend the afternoon reading. After they left, she checked on the baby, then sat in the library, paging through some of the books she thought looked interesting. She didn't get very far before she grew tired and went to join the baby.

Half awake, she wondered again why Gerrit had forgotten her. Why didn't he call? After they bought the farm and she went up north to live while he continued working at the bank in Chicago, she'd never worried about his faithfulness to her. He'd written often and tried to get up to see them at least every other month when the weather was good. How did she ever get through those long lonely days? Helen and Harald were such good neighbors. After Harald died, Gerrit always seemed to have business to talk over with Helen. Maybe he did. She knew he relied on Helen to help with herself and the baby. Kate knew she didn't have the stamina to handle a baby when her own health was so compromised. It seemed Gerrit was tired of a wife who couldn't take care of things anymore.

December 19, 1944

Dear Days,

Some days I feel as if I'm falling down a steep hill. When I get to the bottom, I realize I don't have the energy or strength to climb back up. Sometimes when I wake up in the morning, I realize I've been crying in my sleep. I know it's not because I've lost Ida. I know she's in heaven with our parents. She was such a good sister. Well, sometimes she was a little bossy. But she always looked out for me, even though she was much older than I was and had a lot of friends. I never seemed to have any friends. I'd walk home from school with some of them, but they never came over to my house to call for me. And I never went to their houses, except when I'd call for them when we would walk to school together.

I think I used to lean on Ida rather than make plans to do things with girls my age. She always let me tag along.

Oh, Ida, is there really a veranda where people can look down from heaven like Poppa always told us? I feel like a silly kid asking such a dumb question, but can you really see us?

You have always been my best friend. I wish you were here now so I could talk to you about Gerrit. After your funeral, he went back to the farm because he had budget and tax business to take care of. But he hasn't even called once since then, much less written a letter like he always did when he was in Chicago. I'm afraid maybe he's tired of having to bother with me.

Rest in peace.

Kate

Ψ

Jack and Julia planned to visit family in St. Louis over the Christmas holiday. There were too many memories from a lifetime of Christmases in their own house. Aside from holiday cards, there was no other sign of the coming festivities. Even the door wreath was trimmed in black ribbons.

The neighborhood was blanketed in snow that sparkled in the moonlight as Kate stood at the window of the quiet house. She had to get back to the farm before too many more days passed. She had to at least get to Ida's house so she'd be out of the way so Robert's family could get their house closed up for a week.

But Kate didn't have to raise the issue of leaving. Emily already had the go-ahead from her doctor. "It's time for me to head home," she said to Jackson and Julia. "I'll miss you, this beautiful house, and having a fire in a fireplace, but I think I can manage on my own now. Aunt Kate and I can get where we need to go on the train."

"Nonsense," was Jack's response. "We're planning to drive you up there as soon as we have a day or two when it isn't snowing. Maybe even tomorrow. That way we can drive you right to your house or your mom's house and help you settle in."

Jackson explained that he felt Kate should stay with Emily at her house in Milwaukee until things had normalized, even though Anna was anxious to have Katherine back.

"I remember how Robert used to fuss if he couldn't keep an eye on me," Julia said. "He didn't even want one of his grandmothers or aunts holding him, much less feeding and changing him. Katherine is an amazing little girl, and we are going to miss her."

Jack said he and Julia had been talking about the possibility of driving up to the farm to visit and meet some of the wonderful Amish neighbors they'd been hearing about. But that wouldn't happen until the snow melted and the rosebush and lilacs were in bloom.

With no snow expected for the next couple of days, Emily and Kate started gathering their things for the trip north. The bulk of Kate's luggage was Katherine's. Even with some of it squeezed into a couple of shopping bags, the suitcases bulged.

Emily was anxious to get started, but that bravado quickly wore off as they got on the major north-south highway headed to Wisconsin. Kate watched as her niece opened and closed her balled fists. What did she remember of that horrible trip a month earlier? While it was on everyone's mind, none of them dared mention the significance of that stretch of highway.

Kate had her own unspoken terrors as she thought again of Gerrit. He and Jack had talked several times, but apparently, he hadn't even asked about Kate. She would stay a couple of days with Emily, then take a cab to the train depot. But with what? The couple of dollar bills she still had in her purse wouldn't even cover taxi fare, much less a train ticket.

Emily decided she wanted to go to her own house. The doctor had warned her not to drive in the city because the traffic could be too stressful for her. In another week or so she would be okay to get behind the wheel. Then she remembered that Robert's car was in her garage. They had used her car for the Thanksgiving trip to Chicago because it was larger than his. She remembered how he laughed about Chicago drivers, and how he didn't want to be responsible for getting her pretty robin's egg blue paint scratched.

The legendary Chicago traffic lived up to its expected holiday-week congestion, but it thankfully thinned out the closer they got to the border. There, most of the traffic was heading in the opposite direction toward Chicago.

Emily had called her next-door neighbor before they left that morning to let her know she was on her way home. Not only had the neighbor gone over to turn up the thermostat to warm the house, she'd also set out the tea pot with cups and saucers, plus a fruit bread and fresh butter on the kitchen table. It was a wonderful "welcome home" surprise. Best of all, when Jack's car pulled into the driveway, Emily's neighbor was right there with her arms open wide in welcome.

Jack unloaded the luggage from the trunk and carried it not only into the house, but upstairs to the two bedrooms. A stack of pillows had been piled on one end of the living room davenport so they could keep the baby from falling onto the floor. But that, he could quickly see, was not going to keep Miss K from rolling off. Best thing would be for her to start off on the floor, close to one of the living room radiators.

At early afternoon, as Jack and Julia backed out of the driveway for the trip back to Chicago, Emily and Kate tried to keep their smiles in place. But the reality of what had happened in Chicago made that impossible. It was another hurdle in that long climb back without Ida and Robert.

After getting Katherine settled on her floor quilt surrounded by pillows, Kate stretched out on the couch and covered up with an afghan. Emily went upstairs to nap, promising not to sleep too long—a promise she didn't keep. Later, when Kate woke up from her own nap, she tried to reach Gerrit at the courthouse, but the switchboard said he had a luncheon meeting and wouldn't be back until late in the afternoon. The woman on the phone promised to let him know where he could reach her, then put away her business voice and told Kate how sorry she was about the tragic death of her sister and that she hoped she would be back home soon.

That night it started snowing again—mostly flurries. Julia called after supper to say they'd gotten home safely and were ready to turn in. The snow hadn't started there yet, but it was expected before morning. The next morning when she looked out the bedroom window, low-riding clouds hid part of the landscape. A very heavy snowfall lasted the rest of the day. It was still spitting snow the next morning. Emily's neighbor had not only brought the loaf of sweet bread for their welcome-home snack, she'd filled the refrigerator with fruit, milk, eggs, and a few other necessities. She also had left a note to Emily to make a list of what she needed so she could do some shopping for her as soon as it stopped snowing.

The days flew by, and still no one called to arrange getting Kate and the baby back to the farm. Eventually, someone would have to let them know when they'd be coming to get them. Gerrit never called her back. She knew the operator would have given him her message.

One afternoon, Kate asked Emily what the date was. But Emily didn't have any better idea of the day than Kate did, so she did the logical thing: she called her neighbor.

December 23, 1944

Dear Days,

You'd never guess what we had to do to find out what today's date is. Neither Emily nor I had any clue, so she called her wonderful next-door neighbor, who was laughing so hard I could hear her from across the room. That neighbor is amazing. She was kind enough to stock Emmy's fridge for her return. This morning, she came over to get Emily's shopping list for fresh meat, oatmeal, noodles, some canned goods, and cookies. I think Emily should sell her mother's house and keep this one with the wonderful neighbor. The people who lived around Ida's house were a little stand-offish. Ida's house was larger and fancier, but it was not a place I

would ever want to live after what happened to
my daughter there a year ago.

Today is Dec. 23rd. Maybe Fletcher will drive
down tomorrow to get us.

Emily has her mother's knack for cooking.
She made a kettle of egg noodles and glazed
it with grated cheese. When I finished feeding
Katherine and went out to the kitchen, I
couldn't believe my eyes. There, in the middle
of the table, was a plate of Annalise's dried
apple slices. I couldn't get a word out—the tears
were just streaming down my face. It was as if
everything had landed on my shoulders all at
once...the money she'd earned selling the dried
apples that paid for her high school tuition
and the awful things (but not all awful) that
it brought about. The humiliation of having
to go back home after barely one semester at
the private school, going to school again with
classmates who weren't sure why she'd come back
again. They'd moved on with their lives and
she wasn't part of them. The weeks she'd had to
spend in bed, my stroke and stay in the hospital
at the same time she was there. The routine of
caring for a baby, going to school and trying
to help with the house chores and a new crop
of apple slices. I'd gotten through everything
without breaking down, but the apple slices
brought everything into sharp focus. And once
I started sobbing, I couldn't stop. There were
so many things in my life that had been taken
away with no chance of ever returning. The only
good thing was the little girl sucking her thumb
on her quilt on the living room floor. And now, I
might also have lost Gerrit.

Kate

Emily was taken aback at her aunt's outburst. She hadn't realized the emotional strings attached to those slices.

CHAPTER TWENTY-TWO

The phone rang early the next morning. Kate could hear Emily's hushed voice. It was probably Robert's parents wondering how things were getting on now that she was back home. Kate didn't bother asking who called.

Close to lunch time, she heard someone at the front door, but she knew Emily was downstairs and could answer it herself. The conversation was a quiet buzz at the front of the house, but Kate couldn't make out any of the words. Then she heard laughter. The loudest laugh was Fletcher's. He'd come to get her. She scooped up Katherine and rushed down the stairs. But it wasn't just Fletcher. Gerrit and Annalise had come, too.

"Bet you thought we'd forgotten all about you," Gerrit said, scooping her into his arms. "We were working on a big surprise for Christmas, and we didn't dare talk to you or one of us might have let it slip." She saw tears well up in his eyes as he pushed her away so he could get a good look at her. Kate realized that Anna had grabbed her little girl from her arms and was hugging her to pieces. Regardless of all the time they'd been apart, Baby Katherine certainly knew who her Momma was. They disappeared into the living room and found the rocker.

Fletcher wailed. "This is certainly a tear-jerk occasion. If I'd known everyone was going to be sniffling, I'd have stayed home with the dog and cows." But then it was his turn to give his mom a huge welcome-home hug. "We certainly need you to come home. Things have gotten a little out of hand without you."

That's when Kate noticed that the table was set for five, not two, and the small plate of dried apple slices had been replaced by a bowlful of the prettiest, red-skinned apples. Last year's harvest had been bountiful, especially the Red and Golden Delicious.

After they'd eaten the ham and cheese sandwiches Emily had heated in the oven and snacked on the sun-drenched dried apple slices, they had tea and a plateful of the cookies Emily's neighbor brought over. Despite what the family had been through in the previous year, one wouldn't have been able to tell them apart from any other jovial group at Christmas.

"Fletcher and I need to go over to Ida's house this afternoon to make sure everything is still in good running order," Gerrit said. "I'll do the driving, but Fletcher, our future engineer, will check the mechanicals. We also need to take a close look at the building itself. If you're thinking of selling either of these houses, early spring would be the best time. That will give us a little time to repaint walls and clear out all but the essentials needed to dress them for showing. You won't need both houses, for sure."

Gerrit sipped his tea and then looked around the table. "Anyone else interested in going along this afternoon? I'd rather get an early start in the morning and know that we've taken a good look at both houses so we have a good idea of what needs to be done before spring."

Only Anna and Katherine stayed home that afternoon. Fletcher took a legal pad for making lists of tasks and suggestions for who could do them. Emily was certain she wanted to stay in her own house and put her mom's on the market. While it was not information that would be given to a potential buyer, the main reason for selling Ida's house was because of its history involving Annalise. Emily was also certain Anna never wanted to spend time in that house, least of all stay overnight in her old bedroom.

Ida's house would appeal to someone a bit older, which was a good feature to highlight since the neighborhood had, primarily, an older population. Coming up with a potential price for the property would take a little more thinking.

The next step was to itemize things that needed fixing, repairing, or replacing in Ida's home. Gerrit suggested Emily have a plumber look at all the piping for the bathrooms and kitchen. They checked all the windows and found two that had slight cracks in the glass. Some screens had seen better days, and the glazing around some of the panes was loose and leaking air.

Kate and Emily decided to take a break from examining the house and made tea. Gerrit and Fletcher did a walk-through out in the garage. Ida's garage was considerably larger than Emily's, but it also had been neglected for several years and needed serious work. More items on the to-do list. It was difficult to get a good read on the sidewalks and driveway under the snow, but as soon as possible, they'd need a concrete man to figure out what needed fixing and how much it would cost.

"All it takes is a lot of money," Gerrit said with a grin, and Fletch added a groan for punctuation.

When the gentlemen got back inside, their limbs were numb. "I think we will definitely be staying over tonight, if that's okay with you, Emily," Gerrit said politely. "Maybe Fletcher, you, and Kate should bunk here at Ida's, since there isn't room for everyone at your house. The baby is all settled at your place, so we could just leave Anna there with her."

Gerrit turned to his son. "Fletch, could you contact the local police and ask if they have any weather-related cautions for the entire state in the next twenty-four hours? If not, let's be packed up and ready to roll first thing in the morning."

Gerrit then asked, "By the way, Emmy, were you planning to come up to the farm with us for the holiday weekend? You know, our welcome mat is always out for you. Almost forgot. Ida's car is still in her garage. I think we will need to use that for our trip back to the farm. Baby Katherine takes up more than her share of the room in the trunk. We'll need it whether or not you decide to go with us. But if we can use her car we will not be so squeezed together. That's really why we brought Fletch with us. I figured he could drive one of the cars."

Emily was hesitant to say yes for the trip north. But Kate and Gerrit were not happy at the prospect of leaving her behind. Her first Christmas after the accident needed to be spent with family. And Gerrit knew Kate would be a lot more relaxed if Emily stayed with them over the holidays. Gerrit could drive her back and Fletcher could drive Ida's car back.

Next morning, Emmy's suitcase stood beside the front door.

It was a perfect almost-Christmas day as the two cars headed west out of town. The only thing that could have been better was one large vehicle instead of two smaller ones. It was easy enough to travel in tandem, but it wasn't as much fun in separate cars. But the idea of all of them being together for Christmas made the day almost perfect. Kate and Gerrit rode in Gerrit's car. Emily, Annalise, and the baby quickly settled in the backseat while Fletcher was tucked into the driver's seat, surrounded by boxes and shopping bags. Gerrit and Kate led the way for most of the trip. Kate watched in the rearview mirror and could tell by the way their mouths moved in unison that they were singing holiday songs. While she couldn't figure out what songs they were singing, she mentally sang along—a song of her own choosing. The trip went quickly. Leaving so early in the morning, they missed what would have been a busy holiday travel day.

Despite Gerrit's warm hug, Kate still felt a little uneasy around him. He seemed reluctant to strike up a conversation, and she was too distracted to try to ease into some neutral topic to get him to talk to her. He just drove, and eventually, she rested her head against the back of the seat and fell asleep. When the car shifted into a slower speed, it disturbed her, and she sat up to look around. They were pulling into a gasoline station, but Gerrit just pulled off to the side. Fletcher quickly hopped out and inserted the gas hose into the tank opening.

Anna got out and hurried over to where her parents waited for Fletcher to finish filling. "You two doing okay?" she asked as her mom rolled down the window. "We wish we were all in the same car. We've been singing

Christmas carols, mostly the old classics. Emily has such a beautiful voice. She said they had a pump organ on the farm when she was growing up and she learned how to play. I wish we had a pump organ so she could play when she comes to stay for visits. It would be such fun to watch her play. She said she usually doesn't even need a sheet with the notes on it. She plays by ear. I guess that means she learned to play the notes by listening to how the music sounds."

Once everyone was back in their respective vehicles, Fletcher pulled out ahead of his dad.

"He's a pretty good driver," Gerrit said, more to reassure himself than to point it out to Kate. "Now that track season is over, he's been coming home in your car most weekends to help out. I had a chance to buy a few head of dairy cattle for a good price, so I did. Makes milking time last a little longer every day. I've been teasing Anna that we're going to have to teach her how to milk so we can get done a little earlier. She didn't think she'd have time once Katherine was back."

Gerrit glanced over at his wife, and her lack of response spurred him to speak further. "You look like you're feeling a lot better these days. I know this has been hard on you, but it seems your taking care of Katherine hasn't caused any setbacks. Chandler is anxious to have you stop in for a quick checkup. He also wants us to bring Emily in so they can get current information in their records. Emily didn't bring any of her records along, did she?"

"I don't think so," Kate answered. She had no paperwork with her when she came back from the doc's office at the hospital

"We've really been lucky that it stopped snowing when it did. Can you imagine people trying to drive through snow-covered rural roads on their way to grandma's house?"

Kate's eyelids sank again, but when she noticed where they were, she sat up straighter, looking to see if she could spot their house. She realized they were still too far away. Another couple of minutes, maybe. That train of thought brought back the porch at heaven's front door that had caused Kate, Emily, and Robert's parents to laugh so hard. She tried not to laugh or snicker about it in front of Gerrit. He wouldn't appreciate such a goofy story. She had always been surprised at his indifference to religion. When she and Gerrit had prepared for their wedding day, they never even discussed where the service would be. He knew his role in the nuptials was to do exactly what they'd rehearsed and not offer a second opinion. Even Kate didn't have much of a say in how the service would go. But then, her Poppa had always controlled what happened in his own sanctuary. No one ever argued about it. The church building and what went on inside of it was his domain. That short, gray-haired pastor with wispy curls winging up in the most conspicuous places around his head presided proudly. And when he laughed, smile-lines broke out from his chin to his forehead.

Suddenly, Kate's reverie about her late father shifted and she saw their farmhouse. It seemed like she'd been away for months. Her fears of being useless and forgotten in her own plain-wrapped, square, white house rose up and nearly choked her. She promised herself she would not cry.

Gerrit parked close to the steps leading up to the porch. The rosebush she and Fletcher had planted so many years ago was hidden by the mounds of snow in her welcome garden. While she was still trying to sort out the emotions washing over her, Gerrit jumped out of the car and ran around to her side, and held the door open for her. His smile stretched from ear to ear.

That's when she noticed Helen's car parked in front of the woodshed section of the garage. She remembered Gerrit honking the horn as he turned into the driveway. Helen was waiting at the open door. Something about the porch looked different, but she was helped up the steps so quickly she didn't have time to analyze from the outside. Inside, everything looked pretty much the same except for...the curtains! Even the old chair had a cushion made from the same fabric, and the daybed had a brand new spread!

Fletcher and his passengers had pulled up behind Gerrit's car. They got out and quietly joined everyone in the redecorated space.

Helen stepped aside as Gerrit took Kate's hand and led her into the house. Everywhere she looked, things were the same but looked brand new. The raggedy green shades at the parlor windows were replaced with new lacy ones. So were the shades in what had been converted years earlier into the main bedroom. When she peeked into the back bedroom, she was surprised to see everything changed there, too. They now had a real bathtub and a large vanity with two sinks. Over each sink hung a mirror. There were new towel bars over the tub and next to each sink. There was a new commode and cupboard filled with brand new towels and washcloths. Since the room was so large, there were more cupboards which, she discovered, held sheets and blankets for the beds. There was a bench for sitting to dress after a bath. A door had been installed to close off the under-stairs closet.

In the corner of the main room near Gerrit's rolltop desk was a little feather Christmas tree decorated with blue ornaments that Kate inherited from her parents. The sideboard where Kate had shoved Fletcher when the tornado had roared through, donned new candlesticks standing on crocheted, homemade doilies. Helen leaned close to Kate's ear and whispered, "Grammy Iversen made these years ago and always said she wanted you to have them."

Everywhere she looked, things were new, changed, painted. Perfect!

Gerrit and Kate's bedroom also had a new look. A crib stood in a corner so Katherine would be able to nap there without Kate having to carry her up and down stairs during the day. There were new blinds and more lace curtains to soften the look. There was a rocker in the bedroom and a bench where Kate could sit when she took off her shoes. There was even a closet built into the corner on the wall backing up to Gerrit's desk. Most of it was space for hanging clothes, but there was another spot where coats could be hung. The closets also had space up top for storing hats, suitcases, and other things.

Next, they toured the refurbished rooms upstairs. A narrow closet for Fletcher had been built into what had been Annalise's room. The big old dresser with the handkerchief drawers had been moved to Fletcher's old room for Annalise. There also was a large antique walnut wardrobe for Anna's clothes and a dresser for Katherine's. Out-of-season clothes could be stored in a large cabinet built along the north wall. There were hanging closets and loads of drawers and smaller cabinets. She could tell who had built that—Aaron Mellen and his boys. There was even a large rug on the floor to make the room warmer in winter. There were pretty curtains at the windows and heavy shades to shut out lightning storms and keep the room toasty. New was a rocker and desk where Annalise could study and write in her Book of Days. There was also a typewriter.

Under the eaves was decluttered and now held a nice sitting area. The wooden steps had been sanded smooth and varnished. Carpet had also been laid up the stairs to soften the noise and make them cozier underfoot. There was even a curtain at the window overlooking the garden out back and a shade installed so the cold air could be blocked out.

Besides curtains and mirrors, pictures were hung in all the bedrooms. There was a nice bookcase in Anna's bedroom upstairs and a toybox for Katherine in the downstairs bedroom next to her bed.

Kate had enjoyed spending time in Jack and Julia's beautiful house in Chicago, but here she was, standing in her own beautifully redecorated house.

Finally, Kate sat down at the dining room table and put her head down and cried. Ida's curtains had come to fruition. Windows sparkled. Polished furniture glowed warmly. A new oilcloth had been laid on the long table on the porch and pictures hung above it. A large cupboard stood at the far end of the porch with drawers holding tablecloths and other necessities. Family treasures were displayed on the top. At the other end of the porch was a closet for coats and jackets. The biggest change was a fireplace-style heater to warm up the porch on a cold day.

The farmhouse redecorating project had been hatched when Gerrit and Annalise drove home after Ida's funeral. Gerrit explained, "Annalise and I spent most of the trip discussing how we were going to surprise you when you came home. Nothing much had changed inside or outside the house except for your gardens, and we thought it was long overdue. But I certainly couldn't figure out how to make this a beautiful place for my beautiful wife and family, and Annalise was willing but didn't have the experience to gather up the bits and pieces that would change the comfortable home you'd made for all of us into something that would reflect your beauty and grace."

At that, Fletcher groaned, then laughed.

"Even your son was in on the redecorating effort," Gerrit said. "But the real genie behind this transformation was our dear Helen. When I told her what I had in mind, she told me that she and Ida had been talking about making some changes inside the house for a long time but they couldn't figure out how to get it all done with everything else that was going on in our lives. When I called Emily and told her what we were working on up here, she promised to delay coming back until we had everything finished. We were all afraid we might spill the surprise and we didn't want to spoil our gift to you. Robert's mother offered to shop for the lace and other curtains in Chicago. The ladies at church helped, too. The quilt was stitched as a celebration of Annalise and her commitment to baby Katherine's safe arrival and for your ongoing recovery from the stroke."

A sudden cold draft caught everyone by surprise—and in walked their Amish neighbors, holding their own gifts, including a new rocker for Kate. When it was carried into the parlor, Fletcher took the old one to the little sitting area in the upstairs hallway. Kate took a deep breath and eased down into the beautiful wood that had been sanded and polished to a silky finish.

Kate's voice quivered as she leaned forward in her new chair and tried to thank everyone. "I can never, ever thank you for this unbelievable surprise and gift. About all I can do is promise that I will love you all until my time comes to an end."

Annalise set Katherine in her Grammy's arms and went out to the kitchen. She returned carrying packages of her spiced apple slices and packets of cookies, which she laid out on the dining room table. Aaron and Nellie had brought treats with them, too—Amish cookies shaped like stars and a large loaf of Christmas breakfast bread. They quickly begged off the invitation to eat a light supper with them before heading back to their farm and the rest of their nightly chores.

A month earlier, it would have been Ida at the refrigerator taking out bowls and platters to serve the family and guests. This time, Emily and Annalise carried the food into the parlor and set it out on the table already stretched out to its full length.

"Noah was about finished out in your barn when we got here, so we'll wait until he's ready to ride home with us. Reading the birth of Jesus is a big part of our Christmas Eve," Nellie said. "It's a quiet night when we take time to watch the stars and reflect on what happened that night long ago when he was born. We are so blessed."

"Emily, we want you to know that we will remember Ida and your intended husband, Robert, during our prayers tonight," Aaron added.

The back door opened and closed quickly. Noah had finished and seemed anxious to get home to their family gathering.

Gerrit reached into his desk drawer and took out an envelope. "This is a little extra for your farm fund," he said to his hired man. "We are so thankful for all you do for us here. I'm still trying to figure out why I had to buy a farm when, for heaven's sake, I don't know the first thing about farming."

That interrupted the night with hearty laughs.

Nellie had a little package in her bag that she handed to Annalise. "Sarah wanted to bring this herself, but she had chores to finish so we'd be ready for the Christmas readings when we got back. This package is for Katherine and there is a card for you."

Another cold draft paused the conversation as Chandler and his wife and three boys came into the room. "I had to come and check up on my growing list of patients," the doctor said. He pretended to give Kate and Katherine a quick checkup, then turned to Emily. While he'd teased about his other welcomes, he gave her a silent and cautious hug. Annalise watched as he tried to brush tears away.

Emily reached into her sweater pocket for her crystal rosary beads, a gift from Robert when she'd been baptized a Roman Catholic. She was still holding them when he took her hand. He smiled when he felt what she was holding. "We have to talk soon," he whispered.

"Can we talk for a few minutes now?" Emily asked.

The affable Chandler was at a loss for words. He just nodded.

"I would like to go to midnight Mass tonight," she said in a quiet whisper. "Do they have Mass tonight at your church in town?"

"Yes, they do, and yes we are all going," he said. "Would you like to go with us?"

"May I? Robert often told me about how his family went to midnight Mass on Christmas Eve when he was a boy. When I was baptized last fall, he promised he would take me to Mass to see for myself how beautiful it was. I think he'll be there waiting for me tonight. My car was totally ruined in the accident, and I haven't bought a new one yet, but my mom's car is here and I could drive that into town."

"No," Chandler whispered. "Mass starts with carols at eleven, and the bells ring at midnight for the start of Mass. I will take the kids back into town because the boys are singing in the carol choir tonight. Then I will drive back out to get you."

"What are you two whispering about over here?" Gerrit asked.

"Emily was asking about going to midnight Mass tonight, and I'm arranging to get my boys to carol choir and giving her a ride to the service."

"Could I go, too?" Annalise asked. "I've been thinking about it all day, wondering how I could do that. I want to take Baby Katherine. She should be there, even if she sleeps through the whole thing. The Mass belongs to her more than to most of us here."

"I've been thinking about that, too," Gerrit said. "For little Katherine, I mean."

Fletcher joined in the conversation as he came into the room with a handful of Christmas cookies. "Are we going to church tonight?" he asked.

"Midnight Mass at the Catholic Church in town," Annalise explained. "Emily was talking with Chandler about going to Mass with them tonight, now that she's a baptized Roman Catholic. Katherine isn't baptized yet, but I think of her as a Roman Catholic, too, so I was trying to figure out how I could take her to that church."

"Problem solved!" Fletcher said with a hearty chuckle. "I'll drive Emily, Anna, and the baby into town in time for the services. Just tell me what time we have to be there. I'll join you, too. We have somehow survived so much these last few weeks. I'd heard about Catholics going to Mass at midnight on Christmas Eve. Momma, would you like to go too? What about you, Pops?"

"Can't imagine why not. Mom could sit in the pew next to Chandler so he can keep an eye on his patient," Gerrit said. "And I could probably benefit from a little church-going on Christmas Eve," he added.

"I would especially like to go early to hear the children sing carols," Kate said. Her memory flitted back to the children singing carols at Emily's hospital room door, and the voice that reminded her of Daniel. Kate then added, "I could rest for the next hour, and we'd still get to the church on time, don't you think?"

To ensure that the Jansz family could sit behind them, Chandler's wife Suzanne promised to claim the pew early so there'd be room enough for all of them.

After Chandler and his family left, Kate pulled the Christmas afghan over her as she laid down on the bed. Gerrit came to tuck her in. When he leaned down to give her a kiss on the cheek, Kate held his hand as she whispered something to him: "When you didn't call me, and when Annalise said you were over at Helen's for a late-night supper—well, I can't tell you how upset I was. I thought you'd given up on me and my slow recovery from the stroke. I was so afraid to come back here because I thought…"

"Don't ever think that. We were all so excited at carrying out our plans for your Christmas surprise," he said softly. "I think Ida was here today. I know she was. This started out months ago as her idea. Then when she was dying, I whispered to her in the hospital that I knew what she'd planned to do for you, and I promised her we would make it all happen. Even the indoor plumbing. So, she had to come to make sure we'd gotten it all right. Even without her supervision."

Kate dozed off. Annalise took Katherine upstairs to decide what she'd wear to church tonight. She had almost fallen asleep when she heard Fletcher's footsteps on the stairs.

"Hate to get you up so soon, but I wanted to make sure we were ready to go," Fletcher said quietly. "I know you went to Mass in the chapel at the Catholic high school last year. I was wondering if we should do the same sitting, kneeling, and standing as the regular Catholics do, or if we should just sit and watch? What did you do when you went at school?"

"Just tried to keep up with what everyone else was doing," Anna replied with a smile. "When I'd be a little behind or forget to watch for their cues, no one seemed to mind. I'm sure everyone will be so absorbed in the special event that they won't notice. If we sit in the pew behind Chandler, we can easily keep track of what they are doing. And if you get tired of trying to keep up with them, just sit down. That I know would be perfectly acceptable. And I also know that I'll probably sit during most of the Mass because I'll be holding Katherine. Momma, too."

"Weren't you a little surprised about Poppa? I never would've thought he'd be interested in going to Mass in the middle of the night. Even with everything we've been through this year, he's never been much for going to a church service unless it was a wedding or funeral."

"Poppa's sometimes hard to understand. I never could figure out why he disliked going to church so much. But here he is, wanting to go with us," Anna said, shrugging.

Bundled up in the cars for the trip to town was like driving into a fairyland. The temperature hovered just below freezing. There was no wind, and the starlight shimmered like diamonds on the pristine snow along the road. Church after chores and breakfast on Christmas morning was nothing compared to this holy scene. Annalise would not have been surprised to hear a heavenly choir of angels.

Their footsteps softly crunched as they walked down the sidewalk toward the welcoming lights of the nearly silent church. Suddenly, the sound of children's voices exploded into a rapturous crescendo of "Gloria in excelsis Deo". It took Anna's breath away.

Inside, tall candles flickered on the high altar as the Jansz family walked down the aisle to the pew behind Chandler's. Fletcher had forgotten to ask what they were expected to do when they got to their pew. He noticed some people bowing their heads before going into the pew. Others knelt on one knee, bowing toward the altar and the nativity scene laid out to the right of the altar. A wooden railing with a white cloth stretched along the backside separated the altar space from the pews where people knelt or sat.

Anna laid Katherine on the pew as she knelt to say happy birthday to the infant Jesus. She told him that she'd brought little Katherine for her first visit to the church of her father. Then she picked up the baby again and sat down on the bench. The children's voices were joined by older ones, giving depth to the familiar hymns. She heard sounds from the choir loft and turned around to watch. The adult choir members took their places on the risers, facing the front altar. The director urged the children to move so the adults would be ready to start singing when the altar boy and candle bearers led the procession into church. Kate tried hard to stay awake amongst the lullaby of hymns, fragrant candles, beautiful greenery, and pristine stained glass.

Annalise looked over at Fletcher and saw his eyes were sleepy, too, but she knew that when the priest entered the church, the organ would erupt and waken any tired soul for miles around.

As she predicted, the magnificent organ accompanied by a glorious array of singers was an unbelievable experience. Annalise couldn't imagine anywhere else she would've rather been.

Emily's face glowed. Anna had worried this might be too emotional an experience for her cousin, but instead, she was enveloped in the music. She looked radiant.

Suddenly, Annalise had to sit down, the experience overwhelming and tears coursing down her cheeks. She held Baby Katherine to her shoulder and savored the moment washing over her.

Ψ

Christmas Day brought an unexpected visit that turned lingering sadness to pure joy. Robert's parents called from a two-car caravan. They were about a half-hour away with packages to deliver.

Most of the family lounged in robes and slippers, sitting around Gerrit's mother's old feather Christmas tree. It looked completely at home on Gerrit's desk.

Because the guests miscalculated their arrival by more than fifteen minutes, the shades at the front of the house were still drawn and the porch door locked. Suddenly, the family heard jingling holiday bells. Fletcher jumped up to answer the door.

Jackson and Julia were dressed like holiday elves with silly red hats and long scarves. They carried armloads of packages wrapped in silvery paper with green velvet bows.

The joyful confusion never stopped that day. Katherine was the main attraction for everyone, since it was her first Christmas. Gerrit couldn't remember a happier Christmas. When he was a kid, holidays never measured up to the fun his schoolmates talked about. For Kate, there remained a shadow of sadness—although no one could see it. Her face shined with happiness.

Gerrit kept an eye on her, fearful the intense activity would be too much for her. He needn't have worried. She weathered it perfectly.

Emily, even though mourning the death of her beloved Robert, never stopped smiling. She knew he was there with them, as was her mother.

They unloaded the food they brought from Chicago. (Where was Aunt Ida when they needed her to make sense of such a scene?) The food spread upon the table provided an endless feast throughout the too-short day. If Emily had noticed, she didn't give any indication that she recognized the second car in the driveway.

Late in the afternoon, before they left to go back into town where they had a room at the little hotel, Jack pulled a silver ribbon from his pocket. Julia wrapped her hands around her husband's as they handed Emily the keys to their son's car. It was important for Robert's parents to give Emily that last reminder of him. She'd lost her car but wouldn't need to get a new one.

When she'd seen them walk through the door that morning, Emily knew she would never be far from Robert's family. She didn't know then, and maybe they didn't either, but someday she would inherit everything meant to belong to their only child and the woman he'd planned to marry.

Their gift gave Emily the courage to give Anna a gift she was still too young to use—Ida's car. "In time, you can drive this. But for now, it will be parked in the garage. Or Fletcher could use it for trips to and from college. That's up to you two," Emily said to her cousins.

Ψ

After the excitement of the holidays, Anna was ready to go back to school. Fletcher had already left for college, driving his mom's car. Emily's new car was moved to Kate's old stall beside Gerrit's. Ida's old car seemed content in the woodshed, waiting for Anna to get old enough to drive it.

Kate continued therapy to finish recovering from the stroke. Emily's therapy appointments lasted well into March. Finally, Chandler said he looked forward to her visits when she brought Kate in for checkups.

Once a month, Emily and Annalise drove to Milwaukee to check on the two vacant houses. Then, one Saturday, Emily announced she didn't want to live in either one. Both had too many tragic memories of her beloved lost ones.

Month by month, they sorted and bagged things for donating to charities. Sometimes Kate and baby Katherine went along. Once or twice, Gerrit also helped. In the end, they had only a few boxes of Emily's childhood treasures and another one holding a small stack of Ida's journals she'd occasionally kept. A quick peek at the dates on the covers showed she hadn't altogether stopped writing in her journal after she and Jake married. Most entries were from the first years of Emily's life. Then they suddenly stopped.

"We should take these up to the farm and add them to the journals written by Grammy Conner and your mom," Emily suggested to Annalise.

Little by little, the accumulations of years were packed into Gerrit's car and hauled to the farm. Special treasures were Grammy Conner's silverware and the tea set they'd received as a gift from the parish to use for special occasions. The minister who'd succeeded Pastor Conner had his own tea service, which was used at Ida's funeral.

A month later, Emily's house was listed with a real estate company and ready for its first open house. The family awaited news from their farmhouse up north.

The repainted and redecorated home showed very well, the agent said. No offers had arrived yet, but there were glimmers of hope.

"Everyone really liked the way the house was set up. They liked the paint colors in all the rooms. You never know who's going to come in with an offer or when, so we will just wait and see," the realtor said.

Shortly after, the phone rang—an offer. It was from a newly married couple who had been some of the first through the house. They thought it was well-priced, and they didn't want to chance someone buying it out from under them. They had already been to the bank and had a good down payment, so they wouldn't need much of a mortgage.

"This is one of the fastest sales I've ever had," the realtor lady said. "They merely wanted an inspection to make sure the foundation was in good shape, the plumbing worked and the electrical wasn't a hazard."

The realtor offered to meet her halfway so she wouldn't have such a long trip just to sign paperwork, but Emily said she didn't mind driving down. It seemed the least she could do when she was getting the price she wanted for the house.

"One down, one to go," she told Kate as they had a cup of tea in celebration.

The phone rang again. This time, the real estate agent had a question. "Would Emily consider selling some of the furnishings in the house? The buyers just loved the look of the house. They said they hadn't been married long enough to have much furniture, and the furniture was exactly what they'd like to have in the house."

Gerrit took off work so he could go with his niece who'd gotten an offer to buy her house the first day it was officially on the market. "I think Emily needs a money man in her corner to help with any negotiations," he said.

CHAPTER TWENTY-THREE

A Former Priest's Posthumous Letter

November 21, 1944

Dear Miss Annalise,

This letter is one I have written over and over in my mind for the past year. I cannot delay it any longer. Although it is dated with today's year, 1944, it will not be received by you until my will is probated after my death. These are the thoughts that have troubled me since that horrible night at your Aunt Ida's. While I think I have more than a few years left on this earth, I did not want to take a chance that I could not extend my most sincere apology to you for what I did. I can't blame it on an indiscretion in a moment of passion. It wasn't. It was a carefully pre-planned situation that will haunt me to my dying day.

I have no explanation or excuse for that night when I came to your Aunt's house with the soup and a cruet of 'toddy' in my coat pocket. I knew full well you were home alone, and I took that opportunity to give in to the unforgiveable. I not only committed a terrible crime against you, I violated my vow of celibacy that was part of my commitment to God at my ordination to the priesthood.

I can only pray that you will, in time, forgive a fallen priest, and I continue to pray that God can forgive me for my terrible sin. I know some of the struggles you had in the pregnancy I caused.

Circumstances were such that I had no way of coming to grips with what I had done and what I owed you and the child. My bishop sent me here for counselling. Even after all these months, I'm still trying to sort through how I could harm you and your family and disregard my vow of celibacy.

While I cannot forgive myself, I've taken a first and very sorrowful step by asking the Vatican to absolve me from my priestly duties. That laicizing decree was recently granted, and I am sadly no longer a priest.

There is no way to right the wrongs I've done, but I've put some long-range plans on paper that you will learn about when my will is probated. These bequests will, I hope, help in some way to make up for the horror I put you through. I hope if you have a child, there will be enough in my bequest to cover some of the education expenses for him/her.

I continue to pray for you, your child, your family. I beg their posthumous acceptance of my heart-felt apology.

Most sincerely,

Cleary Nolan

BOOK THREE

Katherine

CHAPTER ONE

Jonathan and Angeline squealed with excitement as big sister Katherine set her school lunch box in front of them. When she unsnapped the lid there were two sandwiches wrapped in waxed paper…one for each.

Jonathan wouldn't be ready to start kindergarten at St. Michael's School for another year. Although Angeline was only three fingers old, she figured she must be almost ready to go to school, too. But today's lunchtime surprise Katherine had fixed for them was their best treat ever. Baby Tim, barely three months old, was snuggled in his buggy under the widespread branches of the red maple that provided cool shade.

Katherine put her finger over her lips to shush their excited chatter so they could eat their sandwiches without raising yowls of distress from their light-sleeping baby brother.

The quiet was a relief after the clank and clatter of the monstrous equipment digging sewer-line trenches from the middle of their street up toward their new house. Eating lunch at the new picnic bench in their front yard was probably not a good idea since dust still rained down from the morning digging. The equipment operators sat together at the edge of the lawn munching sandwiches and whatever else they had in their black, metal lunch buckets, washing it all down with gulps of something from their gray, metal thermos bottles. *Coffee*, Katherine surmised.

She reminded the little picnickers to keep eating and went back in the house for the milk from the fridge and two Mickey Mouse cups.

Momma said she would be back after lunch. Wednesday was her day to collect the timecards from dad's newspaper office downtown. Momma liked to bring them home to work on—so she didn't have to leave Katherine alone with her younger siblings, especially the new baby, for an entire afternoon.

When the paper was ready to run, Annalise could never resist waiting to hear the presses turn on, stopping and starting until the print on the first pages was in focus. Then there was that pause where Art, the pressman, and Carleton, Annalise's husband and the boss, hurriedly scanned the pages one more time, making sure everything was in order. When Art got the thumbs up from Carleton, he slid the controls to full speed, and the newsprint would spin faster and faster until finally, pages that were all assembled for that day's edition would roll off at the other end. The pressroom crew stood ready to grab them up into stacks which were then set aside on a large table where another group would grab the stacks and hustle them off to the next station where they would slide past, one by one, to get the labels pasted on. Another set of hands would grab a sheaf of labeled papers and put them, stack by stack, through the machine that whipped twine around the packages which were sorted by postal and hand-delivered routes. That machine was Albert's domain. His foot pushed down the controller, which tied the bundles, so he could flip them over onto a long table where the crew of ladies would stack them onto a rolling cart, that would ferry them to the box truck parked at the loading dock. From there they would ride across the street to the post office. Literally! Another cart held the papers for city-delivery routes for the carriers.

Annalise loved the sounds, the energy, the smell of newsprint and ink wafting through the roar. It was always as if no one dared breathe until the process was complete, unless the paper ripped, which would cause the whole run to stop. Today that didn't happen, and Annalise went back to her husband's office and picked up the papers and timecards she needed. Then she walked back through the cluttered front office, filled with the roaring sound of the press despite the heavy steel door separating the front office from the back shop. She never tired of the chest-throbbing energy mixed with the sounds and smells of press day of their weekly newspapers.

Annalise's part of her husband's family newspaper was the bottom line. He teased that that's why he married her—she kept the business running in the black.

There was, of course, more to it than that. It was Annalise who had done the research on buying a better rotary press and it was her calculations that convinced him it was not only a good plan for their weekly run, but they could sell press time to other papers still operating with cobbled-together old presses.

It didn't take much convincing. The relatively new offset printing process had revolutionized the whole method of getting type into print. Instead of the cumbersome hot metal pieces that a machine fed into the sentences and paragraphs that were needed to put them on newsprint, the pasted-up pages of the newspaper were photographed and turned into a negative mat that fit on the press to roll the type and graphics onto the newsprint.

The shortened lead time to get the news ready to roll left more time for job printing, newsletters, concert programs, advertising. It was a miracle that still awed those who had worked on both sides of that bridge, but it was just the way the business ran these days. So a salesman was sent out to cash in on printing jobs that kept the presses busy, money coming in, and bills getting paid.

The hours of the back-shop timecards kept adding up, making a stop at the banks around town a necessity for the employees. Imagine! No more envelopes filled with dollar bills and change. Eventually, most of the employees had their checks automatically deposited in their bank account, so they never had to physically carry a check to the bank.

With little support from Carleton, at home and at the office, Annalise was left to do it all…raise children and run a successful business. Even though it was challenging, the children and the newspaper brought so much joy into her life for years. The thrill of watching Katherine, Jonathan, Angeline, and Tim grow into amazing humans, as well as the success of the newspaper, was what kept her going.

CHAPTER TWO

“**H**ello, Gerrit Jansz here.”

“Poppa?”

“Annalise? What's the matter? Where are you?”

“Can the kids and I come to the farm? Now?”

“Of course—you know you can. But what's going on?”

“I can't tell you on the phone. I'm going to pick up the kids from school and then I wanted to drive up to the farm with them. Can I?”

“No! Where are you calling from? Your house? The paper? Ida's?”

“I'm at Ida's house. I can't go back to our house. Oh, Poppa…”

“Pick up the kids and get them to Ida's. I'll come there. I'm leaving shortly, but first I have to notify the county administrator that I'll be out of the office for a couple of days.”

Gerrit's next call was to let Kate and Emily know that he'd gotten a call from Anna and was on his way down to Milwaukee to find out what was wrong. Emily answered the call and, of course, thought she should go with Gerrit.

“Please just stay with Kate. I'll call when I get there and figure out what's going on. I told her to wait at your mom's with the kids. I think this is where I ask you and Kate to pray. Annalise is not one to get worked up over nothing. Once I figure out what's wrong, I'll be in touch. Anna asked if she could bring the kids to the farm, so you know it's trouble. I shudder to think what started this. Fix Kate a cup of tea and try to keep her relaxed. I'll call as soon as I know anything.”

Anna's first stop was the high school to pick up Katherine. Next stop, the junior high at the other end of the campus for Jonathan and Angelina, then the elementary school for Tim. As Annalise's children hopped into the car at each stop, they inquired as to what was happening.

“Get in! Don't ask questions. You'll find out soon enough.”

At Ida's old house, Anna gave Katherine the key to open the front door. She never, ever put that key in the door lock without the incidents so many years earlier racing across her mind. It never got easier. The only good thing: Katherine did not have any inkling of the things that happened there.

When she'd lived there with Aunt Ida, the house had seemed so spacious. Emily eventually decided to hold on to her mom's house rather than sell it when she sold her own. Overall, it made a lot of sense to have a place to stay when they traveled to Milwaukee. It also made a handy place for Kate and Gerrit to stay when they needed to get away for a weekend.

Annalise was upset that Poppa wouldn't let her drive the kids up to the farm where she would feel safe. But she knew he was probably right. More important for them to stay put and for him to drive down to get things squared away.

No sense looking in the pantry or refrigerator for food, but she'd have to get something for her hungry children. She was amazed at her own sense of calm as she made a shopping list of things needed for supper. She knew Poppa would be hungry when he arrived, too. While their menu suggestions were different, she knew all four of her kids would prefer fried chicken dinners from the grocery store deli. She added ice cream and cookies to the list and "fresh veggies" at the bottom. She gave Katherine the list, the car keys, and a handful of cash.

The others moaned that she was given the enviable role of shopper, but they were just as content to lounge in the living room. The only one raising a ruckus about having to stay inside was Tim. He always had twice the energy of any boy she ever knew, including Fletcher.

Fletcher! Should she call him? Probably not. There'd be time enough once Poppa got there and they had a chance to talk.

She set the kettle on the burner and turned on the flame. She hoped there were still a few tea bags in the pantry, but she realized they would be in the refrigerator to keep fresh. She found a whole package there that probably came from an earlier shopping trip. There also were several tins filled with cookies, some from Christmas. The stars and bells sprinkled with colored sugars were a welcome sight for the kids.

A loud knock at the front door scared her. Jonathan jumped up to answer it, but Anna rushed ahead and opened the door. Carleton started to push his way in, but she held up her hand and suggested he wait on the front porch until he was invited in.

Battle lines were drawn. The kids sitting in the living room didn't know what to make of this stand-off. *Thank goodness Katherine isn't back from the store yet,* Annalise thought. Katherine had no way of knowing that something had happened that put her in the center of a domestic battle. Carleton was always quick to react. Annalise usually could take a deep breath and quietly unravel tangled emotions, but that wouldn't work that day.

Annalise suggested the kids go upstairs and hang out in Aunt Ida's old bedroom where there was a small TV on the dresser. "And close the door."

Only then did she open the front door and let Carleton in. "I got your message about getting a letter from an attorney's office. Where's the letter?" Anna asked.

He reached inside his sport coat and pulled out an envelope that clearly had been ripped open. He handed it to her.

She grimaced when she saw the torn envelope. "This envelope is not addressed to you. It clearly has my name on it and Katherine's. How dare you open my personal mail, read it, and then issue all kinds of ultimatums?"

He didn't answer, but a tinge of red worked its way up his cheeks. "And if I hadn't opened and read this letter, how long would it have been before you told me what was in it? Obviously, this is something you've been hiding all these years we've been married. How dare you be so deceptive? How dare you palm off your daughter Katherine into my family without telling me where she came from? You led me to believe she was just the product of bad judgment when you were in high school. Now I find out who she really is and who her father really was!"

"If you please," Annalise said in a voice that belied her emotional chaos, "I would like to see what was in this envelope from the attorney. Or is the letter shredded as badly as the envelope?"

Carleton reached into his trouser pocket and pulled out a crumpled handful of letterhead stationery. He shoved them toward her.

She started unrolling the scrunched papers, then walked into the dining room where she laid them on the table, smoothing them flat. He followed her, then thought better of it, turning back into the living room. He sat on the sofa and waited while she read and reread the pages. The words spelled out the details of a long-ago crisis that had faded into an unmentionable silence. It was the story of Katherine's beginnings, the man who caused it and suffered a lifetime of loss and despair.

"As I told you in my phone message, I will not have the bastard child of a renegade priest in my house." Carleton said from the other room. "Nor can she ever be part of my family. I will do whatever I must, to undo the adoption that brought her into my life. I will not have her bring shame on me and my three legitimate children. I don't care what you do with her, but if you are going to stay in my household as my wife, it will be without her. Period! And if you choose to leave, you will leave my three children in my custody. Your legal connection to them is very tenuous. I will not, do you hear me? I will not have my community presence disparaged by the garbage you've dumped into my life!"

It was a terrible moment for Katherine to come through the back door, excited about the things she'd found for supper. When she heard her father's angry voice, she quietly set the bags on the kitchen counter and tiptoed back out the door. Only then did she notice her dad's car parked at the curb across the street.

She unlocked the driver's door of her mom's car and slid in, taking a deep breath before starting the engine. Whatever was going on involved her and her mom, and the chasm that separated her from 'legitimate' members of the family. She drove to the park where young children were running off energy they'd stored up during a long day in school. She parked the car and walked to a bench near the fountain. There was no way she could figure out what set off the storm, but she knew nothing like this ever disrupted her life before.

She had no way of knowing the time or how long she sat there, but it was getting dark and most of the children had left for home and supper. It was dark enough that she couldn't tell if the Cadillac was still parked around the corner. She was not about to start the car and drive over there to make sure Carleton was gone.

More time passed, and shadows in the park disappeared in the evening darkness. From time to time she cried, but quickly wiped the tears away. A bigger worry was what was going on with momma.

A finger tapped at the car window.

"Grampy Gerrit? Where did you come from?" Katherine asked, surprised.

"Just around the corner," he said. "It's time to come home. Your mom and the other kids are waiting for you so they can eat."

He climbed into the passenger seat beside her and they drove together around the block, then down the street to the driveway alongside Ida's house.

"I think your mom and I have some talking to do, with you and without you," he said before they opened their doors and headed toward the house. "Presumably, whatever it's about should not be discussed in front of the other kids. So, we'll go in and eat and figure out what happens next."

Annalise looked like she'd been crying. Katherine noticed several sheets of letterhead stationery on the living room bookshelf. It was Wednesday, the day mom always picked up the timecards and expense sheets so she could take them home to work on in time to get payroll and expense checks ready for distribution Friday.

Grampy Gerrit kept the conversation going while they dug into the box of fried chicken. There was deli potato salad, cabbage slaw, biscuits with honey. Katherine reached into her pocket for the change from the store.

The phone rang. Annalise motioned to Gerrit to answer it.

"I made good time," he said. "Hardly any traffic. We're having fried chicken from the grocery store deli. Katherine even bought chocolate ice cream for dessert. Annalise thinks it's nice to have a kid old enough to drive a car and do the grocery shopping. The kids will clean up the kitchen and Anna, Katherine, and I have errands to run. I'll call when we get back."

Annalise wasn't worried about Jonathan and Angelina, but Tim was visibly fighting tears. How could she send him back to the house with only Carleton in charge? He'd never been a hands-on dad. During Anna's busy newspaper days, she always relied on Katherine to keep Tim in tow.

"I'm counting on you to stay occupied here with homework, kitchen cleanup, and keeping tabs on Tim," Gerrit said to Jonathan and Angelina.

Just then, Gerrit noticed a car parking out front. "I specifically told her not to come," he muttered, watching Emily walk up to the front door.

"I know I wasn't supposed to come," she said, "but I figured maybe the kids and I could hang out here."

Tim wrapped his arms around her legs and started crying. He was so little—the smallest kid in his kindergarten class. She leaned over and scooped him up. "You and I are going upstairs to see if we can find a movie that Aunt Ida might have left around here somewhere." She nodded at Annalise and the other children as she and Tim started up the stairs.

Gerrit, Anna, and Katherine headed toward the front door. "I'll be back to pick you up and take you home to see your dad," Gerrit said, sliding the key into the front door lock.

Before they went to the ice cream parlor in the new shopping center, they drove around for a few minutes. "Our lives changed a little bit today," Anna told her oldest daughter. "We'll find a quiet booth at the ice cream shop so I can fill you in on some of the details. But first, Grampy will drive me over to the house so I can drop some things off for Carleton. It should take only a few minutes. Then Grampy will drop us off at the ice cream shop, and he'll go back to Ida's house to pick up Jonathan and Angelina to take them home. It will all make sense eventually. So, give me a few minutes with Carleton—I hope he's home. He'll have to do the timecards this week, because I have some important things to take care of tonight and tomorrow."

She squeezed Katherine's hand and got out of the car. It seemed strange to ring the front doorbell of her own home and wait for someone to answer and let her in. Or maybe he wouldn't. Then she heard footsteps crossing the front hall and the security chain slide back before the door opened.

"I wanted to drop off the timecards for you to take care of this week," Anna explained quietly to Carleton. "I picked them up this afternoon before I knew about this mess. I hope to get everything worked out in a few days so I can help with the timecards again next week. If you still want me to."

Anna glanced down and then back to him. "My dad drove down here tonight to help me get Katherine's situation squared away. You won't have to worry about her anymore, because she will stay with me at Ida's house. She only has a few weeks left before graduation, so I'm not going to take her up to the farm until after that. I have appointments with attorneys tomorrow, and I assume most of that financial stuff will be sorted out in a day or two. I never could have imagined that you would turn on me and Katherine with such vehemence. I think Katherine will be fine, but I worry about the others without her, especially Tim. I could keep him with me at Ida's, if that would work better for him."

"There is only one condition in all this," Annalise said, narrowing her eyes on her husband. "You will, under no circumstance, start peddling gossip around town about Katherine and her parentage. If you do, my reaction won't be pretty. I would rather you didn't rush into court next week to institute proceedings to un-adopt Katherine. She will never again live in this house. Tomorrow morning, after the kids are in school and you are at the paper, I will come here to gather up Katherine's things and move them over to Ida's house. Katherine has no idea what is happening right now.

"My father thought you and I should try to negotiate a way to resolve this, but I don't have the slightest inclination to ask you to do anything. I had no idea there was any bequest coming to Katherine or me. I will move permanently to Ida's house. The kids, especially Tim, are welcome to move there with me, or stay with you and you can hire a housekeeper and nanny for them, if that's the case. About the only thing I am still signed on for is doing payroll and overseeing the job printing accounts. I will do that, not for you, but for the kids, because that is their inheritance—except for Katherine, that is.

"Sorry to drop all of this payroll stuff on you at the last minute, but then, I never expected to find out in a phone message that you opened my mail and decided to disown Katherine. By the way, I would caution you to explain to the children that our new arrangement is not to be discussed. If I find that it is, I will go to court for a cease-and-desist order against you."

Annalise turned and walked out the doorway, leaving it standing ajar. There were a lot of words she had never been allowed to say when she was growing up, but a whole string of them went roaring through her head as she hurried down the walk. Gerrit had gotten out of the car to open the door for her. Katherine, she could see, was more puzzled and worried than ever.

Gerrit dropped them at the curb in front of the shop. "I'll come in after I deliver the kids home," he said.

Katherine and Anna noticed that most of the booths in the shop were empty. Thankfully. They took the booth for one beautiful daughter in the far corner where no one could overhear their conversation.

"This is, unfortunately, going to be a life-changing experience for us, Katherine," Annalise began. "I never, ever expected it to come to this. We seemed to be such a wonderfully happy family. That was my intention from the day I first realized you would be coming into our lives. For starters, this letter came today. There is another that you will need to see, but not quite yet."

Katherine skimmed the page from the attorney, then reread it slower. "What does this mean?" she asked.

"Simply that your biological father has left you what I presume is a rather large estate. I don't think it's land, but money. We'll find out more tomorrow. You'll have to take a day off from school since we have a scheduled appointment."

When Katherine didn't look up or ask another question, Annalise continued explaining. "Your dad, um, Carleton had come home over the lunch hour and found the attorney's letter. He opened it and blew up and called me in a rage at work." Annalise bit her lip, closed her eyes, and took in a breath. "I always told you and Carleton that you were a teenage mistake. You weren't."

Katherine's eyes met her mother's, and Annalise found the strength to continue. "When I was a freshman in high school here in Milwaukee, Aunt Ida and Emily had to go up to the farm on business, and I was supposed to be at a district forensics contest. I arranged to stay at a friend's house that Saturday night. Except that morning I woke up with a sore throat and could barely whisper, so I couldn't participate in a speech contest. Instead, I stayed home and slept off and on all day. In the evening, I was awakened by someone pounding on the front door. Whoever it was wouldn't stop, so finally I went downstairs, thinking it must've been Aunt Ida back early from her trip. But when I opened the door, I was surprised to see Cleary Nolan, who was rector of the high school I was attending. He was a family friend and often came to Ida's for Sunday supper.

"He'd brought chicken soup, which he said would make me feel better. I just wanted to go back to bed. Instead, he heated up the soup and sat at the kitchen table, reading the results of the forensics meet while I ate. When I finished, I thought he'd leave. He didn't. I kept insisting that he needed to go so I could lock up and sleep. He insisted he needed to make sure I got safely to bed.

"It took me a while before I decided the only way he'd leave was if I got into bed. That's when he pulled out a wine or water cruet, like those used at Mass in the school chapel. He said he'd brought a sore throat 'toddy' like one his mother made for him when he had laryngitis. He said it would warm my throat and help me sleep. Eventually I did. Fall asleep. Pass out, was more like it.

"The next morning, I realized my pajama bottom was on the floor alongside my bed. I didn't dare tell Aunt Ida what I thought happened. Sadly, a few weeks later, I realized I might be pregnant. Aunt Ida and Emily took me to a doctor who determined that I was expecting a baby. That's when Ida called Grammy Kate and asked her to come down the next day.

"When my mother found out what had happened, she went to the parsonage where she held him accountable for raping me. He denied it adamantly. Her second stop was the bishop's office. Mind you, we were not Catholic. Whether we were Catholic or not, what had been done to me was a crime. But no one paid any attention to what we claimed happened. I'm not sure what possessed me to do it, but I folded my soiled pajama bottoms and top and put them in an empty gift box I found on a shelf in my closet. Eventually, we took the box to the farm. But as a way to get the bishop to admit that the priest had abused me, we told him about the clothing evidence being kept in a safe place until science advanced to where they might be able to figure out whose stains were on the pajamas.

"The priest showed up at the farm the day Uncle Fletcher graduated from high school. He insisted on coming inside to see me. I was already assigned to bed rest and couldn't go to the graduation. He shouted at me and told me to stop accusing him of something he never would have done. He drove past our farm several times, and even called the day you were born.

"Despite our meetings with the bishop and his attorney, nothing ever changed. The attorney kept telling my parents and me that I was lying to cover up for a bad mistake I'd made. And we never saw Father Nolan again. Obviously, he never apologized."

Annalise laced her fingers and set them on the table, watching her daughter. "Eventually, someone told us they'd heard the priest was relieved of his duties at the high school and parish and sent to a treatment clinic. That was the last we heard about him. One of the things the attorney included in his letter today was a letter of apology that Father Nolan had written to me.

I'll let you read that sometime. There's a lot more to this story, but you can't absorb it all at once. He apparently changed his will so that a rather large bequest from his late mother was signed over to you and me. The terms are probably spelled out in the will that will be read tomorrow.

"Today, things are a lot more open about such abuses," Annalise said. "But back when I was fourteen, I made up my mind that I was going to have you, regardless of the consequences. And you turned out to be an absolutely beautiful, wonderful baby. I was your mom, but also your sister. Grammy Kate was your grandmother, but also your mom. It was like you belonged to all of us and we all took care of you."

Anna stopped. Sobs caught in her throat and then gripped her entire body. She couldn't look back up at her daughter, who was staring at her from across the table.

"Momma, why are you crying?" Katherine said gently. "I can't believe how blessed I've been, being born to you and raised in a houseful of moms. None of that will change. Aunt Ida is gone, but her memory is with us every day. Emily has been a surrogate mom to me. So have Grammy Kate and Helen Iversen. No one I know ever had a houseful of moms."

Anna reached for her daughter's outstretched hands, then continued once her crying quieted. "So, now you know about your much-celebrated arrival in our family. There's so much more to this wonderful story. You'll never believe how important you were in our lives from the first day we knew you were on the way. Grammy Kate was so sad that she'd lost so many babies when she and Fletcher were living on the farm alone while Grampy was still in Chicago. You replaced one of those she lost. Tomorrow, we'll hear some other missing pieces of our story, too."

"Ready to go?" a booming voice asked from behind Annalise.

Anna, whose back was to the front door, was surprised to hear her father. "Jonathan and Angelina got home safely; I watched until they got inside."

Annalise and Katherine realized they'd never even gone up to the counter to place an order. Gerrit saw there were no empty ice cream dishes on the table, so he pulled out a bill from his wallet and left it as a tip.

The next morning, Emily and Gerrit were ready to go long before Annalise was even awake. Katherine seemed to have gotten lost in the steamed-up bathroom.

Emily had buttered toast and orange juice ready when they came out to the kitchen. They would, she promised, probably get coffee at the lawyer's office, and they'd definitely stop somewhere for lunch. "I'm sure they won't want me to sit in on the reading, but I wanted to come along, anyway," Emily said.

But the attorney's secretary ushered all of them into a conference room where a Mr. Mueller was already seated at the head of the table. A neatly stacked sheaf of papers sat ready for the morning's business.

"Is everyone here?" he asked, taking a visual tour around the table. "I was expecting five family members. I know we have one unexpected relative"—he nodded to Emily—"but we are missing two immediate family members. By my count we should have Annalise, Carleton, Katherine, and Gerrit and Kate Jansz. Do we know if Kate Jansz will be here?"

Gerrit started to shake his head when the door opened, and Helen Iversen poked her head in to see if she'd found the right room. Behind her was Kate, wearing a mischievous grin.

"I gather this is Kate and probably her driver. Good!" Mr. Mueller said. "Now what about Carleton, Katherine's adoptive father. Is he coming?"

Annalise furrowed her brow, stricken at the prospect of having to explain that her husband had only yesterday discovered his adoptive daughter's real birth father and had refused to even allow the girl into his home.

The secretary stopped pouring coffee and interrupted the proceedings. "Sir," she said, "his office called a few minutes ago to say he'd had a family emergency but would be here as soon as possible."

Anna cringed. Knowing his temper, she could hear him delivering his diatribe about being hoodwinked into adopting his wife's daughter, not knowing the girl's real history. Never one to be a whiner, Anna remained silent as she felt the tears drip down her cheeks. It would just have to play out and be done with. Certainly, his decision to withdraw his adoptive parental status would in no way affect Katherine's expected bequest.

The door, still ajar, opened wider as a little boy ran in, followed by his father. He ran around the table to Katherine and buried his face in her lap, sobbing.

"Sir," Carleton started to greet the attorney.

"Sir," interjected the attorney, "I trust you are Carleton, Katherine's adoptive father. Could you please get this boy under control?"

Annalise felt her mouth open and words start tumbling out. "Mr. Mueller," she said. "This is my husband and our youngest son, Tim. When my husband found out yesterday who Katherine's real father was, he forbade her to stay a moment longer in our house. Tim has always been very close to Katherine, and he's been distraught since he learned Katherine couldn't be his sister any longer. Carleton stated that he will file to have his adoptive-parent status terminated."

"Is this true?" the attorney asked.

Rather sheepishly, Carleton nodded. "I was coming here today to deliver that message, but obviously I don't have to." He glowered at Annalise.

"Can I assume you have not yet made good on that threat?" Mueller asked, tapping his finger on the table.

Again, a downcast nod and more wailing from Tim.

"So, for the moment, your adoptive parental status is still in place, so we will proceed with our task today and let you do what you want after we have finished. I will, however, ask that you not remove any of the papers being handed out today. Instead, please file them in the folder and return it to me at the conclusion of this important gathering. Tim? Do you think you can sit quietly while we do some business here? Maybe Katherine would like to hold you on her lap."

That satisfied the boy. He snuggled down in her protective hug and the proceedings began again.

"Welcome, Kate. I've learned a lot about you from the paperwork I prepared for today. There is no doubt in my mind that without your help and guidance, we probably would not have a beautiful young lady here to receive the bequest of a sorrowful man who could never deliver his message to you all in person. And that is not to diminish a young girl's determination to have a baby, conceived in a very tragic rape. But if there can ever be a happy ending to such chaos, I assure you, this is it."

Carleton remained standing. When the attorney had watched him shuffle and look uncomfortable long enough, he pointed to a chair farther down the table from Katherine. Helen settled in next to Emily, and Kate was already seated next to Gerrit.

Two hours later, after a brief break for a catered sandwich lunch around the conference table, the proceedings were just getting down to the bequests of Father Cleary Nolan's Last Will and Testament. The dollars and cents started off with Nolan's mother's bequest to her son from the extensive financial and land holdings of the family she married into. Originally, the will had been probated by this attorney, with all bequests kept intact in the priest's name. But after the sad chapters that followed his rape of young Annalise Jansz, he returned to the diocese and this attorney to have his entire estate probated over to Annalise and her child.

The entire estate in actual cash value sixteen years earlier had been 1.7 million dollars. Its current value was still too volatile due to market conditions, but it had in recent years grown to 2.2 million dollars.

"The last time I met with Cleary Nolan was four years ago. He was already in poor health but still working. At his request, he was relieved of his priestly vows within a year of the rape incident. He never took a dime of his inheritance and envisioned that Annalise and Katherine would share whatever the pay-out amount would be. If there are any future bequests from those, they would have to be arranged by that recipient and only from that recipient's share."

Annalise watched the attorney glance at Katherine and Tim, then to Carleton.

"I perhaps may be a bit out of line for offering an addendum to these proceedings, but I would like to point out to you, Carleton, that Katherine will be eighteen in two months, and at that point will no longer need any support from you. Money for a good college was one of Nolan's bequests, as Annalise hadn't been able to continue her education at Saint Michael's. And now, Katherine, you are a very rich young lady."

At that, Helen and Emily stood up, both in tears. "Oh, Katherine, if only Ida could be here to see this moment. And Harald. All of Lillehammer."

Annalise watched Carleton gather up the papers in front of him. He slipped them into the folder and slid it toward the attorney's end of the table. He nodded in his direction but didn't wait for any recognition. Instead, Carleton scooted his chair back as quietly as possible and left. His mind reeled at the numbers. If Katherine had no need of his parenting to finance the rest of her life in a way she wanted, neither did Annalise. If he followed through with filing a claim to null and void his adoption of Katherine, he had to assume that Anna would no longer seek his support in any way. But he would suffer without her support—not of the money she'd just inherited, but the experience and effort she provided for the paper. He always bragged about the role she played in the phenomenal growth of the paper. Now, he assumed, he'd have to not only take charge of the weekly payroll, but also orchestrate all of the work she usually did to find new job-printing customers.

Annalise had always overlooked Carleton's lack of commitment for the day-to-day grind of running a newspaper, even a weekly. His parents retired years ago to the Caribbean and rarely came back to visit their son and grandchildren. She was sure he already had talked to them about the "fast one" Anna had pulled on him.

The true victim of circumstance was now Tim. He couldn't go back home without his Katherine. But Annalise would see to it that he would be alright. She considered again filing for custody. And Carleton was just ornery enough to insist on it.

There were preliminaries that had to be sorted through and recorded by a legal transcriber sitting at a small table adjacent to the attorney. Annalise had calmed upon Carleton's exit, but now it was Katherine's turn to be apprehensive.

"Nothing here to worry about," the attorney said. "It's all good news for both Annalise and Katherine. Let's move forward."

He handed copies of the background information he was prepared to read to them so they could follow along. The secretary had folders so they could safely store all the pieces.

The attorney explained Nolan's family's history of companies, including their ships used for hauling iron ore on Superior and Michigan. There had been a great deal of land, as well as a good book of financial investments. How all that got separated out and divided was still to be answered.

Anna knew this was probably way over Katherine's head, but even she was dizzy from the complexity of settling an estate with two people, divided evenly.

The attorney cleared most of his papers from the table and collected the folders that were now stuffed with pages from the long reading of the will. He left briefly and returned with another man in a suit. He introduced the representative from a Chicago investment banking firm that specialized in complicated bequests.

"The company is still finalizing the figures, but we could spend a little time explaining the management of an estate as varied as this."

The representative cleared his throat and began. "Because Nolan was an only child who happened also to be a priest, it was a simple matter to assemble all of the pieces of the estate into one package. Starting with his mother's death and funeral, Nolan was frequently called in to consult on what should be done with investments in the portfolio. One of the first things he did was agree that a buyer should be found for the ore carriers his family owned. It was not something he was at all familiar with, nor did he have any expertise in the whole process. When buyers were found, they reviewed the bill of sale, made a few adjustments, and he signed off. He said many times after that that he felt he'd sold his birthright, but he simply was not equipped to make good decisions about hauling iron ore on the Great Lakes. With that liquidated, the income was added to the cash investment portfolio."

Everyone at the table listened intently.

"Over time," the representative explained, "various parcels of property around the state and even some in Chicago were sold off and the cash added to the invested funds. Finally, he'd sold everything in the portfolio except the original homestead that then belonged to his mother. That was parceled off into a separate account Cleary held until his recent death. He never tapped into the cash value of the property."

The representative paused for a moment, glanced around, and then continued. "That property is still intact, and it was specifically deeded to you, Annalise, upon his death. We are still trying to figure out a cash value so the inheritance taxes can be calculated. You have the option of either keeping it or putting it on the market. We figured you might like to see where the property is located and what it entails. I think you will be very pleasantly surprised."

The bank's representative passed around papers with figures and information. Katherine handed hers to Grampy Gerrit. Math had never been a comfortable subject for her. She and Tim sat quietly and listened.

"We will figure the exact amount of tax due when we get the rest of the numbers. There should be more than enough cash on hand to pay the estate taxes with just a debit draw on the account," Gerrit commented as he sorted through the paperwork.

The banker and attorney nodded.

"It'll be easy to settle it all out, thanks to Father's tenacity at liquidating properties and leaving it, or most all of it, in invested cash. And depending on what you decide on the original homestead property, that tax obligation will be calculated separately. But not until after you visit the property. If you'd like to go over this weekend, I'd be more than happy to accompany you. I often accompanied Father when he went. He lived on that property until he went to the seminary. It was, he always told me, the only place he felt safe. Especially after he left the priesthood."

Annalise looked across the table at Katherine and Tim. The boy had fallen asleep in his sister's lap. A moment later, Emily came to get him and take him to Ida's house.

"May we write the checks to cover *all* the inheritance taxes once the numbers are finalized on the homestead?" Gerrit asked.

The banker and attorney agreed, and Katherine gathered her stack of papers. "Can I take these with me so I can look them over?"

"To be sure," the banker chuckled. "Just remember to bring them with you in the morning. At ten. Here in this office."

"You all look like you've been cranked through the proverbial wringer," Mr. Mueller said. "I think you need a good night's rest, and we'll start again in the morning. We'll be working a few more hours on these calculations. If I could, may I have a telephone number where you can be reached overnight?"

The next morning, Annalise, Katherine, and Gerrit were back in the attorney's office, along with the trust accountant from the bank. That day was his show, played first to Gerrit, who understood the lingo, and Annalise, who'd inherited her father's math abilities. Katherine, however, listened and observed quietly like she had the day before.

What it boiled down to was that both Katherine and Annalise would end up with roughly two million dollars. Annalise inherited the family estate, which was separate from the holdings Katherine and she shared. Anna figured she had been willed his mother's treasure in hopes she would keep it intact rather than convert it to cash. That was a decision she couldn't make until she visited the property and had time to think about the best thing to do with it. First, she had to figure out how to get there.

Their tax liability was totaled. Gerrit checked it over and did some calculations on the machine he'd brought along. Checks were written for taxes and the remainder deposited in trust accounts at the bank which Anna and Katherine could draw from as needed.

They stared at the zeros, but none of it seemed real. Katherine could simply write a check for her entire tuition at Marquette, right then and there. She and her mom could add land to the farm and have an orchard. They could expand the original house with a larger bedroom on the main floor for Kate and Gerrit. Alongside additional bedrooms upstairs, they could even have a full bath. They needed a new garage—without a woodshed. They'd need a new tractor, as they were retiring the old one Harald Iversen gave to Kate the first year she lived on the farm. A bigger kitchen and pantry would help cut down on shopping trips and storing the apple slices Kate still dried.

That dried apple slices business had proven more valuable than anyone had imagined. One of the things Annalise had done when she still lived at the farm as a teen was use her apple money to pay off Dr. Chandler's long-overdue bills for his countless trips to the farm during her pregnancy. It even paid for Annalise's time in the hospital. Chandler had told Kate recently that Anna's apple money had helped pay for his children to go to college, especially the youngest, who was just finishing medical school and starting his internship in general medicine.

CHAPTER THREE

The next day, the family prepared to find the Nolan homestead. Since no one had lived there for years, they expected to have to hack their way in through brush and weeds. Anna, Katherine, Gerrit, Kate and Emily would all go on the excursion.

Gerrit was up early looking for an atlas to help them find the property. He called the Register of Deeds at their courthouse to get some help. The family planned to be back at the farm later that morning, and Gerrit said he'd stop in to see what they might suggest. To save time, he gave them the coordinates from the bank's trust account department.

That was a smart move. By the time they got to the farm, Gerrit's friend had not only found the county the property resided in, but also its exact pinpointed location. According to the deed records, the holdings were very extensive—a lot of land and a lot of buildings. And it overlooked Lake Superior.

They'd skimped on breakfast before they left Ida's place, and it was now past lunch time. A visit to Charlie's Diner was the only answer.

Annalise walked to the drug store to buy a camera and film so she could shoot pictures of her new property…or perhaps her new home.

Annalise pulled out the key to the large iron gate blocking the driveway into the estate. Beyond it, she could see the outline of a palatial home that seemed to stretch endlessly in every direction. Beyond that were barns. She walked over to the brass plate covering the gate lock and pushed the key in as far as she could. It wouldn't turn. Something inside blocked it. Gerrit found a stiff stick that he tried inserting into the keyhole. Whatever was in there wouldn't move. *At this rate*, Anna thought, *this was a wasted trip*. There was no other way to access the driveway.

Suddenly, a man wearing a flat cap and jodhpurs appeared along the inside of the fence. "Good mornin' to ye," he said. "One of you must be the new owner of this estate. If you can hand me your key, I can open the gate from this side. I think there's some greenery that's grown in the lock that needs to be chiseled out. I'm Dugan. I've been caretaker here forever, and my father before me. This is quite a place." The man cracked open the gate. "There, now you can drive in, and I'll lock up again."

Dugan's eyes met Anna's. "You the new lady of the estate?" he asked her as he handed back her key.

"As of yesterday," she said. "But I haven't made up my mind about keeping it yet. Can we take a tour of the house and gardens? Oh, and my name is Annalise." She then introduced Dugan to Katherine, Gerrit, Kate, and Emily.

The new owners drove up to the house. The estate caretaker hiked alongside, declining a ride with them. There was a swooping circular drive around an elaborate array of greenery and a larger-than-life-size statue in the midst of it all.

Stately stairs rose up to the wide veranda. Windows along the porch were actually French doors that provided easy access to all the first-floor rooms on that part of the house. Dugan had a large ring of keys. He selected one and opened the French doors, which opened outward. Annalise and Katherine went inside. The people who had owned the house had exquisite taste and an unbelievable amount of money to create something so magnificent.

Dugan led them from room to room. A huge parlor. A library. Sitting room. Drawing room. An elaborate dining room encircled by painted murals. Beyond was a smaller space that he called a "breakfast room." They stepped through a butler's pantry and into an enormous kitchen, which must have been staffed by a half-dozen cooks. Everything was so massive it was hard to envision sitting down even in the breakfast room and having a bowl of cereal and a cup of morning coffee.

The tour circled the downstairs rim of rooms which fed off a large hallway. At either end were stairs leading to the second floor. "That's the bedroom floor," Dugan explained. "Above that is a third floor with servants' quarters—but mostly attic storage. Are you game to look around?"

Annalise was already a quarter of the way up when the others followed at a more leisurely pace. The colors, like those of the main floor, were breathtaking. The bed linens and curtains were all silk and linen. Several beds had canopies. She lost track how many bathrooms were on the bedroom floor. Or how many bedrooms.

"There are six bedrooms on this floor, and at the far end is the nanny's quarters and a child's playroom," Dugan continued. "I knew a lot about this family, but I have yet to figure out how they amassed such a fortune."

The family was so awestruck they had no words.

"There also are stables for horses, as you might have suspected from my everyday outfit," Dugan said, smiling. "Usually when I answer the gate, I ride down the drive on one of the horses. They used to train horses here for the Kentucky Derby and other major events. These stables were famous for the winners they produced. The grooms who cared for the animals lived in quarters above the stables."

Dugan laid a fire in one of the rooms. A maid arrived from somewhere, along with tea pots and plates of scones and other treats. It was indeed a beautiful home and an amazing property, but Anna couldn't figure out what to make of it. It wasn't a home she could live in. Nor was it possible to operate a bed and breakfast so far off the beaten path. Without a potential use in mind, it would be difficult to find buyers with enough capital to purchase the property, staff such an oversized facility, and run ad campaigns to draw people there to spend a week or two on vacation. It was fun to experience something so grand, especially since it had her name on the deed, but it would be a challenge to keep it afloat.

"Poppa," Annalise said. "I've been thinking we might invite our friends. The ones who've cared for us all these years. Our neighbors. They would probably enjoy sleeping in one of those fancy rooms upstairs and walking the grounds on a nice summer evening. We could hire help from around here if there is some, or have food catered by a nearby restaurant. It would probably add up to a tidy sum, but it would be a nice way to share this inheritance that we could never have dreamed of owning. Jackson and Julia from Chicago. Did you know they're talking with Emily about buying Ida's house? We could invite all the Iversen's. I doubt our Amish friends could stay overnight here, but we could invite them, and they could say no—but would appreciate the gesture, I'm sure. We could hire a bus to give them a ride up here and back. What do you think? I'm sure this sounds as unbelievable as this place appears."

Annalise watched her father's face for a moment, and after getting no response, she voiced another idea.

"This might make a nice clinic for priests who have problems."

Quiet followed.

"*Just an idea,*" Annalise thought.

Annalise found Dugan in the kitchen, filling another plate with fresh bakery. "Do you do the baking? Or is there a full kitchen crew hiding out on the third floor?" she jabbed playfully.

They laughed in an echoing tandem.

"We'd like to bring the rest of our family up here either this coming weekend or the one after. Would that work for you? How do we hire staff when we want to stay here a few days?"

"Your smile is what this house has been missing for too long," Dugan told Anna. "Either weekend is fine with me; I can handle ordering food and staff whenever you need—just let me know when you need them. I've been waiting for this day for such a long, long time. This house needs people like it used to have. During the generations when they were deeply involved in their businesses, customers and potential clients were always invited to spend time here so they could talk numbers in a comfortable and beautiful place." The man shook his head, as if to dispel the memories. "I think you and your family will figure out a way to make good use of this property."

The two smiled at each other for a moment, and then Dugan clapped his hands together. "So, let's have another cuppa, and then you can be on your way. If you carry the date-nut bread, I'll get another cozy for the teapot, and we'll be off for another round of afternoon tea."

Gerrit looked in the rearview mirror as they drove back toward the gate. He could still make out Dugan, standing on the veranda, his hand outstretched in a wave. Annalise's chest fluttered as she looked back at the estate, the beautiful surprise from an unexpected turn of events.

Annalise had found a journal in one of the personal packages prepared by Cleary Nolan. Whenever she read a page he'd written especially for her, she had to duck her head so no one could see the tears. Between the words was a voice of incredible sadness over what his impetuous bad behavior had taken from him. When she'd stood in the mansion's second-floor nursery still decorated with his childhood treasures, she couldn't help wondering what his mother was like. Was she the kind of mother who turned her only child's upbringing over to a nanny, dressed in a crisp white uniform with a small watch face pinned to the pocket of her apron? Or did she join him in the playroom for part of every day while the men were busy with their business dealings, shipping schedules, and calculating their monthly net worth?

Could she also have kept a diary, her own Book of Days? Anna wondered if things like that had been stored away in the attic. Did Nolan's mother write her daily entries in the same type of book that she'd given to her son at every Christmas—so he could start a new journal with the start of another new year? Anna promised herself to ask Dugan about any other journals in the house.

Funny. The mansion was very Scandinavian—Norway, in particular. Yet the men they'd hired to serve as overseers of the property were far from Norway. They'd been drawn from Ireland.

The next week flew by yet dragged on. One morning, when she should have been doing work around the orchard, Annalise took time to place a phone call.

Dugan answered almost immediately.

"Were you sitting in the library waiting for my call?" Anna teased.

"Actually, I was just about to have a spot of coffee and think about you and the decisions you will have to make about your estate. So, yes, I was half expecting your call."

"I should be outside working in our orchards. My mom and I have raised apples for years—our orchard has gotten so big. We slice and dry apples as soon as they start ripening, then package them for sale. They have been big sellers in our community. But the reason I'm calling—I was thinking about Cleary Nolan's mother. There was a journal he'd written for me in one of the packages of letters I got from the attorney. He mentions that every Christmas his mother gave him a new journal, hoping he'd write in it occasionally. He said he'd never even opened the book until he sat down to write one for me. Did his mother write diaries? If she did, are some of them still around? Journaling is a tradition in our family. We've always wanted to compile our journals into stories. I got to thinking as we drove back to the farm last weekend that we might compile one for Mrs. Nolan, if she indeed did keep a diary. It would be a wonderful record of the earliest settlers in these parts from Norway."

"I don't even have to go up to the third floor to check," Dugan replied. "I know exactly where she kept her yearly collection of journals. They are safely stored on the top-most shelves in the library. When you come next, we'll climb up to get them. Or rather, I'll let you climb up. I get a little woozy if I get too far up a ladder." Dugan paused, then added, "I have to say it again. I knew when I first saw you that your mind never stood still. You and I—we shall have a good time studying all those entries, and you can write a book using the things she wrote about. I'm sure she never dreamed that might happen. Wouldn't the Father be pleased to know this? And everything is arranged for your visit this coming weekend. If that is not going to work, my household crew is on notice for it to be the following weekend."

At that goodbye, there was no chance Annalise would wait another week to look at those journals. She could hardly wait to tell Katherine when she talked to her that night. Katherine and Emily had driven to Ida's house so Katherine could get caught up on school. Only six weeks left before graduation. Anna had to make sure Katherine had money to pay her cap and gown rental and for the graduation ceremony. Then she'd laughed at that. After their previous week, Katherine certainly had no need of a cash handout from her mother for graduation necessities.

Still, it would be awkward. For sure, Carleton would not bother to attend her graduation ceremony or party afterward. The three other kids would be there, unless their dad made up some excuse why they couldn't. For Annalise, the thought of this milestone looming ahead sucked the air right out of her. She could still picture herself in bed, sad because she couldn't go to

Fletcher's graduation, and then the frightening sounds of someone pounding on the porch screen door, demanding to be let in. And dear, sweet Sarah who had come to sit with her while everyone else was at the high school. Nice, gentle Sarah, the epitome of Amish peacefulness—grabbing two sharp knitting needles, which Helen Iversen's sudden appearance eliminated any need for. Annalise's memories were still so vivid.

At the last minute, Emily and Katherine decided they should forego the upcoming trip to Anna's new Lake Superior estate. There'd be plenty of time after graduation. Emily also was half-expecting Robert's parents to stop in over that weekend for the graduation and to talk about the possibility of their buying Ida's house, if Emily decided to sell it. Katherine's siblings were indeed planning to spend most of the weekend with their sister. There were plans for packing up Katherine's stuff from the big house and moving it to Ida's.

Fletcher and Cynthia, deeply intrigued, couldn't wait to see Anna's inherited estate. While they explored the paddocks and stables, Anna climbed the library ladder and handed down daybooks from the early settlement days of Nolan's prominent Norwegian family. Anna refused to open even one of the books until she had them all down and lined up on the library floor in full-year increments. The first years were written by the original settlers, the men who built the ships and developed the iron ore mines. There, she would find the details of their banking in those early years, the tremendous sums borrowed to build their huge ore-carriers and payments made back to the lenders.

For men who loved horses in their native Norway, it was logical they'd built stables to fill with prize horseflesh and special shelves in the library to house all the winning steeplechase trophies and ribbons they brought home.

The lavish lifestyle of the original Nolan immigrants increased in splendor except for one thing: each succeeding generation produced only one son, including the last one, and that final son went to seminary and became a priest, much to his mother's delight and his father's chagrin. That, he knew, would spell the end to a family dynasty that had done nothing but flourish since his great-grandfather and his four sons first stood on the bluff of their American home, trying to envision what their dreams would look like when they took root.

Initially, they'd camped so they could overlook the inland sea, but as the weather turned cooler, they had to move inland for shelter or risk freezing to death and blowing away in the inevitable howling winter storms. As the ore ships took shape over winter, the brothers and their aging father turned instead to designs of brick and mortar, each variation more palatial than the last. By the time they had a contractor to stake out the design on the hilltop, the estimated cost ate up practically all that was left from their first season of mining and hauling ore. Before the first phase of their home was completed, the patriarch of the clan died in his sleep. There wasn't much time for the brothers to mourn his death.

Their father taught them well to manage their money. In the early years, when their expanding home was under construction, they stuck to their original plan to spend only as much in one year as they could afford to pay for in cash. Good Norwegian economy of scale. The small house grew larger, and as years went by, it was so big that one could not gather its full length in one glance. It was almost as if each brother had a mansion of his own, somehow all connected with doorways.

By the time the future Father Nolan was born, the earliest brothers had long ago died off, with later generations only growing smaller. Instead of related families sharing this palace, the one family left in the house closed off most of the castle, opening spaces only when they were planning to entertain prominent guests, potential customers, and clients. Then, all too soon, the priest's father died of a stroke while hiking along the bluff on a beautiful late fall afternoon, leaving only the priest's widowed mother, a modest house staff, and Dugan, the latest overseer, the third generation of the same family.

It was a good thing the house was so large. There were so many generations of records spread out on the floor of the library there was no room for anyone to stroll around, looking for a good read. From then until Anna had time to read the contents of each diary, the books spread wall to wall were off limits. "Even to you, Fletcher," Annalise admonished her brother. She could tell from the way his eyebrow flicked up that he would not pay any mind to her orders.

She pretended to lock the door at day's end, but she had absolutely no idea if a key for the library even existed.

The next morning, Anna thought she'd be the first one downstairs to start poking through the Norwegian daybooks. She quickly ducked into the breakfast room, where she saw a large urn of coffee on the sideboard for everyone to share. There were eggs and toast in large silver serving dishes under covers. There were muffins with jelly and a large bowl of fresh cooked oatmeal. She took a piece of toast and her coffee into the library, where she found Fletcher stretched out on the floor behind a chair, flipping through a stack of books from one of the first years.

"Fletcher! Who gave you permission to peek into my books?"

No answer.

Annalise didn't wait for one. "I insist you erase all memory of the facts you've been trying to memorize. This is bona-fide private property, which has been bequeathed to me—and me alone. It's interesting stuff, though, isn't it? Katherine and I are going to use our family's daybooks as fodder for a history of the early days, including momma's at the farm when you were a baby. I might give you a few shekels of royalties if we ever sell a book or two."

"I won't need your shekels," he said coyly. "I've got my own daybook as source material, and since I never wrote much in my journal, I'll get it all published long before you even decide on the point size of your typeface."

"If you don't help yourself to any of the words from these early editions, I'll incorporate your words into one of momma's books. Fair game?"

"About the only thing I ever wrote about was long after the fact—my recollections of the tornado and hiding under the sideboard while momma knelt by the white rocker, clutching her grandpa's Bible and begging God to save us. Hardly worth a paragraph of type. Sorry to be peeking into your bequest, but I'm always blown away by what people write in plain and simple English that adds layers and layers to family history. We are so lucky to have such literate people in our lives. And if I were smart enough to know a little Norwegian, I'll bet these Scandinavians had the same good sense to document their experiences in their new homeland. So, since I can only figure out a word or two, there's not much plagiarism I'll be translating."

"Let's go to the other room and eat a proper breakfast. Cynthia not up yet?"

"She'll probably not be up until closer to noon. I think she forgot there are a couple of horses out in the stables we might get Dugan to help us saddle up."

"Not to worry," Cynthia's voice called from the dining room. "I've already finished eating, and Dugan and I are going out to check on the horses."

"Maybe we should just grab a couple slices of toast and bacon and get out to the stables. Dugan told me earlier that this estate was coming back to life. He said he hoped you weren't thinking of selling. It's a beautiful example of how these early Norwegians lived and succeeded in a new land."

Dugan and the livery grooms had four horses ready to ride. Kate said she was tempted but decided she hadn't ridden in so long it wasn't worth the risk. She would take a walking horse ride on a future weekend.

"Everyone seems to believe I am keeping this property simply for weekend escapes," Anna said with a nod and a smile. "This isn't the most carefree place to spend a couple of days once or twice a month. I'll have to assign teams to shop for groceries and others to take care of the beds and bathrooms. Any volunteers for our next outing?"

As the line of horses paraded out of the stable, the show of hands for volunteers was sidetracked. No matter. It was a slow entourage, although Fletcher and Cynthia seemed anxious to take off on their own route.

"Stay together," the groom shouted. "You have no idea where you're going on this first outing, and none of us wants to climb down an embankment and hunt for pieces of what's left of you. It may sound funny, but it has actually happened, and it's not pleasant." After that, everyone kept to their place on the trail. Even Fletcher.

An hour later, they returned to the shade of the gravel drive. Kate and a pot of tea on a small table were nestled under the trees. Gerrit slid down from his horse and handed him over to the groom.

"Kate?" Gerrit whispered. "We're back. Are you napping? The wheelchair is here to give you a ride back to the house where you can take a proper nap. I'm thinking of joining you. All this fresh air has worn me to a nubbin'."

He scooped his wife into his arms and set her down in the wheelchair. The embroidered summer afghan was the perfect weight to lay over her shoulders and knees. The gravel path was a bugger for making any headway with the wheelchair, but the sidewalk made short work of the walk to the house. A young man wearing a tan linen jacket and dark brown slacks helped him lift the chair up the porch steps and into the house. A stair chair made the climb to the second floor easier than carrying her upstairs. Once she was stretched out on the bed, Gerrit lay down beside her. The young man with the tan jacket came in and covered them with a light blanket. Gerrit nodded his thanks, then snuggled down with his arm over Kate.

Kate and Gerrit both slept through lunch, but then, no one had bothered to wake them. Their soup and sandwiches were set aside for later.

When they came down mid-afternoon, the kitchen help brought their late lunch into the breakfast room with lemonade. Upon hearing dinner would be downtown, they decided to skimp on lunch so they could try local food at the restaurant. They wandered around on the main level but didn't find anyone else until they got to the library. Cynthia was stretched out on the floor, studying the Norwegian brothers' records. Cynthia was one of the very few Iversen's who studied the old Norwegian language. Some words, she thought, might have been an even earlier dialect, but because she'd had the good fortune of talking often with Grandpa Harald, she knew what some of the strange combination of letters said. Kate and Gerrit sat quietly, listening to the musical notes of the language.

By sundown, the family had prepared for their evening out in local society. Annalise, who was the hostess, suddenly realized she was the only one without a partner. She hadn't really missed him. Until then.

"Dugan," she called down from the upstairs landing. "Would you mind standing as my dinner guest date this evening?"

From somewhere below, she heard his lilting Irish voice. "'Twas plannin' on it," he said, appearing at the grand stairway. "I want you to know that this evening's meals and entertainment are on the house. The Father's mother always left an account in my name for entertainment expenses. I haven't used it in years, and this seems like the perfect opportunity. There will be plenty of opportunities to entertain guests on the town, but it's my turn to give you and your guests a welcome present. There are some nice evening automobiles in the garage, and the drivers have them all cleaned up and ready. We mustn't stay out too late, though. Church tomorrow in the little chapel in our garden. I didn't ask your faith, but in honor of the priest who willed you his family's home, we will have a Roman Catholic priest say Mass."

That was just fine with Anna.

It seemed that everyone for miles around knew that a new family had inherited the mansion and considerable acreage. Many weren't shy about asking how they'd known the priest. Most seemed to think they might have been Norwegians like the Nolans. Naturally, the family gave nothing away and remained politely quiet.

With a sign from Anna, the small party said they had an early start for tomorrow and would need to drive back to the house and get some sleep. Especially Kate, who perhaps had the most fun greeting all the people who stopped at their table.

In the morning, Anna and her mother and brother dressed quickly and went out to find the chapel. Dugan found them and led the way to where the little chapel stood in a small grove of trees. The priest already wore his vestments. The woman who had staffed the breakfast room the day before played the little organ and sang several hymns. The priest was a little taken aback that only one person received Communion—Annalise. "My daughter, Katherine, is getting ready for her high school graduation, so she couldn't come this weekend," Anna explained to the priest. "Nor next. But she will come soon, and she always takes Communion. I thank you, Father, for celebrating our first Mass here and the beautiful music I hope to hear often. Whenever we plan to come for a weekend or longer, I will let Dugan know well in advance. I hope you will find time to be a guest when we are here." Annalise then introduced the priest to her parents.

As they stepped out the chapel door, Anna gazed at the beautiful house. Her house. It was such an awesome sight that she had a hard time believing it was real and not a fairytale dream.

On the way back to the house on the summit, they discussed that the time to review the situation had arrived. Even though the family had enjoyed fun and games, it was time to get down to work.

Once at the house, Annalise announced, half to herself, "Now comes the hard part." I have been struggling for the last couple of weeks with what to make of this unbelievable gift. Whatever I ultimately decide will not come easily. There are so many options, beyond just accepting the gift and enjoying it for ourselves and generations to come. But besides that, is there something else that should take precedence? It could be a dedicated memorial to those early Norwegian families who left everything to settle here. Many surrounding counties also owe much to those Norwegians—and one family that has been part of ours since Mom and Fletcher first came to Lillehammer."

All heads nodded in agreement.

"But one thing in particular has been nagging me since we first came here," Anna continued. "The former priest who hoped this place would help me recover from the evil I've done to myself. These ideas are all huge crosses on my shoulders. Regardless of what I ultimately decide, you all will help me carry them."

Annalise caught her parents' supportive gazes and then pressed her palms together. "First, which of you would prefer that we keep this estate in our family? It will be well used, especially with our connection to the wonderful Iversen clan." No one responded. "Momma?" Anna inquired.

Kate almost nodded instinctively but then held up. "I am not ready to give an answer."

"Poppa?" Anna asked.

"It would be wonderful if it could be used for a variety of things, including our family's enjoyment. But until we have some idea of what those other uses might be, I'm not ready to decide, either," Gerrit said thoughtfully.

Fletcher was next. "I've certainly had a marvelous time here this weekend. Everything is like a fairyland. The stables. The beautiful rooms. Those fantastic journals. Personally, I think that any decision to find another use for the property should have to wait until those journals are translated and the story of their dreams and struggles are fully understood. Yet I do see this place being useful as some sort of social service facility, too, Annalise."

"Cynthia? Did any other of your living family study the language?" Annalise asked.

"I think I was the only one who had any interest in learning the Norwegian dialect. When I was trying to decipher some of the words in that first journal, I realized how little I really know. There are phonograph records that I can use to brush up. I will make some calls to book stores in Chicago to see how to find one. Seeing all those journals spread out on the floor of the library was such a thrill." Cynthia paused, and then a light sparked in her eyes. "The thought just occurred to me that maybe Helen learned some of the language from Harald and his mother. I wonder if Harald's mother kept a diary. Or were there diaries kept from those early Iversen's who settled that county? You know, Harald's twin brother was always the studious one of the family, and given his interest in keeping records, he might have kept a diary of information. Maybe even a diary written in their native language."

"This quest is getting more interesting by the minute," Annalise said, bemused. "We could build a first-person account of those early settlers who logged their experiences in journals for more than a hundred years. What a monumental undertaking that'll be. History in their own words."

Annalise turned to her brother. "Fletcher, could you find time to do a little research on some of the Norwegian genealogy and history across the border in Minnesota? We know that was the first location for most of the Norwegians who settled here. Except for Harald's ancestors, of course. There might be some histories written that already chronicle those early settlements. See what you can find in books already published. You know, though, perhaps the estate's library might already have an extensive collection of such material. After Katherine's graduation, she and I will drive up there and start looking. I think this will be a very busy summer."

Then it hit her. They'd already agreed to start writing their own family history that summer. Now she'd sidetracked that long-dreamed-of novel for someone else's family journals.

"I think," Anna started again, "we've done enough dipping into those other family histories for a few weeks. It's enough to give me a migraine."

No one argued that point and it was time to head back to Lillehammer Anna leaned into the corner of the car and drifted into a nap until they pulled into a gas station somewhere. From there, they could walk over to a little coffee shop that promised an assortment of soups, sandwiches, and even homemade pies. Fletcher pumped the gas and Annalise went inside to pay the bill before they joined everyone else at the shop.

Coffees were poured all around. Kate knew what Anna's choice would be and had already ordered for her. Egg salad on wheat bread. She didn't realize until they brought out the orders that it was an Amish restaurant. Their preference for kerosene lanterns, iceboxes, and cookstoves didn't seem to interest the Englisher travelers, who were used to overhead lights, refrigerators, and freezers. Eating meals in the estate's grand dining room had been a rare experience, but so was having an egg salad sandwich with homemade fries in a little diner.

"Room for pie?" the waitress asked. Swishing around the table in her long blue skirt topped with a darker blue apron, she jotted the orders on her notepad and went off to get the slices dished up and topped with whipped cream.

Kate smiled as she watched the young waitress; she reminded Kate of Anna's longtime friend, Sarah. Did Annalise see the similarity? She could still see Sarah, clutching the knitting needles to protect her friend from the man who'd stormed into the little farmhouse. *So long ago*, Kate thought as she put her hand on Gerrit's knee under the table.

One by one, the weekend visitors turned their vehicles off the highway, heading home. Cynthia and Fletcher continued south, dropping Anna and Kate at Ida's house. After she got her mom settled for a rest, Anna went up to Ida's old bedroom and dialed a phone number.

Maybe he isn't home, Anna thought as she raised the phone to her ear. But he was.

"Carleton, Anna here," she started when her husband answered. "I hope this isn't a bad time. I just got back from a weekend at the Lake Superior estate. I'm still trying to get my head around all this stuff. But that's not why I'm calling."

Anna cleared her throat, paused to see if he'd say anything, and continued when he didn't. "This coming weekend is Katherine's graduation. I wasn't sure if you wanted to be part of the festivities. I hope the children will be interested in going to the ceremony, at least. I thought since Katherine and I are no longer at your house, you might have forgotten that her graduation is coming up. I hope you will still consider celebrating her considerable accomplishments. She was, after all, an important part of your life for the better part of ten years."

Carleton simply breathed into the phone, waiting for her to continue.

"I've ordered a large white tent with tables and chairs," Annalise explained. "It will more or less fill the entire backyard. I've invited your sister, her family, and a few of the cousins we've always done things with. But for the most part, I think it will be a grandkid's affair. You don't have to give me an answer now, but I want you to know I would love it if you could at least stop in. The graduation starts at one thirty with the processional from the school to the field. Katherine is one of the speakers for the class. We'll head to Ida's after the ceremony. I really hope you can be there. I also have something I want to share with you and hopefully get your reaction and input"

He mumbled, "We'll see." His goodbye was less than enthusiastic when he hung up.

She wasn't surprised by his lack of interest in speaking with her.

On Sunday afternoon, Annalise arrived early to get good seats for her family. Jonathan and Angie were also there early, parked on either side of their grandparents. Tim sat between Grampy Gerrit and Annalise.

"Your Poppa coming?" Anna asked her son, leaning down close to his ear. He only shook his head.

"That's too bad," Anna said with a sigh. "But I know some of your cousins are coming, so you guys will have a good time. Katherine has to give a really big speech today, so we'll have to clap really hard so she'll know we listened."

The school concert band had been playing as the bleachers filled. The chairs behind those for the graduates had long been staked out by people who parked hats and jackets as place-savers. When the music stopped momentarily, family members hurried forward to claim their 'reserved' seating. The band then began playing *Pomp and Circumstance*. Everyone stood, craning their necks to look for the graduates they had come to applaud. The procession from a doorway at the back of the high school to the stadium seemed never ending. Finally, the faculty wearing special caps from fancy universities signaled the graduates to be seated.

First, introductions of guest speakers and honored students.

Next, the salutatorian was introduced, followed by her brief but very articulate remarks. Then her co-salutatorian offered a different twist on the same message. Finally, Katherine, the valedictorian, was introduced. She walked across the stage, then climbed the stairs to the podium platform. That's when Tim started cheering, shouting her name. She turned to the sound of his voice and raised her hand in a salute in his direction.

Anna had heard Katherine practice her speech for several days. She had such a wonderful way with words and such a unique way of weaving her thoughts into brilliant details that held everyone's rapt attention. When she finished, her classmates stood and cheered, and the parents seated behind the graduates jumped to their feet in applause. Poor Tim couldn't clap hard enough for her to hear him.

Before the first row of graduates stood to receive their diplomas the vice-principal began announcing names. The robed students climbed the stairs and crossed the stage to where they paused to collect their diploma and flip their tassels to the opposite side of their mortar boards. That's when Anna noticed Tim was gone. He'd obviously dropped down between the riser on the bleacher step and scooted out at the end of the row. Before anyone could reach him, he'd found Katherine and knelt next to her.

A couple rows later, it was her turn to go on stage for the diploma and tassel routine. Anna needn't have wondered what was about to happen. Katherine took her little brother's hand and they climbed the stairs and crossed the stage together to where the school board president presented her with her diploma. Tim gave him a big salute. The school board president shook not only Katherine's hand but also her little brother's. The crowd broke out in a huge cheer.

That's when the paper's photographer got up close to capture the publisher's son escorting his sister down the steps and back to her chair. That's also when she saw Carleton, looking not too happy with Tim. But at least he was there.

And he came to the party at Ida's house. He not only seemed to relish the reaction to his youngest child's love for his big sister, but he was equally pleased that Katherine, wearing her highest-honors stole, thanked him profusely for coming. He even asked his staff photographer to take a couple of photos of him with Katherine and Anna.

The celebration with family and neighbors finally settled down to quiet conversations in the big white tent. Tim had gone inside along with Grampy Gerrit and Kate for a well-earned bedtime.

The caterer had long since removed the dishes and leftovers. The teenagers, Katherine included, had gone off to another gathering. "Graduation nights are a very scary time for parents," Anna whispered to her daughter before she left. "Home no later than eleven," Carleton added. Since Katherine had moved to Ida's, Carleton wasn't responsible for her curfew. But Anna wasn't the least bit worried. She had raised Katherine to always err on the side of caution.

Carleton also issued his curfew to Angelica and Jonathan. Annalise knew they wouldn't dare be a headline in tomorrow afternoon's paper. But she also knew that the candid shot of Tim and his sister on stage would not only make the local paper but probably also hit the wires.

And that's indeed what happened. Katherine gave a lot of interviews to newspaper and TV reporters around the country. Jonathan checked all the newspaper racks at the drugstore and kept flipping the TV channels to see where Katherine was being shown. The excitement went on for days.

CHAPTER FOUR

School for the other grades did not close until noon the following Wednesday. They had a couple of final exams to finish up, and then there was the usual celebrating with the all-school picnic. At the end of that day, Anna collapsed in the old rocker on the front porch for a quiet conversation.

"Well, Aunt Ida, you can see we made this first milestone," Annalise whispered to her aunt. "Next, she's off to Marquette. Imagine that little pipsqueak going to what was my dream college when I was that age. But a high school graduate with a four-year-old can't always afford her dreams. Now look at us. She and I both have money in the bank. But that's what I've been wanting to talk with you about. I called the bishop's office earlier this week for an appointment. You know I now own Cleary Nolan's family home up on Lake Superior. It's unbelievable. I keep thinking it should be of more use than just a weekend getaway place. Nolan also left a most beautiful letter for me about how he finally was able to face up to what he'd done and how he'd spent the rest of his life trying to make amends. I think I'd like to enjoy the estate for maybe a year or two, but these last couple of weeks, I keep thinking that's probably not the best use for it. I got this idea in my head that maybe it could be a place where priests who have violated their vows can spend time in prayer and therapy to get their lives straightened out. Dugan hinted that Cleary Nolan was a frequent visitor at his childhood home after he left the priesthood. There's a chapel in the garden where a priest came to say Sunday Mass when we were there last."

Annalise took in the quiet for a moment and exhaled. "So, this is my plan. I want to talk with the new bishop about the possibility of eventually turning the property into a treatment center for priests. They keep saying that priests who do things like he did to me never really get over it. But I know he did. He removed himself from his beloved priesthood and from any and every opportunity to offend again."

Bugs buzzed around the porch. "All those times the bishop blew us off still upset me. But Nolan explained the anguish he suffered when he eventually decided he had to leave the priesthood. He wrote about his sorrow for what he'd done and his determination to take charge of his addiction so he would never again be tempted. Nolan did a lot more than the bishop ever did. The bishop didn't even apologize. Accused me of lying. I think the church was worse than Nolan, when all was said and done."

Annalise folded her hands in her lap. "I don't think we could ever have made it without all the people who circled around us. You, Ida. And Emily. Helen. Dr. Chandler and the cardiologist. For all he did for mom, I always struggle trying to remember his name. And how could I ever thank all those in the Amish community for their prayerful love and assistance? But the proof of all their hard work in standing with us is our Katherine. Father couldn't figure out how to deliver his message of sorrow to us, but his bequests to us say what he couldn't express in person."

Annalise sat in silence for a moment, savoring the breeze. "So, just hope with me that the new bishop might talk over setting up a treatment center for priests at the estate. And you, dear Auntie, your help all those years ago is still legendary. You are quite a lady. I know you've been around all these years, peeking over that porch up in heaven. I hope you like our Katherine. She has a lot of you in her. And wait until I tell you someday soon about the books she and I are going to write."

Annalise got up to go inside to answer the ringing phone.

"Momma? Are you up to talking for a bit?" Annalise called out. "That was poppa on the phone. He was calling from the courthouse. He wants you to stay here with me for a few days so he can get some of his work caught up. He said to tell you he'll miss you, but he knows I have something to talk over with you."

"I wouldn't mind some tea and a talk right now, if you'd be so kind," Kate said. "You always have such interesting tea and your pots are so pretty. I keep thinking I should get a new pot sometime, but I'm always just fetching the old one out of the cupboard. If Ida were still here, she'd have those new cupboards filled with a whole new set of dishes and a matching teapot."

"Well, momma, you know we can go shopping anytime you want. Tim is off somewhere with Katherine today. She said something about getting him some new summer clothes and sandals for the Lake Superior beach. You know, they have all those stones along the beach, and all four kids are talking about their next trip up there to start collecting agates. Maybe you and I should go looking for some summer beach things ourselves."

Tea was prepared and the two women sat down together. "But—what I want to talk with you about," Annalise said to her mother. "is that I'm still trying to wrap my head around the estate. It is so impossibly large and luxurious. I am thrilled that it's big enough that lots of us can be together and not feel crowded. For all of those months when we were so frustrated and scared about what had happened to me and then to you, this is such an amazing turnaround…"

Kate nodded and sipped her tea.

"Anyway," Anna said, collecting herself, "here's the scoop. I called the bishop's office this morning. You remember that the one we used to see died a couple of years ago. I called to make an appointment—not about past events or frustrations, but about that idea I've been trying to piece together. I know I mentioned it to you a while ago."

Kate set her cup down, her eyes intent on her daughter.

Annalise leaned forward over the table. "In a special journal, Father Nolan wrote about when he finally admitted to himself what he had done to me, to all of us. That didn't happen until much later in the year, after he'd been escorted down to West Texas. I'm not sure where he went after giving up his priesthood, but Dugan hinted that he'd gone back to the estate, where he was safely away from any temptation."

Annalise cleared her throat and glanced at the tabletop. "I just keep thinking that we should consider offering the property to the diocese for a similar use, where wayward priests and religious people may seek refuge. So they would have somewhere to go where they could at least offer the rest of their lives to prayer and sacrifice."

The room was quiet for a moment. Annalise's thoughts were still a little jumbled. "I don't know," she said, sighing. "I have no idea if there is any hope for that to happen—that a priest can actually recover from those terrible problems. Now, as a brighter light is being focused on the transgressions of priests, is there any hope for a cure? Was Cleary Nolan ever cured, or was his removal from society the next best thing? I simply don't know. Maybe the bishop doesn't either. But he has resources he can tap to get some of these answers. If there is any likelihood a cure might be possible, at least for some, then making the estate available on a trial basis might be worth considering."

Kate nodded hesitantly as Annalise spoke.

"Would you be interested in joining me on this fact-finding mission?" Anna asked her mother with a smile. "I certainly don't want to make any rush decisions. After all, we have barely gotten acquainted with the property, and we certainly have plenty of interest in enjoying such a rare place for a good long while. What if we could parcel off a chunk of the land where the diocese could build its own facilities for patients? Housing and offices for counselors and therapists. It could even be situated so it would have private access to the garden chapel."

Annalise sat quietly, waiting for her mom to comment. As loquacious as Annalise was, Kate was equally introspective. Anna could see from Kate's eyes that she was turning it over and over in her mind.

"For starters," Kate said finally, "I look forward to going with you. Let's see what this bishop has to say. We never got much satisfaction out of the other one. Fat lot of good all of those trips were."

The women smirked at each other knowingly over the table.

"I want Katherine to go with us," Kate continued. "I think this bishop needs to meet her. My name must certainly be familiar to him. Or maybe not. Maybe he was brought in from somewhere else when the old bishop died. I understand that sometimes happens. But we'll start from the beginning and see if we can get a few minutes of his undivided attention. Now let's finish our tea, as promised."

Mid-afternoon, Anna suggested her mom take a short nap. Kate didn't argue.

It was close to suppertime when the front door opened and Katherine and Tim came in, dragging large bags.

"Momma, you should see all the stuff Katherine and I bought," Tim exclaimed. "She said it would be good stuff to take to the big lake when we go up there again. Most of it I can wear around here, too. It was so much fun."

The happy voices brought Kate downstairs. Tim gave her a quick peek into the biggest of his bags before running for the door.

"Supper in a few minutes," Katherine reminded her little brother. "Don't wander off."

"Anna," Kate said, pulling her daughter aside. "A thought for you. I don't mind if we go see the bishop tomorrow, but I still have such anger with what happened to you and then how we all were treated. *Liars*. That's what he called us. I know it was a different bishop and a very long time ago, but regardless, the damage was done. To this day, even the thought of that man standing behind that huge desk makes me so angry I could cry."

Kate closed her eyes and steadied her breathing. "My voice is only as a bystander," she concluded to Annalise. "The house is yours to do with as you choose. But I see no reason for handing over that valuable property to a religious organization that treated us all so badly."

When Annalise, Kate, and Katherine arrived at the chancery, Annalise realized she was shaking. Memories of the last time she'd been there were so overwhelming she could hardly speak to this new bishop.

"Sorry, Your Excellency," Anna said in a quiet voice once they'd entered the bishop's office. "I was sidetracked by memories of what happened the last time I was here."

The bishop nodded with a slightly confused expression. They remained standing until Annalise could explain why they'd come.

"I am Annalise Jansz," she said, finding her strength again. "This is my momma, Kate Jansz. This young lady is Katherine, who will turn eighteen in a few days. She's just graduated high school. My poppa is the County Treasurer where we live, and he regrets not joining us today. The last time we three were here was when Katherine was a newborn. Our visit today started with an unexpected letter Katherine and I received from an attorney a few weeks ago. Visiting that attorney changed our lives entirely. Sometimes I feel I didn't deserve such a blessed fate, but…"

The bishop motioned his visitors to have a seat as Annalise paused.

"I thought perhaps you were waiting for the diocesan attorney to arrive," Annalise said.

"Why would you think that?" this bishop asked, even more confused.

"Because," Anna said, "the other bishop always had him at the meeting whenever anyone from our family came here. We never started meetings until the attorney arrived to take notes and record everything. But I doubt those records will ever surface again."

The bishop shook his head and again gently motioned for the three ladies to sit. They did.

"The jaw-dropping information Katherine and I received at the attorney's office was what we inherited from Father Cleary Nolan's will—he was the old rector at Saint Michael's and a priest in this diocese when I was a teen. You see, Cleary Nolan left his family's entire estate to me. I don't mean just the cash bequests, but rather the enormous grounds and palatial home on a bluff overlooking Lake Superior near Duluth and Ashland in Wisconsin. It is so grand, so unbelievable, that I thought I could never accept it. I've been trying to figure out what to do with it, rather than just keep it all to myself. Yes, it would be fun to share such a place with family and friends. But then again, such an amazing property should have an equally amazing use—like the West Texas clinic where Father Nolan was hauled off to for treatment, with instructions never to come back."

The bishop raised his eyebrows, clearly mentally linking the offered details together.

"Father Nolan left me a notebook detailing some of his struggles while coming to terms with what he'd done to me. Those struggles caused him to leave his priesthood and enter a life of service—and they continued for years."

Annalise took in a breath and then smiled with embarrassment. "I'm sorry. I realize I keep referring to him as Father as if he's still a priest. I know he isn't either a father or a priest anymore, but it makes telling the story easier."

Annalise gazed at her mother and daughter, who looked back at her with gentle, supportive eyes.

"I have worried and prayed over this, day after day," Annalise said. "Eventually, I figured there was only one way to make some sense of all this, and that was to start at the top. To ask you and your resources what the current expectation is for curing rapists and pedophile clergy. And if my opening a center for them on my estate would be of any use. I could look for advice from psychologists and the like, but I expect you would have a closer handle on how well treatment works and what kind of treatment is even available at this point."

The bishop tapped a finger on the side of his head thoughtfully and leaned back in his chair.

"So, that's why we're here. I'm not sure how any of this would work with the property I inherited, but I needed to start my research somewhere." Annalise bit her lip and gazed down at her hands. "And while I came here looking for your advice, I never expected to have the past slam me in the face again, after all these years. I feel the same tension and humiliation and disparagement I did years ago. I had been forced to come here and tell the bishop face-to-face that I'd been raped, my infant daughter that came after in my arms at the same time..."

Kate reached over and gripped Annalise's hand.

"But I'm as tough as my Momma and decided I'd get through it," Anna said and looked directly into the bishop's eyes. "I even brought a package of the dried apple slices I'd made and sold to raise money so I could attend the Saint Michael's here. I wanted a good high school education so I could get into a good college. I laid the package of apples on his desk in front of him, but he never acknowledged they were there. I figured he'd probably just throw them away. He and his attorney simply called me a liar and didn't consider a single word that came out of my mouth. We were then dismissed."

Annalise held her gaze on the bishop but sat back suddenly. Her posture straightened. She looked at her mother, then her beautiful young daughter, and then turned back to the bishop. "You know what?" she began. "Rather than giving my estate to this diocese to set up a clinic for wayward priests, I think I will use the estate as a quiet place to write a book about how not to treat someone who has suffered abuse, not only at the hands of a rapist, but also at the hands of a bishop and others in a diocese. I hope to write a book about how to avoid being like those who refused to even acknowledge that a crime had been committed against me—and every other young person who experienced the same horror. I know none of this is your fault, but I came here with the best of intentions…to help pedophile priests…but I think I will be better served to deal with my own frustrations at the nightmare I am still trying to put behind me."

Annalise looked over at her Momma to make sure she was okay. "My mother came along for my command performance with the other bishop, even though she was still struggling to recover from a stroke. She's still struggling, and all because her little girl was raped by a Catholic priest and was determined to have the baby rather than an abortion. I spent six months in bed, occasionally in the hospital. I was only fourteen years old."

Kate squeezed Annalise's hand tighter, and Anna smiled at her. "People in my family and all our neighbors were endlessly generous with helping us. Even a whole Amish clan befriended us Englishers during that difficult time. If there was one good thing that came out of all that happened to me and my family, it was that Katherine came into our lives and never knew until recently anything about the horror of her conception."

The bishop pursed his lips and watched the three thoughtfully. He remained respectfully silent.

"I'm so sorry for wasting your time, Excellency," Annalise said. "But it hasn't been a waste of time for me. I was about to make a very serious mistake. While I still think a treatment center, like Cleary Nolan was sent to, might be helpful for this diocese and others. I just can't see it happening on my land. You know, my mother has often wondered how I could practice a faith that treated me so badly, but I'd already decided on the faith I wanted before I was raped. My faith is centered in God. That's all that matters."

Annalise rose from her chair. As she helped her mother up, Annalise said, "You have been so gracious in allowing me to just prattle on and think aloud, Excellency. I don't mean to be rude, but do you plan to put down on paper some of the things I've said? I wouldn't be surprised if you didn't see any need to do that."

"Annalise," the bishop spoke gently for the first time in more than thirty minutes, "I can assure you that there will be a record, written—typed, even—by me. I am also going to go on the hunt to find out everything I can about the records from your family's ordeal eighteen years ago. Regardless of the outcome of that search, I will be back in touch with you on what I find out. I was not part of this diocese back then, so I have no first-hand knowledge of who this priest was nor what the official diocesan records give for his leaving."

He rose from his chair and squeezed his hands together as he continued. "My heart breaks for what you had to deal with, but I keep looking at your beautiful Katherine, and I'm sure the Lord is as happy as I am that you made the decisions you did. In my years in the ministry, I've never seen such courage from someone so young as you were. If I find something—anything—I will be in touch."

"Thank you, bishop," Annalise replied. "I realize you had nothing to do with how shamefully we were treated, but I can't thank you enough for helping me—no, us—move forward from what endured."

"Mrs. Jansz, I can't tell you what a great pleasure it has been to meet you and part of your family," the bishop said and reached out to touch Kate's hand. "I hope you can come again so we might have lunch together here at the chancery. You have raised one amazing daughter, and I foresee that carrying on to the next generation."

"Oh, by the way, Bishop," Annalise added as they moved toward the door. "I nearly forgot to show you these two pictures. One is of Katherine as a baby on the day we came here for that final meeting, and another that Cleary Nolan included in his folder for me. A baby picture of him with his mother."

The bishop carried the two pictures over to the windows overlooking the back gardens. "Oh, my gosh," he said. "Oh, dear God." He stood for a long time, staring and comparing the two photographs. When he finally handed them back to Annalise, she was shocked. Tears streamed down his face.

She reached out to shake his hand that was still extended from handing back the pictures. But he didn't take her hand. Instead, head bowed, he put his arm around her. "I thank God for sending you here today," he said. "I will call you in a few days after I've had a chance to dig through some files. You are wonderful, strong, good people."

After a formal bow to Kate, he wished Katherine well in her coming enrollment at Marquette and stepped aside so they could leave.

Halfway across the parking lot on the way to their car, Annalise stopped.

"Momma," she said. Did Poppa ever bring that box with my pajamas home from the courthouse vault?"

Kate frowned. "No, I don't remember that he did. It's probably still on the shelf way in the back."

"Momma," I think it is time for us to take this horrible memory and put it on the shelf way in the back of our memories.

Kate nodded in agreement and smiled as they got in the car and drove home.

THE END

FATHER CLEARY NOLAN'S JOURNAL

January 10, 1944

Each year after my ordination, my mother gave me a journal in which she hoped I would write down things I wanted to remember. She once told me it would be a good place to keep a record of conversations I might have with our Lord or His Blessed Mother. Never happened.

I could always find time to write a pastor's item for a bulletin or reports from a parish or diocesan meeting, but there was something about those little booklets that prevented me from writing even a single note about a snowstorm or beautifully sunny day. The empty books just gathered dust on the shelf.

Until now.

After the most terrible transgression of my priesthood, I felt compelled to write at least a few pages to help me find a way to deal with my shame and horror. I don't know if anyone will ever read these sentences, but I pray they eventually will find their way to little Annalise. She is such a lovely young lady, who, when she enrolled in our high school, was almost always at my daily Mass in the chapel. She wasn't even Catholic.

At the first open house of the semester, she introduced me to her Aunt Ida who, she said, was the daughter of a Methodist pastor in Iowa. We chatted about our common interest in the differences and similarities in various sects of Christianity.

So, when Ida invited me for a Sunday night supper, how could I say no? Annalise almost always joined us at the kitchen table but didn't stick around after she finished eating. I think our discussions bored her.

Ida knew a great deal about so many different faiths and one night surprised me when she said she'd always planned to go into ministry—but her brother Daniel beat her to it.

The Sunday night suppers we shared were such a pleasure, not only because of the stimulating conversation, but because it gave me something to fill my otherwise lonely Sunday evenings.

The entire week is geared toward Sundays. Sermons. Bulletins. Music. Sometimes after-Mass gatherings. Then everyone leaves to spend the day with family, friends. Even pastors of other denominations who are married have special family time on Sunday nights. But not Roman Catholic priests.

One weekend, Ida's sister Kate was there to visit her daughter, Annalise. Kate wasn't quite as caught up in discussing religions as her sister, but she was no slouch when it came to knowing the structures of different faiths.

Annalise had discovered forensics, something she'd never known at the public schools in her town. They had sports, a chorale, band, theater, but nothing like debate or storytelling. She was forever practicing her speeches, trying to overcome nerves and get the tempo just right. Her coach said she'd done well in early contests but was a little unnerved about an upcoming district competition.

Ida and her daughter Emily had plans to visit her sister the weekend of that district competition, so Annalise had made arrangements to spend the night with one of her teammates. Anna then came down with a terrible sore throat and could barely talk above a whisper, so she couldn't go with the speech team. Anna didn't call her mom to let her know she was home in bed, so Ida and Emily didn't know they should have gone home since she was all alone. Although Annalise called to tell the forensics coach she was too sick to go, she forgot to pass along the message that she wouldn't be staying overnight at her friend's house.

Mrs. Porter always left soup or a casserole in the fridge so I'd have something I could heat up for my supper. I've played this whole sad story over and over in my mind, but I still don't know how I let myself lose control. It had been years since I'd given in to temptation. Before, there never seemed to be any personal connection between me and the victims I hurt. I should have remembered how I suffered after those earlier transgressions, but it was as if my body just took over. I knew Anna hadn't gone to the forensics event because I'd talked to the coach that morning, just after she got the call about Anna being sick. I remember she said Anna's voice was so bad she could hardly hear her over the phone.

I'd spent the day reviewing my sermon and making a few last-minute changes.

3

Mrs. Porter only worked until noon on Saturdays. I heard despair confessions from one to three that afternoon. That should have triggered something in my brain to keep me from falling off my promise to never, ever rape a young student again.

But I did.

I heated the soup and put it in one of the jars in the pantry. I'd already put rum and some orange juice in a cruet. I planned to add warm water when I got to the house so it would be soothing to her sore throat.

I wrapped the jar in a terry towel to keep it warm and carried it in the leather satchel where I kept my parish paperwork for meetings. The cruet was in a pocket in my coat. I knocked on the front door, but it was a few minutes before Anna opened it. She seemed startled to see me. I told her I'd heard she was sick and couldn't go to the forensics meet, so I brought some of Mrs. Porter's chicken noodle soup for her supper. I could tell she was uncomfortable that I was there, but I distracted her by reading the results of how our school fared in the day's events. Three of our seven speakers moved on to state competition.

I put the empty jar back in my satchel and carried Anna's dish over to the sink. When I said, "Let's get you back into bed," she grew very fearful. She followed me to the front door, except I started up the stairs. She held the door open for me to leave.

I said: "I can let myself out after I make sure you get back upstairs and safely into bed." Too late, I realized what I'd just said. I'd have no key to lock the door from the outside. But she was too distracted to think that far ahead.

Upstairs, I quickly poured some of my toddy into a glass on the table next to her bed. I recited my little story about my mother's toddy for my sore throats when I was a boy and convinced Anna to try some. She had no idea what alcohol tasted like, so my story about it being sore-throat medicine worked. Before she finished what I'd poured into the glass, she was starting to doze off. I sat in the rocker I'd pulled over next to the bed and waited until I was sure she was sound asleep.

Before I left, I took the glass into the bathroom and carefully rinsed it out, then after rubbing the sink bowl with a bar of soap, I rinsed it again.

I'd thought about putting her pajama bottoms back on her, but I needed to get out of there. Instead, I kicked them under the bed and hurried down the stairs. Before opening the door, I found a key on the plaque that fit the lock. Next, I made sure no one was out and about in the neighborhood to see me leave. Everything seemed quiet. I walked quietly down the front sidewalk to the street, then hurried in the opposite direction from where I was going.

Back at the rectory, I washed the soup jar carefully in the sink. The cruet was a spare from the student chapel, so I left it in my bag to wash up later. The events of the night had worn me out. I took a shower, set the alarm for an early wake-up, and crawled into bed. The pleasure I'd expected from the evening was lost in my deep despair at what I'd done.

I'm writing this long after it occurred. At the time, I felt no need to document what I'd done, but when the despair started, I knew I'd have to keep a record of what actually transpired. But that night— and the days that followed—gave no hint that it had all gone horribly wrong.

The shame and horror consumed me...
but not enough to make me find a confessor
to whom I could tell my fall from grace—
again.

January 27, 1944

I tried to make arrangements to find
a confessor so I could put myself right
with my vows, but I couldn't summon the
courage to actually make that phone call.

Then, out of the blue, I had an
unexpected visitor storm into my office
at the parish. It was a beautiful sunny
Saturday morning, and I'd planned to get
my bike out of the garage and ride the
trails in the nearby park. At first, I didn't
remember who she was, but as soon as
she reminded me that she was Annalise's
mother, I thought my heart would fly
right out of my chest. This was something
I'd never even considered...that Annalise
might become pregnant. How could I have
been so stupid? Just because it had never
happened in the past didn't mean it wasn't
always a possibility.

I tried to invite her to have a seat, but Kate just stood there, leaning over my desk, her voice rising the more she struggled to find the words to accuse me of raping her daughter. She obviously had just found out. I tried to deny that I would ever have done such a thing, but she wasn't buying it. They had a doctor's confirmation that Anna was pregnant, and the timing matched the forensics meet Anna didn't attend. While she had no recollection of being raped, Annalise certainly would have figured it out when she learned she was pregnant.

Kate's words regarding my raping her daughter will never leave my brain. She said, "My next stop today is with your bishop. I don't care how many times you deny it, there is no other way my daughter could be pregnant without knowing anything about it. She said you had a toddy in an offertory cruet from the school chapel. So just keep denying it, and we are going to keep right on accusing you until you own up to this terrible thing you did to our Annalise and our family. You have destroyed her future! And you and your diocese will have to pay for what you have caused."

She didn't say goodbye. She slammed the door as she left. The housekeeper stood there, gasping.

I often wondered how Anna's mother found her way to the chancery office that morning. But I knew she did because I got a phone call from the bishop after she'd delivered the same message to his surprised ears.

Enough for now.

January 28, 1944

Ida showed up unannounced first thing Monday morning. I knew her as a gracious Christian lady, well-trained in being the daughter of a Methodist pastor. That day, her eyes were fire and brimstone. She stormed into my office, announcing that she'd come to collect Anna's belongings from her locker and return her textbooks and library books. She said to me, "I rue the day I invited you to share Sunday night suppers and conversations at my table."

Since I hadn't received a call from the bishop that morning, I figured Ida hadn't driven to the chancery to add her loud notes of displeasure to him. Even if she had, His Excellency would've denied vociferously before suggesting he was busy, and she should be on her way. Instead, I called him, but only got as far as his office receptionist, not even the bishop's personal secretary. Things were looking up!

But Annalise's family continued pushing the issue. Despite the bishop's promise to look into their accusations, it seemed unlikely that a highly respected high school rector could have done anything so craven to a young student. More likely, the girl was just trying to find someone else to blame for her indiscretions. The bishop was obviously just avoiding the issue as much as possible.

Over the months that followed, the family tried repeatedly to get the diocese to at least admit that what she claimed had occurred. There was no doubt she was pregnant and was smart enough to save the pajamas she'd been wearing that night.

After a visit from Anna's father and Ida, the bishop was so incensed he could hardly talk when he got me on the line. He handed the receiver to the attorney and asked him to explain. He instructed, after telling me that the girl had saved her pajamas from that night, that I had to get into that house and retrieve the evidence. "I don't care how you do it, just get those pajamas in that box from a closet shelf in her old bedroom."

I didn't know it at the time, but even though Ida had left her house, her daughter was still there. After dark, I took a hike around the block and after confirming the house dark and unoccupied, just like most of the neighborhood, I walked up to the door and tried to open it. But the key I'd had made for myself wasn't working. I kept jiggling it until an upstairs light turned on. I'd barely ducked around the corner when I heard a car approaching—a squad car. Followed by a second one. In my black clothes, it was easy to disappear in the dark.

I had to find that box. I tried again a few days later. That time, the key worked on the first try. But there was nothing in that closet. The dresser drawers were empty. I grew more and more frantic. I pulled clothes out of closets and dumped drawers all over the floor. I searched every corner of that house but found nothing. They must have taken them up to the farm for safekeeping, thinking I wouldn't dare try to break in up there. It was driving me nuts.

Who cared if they kept the pajamas? By the time they'd invent something advanced enough to test my semen on the pants, I'd be long gone.

ABOUT THE AUTHOR

Patricia Raab grew up in Central Wisconsin where she lived with her parents, Hartlan and Ruth Gowey, along with her five sisters and one brother. She attended parochial schools, which developed her strong character and drive. After high school, she earned a bachelor's degree in Journalism from Marquette University and made use of those credentials for a successful lifelong career as managing editor, reporter, and columnist for community newspapers in Wisconsin and Illinois. Not only was she an outstanding journalist, but also a wife, to William, and a mother of six children. Patricia was an avid member of local charitable organizations, and her church, serving on numerous boards and committees. Later in her life she was a part-time copy editor at the Milwaukee Journal, where she eventually retired. Currently, her favorite pasttimes include gardening, writing, and spending time with her family.This is Patricia's first published novel.

Made in the USA
Middletown, DE
26 June 2022